LABOR OF LOVE

LABOR OF LOVE

❀

Arlene J. Warner

iUniverse, Inc.
New York Lincoln Shanghai

Labor of Love

iUniverse, Inc.

For information address:
iUniverse, Inc.
2021 Pine Lake Road, Suite 100
Lincoln, NE 68512
www.iuniverse.com

All Scripture quotations are taken from the King James Version of the *Bible.*

ISBN: 0-595-28708-5

Printed in the United States of America

In memory of my grandparents, Harter and Bessie Green.

Remembering without ceasing your work of faith, and labour of love, and patience of hope in our Lord Jesus Christ, in the sight of God and our Father." First Thessalonians 1:3

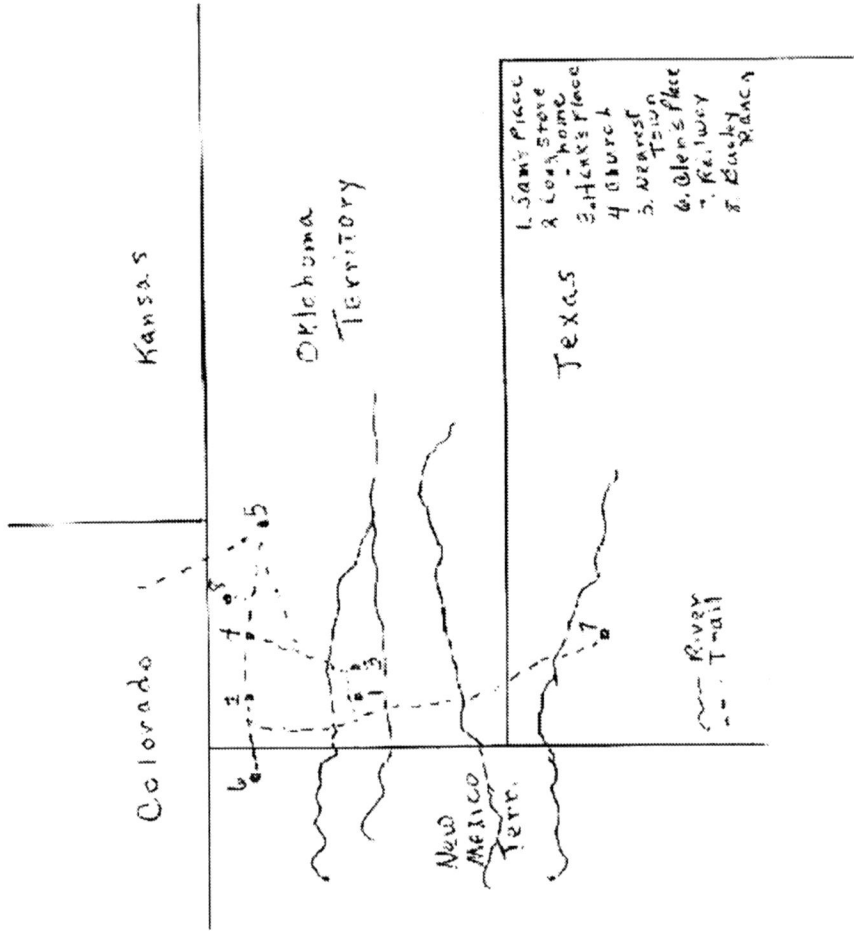

Colorado

Kansas

Oklahoma
Territory

6 • 1
  2
    3 • • • 7 • 8
            4 5

3

6

Texas

1. Sam's Place
2. Log Home
3. Hicks's Place
4. Church
5. nearest
   Town
6. Glen's Place
7. Railway
8. Bucky
   Ranch

New
Mexico
Terr.

7

~~~ River
--- Trail

C H A P T E R   1

⚜

Samuel Butler Jackson dismounted, tied his bay horse Gallatin to the cedar rail, and entered the Long Country Store. He waited for his eyes to adjust to the dimness, then removed his dusty hat and pulled a crumpled scrap of paper from the pocket of his worn jeans. He had labored over the list of supplies for a half-hour last night, painstakingly printing each item with a stubby pencil, and now he could barely make out the smudged letters.

The dignified proprietor approached with a smile. "Good morning, Sam. What can we do for you?"

"Morning, Mr. Long. Need a few supplies." He handed him the paper.

Owen Long scanned the list and briskly ticked off each line with his pencil. "I think we have all this. See you got seed here: corn and…sorghum is it? You have your claim ready for planting this spring?"

"Got about forty acres broke out of the sod. Sure hope there's enough rain for corn to grow, and I need the sorghum for feed."

"Fine, I'll get this together for you right away." He fingered his dark brown moustache, then moved toward the rear of the store.

Sam wandered around the long, narrow room as he waited. Three sets of small, dusty windows set just below the rough, vaulted roof on each side wall, plus two larger ones at the front, gave just barely adequate light. *The little general store back home in Tennessee was half this size, yet held twice the merchandise offered here. Wide open spaces seem to define this country.* He grinned. *Makes a man feel free.* He ran a calloused hand along the side of an elaborately tooled saddle, which appeared out of place with the mostly functional items surrounding it, shook his head at the price, and deliberately turned to a counter displaying tin dinnerware and cooking pots. The wide-board pine floor squeaked as he moved toward a table holding articles of clothing: overalls, cotton shirts, and heavy wool socks. Long woolen underwear lay discreetly folded on the shelf below. A wire rack at the far end held bolts of colorful cotton goods. He breathed in the pungent smell of the new-wood handles on the hoes, spades, hatchets, and axes hanging on the wall.

A soft swish of sound to his right drifted into his consciousness, and he turned to see a girl saunter toward the storage area in the back, swinging a feather duster in one hand. *Must be one of Long's daughters. Heard he had two or three.* Curly black hair cascading to the middle of her back grabbed his attention as he watched her tall, slim figure turn the corner and disappear. An involuntary shiver ran the length of his stocky, twenty-three year old frame.

"Is there anything else, Sam?"

Sam started and realized he was staring at an empty aisle. He gave Mr. Long a sheepish grin. "No that's all this trip."

"Would you like to set up a monthly account? You've been coming in steady for a year now, so I could…"

"No, thanks. I'm paying cash."

"Very well. If you change your mind let me know." He led the way to the counter in the rear of the store.

Sam counted out bills and coins, then thrust his old, crumpled, brown hat on his head. He heaved the sack of seed onto his left shoulder and gathered his other purchases in his right hand. When he turned, she was standing behind her father. With a quick intake of breath, he nodded and gave her a reserved smile. Her vivid blue eyes met his for a moment only, then swept past. Sam straightened his back and lurched toward the door. *Those eyes—a man could drown.*

As he stepped into the bright sunlight, he heard Mr. Long's voice. "Nessa, did you finish dusting?"

"Hey, Sam, need some help?"

Sam squinted up as Hank Moran, his friend and neighboring homesteader, stopped his horse at the rail.

"Howdy, Hank. I'll manage." Sam dumped his purchases into two gunny sacks and tied them behind Gallatin's second-hand saddle.

"You all right Sam? You look like you jest found a pot of gold, and I don't figure they have that for sale in there."

"I just saw the girl I'm going to marry." He pursed his lips and bobbed his head in affirmation.

They glanced toward the general store at the creak of the screen door opening. The young girl with black hair and blue eyes stood in the open doorway staring at them.

"That kid?"

"She'll grow up."

"Yeah, well."

Sam ignored the doubt in his friend's voice, mounted, and turned his horse into the western sun.

"Hey Sam, you fixin' supper tonight? Thought we might play some dominoes."

"Come on over," Sam called over his shoulder and waved without looking back. He held the reins loosely and allowed Gallatin to set his own pace toward home.

Hank's right, she is kinda young. Probably no more than fourteen. Her blue eyes, dark and bright at the same time. What name did her father call her? Nessa—different. Definitely one of a kind. He smiled.

Sam had labored on his hundred and sixty acre homestead in the Oklahoma Territory for almost a year. He spent weeks last summer cutting the tough buffalo grass with a rented team and mortar board sod cutter. More weeks in digging the hole for his house. Last fall and winter he had worked on a ranch making good money–twenty-five dollars a month. He now had a tiny dugout–dirt walls and floor, capped with a layer of cedar planks covered with tar paper, and blocks of sod salvaged from the field. Forty acres of land were ready for seed, in addition to a sizable plot for vegetables. He had built a lean-to for Galatin and a small coop for the rooster and six hens he received as payment for three day's work at the neighbor east of his place, the same one who had rented him a plow horse for fifty cents a day. He had purchased the plow from the nearest town, twenty miles east. His place had no well, and Sam hauled water from a spring—five miles each way. "Truly," Sam remarked to himself, "This is a big country."

All this passed through Sam's mind as he was carried along the rutted track. He had been proud of his accomplishments. Now...

"It's not much, Gallatin. Not enough for a woman. And I've spent most of the money I earned last winter." He shook his head and stared at the golden horizon until Galatin stopped at the dugout entrance.

Sam started the outside fire where he did his cooking during warm weather, and tossed thick slices of salt-bacon into a frying pan. He mixed dough, molded it into flattened rounds, and arranged the biscuits in another frying pan with a tight-fitting lid. A precious tin of milk, half full and diluted with water would make enough gravy, he hoped. The bubbly mixture began to thicken as Hank arrived just after sunset.

"Smelled that bacon clear over to my place," Hank said by way of greeting as he swung down from the saddle. "You got biscuits, too?" His blue eyes gleamed in the firelight. "Man, you're gonna make somebody a good wife!"

Sam grinned and handed his lanky tow-headed friend a tin plate and a cup for coffee. They piled bacon and biscuits and gravy onto their plates and squatted on the packed dirt. Sam gave thanks to the Lord for the food.

Forks scraping against tin, the hooting of an owl, and the clucking of chickens jockeying for position on the roost were the only sounds.

"I ain't got the knack for cooking," Hank rubbed his stomach and rose to his feet to get a second helping.

"There's molasses in that tin there." Sam set his plate on the ground and reached to pour a cup of coffee.

Hank nodded and drizzled a hefty stream on his biscuits. "Yeah," he continued. "Gotta get me a wife one of these days. But none of them girls in town want to live way out here. Even if I had a decent house, which I don't."

"What do you know about the Long girls?"

"Not much. There's three of them. But like I said this afternoon, they're just kids, Sam. That one today, she's the oldest I think." He shook his head. "You want a real woman."

Sam smiled. "Uhuh, and what does a twenty year old kid from Illinois know about real women?"

Hank snorted.

"Never mind. Let's get the game going." Sam fetched a piece of canvas and a box of dominoes from inside the dugout. He spread the canvas on the ground between them and dumped the dominoes on it, then took a lantern from it's hanging post, lit it and hung it so the light fell on the makeshift table.

After an hour spent playing dominoes, discussing the weather, and swatting at the insects drawn to the lantern, Sam pulled out the pocket watch his grandfather had given him on his twelfth birthday.

"After nine." He placed the coffee pot back on the coals to heat, then gathered the dominoes into the tin box. After pouring cups of the bitter brew, he sat beside his companion, sipping and enjoying the cool breeze that sprang up from the southwest.

"She may be young," Sam began without preamble, "but she's the one for me. I knew it when I saw her walking today, and those eyes…"

"You got it bad, Sam." Hank grimaced and shock his head. "I can see that, even if I can't see the why of it."

"Yeah. I gotta figure a way to get this place ready for a woman."

"I don't mean to splash cold water on your dream, Sam, but I heard Mrs. Long's parents had a good-sized place in Georgia afore the war. Guess they were nearly wiped out by the time she married Owen Long. Anyway, he came out here for a fresh start. Word has it she didn't want to leave the south." He sipped the last of the coffee in his cup and spit grounds into the fire. "Had some money though, to open that store."

"Yeah." Sam frowned and picked at a callous on his thumb. "I reckon she's used to more than I got, but I'll work it out, with the good Lord's help."

Hank snorted. "Well, I wish you luck." Sam heard but ignored his friend's whispered "You're gonna need it," as he threw the grounds from his cup into the night and got to his feet.

"Thanks for the supper; sure appreciate it. Sorry I beat you so bad at dominoes. Maybe your head'll be cleared up some next time we play." He cinched up the saddle on his horse, mounted, and disappeared into the darkness.

Sam sat holding his half-filled cup of lukewarm coffee, and looked into the heavens. "Lord, I sure thank you for keeping me healthy and getting this place started. I've never asked you for much before. Now I'm asking real serious for your help. I haven't given much thought to girls. Just thought someday I'd probably get a wife. What I'm leading up to Lord is–will You help me do what's needed to win that girl I saw today? I think her name's Nessa, Lord, You know the one I mean. And there's something about her...Anyway, I'm asking, Lord, and I sure do need some help. Thank you for listening. Amen." He kicked dirt over the fire, took the lantern from it's peg and went down into the dugout.

CHAPTER 2

❁

Nessa flipped a stray tress of raven hair over her shoulder with slender fingers, and strode back inside the store.

"Papa, who was that man?"

Her father looked up from his ledger. Nessa squirmed under his scrutiny.

"Except for your hair, you look more like your mother every day but you're already taller than she is, aren't you? Take after your grandmother there." His gaze shifted to somewhere over her head and he smiled. Nessa tapped her foot on the wooden floor. "Oh, you asked about the man who just left? Why that's Samuel Jackson. Has a place about three miles south. Came here about a year ago from Tennessee. Hard worker, I hear."

"Samuel…Sam…Jackson," she said slowly. She liked the flavor of his name rolling in her mouth. "He looks awful poor and kind of old."

"Old!" Papa's hazel eyes gleamed with humor. "Not much more than twenty, I suspect." His apparent amusement gave way to disapproval, and a furrow appeared on his brow. "And most everyone around here is poor by some standards, child."

Nessa dropped her gaze and ran to the family kitchen where her mother stood in front of the cabinet peeling potatoes for the evening meal. Nessa leaned on the worktable beneath the window and frowned at the meager back-yard and bare fields that stretched to the horizon.

"Mama, remember the trees and pretty flowers and the warm rains in Georgia? The big house and my bedroom? It had a full-length mirror and I didn't have to share it with Ellie and Opal."

"Oh, yes, I remember." Rebecca Long placed the pan of potatoes on the stove." She tucked a strand of honey-colored hair into the bun at the nape of her neck. "And I remember our last winter there when we had little to eat. Most of the land was sold to pay the taxes. Your father feared the house would be next to go and we would have nothing." She wiped her hot face with a corner of her apron and sighed. "I remember. Thank the good Lord we were able to save some of the furniture and this old range."

Nessa's vision wavered at her mother's words, and another illuminated her mind. The house she would preside over one day. Tall, with white columns, a wide verandah, polished oak floors with oriental rugs, silky damask or rich velvet hangings over the multi-glassed windows on bright brass rods. A handsome husband hovered in the background, eager to supply her every need and grant her every wish. Her frown deepened. No, she didn't want to be treated like a piece of china. Sitting in the parlor pouring tea would bore her. She wanted to fly across lush green pastures on a spirited horse, or take a train to faraway places. She wished she had been born a boy. No, she wished girls were allowed to do boy-things.

"Better quit dreaming and set the table for supper."

Nessa's reverie splintered into reality at her mother's words, and she hurried to obey.

Later that night, Nessa sat quietly on her narrow bed and stared at the stars through the open east window on the second floor. Darkness had scarcely dispelled the heat and the cotton pink and blue flowered curtains caught no hint of a breeze. She glanced over her shoulder at her younger sisters. Eleanor and Opal slept soundly on the double bed across the room. Nessa's lips thinned as her gaze circled the dimness of the room with its white painted walls, and multi-hued rag rugs on the pine floor, the old-fashioned wardrobe standing beside her bed, and the rustic pine table holding an enameled basin and pitcher.

Nessa dismissed the room with a sniff, and turned back to the open window. She knew in her heart her family fared better than most in this newly settled land. But it didn't compare to the richly appointed boudoir of her dreams. She stared into the heavens. The brilliant stars in the moonless sky seemed to stare back at her.

"Are you there, God?" she whispered. "I mean, I know You're there, but do You know me, Nessa? I asked Jesus into my heart two years ago after Mama explained about Him dying on the cross for me. And I try to listen when Papa reads the Bible every night and a whole half-hour on Sunday. But I've never even been to church. It was too far to walk back in Georgia, and now we're twenty miles from the nearest town. Grandmama told me stories of the family before the war; about the carriage, pulled by beautiful black horses, the family used to ride in to church, and to parties, and even to shop in Savannah, but they were sold long before I was born."

The silence increased her doubts. "Am I really saved? I don't think I am. Mother says Christians have pure thoughts." She winced. "I get angry sometimes with Ellie and Opal; and I don't always obey Mama and Papa. Sometimes I even lie, like the time I told Mama I had been weeding the garden and actually I had been riding my pony."

Her shoulders slumped. "You won't help someone like me. How can You, when you're so Holy? And Mama and Papa can't help me even though they do the best they can." Tears trickled down her cheeks and fell on her folded hands. "I want things to be like they used to be."

Nessa threw herself on the bed, and hid her face in the pillow, shaking with muted sobs. *Nothing works for me; no one cares how I feel. Grandmama, why did you leave me? If you were alive, Papa wouldn't have brought us to this place.* Gradually her body stilled and her thoughts leapt to this afternoon.

The man in the store, Sam somebody, she'd forgotten his last name. But he couldn't mean anything to her. He had less than she did. Still, something about him intrigued her. He wasn't overly handsome—nice looking though: medium brown hair, brown eyes. Not so tall, but he seemed much taller when he climbed on his horse and rode away. Maybe it was the way he sat in the saddle, straight as a fence post, like he was in charge, and could handle whatever came his way. His shoulders weren't slumped like most of the men she knew. He's too old though; around twenty, Papa said. She sat up and hugged her knees to her chin. Or maybe that's it! He didn't act silly like the boys her age. They stumbled and turned red when she glanced at them.

"Sam," she said in a low voice. It had a nice clean sound. And Sam had looked her straight in the eye and smiled and nodded. He had treated her like a grown lady, not a child.

A wisp of cool air crept in through the window caressing her bare arms and feet. She shivered in surprise and delight and closed her eyes.

❦   ❦   ❦

Owen Long sat in his rocker reading the month-old April 1898 Atlanta newspaper a farmer had brought earlier today along with some supplies from the railway station almost sixty miles north. A front page article about an invention caught his attention.

"Listen to this Rebecca, a man named Judson invented a device called a zipper a few years ago. Looks like two strips of cloth with teeth-like metal pieces down the side somehow join together. According to the article, this zipper can be used on clothes in place of buttons and hooks. It's predicted to revolutionize the clothing industry. There's a drawing here–it's odd-looking." Owen lowered the paper and gazed at his wife sitting across the room.

Rebecca continued to sew on the blue flowered fabric in her lap. "Interesting. I'll read about it when you finish the paper." She dropped her hands in her lap and looked up at her husband with soft hazel eyes. "What I'd like is a sewing machine."

"I know, dear." Owen gave her a fond smile. "With the new settlers around, business is increasing. I'm sure I can order one by the end of the summer." He pursed his lips and gently chided her. "But, remember, you chose to make room for your piano rather than the old sewing machine when we moved."

"Yes, I did, and I would make the same choice today." She smiled at her husband. "That piano gives me great pleasure."

Owen bent back to his paper, but after reading an article on the production of cotton for the second time without comprehension, he dropped the paper on his knees. "Speaking of sewing. Have you noticed how Nessa has grown? She's taller than you and the dress she wore today—well, Rebecca, it fit kind of tight at the top. Uh—I mean…don't you think she needs a new dress?"

"That's one reason I would like a sewing machine." Rebecca laughed and held up the unfinished garment. "I'm sewing as fast as I can on this dress for her. She's outgrown everything from last summer."

Owen sighed. "She's almost fifteen. I guess I hadn't realized. What got me to thinking was the way that young man, Sam Jackson, looked at her today."

Rebecca's head jerked up. "What do you mean?"

"Oh, there wasn't anything wrong about it, exactly. It just wasn't a look one would give to a little girl."

"You have to face it, Owen. She's not a little girl any more. I was sixteen when we got married."

He stood, went to the hall-tree standing by the front door, and took a woolen jacket from one of the hooks. "There's a chill tonight. Maybe I should have lit a fire." He slipped the jacket on and turned back toward his wife with a gleam in his eyes. "Yes, and you were barely fifteen when we started courting. Hard to believe it's been almost eighteen years." He fingered his moustache. "You seemed more grown-up than Nessa is."

Rebecca sighed and rested her hands in her lap. "She has a stubborn streak like your mother, Owen, and she seems determined to resist taking responsibility for a girl her age. Apparently, she also inherited my mother's penchant for not facing reality. She's always off in a daydream, or riding her pony lickety-split. It's a miracle she hasn't killed herself."

"Well, give her a little time to grow up." He rubbed his jaw and laughed. "It'll have to be a strong man that takes her on, though." His face sobered when he saw the disapproving look from his wife. "Oh, don't worry, Rebecca. She'll be fine."

"I pray you're right." She yawned and rubbed the back of her neck.

Owen glanced at the mantle clock. "Almost ten. Guess it's time to get to bed."

Rebecca smiled and gathered her sewing into a bundle. "I'm ready."

C H A P T E R 3

❀

Before dawn, Sam ate cold biscuits and bacon, and at sunrise, he began planting the corn seed in furrows of rich soil. It was hard work. Dig a shallow depression with his hoe, drop in a seed, cover it, take a step, and do it over again. Each time he made a round trip, he drank deeply, from the jug of water he left at one end of the field, then dampened his handkerchief and wiped his face.

"This heat's good for corn, but it sure wipes out a man," he said to the sun, stuck his sweaty hat back on his head, and picked up his hoe.

The last twenty yards were sown after dusk, more by habit and experience than by sight. At the end of the row, Sam bent once more to pick up the empty water jug and trudge toward the dugout. After fanning the few feeble embers in the rock-rimmed fireplace into flames, he filled the blackened pot with water and added a scoop of coffee to the old grounds. While it heated, he gathered eggs. Five today, the hens were adapting to their new surroundings. But even this bonanza failed to energize him. He dipped cold biscuits in the bitter hot coffee, chewed methodically, and snuffed out the fire. Then, with muscles protesting at every move, he clumped down the steps and fell onto the flattened corn shuck mattress covering the narrow wooden slab that comprised his bed.

Sam spent ten days in back-breaking work, planting corn, and sowing sorghum. Vegetable seeds squirmed upwards in their garden bed, and already tiny spears of green poked out of the furrows and opened their arms to the nurturing sun. Sam rose at dawn and thanked his Creator for the good planting weather, then raised his hands toward the golden sky, and prayed for a gentle rain to make the crops grow. Then he headed for the barn. *No time for dwelling on past accomplishments.*

Hank had come by the previous evening to tell Sam the drilling rig would arrive at Sam's place the next morning. *I'm glad I set the money aside last month when I ordered the well. Savings are running low after buying seed.* Sam stretched the muscles in his arms and legs, then, grinning at the thought of having all the water he needed, he picked up a bucket and strode toward the water barrel.

The thought that his funds might run out before water was discovered sobered Sam. He knew it could take up to three days to drill with the steam-driven rig, and some wells in the area were over a hundred feet deep. Sam had enough money to drill ninety feet. If a good source of water was not found within that depth, the drilling would cease. Sam prayed again, as he had several times a day for the past week, that the Lord would grant him a well of abundant sweet water within the ninety foot limit.

The driller and his helper, arrived with the rig a little after nine, accompanied by Hank, who said he came to give moral and verbal support. Sam grinned. He suspected Hank was simply curious about the machinery. After greeting the driller, Sam gestured toward the spot where he wanted the well. The assistant brought out a forked stick, pointed it at the ground, and began walking over the area.

Sam gazed at him a moment and his brow furrowed. "What's he doing?"

"Ah, he's witching for water. That stick he's holding is supposed to dip if there's a good supply of water below." The rig owner winked. "If you believe in that kind of thing. Me, I figure there's underground water everywhere, you just have to go deep enough to find it. Some folks swear by that stick, though, and you're as apt to find water where he says as any where else, I reckon. But, you decide where you want to dig, and we'll dig."

Sam watched the man with the stick. "Have you actually seen that stick dip toward the ground?"

"Well…I guess I've seen it bend a bit, but what caused it is another question."

"What's supposed to cause it?" Sam removed his hat and scratched his head. "Scientific like I mean."

"I don't rightly know." The driller chuckled. "The water witch, I reckon."

"Witch! I want nothing to do with that. And why would a water witch want to help me out? Witches!" He crammed his hat on his head and strode to the assistant's side. "Find anything?"

The man jerked his head up at the sarcasm in Sam's voice. "Uhh…nothing yet."

"Good. You can stop that witching nonsense right now. Even if there is anything to it, I don't want no witches any where near my place."

"But," the man sputtered and Sam caught the alarm in his voice, "there's no harm in it! I been doing this for more than ten years and I never saw hide nor hair of a witch. It's just an expression, mister."

Sam stared into the older man's eyes with a grim face, but his eyes twinkled. "Oh yeah, how can you be sure?" He turned away to hide a grin and called to the driller. "We'll dig over there to the left of the dugout."

Hank edged up to Sam and whispered, "Sam, you likely made a big mistake there."

"What do you mean?"

"Well, if there is something that makes that forked stick tell where the water is, you shouldn't have made it mad."

Sam snorted. "Hank, you're not such a fool as to believe that mumbo-jumbo are you?"

Hank shifted his gaze to his feet. "I dunno. There's a bunch of strange stuff around, like that 'lectricity I heard about."

Sam shook his head and walked toward the men setting up the drilling machine. Finally, they were ready; one man spit on the ground for good luck, and the other muttered to himself while kicking a few rocks aside. Sam silently sent up yet another prayer that water would be found within eighty feet.

At mid-morning they hit a shallow water table at twenty-three feet, an inadequate supply, and the drilling continued. They worked through lunch rather than shutting down the machine, and by late afternoon, the drill had reached a depth of sixty feet, having just pierced a two foot barrier of stone. An hour later, the driller let out a whoop.

"We hit a big water table. Should be enough water for anything you want to do."

A wide grin split Sam's face and a silent prayer of thanks shot upward. Now they could take a short break.

Sam glanced at the friendly teasing clouds which covered the sun intermittently, then joined the others as they swatted their jeans with their hats to free some of the clinging clay. After cooling off by pouring dippers of water over their heads, Sam set out cold biscuits filled with thick slices of salt pork. They squatted or sprawled against the wagon, and ate the simple fare, washing it down with cup after cup of water drawn from the barrel Sam had labored to fill and haul from the distant spring.

Then, with a minimum of grumbling, the two men went back to work, while Sam and Hank watched with interest. By dusk, Sam smiled at the sight of the piping and hand-pump gleaming in it's new location.

The driller stepped away and motioned to Sam. "You have the honor of bringing up the first bucketful."

Sam lifted the handle of the primed pump and worked with a steady up-and-down motion until a stream of water gushed out into the bucket under the spigot. He filled several buckets and set them aside for the garden before the water ran clear and cold. Then he filled a tin cup and sipped the sweet liquid. "Never tasted anything so good!" He passed the cup around and each man drank and responded with a nod and a smile. Sam had his well.

Sam prepared supper for the two drilling men and Hank, who accepted the invitation to stay for the meal with alacrity. "Good men and a good neighbor—and a good day's work. Thank you Lord," Sam murmured as he mixed dough for biscuits.

The men ate with relish and in silence, leaving only a few crumbs for the birds. Sam poured coffee and they sat on the ground around the fire, gorged with food and the satisfaction of a successful day of labor, and swapped tales for an hour. Hank rose, retrieved his horse from the pen, slapped the saddle on it and headed home into the night. The driller and his helper spread bedrolls on the ground near the fire.

"We'll be up and gone at first light," the driller told Sam, "have a well to drill way down south."

Sam shook his hand, thanked him, said goodnight, and went into the dug-out with a smile on his face.

❦   ❦   ❦

With a water supply, Sam could care for additional animals and the cash left from the digging of the well would give him a start. The next morning, he jubilantly saddled his horse and rode to the general store to ask Mr. Long if he knew of any cows and pigs for sale. He also intended to inquire about another matter; one close to his heart.

After learning of several farmers with animals for sale, Sam gripped his hat tightly in his left hand and drew a deep breath.

"Mr. Long, there's something else on my mind."

"Oh? Something else you want to buy?"

"No, sir, not buy…and not some thing…it's about your daughter. The one with the black curls."

"Nessa?" the storekeeper scratched at his ear. "I'm afraid I don't understand, Sam."

"I've got…I'm trying to…I'd…I'd like your permission to court your daughter, sir."

An arrow of breath issued from Mr. Long's mouth. He pursed his lips, and Sam's heart plummeted into his boots, but he squared his shoulders and looked Mr. Long in the eye. He waited.

"You know, Sam, she's not yet fifteen—a child really."

"Pardon me, sir, but I reckoned she was too young for a bit yet, but I'm willing to wait. I just wanted to let you know where I stand. I intend to marry her when she's grown some, maybe a year or so." Sam's steady gaze wavered and he looked at his feet. "I'm working real hard on my place to get it ready for a woman, and I promise I'll take good care of her." His sun reddened cheeks darkened and a trickle of sweat ran down his back making him shiver. "She's the one for me, Mr. Long. I'll wait til you say the time is right."

"I see." Mr. Long bit at his lower lip, then bit at his upper lip, and his eyes stayed focused on Sam's face. "Well, Sam, I must say you caught me by surprise. From all I've heard, you're a fine young man. If my daughter is willing, then you have my permission. But, mind you, she's young, and," he sighed, "she's got a mind of her own, son." He uttered a short laugh and held his hand out to Sam, who took it firmly in his own.

"I'll call Nessa out here, and we'll learn what she thinks about this."

Nessa entered the store in response to her father's voice, stopped inside the doorway and looked at Sam.

"Nessa, this is Sam Jackson. He's asked if he could speak to you."

Nessa lifted her chin and stared at him, unsmiling, but Sam saw the laughter in her eyes. Her mockery frightened him more than her rigid figure and her tight lips. *Help me Lord!* "Nice to meet you, Ma'am. Pretty name—Nessa. I never heard it before." Sam's gaze wobbled to the ceiling, and back to her left ear before settling on the blue merriment above her nose. *She knows! She's enjoying watching me make a donkey out of myself. Well, we'll see about that!* He gave her a slight bow and turned to her father, who rearranged his open mouth into a grin.

"Thanks for the information about the cow and pigs, Mr. Long. I'll be back."

Mr. Long smiled and nodded. "See you Sam."

❧   ❧   ❧

"Well, of all the nerve." Nessa shook her curls and flounced into the living area. By the time she reached her room, pea-sized tears were racing down her cheeks.

"What's wrong, Nessa?" asked nine year old Opal. She and Ellie sat cross-legged on the floor sewing on their samplers.

"Not a thing. I just need a little privacy."

"Let's go outside, Opal." Twelve year old Ellie got to her feet and pulled her little sister from the room.

Nessa closed the bedroom door with a bang, threw herself across her bed, and muffled her anguish in the pillow. A few minutes later she heard a tap on the door.

"Nessa? Are you all right, dear?" Her mother entered and stood beside the bed. "Your papa told me what happened."

Nessa kicked her feet in frustration and buried her head deeper into the pillow. At her mother's touch, she sat up and fell into her arms.

"It will be all right, child." She caressed Nessa's shoulders. "Tell Mama what is troubling you."

Nessa pulled away and lifted her eyes to met her mother's concerned ones. "Mama, why do I do things that make me miserable? I heard Sam talking to Papa." She paused at her mother's audible intake of breath. "Oh, I know it's wrong to eavesdrop and I didn't intentionally. I went to the store and I heard my name, and well…then I stayed behind the door until Papa called me. I'm sorry, Mama, but that's unimportant right now." Her shoulders slumped forward. "I think I'd like to get to know Sam better and I wanted Papa to agree we could step out." She bit her lip. "But instead, I drove Sam away." Again, she crumpled into her mother's arms.

"Nessa, you're very young and some lessons you have to learn the hard way. I've tried to teach you to be considerate of other's feelings, and to think before you act." She grasped Nessa's shoulders and tugged her upright. "It's not the end of the world, dear."

Nessa raised her head, soothed by her mother's lilting voice. "I'm sure Mr. Jackson will be back. If he is really interested in you, he'll return. If he chooses not to, then he's not the man for you. More importantly, you must begin using the sense the good Lord gave you and stop trying to be someone you're not. And think of someone besides yourself, Nessa. I admire your spirit, you remind me of your grandmother, but if you use it in the wrong way, it will lead to unhappiness. Ask the Lord to guide you."

"I don't think He hears me any more." She swiped at her wet cheeks with a fist and noticed Mama's brow furrowing.

"Now who put that idea in your head?"

"I've done so many wrong things that the Bible says He hates, so He must hate me, too." Nessa's gaze dropped to her lap.

"Oh, Nessa. God doesn't hate you if you do something wrong! What kind of father would hate a child because of a mistake? The truth is none of us would be saved without his mercy." With an index finger, she lifted Nessa's head and gazed into her moist eyes. "Get on your knees and tell Him you're sorry and promise to do better. He'll let you know how much He loves you and wants what's best for you. You must read your Bible more. Begin with John."

"You really think He still loves me?"

"I know He does, but you need to get to know Him for yourself. Go to Him now, Nessa."

❦   ❦   ❦

Owen looked up from his account books when he heard Rebecca's quick steps. She seldom appeared in the store before lunch, and his brow furrowed as she stopped in front of him and took a deep breath. "Owen, I need to talk to you."

Owen's frown deepened at her tone of distress. "Of course, dear, what has distressed you?" He rose from his desk and strode to her side.

"It's about Nessa, and that young man, Sam. I'm sorry, I don't recall his surname." She blinked and gazed into her husband's eyes. "Owen, why did you give him permission to court Nessa? He has nothing to offer her." Her lips lengthened into a rare grim line.

"I'm sorry, Rebecca. I don't quite understand. Sam's a fine fellow; hardworking, doing real well with that homestead of his. Done more in the last few months than most men in a year." He took his wife's arm and led her to the chair behind his desk.

Rebecca sat and wrung her hands. "Oh, Owen! You know what I mean! He's just not the right person for our daughter."

"Rebecca, think what you're saying. Every family out here, with the exception of two or three ranchers, are homesteaders. Good people; making a home, raising their children." He bent, took her hands in his and smiled. "Rebecca.

This is our country; we won't be going back to the south, not back to the way things were years ago. Our destiny is here. We're helping to build a new land in America. Right now it's a little backward, but remember what our ancestors found when they came to Georgia almost two hundred years ago."

"Owen! Please don't mention that. You know how it pains me." She clutched at his arm. "We cannot allow our girls to endure such hardship. They must have the chance I never had." Tears trickled down her cheeks and she hid her face against her husband's chest.

Owen placed one arm around her convulsing shoulders, pulled a handkerchief from his pocket with his other hand, and placed it between her fingers. "Our girls will be all right, Rebecca." He frowned. "Sam's a good boy and he seems to care a great deal for our daughter. He's willing to wait until she grows up—a year or more. He's a patient, honest, hardworking, Christian. What more could you want for a son-in-law; and for your grandchildren's father?"

Rebecca raised her head. "Owen!" She wiped her eyes, and discreetly blew her nose.

He laughed and brushed a stray tear from her cheek."Well, it's something to think about, isn't it?" He kissed her forehead, pulled her to her feet and into his arms. "We can have a fine life here, Rebecca. I'm sorry I can't return to you what your family lost, but Oklahoma will be a great state one day, and we'll have a part in that, as will our daughters."

Rebecca sighed, pulled away and searched his face. He met her gaze with eyes full of honesty and love. She gave him a watery smile. "Forgive me, Owen. You're right, of course." She brushed a damp lock of hair back into place. "Sometimes I miss our old home so much–old friends, old ways." She caressed his cheek with gentle fingertips. "But those times are few and don't last long. You are my happiness. I chose to follow you a long time ago, and I've never regretted it." Her face softened and her brown eyes glistened. "I love you, Owen, and I trust you to know and do what is best for all of us."

She relaxed as his arms tightened around her slender form. At last he released her and kissed her lightly on the mouth, then held her at arm's length.

"That's my girl. The sprightly miss who stole my heart seventeen years ago."

"Ahem. Mr. Long, are you busy?"

The sound of a customer's voice sent Rebecca scurrying through the door to the living quarters.

❧   ❧   ❧

Sam urged Gallatin to a gallop and fumed most of the fifteen minute ride to the nearest farm with animals for sale. He slowed Gallatin to a trot and shed his provoked posture. His shoulders lifted and he prepared to get down to business.

After a half hour's negotiation, he owned a young Guernsey cow due to calf soon, and had put a down payment on two piglets to be picked from a litter expected in a few weeks. The fourteen dollars remaining in his jean's pocket would have to carry him through the summer until he could sell his corn crop. He fashioned a halter around the cow's neck, tied the other end of the rope to the saddle horn, and began the hour's journey home at a slow walk.

Satisfied with his business deals, Sam's thoughts turned to Nessa, and his face alternated between a frown and a smile. *She sure is feisty. How did she know what I was going to say? If she can read me so easily, it could be troublesome. She's bound to be intelligent and probably witty. Can I keep up with her?* He grinned. *She's going to be a handful, though.* Before reaching home, he had it worked out to his satisfaction. *I'll go back next week and pretend this morning never happened. We'll keep company in a friendly way for a few months. That'll give her time to grow up and me time to get smarter.*

He arrived home just before mid-day. After fetching a bucket of water for Gallatin and the cow, he staked her in the grassy twenty-acre pasture on a long rope.

"This is your new home, cow. Hope you like it. Sorry about the rope, but I'll have to wait until after corn harvest to put up a fence." He scratched the stiff hair between her ears. "How do you like the name Dolly?" The honey-hued mother-to-be stared back at him. "Yeah, you look like a Dolly."

Sam spent the next week hoeing the weeds coming up with the corn and tending his garden and livestock. The sun-warmed days grew longer, but the amount of necessary labor seemed to increase rather than diminish. He expanded the shed to give Dolly more space and arranged additional sod on the roof of the dug-out. He planned to add another room next spring. It would be at least two years before he could build a proper house, he surmised. At dusk on Friday, Hank came for supper and dominoes.

"Fried chicken and biscuits and gravy. About my favorite." Hank peered into a pot set at the rim of the fire. "What's this green stuff?"

"Wild chickweed greens. Just picked them from the pasture this evening. Don't you have chickweed in Illinois?"

"Chickweed greens." Hank lifted a spoonful, frowned, and dropped it back into the pot. "I can't say I ever heard of it. Guess I'll pass."

Sam hid a grin. "All right, leaves more for me."

They ate without speaking by the light of the fire, then concentrated on their dominoes. After Sam won three games, Hank tossed his dominoes onto the playing board.

"I quit," said Hank. "You must have got that little black haired girl out of your system."

"Nope. In fact I asked her pa if we could keep company. I'm going to see her tomorrow."

"Humph. I'm telling you, Sam...Ah, never mind." He scratched his head. "I was going to ask you if you wanted to ride over to the social at the Bagley ranch."

"Yeah, I'm thinking of going. They're raising money to build a church across from the schoolhouse." He grinned and shook his head. "I don't have any money but I'll volunteer some labor."

"I imagine most everybody in the area will be there. Should be quite a shindig. Want to come by my place about six?"

"Sounds all right."

"Well, I gotta get some sleep so I can outrun all those pretty gals chasing me tomorrow." He grinned, set his empty coffee cup on the ground, and went toward his horse.

"Yeah, Hank. I can't wait to see that." Sam chuckled and watched his friend gallop across the grass.

CHAPTER 4

❀

Nessa took a deep breath after fastening her blue dress. *It's a little tight and a year old, but it's the only party dress I have.* She stepped to the dresser where Eleanor and Opal were maneuvering their heads so each could claim a face-sized segment of the mirror.

"Ellie," said Nessa, "you helped Papa in the store this afternoon. Did Sam Jackson come in?"

"I don't know any Sam Jackson, but he didn't come in while I was there. I knew everybody." Ellie brushed a shiny strand of brown hair into a smooth curl. "Henry Jones asked if you were going tonight." Her gaze met Nessa's in the glass. "Who's Sam Jackson?"

"Henry." Nessa's voice dripped with disdain. "Who cares about him any more, after Louise threw him over?" She yanked the blue ribbon from her hair, smoothed it with her fingers, swallowed her impatience, and retied the length of shiny satin into a perfect bow.

A knock on the door, followed by her father's voice, interrupted. "Daughters, finish your dressing and come downstairs right away. We will be late."

Papa helped his ladies settle in the buggy, took up the reins and flicked them, signaling the matched pair of chestnut horses to proceed. When Rebecca turned to look behind her, Nessa closed her eyes and silently mimicked her mother's words as she spoke them.

"Remember your manners at the party, girls. Decorum, decorum, decorum. I expect you to be on your best behavior." Nessa opened her eyes when her mother continued. "This is your first social outing. Nessa, you and Ellie have been practicing the steps of several of the square dances. There will be others you don't know, so don't act like silly geese if you make a mistake. Watch the other women. Opal, you're too young to dance, but you can watch and learn or play with the other little girls, but mind you care for your new shoes."

When they reached the ranch house, Papa secured the buggy beside one of twenty or more other conveyances and joined the group of older men near the corral, Mama carried the basket of food to the long tables set out on the grass in front of the house, and Opal ran toward the children playing in the orchard. Although Nessa had visited her best friend, sixteen-year-old Louise Bagley, several times, she was again impressed by the imposing two story rock house. Papa had told her the Bagley's were one of the first families to come to this remote part of the Oklahoma Territory. They ran several hundred head of cattle on a thousand acres of federal range land, in addition to the hundred and sixty acre plot where the ranch house stood.

"There's Louise." Ellie pointed toward the corral. "I wonder where the other girls are."

Nessa looked at the crowd milling around. "Everyone in the area must be here. Do you see any of your friends, Ellie?"

"I think so, way over on the other side of the house. See you later."

Nessa walked toward the fragile looking blonde who stood gazing up at two young cowboys sitting on the top rail of the corral fence. Louise gave the fellows a little wave and strolled toward Nessa.

"Hi! I'm glad you're finally here." She fingered the wide lace around her neckline. "Your last year's dress looks very pretty."

"Hello, Louise." Unsure whether she had been put down or complimented, Nessa lifted her chin. "Thank you." Although Louise was her best friend, Nessa was fully aware of her sharp-tongued propensity to always put herself in a good light, sometimes at the expense of others. At the same time, she valued Louise's friendship and tried to pattern herself after her acknowledged sophistication.

"Your new dress is pretty. I'm glad you finished sewing it in time." Nessa eyed the dress of pale green patterned with yellow rosebuds. It sets off her fair coloring, thought Nessa, but my figure is better. She stretched to her fullest height and looked down at the top of Louise's head. "Your dad's social sure drew a crowd."

"Yes, poor Mother is beside herself. She's afraid someone will trample her flower garden." She frowned and discreetly pointed to the two men at the corral. "And those two, they're from Texas, just traveling through. One of them asked me to eat supper with him." She lifted her chin. "Of course, I had to say no, Father would have apoplexy if I sat down with a drifter. I hope he didn't notice me talking to them." She raised a slender hand and flipped a tress of hair over her shoulder.

Nessa watched the sun glint on the golden curls. *She looks like Mama's treasured china doll. It's not surprising she has so many admirers.* Nessa had no illusions about Louise's ability to take care of herself; she could ride a spirited horse and drive a team and buggy—when no young men were watching.

Musical sounds emanated from the barn, and the girls made their way through the streams of children playing tag to the huge open door. Nessa stood eying the thin layer of scented clover covering the barn floor, and the bales of hay lining the perimeter, while her eyes adjusted to the dim interior. She tapped one foot as two men tuned up their fiddles and a third played a lively ditty on his guitar. Young wives appeared with husbands in tow and formed two squares at the far end. A young man claimed Louise for his partner and Nessa looked around for someone she knew. Henry Jones appeared, bowed, and held out his hand. She followed him to the floor where three couples waited to complete the fourth square. The caller took his place in front of the musicians and the dance began.

The barn became warm and dusty despite the floor covering, and after three rounds, Nessa slipped out for a breath of air. The mellow night, with a quarter moon hanging in the eastern sky, reminded her of a gigantic field dotted with a million tiny campfires. A wisp of wind, carrying the sound of voices, focused her attention on the corral where two men were unsaddling their horses. Nessa recognized the shorter one. Sam Jackson. She ducked back inside and made her way to a shadowy corner.

She watched as the young men chose partners. Sam danced with Louise twice and Opal once. He never came within ten feet of her hiding place and her countenance fell.

The clang of the supper bell blotted out the music, and laughing couples ran to grab early spots in the line queuing up in front of the laden tables. Nessa slowly moved forward. A rancher's son sprinted by with Louise in tow. She slowed to speak to Nessa.

"Speak with me later. I want to ask you about Sam somebody. Opal says you know him."

"What do you…?"

"He's hmm—you know!" Her blue eyes danced as she was pulled along by her escort.

"How about having supper with me?" said a voice behind her. She turned to find Sam grinning at her. She stared at him in surprise, and an uncommon feeling of confusion caused her stomach to lurch.

"What's the matter, cat got your tongue? Let's go before the roast beef's all gone."

She didn't resist his forceful grasp of her arm as he led her outside.

When they reached the first table, Sam took a slip of paper from his pocket, wrote: 'Twenty hours labor, Sam Jackson,' and dropped it in the basket provided for donations to build the church.

After heaping their plates with succulent roast beef, ranch beans, potato salad, cole slaw, and biscuits, Sam motioned toward the side of the house. "It's less crowded over there."

Nessa sat on the ground and smoothed her skirt over her legs while Sam squatted beside her. They ate in silence for several minutes, then spoke in unison. "I'd like to apologize."

"You first." Nessa gave him her sweetest smile.

"All right." Sam cleared his throat. "I need to apologize, and I do right now, but tell me how you knew I had asked your father if I could call on you?"

Nessa attempted to tuck her crimson face into the collar of her dress without success. "I didn't mean to eavesdrop, but I heard you talking to Papa." Her voice rose and quavered. "And then, I don't know what came over me, but I'm sorry I was rude." Her words faded into silent embarrassment.

Sam chuckled. "And I thought you might be one of those mind-readers. Scared the dickens out of me to be truthful."

Nessa speared a bite of meat and chewed, avoiding Sam's gaze. "I didn't think you were coming tonight. Did you just get here?"

"Been here quite a spell. Didn't see you though, til after the last dance."

Nessa sensed the question in his voice and knew he was looking at her but she kept her gaze on her plate, and simply said, "Oh."

After a few minutes of awkward silence, he asked, "Who is Louise?"

Nessa stopped chewing, swallowed hard, and a morsel of salad slipped down her throat. Not again! She battled the pain and fury watering her eyes. After several moments, she looked squarely into Sam's eyes. "Louise? She's the daughter of the man who owns this ranch, and my best friend."

Sam looked at his empty plate. "Yeah. That figures."

"What do you mean?"

"I hear the music starting. You ready to dance?" He grasped her hand and lifted her to her feet.

They danced two squares then Sam led her to the side. "I have to leave now. It's a long ride home, and morning comes early." He looked around the barn. "I wonder where Hank is."

"That fella you rode in…I mean the one…he's in the corner talking to Louise."

Sam raised his eyebrows and grinned. "Yeah, the one I rode in with. I'll see if he's ready to leave." He took Nessa's hands in his. "Thanks for the dances. I might be able to come by your place tomorrow afternoon. We could go for a ride if you like. You do ride, don't you?"

"Of course I ride!"

Sam squeezed her hand. "Good. See you tomorrow." He gave her a slight bow and strode toward Hank.

Louise gave Sam a coy smile when he halted beside her, and laid a dainty hand on his arm. Nessa glared at Louise's back.

CHAPTER 5

⚜

Sam read the Bible for an hour after doing chores and eating breakfast, then spent the remainder of the morning working in the garden. After lunch, he hauled the big wash tub behind the animal's shed, filled it with buckets of hot water heated on the outside fire, and bathed for the second time in two days. He dressed in his best jeans and shirt, banged the dust from his hat by slamming it against the side of the wagon, and saddled Gallatin.

Mr. Long, dressed in his Sunday suit, stiff-collared white shirt, and black string tie, sat in an ancient rattan rocking chair under a cotton wood tree reading a newspaper.

Sam dismounted, ambled toward the older man and removed his hat. "Mr. Long."

"Hello Sam. Nice weather we're having."

"Yes, sir." He leaned against the tree and shuffled his feet. "Is Nessa home? I thought we might take a ride, with your permission."

"She's in the house, Sam." He motioned toward the front porch. "Go ahead in and ask her." He smiled. "Be back before supper time."

"Yes, sir. Thank you." Sam tipped his hat and took the steps two at a time to the front door.

Mrs. Long answered his knock. "Sam, isn't it? Please come in."

"It's Nessa I came to see, ma'am."

"Have a seat and I'll fetch her."

Sam stood by the fireplace, fumbled with his hat, and feigned an interest in the richly carved grandmother clock while listening for Nessa's footsteps. When she appeared at the parlor door, his heart missed a beat.

"Nessa. Like I spoke of last night, I came to take you riding if you're willing." Her cool blue eyes met his and he held her gaze for a long moment.

"Oh, did you?" Her skirts swished from side to side as she strode to stand in front of him. "I thought you might have something better to do."

Sam frowned. "I don't believe I get your meaning."

A smile of mystery flashed across her face and her eyes glowed. "I'll tell Mama and change into riding clothes. Saddle Nellie for me." With a swirl of skirts, she turned and disappeared.

After a moment of stunned immobility, Sam wandered outside to obey her command.

"Nessa told me to saddle her horse," he told Mr. Long as he walked toward the barn.

"Ah. Her saddle is hanging on the north end of the shed." Sam felt Mr. Long's gaze on his back and he quickened his steps. A few minutes later he led Nessa's little black mare to the front yard and tied her next to Gallatin.

Mr. Long rose and took a few steps toward him, shielding his eyes from the sun's glare with one hand. "Where are you two planning to ride?"

"Not far. Down the trail toward where the church will be, probably. Don't worry, sir, I'll have her back early."

Nessa appeared dressed in a deep-green, lace-trimmed riding outfit, and polished black boots. Her raven curls were swept up and under a man's felt hat. Sam stared at her headgear. He grinned and was rewarded with a scathing look.

"Don't say a word. Mama insisted I wear this to protect my complexion."

She snatched Nellie's reins, stalked to the mounting block, and stood waiting with head held high. Sam shrugged in amusement and hoisted her to the saddle. Before he could step away, she slipped her feet into the stirrups, slapped Nellie on the flank and said, "Go, girl." She yelled over her shoulder at Sam, "Race you to the end of the cornfield." Nellie obeyed the call and broke into a gallop.

"What the…" muttered Sam. He hiked himself into the saddle and gave Gallatin a full rein. The horse reared in response and took the challenge.

When Sam pulled up beside Nellie at the edge of the field, Nessa was picking the buttercups growing along the edge of the road. "Took you long enough," she said and grinned, revealing a mouth filled with even white teeth.

"Don't you know better than to run your horse without letting her warm up?"

"Oh, fiddlesticks. She's been running in the pasture all day; I just brought her into the corral a half hour ago." She turned back to searching in the weeds, then gave him a side-long look, "You're just mad because she outran that big old monster of yours."

Sam watched her and wondered how one little girl could cause such conflicting emotions in a grown man—one glimpse of her eyes and his heart thumped, then with one word or action, she became the most maddening creature he'd ever come across.

"You shouldn't pick buttercups. They wilt before you can get them home."

"I know." Her slight southern drawl became more pronounced. "I should leave them for every passerby to enjoy." That's what Mama told me." She straightened to her full height and looked at the drooping yellow petals. "She's right. I'm sorry, pretty flowers. I won't pick you again." She dropped them at her feet and turned to face Sam.

"What do we do now?"

Sam sighed and dismounted. "Let's sit awhile."

Nessa sat on a cushion of weeds, removed her hat, and shook her curls loose. Sam squatted beside her. He picked up a pebble and drew circles in the sandy soil. "I'd like us to get acquainted and I guess the best way is if we talk about ourselves some." He glanced at Nessa whose unwavering gaze monitored the progress of a red ant crawling across the toe of her boot.

"About me. My family has a farm back in Tennessee. I have three brothers and a sister besides my ma and pa. I came out here over a year ago and bought a little homestead. I'd heard stories about Oklahoma Territory since I was a boy and there wasn't much future at home. All the good land is taken. Anyway, I worked on ranches on the way west, and when I got here I stopped. I want to have a nice place to work and grow things and a family. I only went to the fourth grade in school but I'm good at figures and I read whatever I can find, mostly the Bible right now, but Ma had some books and the school teacher let me borrow some of hers. I liked the history books, and *The Prairie*, and even a little Shakespeare." He paused for breath and gazed at his companion.

"I don't read much, but I like poetry. Have you read Lord Byron's *She Walks In Beauty?*"

"Lord—?" Sam felt heat rise from his neck to his ears. "I can't say I ever heard of him."

"Oh, well. It hardly matters. He's been dead for years." Nessa leaned back and took a deep breath of the cooling air. A horse snorted and she looked at

Sam's big bay. "Gallatin sure is a funny name for a horse. How'd he come by it?"

Startled, Sam turned to meet curious blue eyes. He searched their depths for mockery a moment of two, then finding none, he stared at the ground between his feet. "It's a long story, and I…"

"I'm not doing much of anything in the next half hour."

"Do you ever let a person finish a sentence?"

She flushed and studied her fingernails. "Forgive me. I confess I'm a little nervous."

A side-long glance convinced him she wasn't pulling his leg, and her sunny smile caused his stomach to do a cartwheel."Okay," he said in an amused voice, "you asked so I'll tell you." He got to his feet and looked at the horizon for inspiration. "The story's told that my great-grandfather lived among the Indi-ans in western Tennessee—sold supplies to them, went hunting with them. He ended up marrying the chief's daughter, a princess." A nervous chuckle burst from his lips and he turned his face away from Nessa.

"Oh! A real princess?"

Her apparent interest surprised Sam and bolstered his confidence. He returned his gaze to her face and basked in her smile. "Yeah, that's what my grandpa told me. He didn't know her Indian name but my great-grandpa called her Jewel. Ma has a picture of her—a good-looking woman. Anyway, an influential man from Washington went out there around that time, maybe before, I'm not sure. A man named Gallatin, and I guess he did a lot to help the Indians. And my great-grandpa and the princess called their first son Gallatin. He was grandpa's oldest brother. I never knew him, but I remember the first time I heard his name. On my seventh birthday. Grandpa gave me a pocket knife and told me the story of his parents. I couldn't get the name Gallatin out of my head so when Pa gave me this colt, that's what I named him. Pa laughed. Said it was too regal for a plain old horse. But I didn't pay no mind. I thought it suited him fine. So, that's the story." He gazed at Nessa with narrowed eyes. "Are you going to laugh, too?"

"No, Sam. I think it's a beautiful story. So romantic." Her eyes searched his features. "And that's where you got the bronzy glow to your skin and those deep brown eyes." She jumped to her feet, placed her hand on his arm, and peered up. Her slightly open mouth, and pink lips curved inches from his.

Sam took a hurried step backwards. "Drat it, Nessa, don't do that!"

"Why, whatever do you mean?" She squinted at him through lowered lashes. "I guess you better take me home, Samuel Jackson." She slammed her hat back on her head, lifted her chin and gazed at the horizon.

Sam studied her unwavering profile. Would he ever know what this girl was thinking? "Yeah, it's getting late. I promised your pa I'd have you home before supper." He helped her mount and drew himself into his saddle. They tilted their hats to shield their eyes from the harsh rays of the sun and trotted back the way they came.

Mr. Long met them at the corral gate. "I'll take care of Nellie, you go on in the house," he told Nessa, after Sam helped her dismount.

"Goodby, Sam." Nessa casually waggled her fingers in his direction. "Thank you for the ride."

Sam tipped his hat and turned to Mr. Long. "We're not late are we?"

"No, young man. Nothing like that. Nessa sometimes neglects to brush Nellie down if she's in a hurry or excited." He grinned. "I noticed a sparkle in her eyes."

Sam felt heat rise up his neck and lowered his eyes to the ground. "I took good care of her, sir, like I promised."

"Oh, I don't doubt that. And you seem to have caught her interest."

"Yeah, well, we talked about our families. Mine back in Tennessee, mostly. We never got around to..." He shuffled his feet. "If there's nothing more, Mr. Long, I need to get home and do my chores."

"That's fine, Sam. Come again."

"Yes, sir. Thank you."

❧   ❧   ❧

Nessa blew into the kitchen and tossed her hat on the table. "Mama! You'll never guess—Sam's great-grandmother was a princess."

"Nessa, please put your hat away properly. What are you saying? We don't have princesses in the United States of America."

"It's true. His great-grandfather married an Indian princess. And she named her son..." Nessa stopped at her mother's expression when she turned from the stove and pushed a strand of hair from her perspiring brow.

"An Indian princess? Nonsense, child." Mama shook her head and vigorously stirred the stew. "Now, I could use some help. Ellie has gone off somewhere. Pour the milk and cut some bread."

"Yes, Mama. But isn't it exciting? I never would have thought…And Sam looked so handsome today. His eyes are so brown." Her mother turned to her with a frown and Nessa hurried to get the milk from the well house. She lifted the gallon jug from the shallow water-filled trough running the length of one wall, and noticed the almost full bucket of cream her mother had skimmed from the milk. No doubt she or Ellie would have to churn it into butter the next day.

Papa dominated the conversation at supper, talking about two new families who had moved into the area and how much material and labor had been donated for the church. Nessa fidgeted and pushed the food around on her plate, forking a morsel into her mouth only when her mother's gaze settled on her. She received a smug smirk from Ellie, when their glances met across the table, but her afternoon with Sam absorbed her and she ignored her sister. At last they finished eating. Papa went to the parlor while she helped Mama and Ellie wash and dry the dishes.

When they finished, Nessa followed her mother into the parlor and sat in a chair across from her father. He took the family Bible from a shelf and began the traditional Sunday evening reading. Nessa struggled to pay attention, knowing her father would question her and her sisters on what the text meant, but her thoughts kept wandering. Fortunately, she knew the story of Joshua and how the Lord gave him extra time to win a battle by causing the sun to stand still. She fidgeted during her father's prayer of praise and thanksgiving for caring for his family the past week, and petition for blessings during the coming one. When he rose to replace the Bible, Nessa spoke without preamble.

"Papa, did you know Sam's great-grandmother was an Indian princess?"

"Um, a princess you say? No, I didn't know." He returned to his seat and picked up the paper laying on the table beside him.

Nessa strolled across the room, sat on the arm of his chair and related the story Sam had told her. "Isn't it wonderful?"Dubious silence filled the room.

Papa tipped his head to one side and smiled. "How about that! I don't know how wonderful it is, but it helps to explain Sam's forthright bearing and the pride he tries to keep hidden."

"I don't care about all that, Papa, but he…"

"Listen, Nessa. It's true a man is part of his background, his heritage, but the important thing about Sam is not that there was a princess back somewhere in his ancestry. The important thing is what kind of man he is."

"Oh, she thinks he's the right kind of man," said Ellie. She lowered her head and giggled.

"What do you mean?" Nessa jumped from her chair and confronted her sister with arms akimbo.

"You were sitting awful close to him, and then you…"

"What do…how do…were you following us?" Nessa raised one hand, stepped toward Ellie, then whirled to face her mother. "Mama!"

"Ellie, where were you this afternoon?" Nessa's eyes widened at her father's stern voice and she watched her sister's face pale.

Ellie failed to meet her father's glance and twisted her hands behind her back. "I just went for a walk. It's not my fault they were over there by the field."

"O-o-h." Nessa grasped her skirts with clenched fingers and raced up the stairs.

Her mother's voice penetrated her distress as she sped down the hall toward her room. "Ellie, your father will speak with you."

Nessa lay sprawled across her bed, her fists beating a ragged rhythm on the coverlet when her mother knocked and entered the room.

"Nessa?"

She turned her face to the wall and wailed, "How could she be so mean?"

Mama sat on the edge of the bed. "Nessa. It was unkind of Ellie to follow you, but I don't believe that's the true reason for your distress. Would you like to tell me what's really troubling you?"

Nessa sat up and rubbed her eyes with anger-curled fingers, then threw herself into her mother's arms. "Mama, I'm so miserable. How can something wonderful make me feel this way?"

"Mercy, Nessa. Just tell me what you're thinking, and perhaps I can help."

"Sam is nice, Mama, even I can see that. And I like him a lot. But, Mama, I…I've been praying God will change me so I'm not angry, or envious, or any of those other things I do that are wrong. But I still do them sometimes, and I don't want Sam to find out what I'm really like. He would have nothing to do with me if he knew."

"Honey, God loves you and He is changing you. But it won't happen over night. He's changing your heart right now; that's why you feel hurt inside. You know it was wrong to raise your voice to your sister. You'll feel better when you tell her you're sorry."

Rebecca brushed tendrils of damp hair from Nessa's face. "You're growing up, child, and I know you're going to be a fine woman. As for Sam, if he's half the man your father thinks he is, he knows more about you than you realize and he keeps coming back. He sees something in you that won't let him go. I think he'll wait until you grow a little more."

Nessa looked into her mother's eyes. She saw love and no doubt. She smiled through the tears. "Do you really think so? If only…Why is it so hard to grow up, Mama?"

Her mother laughed. "I wish I knew, Nessa. All I know is everyone has to do it, and most of us make it through. You will, too; I promise."

❦   ❦   ❦

Shortly before midnight, Sam fell into his bed, tired but animated by Nessa's response to him. She intrigued him more deeply with each encounter. Her vitality and intellect fascinated him. And today. Her lips, so close. Not his to explore…yet. He mentally counted off the remaining months before her sixteenth birthday. Fourteen to go. A long time. He sighed and rolled onto his back. He had much to accomplish before bringing her to his home. He must keep his mind on those tasks. He sighed again, said his prayers, and turned on his side.

CHAPTER 6

More than a dozen men gathered at eight in the morning with shovels, picks, and other construction tools to begin erecting the church. Sam helped dig the basement, line it with rocks, hauled from the foothills twenty miles to the northwest, and cover them with rough plaster. The next day, Sam and Hank knelt side by side pounding nails into the rough flooring, while others constructed the framework for the outside walls. Wives and daughters arrived at the church site before noon each day, in wagons laden with food for the hungry laborers.

Sam caught the scent of fried chicken and raised his head to gaze into Hank's grinning face. He sat back on his heels, swiped at his perspiring face with a gloved fist, and pulled his old watch from his pocket. Hank shaded his eyes with his hand and peered at the sun overhead.

"Almost noon."

"Quarter to." Sam replaced the watch and picked up his hammer. When the ding, ding of the brass bell announced dinner, he rose to his feet, rubbed his sore knees, and looked about him. "We'll finish this in another hour, and looks like the walls are about ready to be raised. We should have them up by sundown."

"Yeah, I'll be glad for that. This is harder than hoeing corn. The good Lord didn't make knees to be walked on." He took a few tentative steps. "Well, come on, let's get something to eat. I'm starved."

"Coming. I have to wash up and get a drink first." Sam went to the barrel of water and drank deeply from the tin dipper, then poured a small amount into his hand and splashed it over his head.

"Here's your plate, Sam. I got you a big piece of chicken breast before it was all gone."

Sam turned. Louise, stood just behind him, smiling and offering a plate piled high with chicken, potatoes, corn, and biscuits. The sun glinted off her golden hair caught on top of her head with a pink ribbon.

"Louise." He stuffed the handkerchief back in his pocket. "Uh, thanks." He took the proffered plate and strolled toward a group of men sitting on the ground in the shade of a wagon.

"We could sit over there in our buggy. The top will shade us and we're high enough to catch a breeze."

He looked down into seemingly innocent blue eyes, but a hint of challenge tinged the upturned pink lips. Sam covertly glanced around but saw no path of escape. "Uh, okay, but where's your plate?"

Louise moved toward the buggy and, with an over-the-shoulder look, said, "I'll eat later." Sam found himself following the bouncing pink bow. She stopped and Sam eyed the shiny black metal carriage and the leather covered seats, shaded by a heavy black cloth top.

"I can't sit up there; I'm all dusty and sweaty."

"Oh, bother! You can sit on my shawl."

"I haven't seen you since our party," said Louise after Sam helped her up into the buggy and sat beside her on the back seat.

He chewed, swallowed, and kept his eyes on his plate. "Been busy with my crops. Had to finish hoeing so I could help out with the church."

"I've been here every day this week, but you never even said hello." She inched closer and fluttered her eyelashes.

Sam pressed himself against the side of the buggy. "Look, Louise, you're a pretty girl, but I…"

"Oh, never mind!" Louise slid to the far side of the seat and stuck out her lower lip. "I guess you only have eyes for Nessa."

Sam frowned and watched her bosom heave up and down for a moment, then turned back to his plate. The food no longer interested him, and he shifted his legs to rise. Louise turned her face and their glances met. Her pale blue eyes sharpened to green jade. "I don't know why. She's such a child."

Sam looked away and inhaled deeply. "Yeah, well, I guess I better get back to work. Thanks for bringing my dinner." He nodded to her, jumped from the buggy and without breaking stride, ran toward the work site.

"Go on, then, if that's what you want. Bet you'll be sorry!"

Hank intercepted him. "What's going on? What did Louise mean, 'you'll be sorry'?"

Sam's glare effectively halted further questions, and Hank threw up his hands. "Okay, I'm sorry I mentioned it. Let's get this floor done."

❧   ❧   ❧

Nessa watched Louise waylay Sam and kept her gaze on them while pretending to eat.

When Sam walked away, she ignored her mother's direction to hurry and finish so they could pack up and go home, slammed her plate on the wooden trestle table, and stormed toward her blonde friend. She stopped a few inches from the ornate carriage and Louise bumped into her when she stepped down.

"Nessa! I didn't see you."

"I'm not surprised." She took a deep breath and faced her rival. "Stay away from Sam Jackson, Louise."

"I don't know what you mean." She straightened her skirt. "And, anyway, I didn't see your brand on him." She attempted to sidle around Nessa.

Nessa stood her ground and her steely gaze penetrated the older girl's poise. Louise paled and whirled away, brushing against Nessa's shoulder. Nessa lips curved, but the flint lingered in her blue eyes.

❧   ❧   ❧

Sam worked beside Hank in near silence for an hour, and then left to help the men raise the walls. At sundown, he lifted sore muscles into his saddle and left the skeleton church, with Hank by his side. Sam had regained his composure and he jokingly related the incident with Louise as they trotted toward home.

Sam dismissed the smudge of clouds barely visible above the western horizon. The weather had been hot and dry for two weeks and he had sent prayers to heaven daily asking God to delay the rain until the end of the approaching corn harvest. He smiled at the memory of corn towering above his head and sorghum swinging its thick, succulent green leaves in the wind, when he checked his fields early this morning.

"I figure I can work the rest of this week at the church, then I'll have to gather my corn." Sam tilted his hat back, surrendering his forehead to the cool breeze. "If it does as well as I think, I can add an above-ground room for cooking."

"My corn's about ready, too. You want to work together to get it in? I planted mine two days after you did, so we could do yours first."

"Sounds like a good idea, Hank. I'll be hauling most of it to a fellow down south who promised to buy what I don't need to keep for seed. You planning to sell all of yours?"

"Most of it. I have a buyer, too. Looks like we'll have a little silver to jingle in our pockets this winter." Hank let go with an exuberant, "Yippee. I can go to town every Saturday this fall."

Sam shook his head.

※   ※   ※

Yesterday's hint of clouds had erupted into a dark cauldron threatening the lowering sun, Sam noticed the next afternoon when he stopped hammering long enough to get a drink of water. Still miles away. He looked over his shoulder at the burgeoning structure. Today's community teamwork had successfully anchored the walls, raised the roof joists, and covered about a third of the opening with rough sheathing. Sam hurried back to his task. They must finish closing in the roof and sidewalls before the rain storm.

Menacing thunder heads overspread the western quadrant of the sky by the time Sam and Hank reined their mounts toward home. The cooling air seemed charged with an ominous breath of warning.

"Looks like we're in for a storm. Glad we got the roof closed in." Hank eyed the sky and urged his horse to a trot.

Sam studied the glowering clouds as Gallatin increased his pace. "It's moving fast and coming from two directions. If we don't hurry, we'll get a soaking." A wind gust blew a tumbleweed across the trail, and he yelled at his friend. "See you tomorrow, Hank."

Wind-driven raindrops the size of nickels pelted Sam a quarter mile from his place. Gallatin leaped into a full gallop and Sam scrunched his old hat down to his ears. He rode to the gate of the small corral enclosing the lean-to barn, and removed Gallatin's saddle and bridle. The cow stood bawling out in the pasture with her calf huddled beneath her belly, and Sam ran to let them into the shelter. The piglets lay safe in their shed, and he slammed the door shut, then sped by the chicken coop, secured the door, and raced to the dugout.

Experience led his feet down the dark stairs and to the chest where he lit an oil lamp with shivery fingers. After stripping his lean body of wet clothes, he chucked a scoop of coal into the little stove, added a few dry twigs and struck a match to start the fire. The noise from the storm penetrated the earthen roof like a cattle stampede. When the stove gave off heat, he broke eggs into an old iron-cast skillet and put a couple of yesterday's biscuits in the oven. He ate sitting in the old rocker, then rose to pour a cup of stale coffee, and again sat, rocking and listening to the turbulence above his head.

A dripping sound near at hand brought him to his feet. In the feeble lamplight, he saw trickles of water on the west wall of the dugout. The rain had penetrated the roof covering. Even as he watched, frowning, more rivulets appeared on the west ends of the north and south walls. He pulled his bed and the chest holding his clothes into the middle of the room. There was little else he could do. The water would soak into the dirt floor, but too much on the walls might cause portions to become saturated and break off. The stove, safe against the northeast wall, dispelled the chill of gloom with radiant heat. He moved the wooden box which held flour, sugar, and coffee to the top of the chest, and anxiously paced back and forth along the dripping walls. The little streams did not seem to widen, and no new ones appeared. *Thank you, Jesus.* He returned to his chair, not rocking now, as there was no space with the chest in front of it and the bed behind. Every few minutes he moved his lips in silent prayer, as he waited out the storm.

When the roar diminished to intermittent howls, he glanced at his pocketwatch—almost nine o'clock. In stocking feet, he ascended and pushed back the east-facing door. A few dislocated drops of water trickled down his nose when he stuck out his head. The heavens were as thick and black as tar overhead, but lightning followed by bellowing thunder traced up, down, and sideways across the eastern sky like a hundred fourth of July celebrations. He glimpsed the outline of the barn and sheds during a light display. Sheets of rain distorted the scene and he descended, banked the fire, undressed, and scrambled under the bed quilts to banish the chill of his arms, legs, and foreboding. Before going to sleep, he prayed for safety for himself and for the animals under his care.

🍁   🍁   🍁

After supper, Rebecca and the girls left the dining room to clean the kitchen. Owen dawdled over a cup of coffee and kept an ear tuned to the sound of the storm. When the dishes were done, he suggested the family stay together in the parlor. The clangor of the storm prevented conversation. He read his paper between apprehensive glances at the draped window, and Rebecca's embroidery needle moving up and down through the pillow case on her lap, keeping time with the crashes of thunder. Ellie and Opal played an almost silent game of checkers, tensing with each blast of sound, and Nessa held her book with stiff fingers.

The mantel clock showed 9:23 when the sound of the wind-driven rain lessened. Opal pulled aside the curtains to stare into the night. "One-thousand, two-thousand, three-thousand," she said and turned to her father. "The lightning is three miles away now, Papa."

"Good. Think I'll go out and look around a bit." Owen took a small lamp from the table by the front door and walked onto the porch. Intermittent drops fell from the trees, but the rain appeared to have gone with the lightning and thunder that still brightened the sky to the east. He held the lamp high and noticed a spate of water hurtling down the shallow depressions on each side of the road. Pools overflowed one into another between the house and the barn. He estimated the rainfall at over two inches and sighed. Some farmers' crops were undoubtedly flooded, which could mean a hard winter, especially for newcomers.

Owen stood looking into the night and seeking the future. How much credit would he be asked to carry in food until the next harvest? How much could he carry without endangering his own family? *The Lord will see us through. All of us who trust Him. I hope the church building isn't damaged. People will need a place of peace and fellowship.*

CHAPTER 7

❀

Sam woke, added a handful of coal to the fire, and carefully stirred the embers with the poker. Hot coals blazed from under their ash coating. He replenished the coffee pot and set it near the back of the stove where it would not boil over, but would be ready by the time he finished his chores. After dressing quickly, he donned his hat and started up the steps.

A warning hiss stopped him with one foot in mid-air. A rattlesnake lay curled at the top of the stairs. Its signature tail rose from the center of the coils singing a challenge. Sam retreated, one, slow, methodical, pace at a time. When he reached the floor, he ran to the chest, shoved the rocker aside, grabbed his pistol from the top drawer, and stealthily climbed upward.

The sound of the shot echoed around the tiny enclosed room causing Sam's ears to ring. He shook his head and peered into the shadows at the writhing serpentine form. It slid down a step, then another. Sam did the same.

When the flailing grew less violent, Sam took a cautious step upward, and studied the feeble contortions of the headless body. Still gripping the pistol in his right hand, he grabbed the poker, hooked the convulsing carcass, and carried it to the top of the stairs. The rattler's head lay where it had fallen from the blast. After tossing both parts outside for later disposal, he took a deep breath and left the door open, allowing the morning to disperse the shadows while he inspected each step. He knew the reptiles usually traveled in pairs, and he meant to search every inch of the room. Finding nothing after fifteen minutes, he returned the pistol to the drawer, poured a cup of coffee almost as weak as his knees, and perched on the edge of the bed.

Dolly's bawling brought him upright with a jerk. He slammed his cup down on the table and hurried outside. Dolly and Gallatin stood at the fence staring toward him, no doubt wondering why he was so tardy with their breakfast. He grinned, waved at them, and yelled, "Coming. Sorry I'm late, but I've been kinda busy."

Chores finished, he headed back toward the dugout to fix his breakfast and enjoy a strongly brewed cup of coffee. He glanced to the north, stopped, dropped the feed buckets and ran toward his corn field. At its edge, he fell to his knees in shock. A swath of destruction lay before him. The six foot stalks of corn were gone. Parts of the field lay barren as though swept by a giant's broom. Piles of golden stubble, broken and pointing in all directions, lay here and there. Beyond the corn field, the sorghum glistened peacefully in the morning rays of the sun. Sam's gaze followed the route of devastation. It stretched from southwest to northeast as far as he could see, a hundred yards wide.

He squinted into the sun's glare. *What happened to the trees down by the river?* A gaping nothingness appeared where three huge old cottonwoods had stood yesterday—a landmark for folks in every direction. Gone, just like that! His eyes widened with understanding. *A twister! A twister came through here.*

He stared at his ruined field for long minutes. Finally, he looked at the healthy field of silage, then turned to look at his livestock, his plow, his vegetable garden, and his home. He rose and lifted his arms toward heaven.

"Thank you, Jesus, for protecting the animals, the garden and the feed crop. I really needed the money from a good corn harvest so I could fix this place up for Nessa. But You know everything, and I guess it wasn't meant to be. I'll trust You to tell me what to do now. I feel kinda down, but I know You're there, so I'll make it all right."

He straightened his shoulders and strode back toward the dugout, shoveled up the rattler's remains, carried them to the edge of the ruined field, and tossed them as far as he could. After a quick cup of coffee, he stuffed a biscuit into his shirt pocket and went outside to saddle Gallatin. He would check on Hank first, then the families who may have been in the path of the tornado.

The sandy track had washed out in places and pools of water stood in the low spots. He topped a rise and saw smoke billowing from the pipe in the roof of his friend's dugout. A grin spread from ear to ear dissolving the distress in his brown eyes.

"Hank!" He urged Gallatin to a canter, and rounded the end of the corral without slowing. Hank's startled figure emerged from the lean-to which sheltered his horse, and dropped the buckets of feed and water he was carrying.

"Sam! What the dickens do you mean yelling like that?"

Sam brought Gallatin to an abrupt halt, leaned back in his saddle and grinned. "Guess you're all right, as ornery as ever."

"And why shouldn't I be?" demanded Hank. "You scared me out of five years good life. What are you doing here? You never go visiting before a full day's work, and it's just past breakfast."

"A twister came through last night. I rode over to see if you'd been hit." He surveyed the area. "Appears to have missed you all together."

"A twister? Just a hard rain here, a little hail." His eyes narrowed. "Are you joshin' me?"

Sam sighed. "Nope. Wish I was. Took out most of my corn field. Everything else is okay at my place, but some may not have fared so well. Looks like the twister headed straight for the Lukinbill's place. I'm riding over their way. Want to come along?"

"Sure. Wait till I saddle my horse."

They rode side by side, quickly and silently, down the side of Hank's sorghum field, then cut across open pasture, heading toward the unnatural gap in the trees ahead. They slowed the horses to a walk, then to a stop, a hundred yards short of the destruction. Jagged tree trunks poked their nakedness out of the debris of limbs and leaves.

"Let's get moving. The house is just on the other side of the grove," Hank said in a somber voice.

"Yeah. John just finished building that house last fall. Took him two years. He has one of the most prosperous farms around." Sam reined Gallatin to the side and picked a path through the trees on his left.

"Yeah. Some folks were sort of envious. Over two hundred acres planted in corn, wheat, feed and a huge garden."

Sam frowned. "Not to mention his herd of white-faced cattle, hogs, chickens, turkeys, and ducks. When I worked for him last spring, I took my pay in chickens and horse feed."

Now the view in front of them was grotesquely altered. Only half of the barn remained. A cow and calf, legs twisted, lay in a heap. Black, brown, gray, and white feathers littered the ground as though an unruly rabble of children had conducted a gigantic pillow fight. The house stood with a portion of the roof missing, but a spiral of smoke issued from the undamaged end, causing Sam to heave a big sigh of relief.

"There's Mrs. Lukinbill." Hank pointed to the woman standing at the edge of the decimated yard where roses once had been coaxed to bloom.

"Morning, Ma'am." Sam tipped his hat and searched the area for the rest of the family. "You folks all okay?"

Mrs. Lukinbill, trance-like, pushed strands of limp hair from her eyes. A trace of a smile emerged and disappeared in the space of an eye-blink. "Sam, Hank. We'll do, thank the Lord. Nancy's making breakfast for the other children. I had to get outside. Couldn't take the smell of food this morning."

"Where's John?" asked Hank.

A tear escaped from the corner of Lucy Lukinbill's eye and spilled down her cheek. "Janet Jones came for him an hour ago. Her pa was checking his stock when the twister hit. She and her ma looked for him all night after the storm went through. She asked John if he would come help move some of the heavy barn timbers. I guess they lost everything but what was in the dugout, and its roof blew off."

Sam cleared his throat, breaking the heavy silence. "If there's nothing we can do for you right now, we'll head over there."

Lucy stared at the ground and nodded, and Sam followed Hank along the clear-cut trail of fury leading to the Jones' farm.

All they had seen this morning did not prepare Sam for the scene in front of him. The storm had apparently intensified just before reaching the farm. It no longer resembled a patch of earth tended by human hand.

"That's what I picture the Sahara Desert looks like, except for that one pile of wood way over there," said Sam in a subdued tone of voice, and kneed Gallatin to a gallop.

"Yeah. It's like no one ever lived here; nothin' left. The ground looks like it's been scraped with a razor." Hank's harsh voice carried above the sound of thudding hooves.

They jumped from their mounts and sped toward blotched earth where Mrs Jones, Janet, and John Lukinbill scrabbled at a mountain of rubble. John turned at the sound of their footsteps, removed his hat, and wiped his sweaty brow with scratched and bleeding fingers.

"Hank, Sam, glad you're here." He sighed and held out a hand of welcome.

Mrs. Jones seemed not to notice their appearance, but Janet gave them a stone-faced nod and yanked another broken board from the heap.

Soundlessly, Sam and Hank dropped their horse's reins and set to work. Mrs. Jones adamantly rejected John's plea that she wait in the dugout while the men searched. Another half hour of concerted labor revealed the tragedy: Mr. Jones had apparently been crushed beneath one of the barn timbers when it collapsed. Mrs. Jones moaned and fell to the ground. Janet stared wide-eyed at her pa's body, while a torrent of tears streamed down, leaving muddy trails on her motionless face.

Within an hour, Sam escorted Janet and her mother to the Luckinbill's farm and placed them under Lucy's care, and John headed toward the church with Mr. Jones' quilt-wrapped body in the back of his wagon.

Sam and Hank continued in the twister's path to help where needed. They learned five more neighbors had lost their lives, and several others had damaged property. They turned weary bodies and horses toward their homes at sundown, assured that everyone was accounted for and was receiving food and shelter.

❧   ❧   ❧

Nessa took the plate her mother handed her and ran the dish cloth over it while gazing out the window at the wind-blown garden.

Papa rushed into the kitchen. "Rebecca. A tornado struck south of here last night."

Rebecca gasped and the handful of silverware she held splashed into the hot soapy water.

Nessa stood stock still. South meant Sam.

"Papa?" She twisted the cloth in her hands.

"I heard Sam is okay, daughter." He turned to Rebecca. "But some folks were injured. I'll hitch up the wagon and gather some tools and ride out to help."

Rebecca dried her hands. "I'll get food and blankets and go with you. Nessa, you can mind the store."

Late in the evening, Nessa heard the wagon approaching and ran out the door. Her father, looking tired and dispirited, helped her mother from the wagon. She squinted into the darkness, when she noticed figures sitting on the wagon bed.

"Papa? Mama? Are you all right?"

"We're fine." He turned to assist the others.

Rebecca walked up the steps toward Nessa. "The Martin family lost everything, Nessa. They'll stay here tonight and then we'll decide what to do."

Nessa covered her mouth with her palm. "How awful!"

"We'll put Mr. and Mrs. Martin and the baby in your room. Make sure it's clean and orderly. Get the rest of the blankets and linen out of the closet and make pallets on the parlor floor for you three girls. The two Abbott boys can sleep on pallets in the back of the store. That's the best we can do tonight." Rebecca sighed and put an arm around Nessa. "I'll go start supper."

"It's ready, Mama. But there's not enough for four more and a baby."

"I'll take care of the food." She patted Nessa's shoulder and walked into the house. "See if Mrs. Martin needs help with the baby."

After helping papa get the Martin family and the young orphaned Abbott brothers settled, Nessa sat at the corner of the table and bowed her head. Papa prayed, thanking God they were safe and asking Him to comfort those who had lost loved ones and property. They ate the simple meal in thoughtful silence.

Later, Nessa and Ellie lay side by side on the floor pallets, whispering so as not to wake Opal.

"I can't believe it, Nessa. Just like this," she snapped her fingers, "people are gone. What if it had hit us? What if we had no home, or…" She stuck her fist in her mouth, muting the sobs.

Nessa gently squeezed her shoulder, and swallowed hard. "You think you have your whole life ahead of you. You can put things off till tomorrow or next week. But maybe you won't have tomorrow or next week."

🍁   🍁   🍁

The next day, neighbors gathered to say good-bye to six victims. They crowded into the unfinished church, and when it could hold no more, they stood in the muddy yard to pay their respects. Nessa huddled next to her mother, clasping Ellie's hand and staring at her feet. She heard a woman behind her whisper, "I wonder if so many would be here if we were dedicating the church today."

The preacher was unavailable at such short notice, so Papa read the twenty-third Psalm, several friends gave eulogies, and a group of women sang hymns. Sam, looking exhausted, told Nessa that he and Hank, along with several other young men, had spent the early hours digging six graves in the soggy earth, in a hastily cleared area behind the church. At last the ordeal drew to a close, and Nessa trudged with the others toward the various conveyances strung up and down the trail. Papa stood on the church steps, with other prominent men of the community.

"Folks, we've decided to begin services on Sunday despite the lack of pews and glass in the windows. We'll meet after church to decide what can be done to help our neighbors hardest hit by the storm." He raised his arms. "May the Lord bless each of you."

Bleak-eyed men and women echoed his Amen then turned to leave.

❧   ❧   ❧

Parishioners overflowed the little church on Sunday. After prayers, Bible reading by one of the ranchers, and singing of hymns, Papa and the other men left for a meeting in the churchyard. The women remained huddled in the church, and Nessa stayed close to her mother's side. Most of the younger children scampered outside to play. The women decided to meet at the Long's to quilt and promised dozens of quarts of home-canned food. Nessa's heart warmed. The community was drawing together, as they had to build the church.

Nessa quietly left the women's circle and stepped outside. She wanted to find Sam. He stood at the edge of the group of men with his hands folded on his chest, staring at the sky.

She stopped just behind him. "Sam," she whispered, "can we go somewhere and talk?"

Sam slowly turned to face her. "Nessa. Sorry, I have to get home. Glad you and your folks are okay." He dipped his head in a polite salute and walked toward his horse, as she watched in numbed silence. She whirled around at Louise's voice.

"What in the world did you say to him, Nessa? Maybe he finally realized you're just a child."

"You…you…ooh," she sputtered and ran back to the church.

Ellie met her at the door. "Where have you been? Mama needs her shawl from the buggy."

"I'll fetch it. No, come with me and bring the shawl back. I don't feel well."

Her sister's eyes opened wide and she tilted her head to peer into Nessa's face. "Nessa, what's wrong? You look like a sick kitten. Shall I tell Mama?" She frowned.

"No! Please don't say anything to Mama. I'll just sit in the buggy." She climbed up, handed the shawl to Ellie, and plopped down on the seat. Furrows deepened in her sister's brow and she stood staring at Nessa.

Nessa sighed. "Go on, Ellie. I just want to be alone."

After Ellie obeyed with obvious reluctance, Nessa allowed the tears to run unchecked for several minutes. The sound of voices shook her from her cocoon of misery. The meeting was breaking up. She hastily rubbed her cheeks with tremulous fingers, pulled the old robe off the wooden seat and wrapped it around her shoulders, hiding her face.

"Nessa, dear! Are you all right? Why are you wrapped up like an Eskimo on such a warm day?" asked her mother.

Nessa adjusted the shawl to reveal one eye and met her mother's questioning gaze. "I felt a chill."

"Mercy, what next!" Mama climbed into the buggy. "Let me feel your forehead." She tugged the shawl from Nessa's clutched hand and pressed an experienced palm on Nessa's brow. "You do seem warm and rather clammy. Ellie, hurry your father along, we'd better get her home." She sat and took her daughter into her arms. "It's okay, baby."

Baby! Nessa burst into tears.

❦   ❦   ❦

Sam allowed Gallatin to choose his pace after he turned him from the church toward home. Sam barely noticed the animal's change of gait from slow trot to canter to gallop and down again, as though the horse progressed through a self-imposed training exercise. Sam stared unseeing at the lightly-held reins in his hands. He saw only Nessa's stunned face; the shadow covering her bewitching blue eyes. It was over; at least for years, and Nessa would not wait years for him to get on his feet. Some guy would rush her off her feet into marriage and Sam only hoped he would treat her well. His head fell lower; his shoulders slumped. No corn, no money, no Nessa—as simple as that.

Gallatin stopped at the side of the dugout and Sam instinctively heaved himself from the saddle, took a deep breath, and began the evening chores. Plenty of hard work would keep his body busy, but what about his mind, his thoughts? Sam sighed. *Only God knows, and right now I'm too tired to even ask Him.*

The next week Sam spent hours working his garden, tending the animals, and strengthening the fence weakened by the wind, but with no corn to hoe, he found himself searching for jobs to fill the daylight hours. Early Thursday morning he caught three hens and tied them in a gunny sack, gathered up a couple of feed sacks filled with vegetables picked late on Wednesday and rode to Hank's place.

"Here's some things I pledged to help out the families. Could you take them to the Long store for me?"

"Sure, Sam, but why don't you take them, and mine too? You would have an excuse to visit that little girl you're always talking about. I planned on going to town this evening."

"I've never asked much of you, Hank, but I'm asking you to do this for me, and I'd appreciate it if you went easy on the questions."

"Okay, Sam. Whatever you say." Sam ignored the puzzlement in Hank's voice."I can go to town some other time. Why don't you come with me on Friday? Stay in the hotel, and get home late Saturday, or Sunday for that manner. It'd do you good, Sam. You need to let go and have a little fun."

"Yeah, Hank. You know I don't hold with that kind of thing. I keep telling you you're going to get yourself in a jam." Sam pulled the sacks from behind the saddle and placed them in the shade. "Thanks for taking them in, Hank. I owe you. There's chickens in the sack that's moving. They won't last in the heat. Will you be leaving soon?"

"I'll get my stuff and go right now, Sam. Think about what I said."

Sam mounted his horse, gave Hank a short wave, and turned toward home.

He slid off Gallatin, unsaddled him and turned him into the small but lush pasture. Then he sat on a rock in front of the dugout and allowed his chin to fall on his chest. No real use in working at anything. No real reason to fix anything. Nobody to see it but him so why bother. The sun was waning when he stirred himself to stagger through the motions of completing chores. Supper consisted of warmed over coffee and cold cornbread. For the first time in years he fell into bed without praying.

❧   ❧   ❧

Owen Long threw the last sack from the wagon over his shoulder and carried it into the storage shed attached to the side of the store. He trudged back outside, rubbing his lower back. Men, women, horses, and wagons filled the area in front of the store, as well as the grassy expanse near the barn. Neighbors milled about, collecting and distributing the donated items as they were needed. Owen watched Hank trot in with several sacks tied in back of his saddle, and he sauntered toward him.

"Thanks for your contribution, Hank. Folks have been real generous, I'm happy to say. They've pledged materials and labor for repairing and rebuilding homes, donated livestock and promised to loan farm equipment. It speaks well for the future of this community. I'd say inside a month the displaced families will be able to put their lives back together on their own homesteads. A couple of them are going back east where they have relatives, including Mrs. Jones and Janet, but the others are staying." He grabbed a couple of the bundles and Hank snatched up the rest.

"Yeah, I heard. Most people who make it this far are tough old birds. These sacks are mostly from Sam Jackson, Mr. Long. I brought a couple of pots and a few old tools. I don't have a garden, and no chickens." He handed the sack of squirming fowl to Mr. Long. "Always thought chickens were a mess of trouble to care for, although I have to admit I sure fancy eatin' them fried," he said with a disarming grin.

Owen nodded and chuckled. "Reckon you're right on both counts. Somebody has to do the caring, though, and the frying." He ran a finger between his neck and the collar of the white shirt he habitually wore. "Going to be another hot one. How is Sam, by the way? Haven't seen him for several days. His place wasn't damaged was it? He never said anything about it."

"Oh, he's okay I guess. His corn got wiped clean out. Sam's not one to talk about his troubles, though. He's sort of holed up out at his place it seems to me. Ain't natural, for a man on his own."

Mr. Long laughed. "Maybe not for you, Hank, but some young men are pretty serious about life." He lifted the lively bag to his left hand. "I better get these chickens out in the air. Tell Sam hello, and we expect to see him at church on Sunday. Like to see you there, too."

"Thanks, Mr. Long. We'll see, but don't count on it." Hank climbed onto his horse, and with a grin and a wave, disappeared in a cloud of dust.

Mr. Long shook his head and plodded toward the chicken pen. He stooped and released the captives, then idly watched them run to the pan of water. Nessa's voice behind him jerked him upright.

"What did Hank say, Papa? Did he mention Sam?"

"Yes, he did." He gave his daughter a thoughtful look. "Nessa, did something happen between you and Sam?"

Nessa reddened and looked at the ground. "No, nothing happened, Papa, nothing at all, and that's the problem."

"What do you mean, young lady?"

"Oh!" Her cheeks flamed. "Nothing like you think. I just mean he acted like he didn't even know me—just walked off and left me standing there like a…a fool." She turned and hastened toward the kitchen door.

Mr. Long sighed and mumbled to himself, "Always one thing after another around here!"

CHAPTER 8

❀

Sam noticed that strips of canvas still shielded the church windows when he reined Gallatin to a halt. He made a mental note to find out when his labor would be needed to help rebuild the houses and finish the church. He had struggled with himself since daybreak whether to make the effort to attend this Sunday morning. Something he didn't question had moved him to do so.

He dismounted, fighting the urge to turn and ride away. The lamp-lit church appeared full when he stepped inside, and he removed his hat and waited for his eyes to adjust to the dim interior.

"Hello, Sam. I'm glad you came." Sam squinted at the dainty blonde standing in front of him. "There's room for you to sit in my family's pew."

"Morning, Louise. Thanks, but I'll just have a seat here in the back." He nodded to two young men who slid over to make room for him. "I see the pews came in."

"Yes," said one of the men. "My father had me pick them up at the railhead Friday."

The service began. A man Sam had not noticed, and did not know, ambled to the front and faced the congregation. He introduced himself as Brother Langtry, and said he traveled to rural churches in the territory.

"Brother Long invited me to your new church and I'll be delighted to come about once a month, if you want me." He held up his hand and grinned. "Don't decide now. You better wait until you hear me preach." When the laughter abated, he prayed, asking a blessing on the congregation, then began the sermon he called *Running the Race*.

As Sam listened to the preacher enumerate the trials of Saint Paul, he shifted in his seat. I've been hanging my head because I lost a little field of corn, he thought. A man of God was beaten, stoned, shipwrecked, and put in prison, and he never gave up. And God never turned loose of him. Sam bowed his head and asked the Lord to forgive him for his faithlessness. "I'm not as good a Christian as Saint Paul by a long shot, but I know how to stand firm. I just lost my bearings there for a bit, but I promise, Lord, I'll run this race as best I can and I'll never quit on You again."

Mystified at the warmth filling him, he slipped outside after the closing prayer and climbed on Gallatin's back.

"Sam, wait up!" He turned to see Mr. Long waving his arm toward him. "I'd like a word with you, please. All right if I ride over to your place this afternoon?"

Sam sighed, and a chill supplanted the comfort inside him. "Yeah, Mr. Long. We need to talk. I'll be home. Come anytime."

"Good." Mr. Long tipped his hat and smiled. "See you."

Best to get it over with now, then I can decide what to do. He turned his horse into the track leading home. A hymn surged through his mind and he began to hum, then the words formed and spilled into the brightness of noon, causing Gallatin to jerk sideways in confusion at the sound of the tenor voice he had not heard before.

"Whoa, boy! Sorry about that, but you better get used to it. I've got a lot to sing about, blessings I never even thought of before. I've been following the same tracks for months, Ole Friend, and it's time I get on another trail. Pipedreams don't last very long; they disappear into thin air just like smoke from a camp fire, like they were never there at all."

He ate a cold lunch of bread and meat when he reached home, then sat cross-legged beneath one of the cotton wood saplings, whittling on a stick with his pocket knife.

Sam closed his eyes for a moment, straightened his shoulders, and took a deep breath, when the sound of the buggy reached his ears. *Just a little while and we'll have this over with.*

He greeted Mr. Long with a forced smile. "Welcome. It's not much to look at, but it's home."

"You sure have done a lot of work in such a short time, Sam."

"Yeah, well, thanks. I thought we could visit in the shade over there. The apple seedlings I brought from Tennessee and the cottonwoods I dug up by the creek are still too little to cast more than a shadow." Sam gestured and began to move toward the east side of the barn and Mr. Long followed. "Brought this old chair out for you; hope it's not too dusty." He removed his hat and ran his fingers through his hair. "Would you like some cool water to drink?"

Mr. Long sat in the chair Sam had made from split logs. "A drink of water would be welcome."

After fetching a cup of water from the well, Sam squatted on the ground beside his guest, wondering how to begin.

Mr. Long cleared his throat. "Sam, I'm real sorry about you losing your corn. I think I know what it meant to you."

"I wanted to talk to you about that. The twister set me back a year or more. I'll have to sell my cow and the chickens and work all winter somewhere, maybe all next summer. So, I'll not be over to see—"

"Now just a moment, son. Let me get a word in here." Owen raised a hand and held it, palm outward, toward Sam. "I have a proposition to make you."

Sam opened his mouth to protest, then closed it when his guest waved both hands. "Now hear me out, Sam, before you say anything. I've been thinking on this for months. Ever since I heard they were putting in a railway line down south. But I didn't quite know how to go about it. It came to me the other day."

Owen stood and paced back and forth in front of Sam while he spoke. "You know, Sam, it's difficult to keep the store supplied like it should be. Folks around have been real helpful at bringing orders from the railway up north, when they happen to be up that way, but it's a hit and miss situation at best. Sometimes a tool a customer needs sits at the depot for weeks. This is my plan."

Sam rose to stand beside the tall, soft-spoken man whom Sam considered a friend. "Mr. Long, I can't take…"

Owen again raised his hand, palm out, to halt Sam's speech. "Just listen, Sam. I need someone I can trust to drive a freight wagon to the new railway and back once or twice a week. I can think of no better man than you. I'll furnish the wagon and the mules, and pay your expenses, plus five dollars a trip. You'd be responsible for the care and feed of the animals. And I'm sure folks would be grateful to receive their mail regularly, so you could fetch that too, and probably a lot of other needed items. You could freight in whatever you have space for, and I'll still pay the five dollars, plus whatever other folks pay for their deliveries." He pursed his lips and gazed into Sam's face. "Think about it, Sam. Also, I calculate that over the winter and spring, the mules and wagon would be paid for and would belong to you."

Sam stood stunned from head to toe, too astonished to speak. His mouth moved, slightly, but no words issued forth. He gave up, pressed his lips together and held his hands wide in defeat.

Mr. Long chuckled. "I know you need to think on this for awhile. Maybe you've got other plans. You could let me know by tomorrow evening, couldn't you? Why don't you come for supper? Rebecca would be glad to see you," he said with an enigmatic grin.

Sam dug at an ear with a broad finger to free himself of the stupor holding him prisoner. "Tell Mrs. Long thanks and I'd be honored to come for supper."

"Good! See you tomorrow and I'll be praying for the right answer to my proposition."

He walked to the buggy, climbed in and with a cheery wave, turned and drove away.

Sam slowly lowered himself into the chair. His thoughts churned counter to the churning of his heart, leaving him light-headed. The dream that had slipped off the edge of reality into black nothingness, now glimmered on the horizon of hope, faint but gaining in intensity. If he moved it might vanish. He must embrace it gently until his thoughts stopped their bizarre twisting, and formed a straight line of possibility.

❦   ❦   ❦

Owen found Rebecca in the kitchen when he returned.

"Were you successful in your mission?" she asked.

Owen sank into a chair at the table. "We'll know for sure tomorrow. I invited him for supper, and he'll give me his decision then. I think he'll agree if he doesn't let his pride blind him." He sighed and sipped at the coffee she placed in front of him. "I'm exhausted. Felt like I was walking on raw eggs—one wrong word, or gesture, or expression, and he would have rejected the whole thing."

"I'm proud of you, Owen. Not many fathers would have taken the trouble."

"He's a good man, Rebecca, and after all our prayers, I know he's exactly the right one for Nessa."

Rebecca sighed. "Perhaps. I only hope Nessa is the right one for him."

"Don't worry. He'll help her develop and check her high spirits, when they get out of hand, but so gently she won't realize it. At least that's the way I see it." He rose, stepped behind his wife and hugged her to him. "We can only pray they have as good a life together as we do." He lifted a damp tendril of honey brown hair escaping from its pins and kissed her neck.

"Don't start something, Owen Long." Rebecca giggled and continued stirring the gravy in the skillet in front of her. "Supper is almost ready."

Owen gave her a playful swat. "Good thing, too, woman. I'm starved!"

❦   ❦   ❦

Nessa sat at the table clasping her father's hand on one side and Ellie's on the other and paying little attention to her father's prayer of thanks. *Ten years from today I'll probably be sitting here, old and unmarried, frowning, and getting wrinkles.* She glanced at her mother's smooth brow and cheeks, just as Rebecca smiled, then spoke.

"Girls, we're having company for supper tomorrow. Sam Jackson is coming to see your father."

Nessa's checks burned. Coming to see her father! Maybe he…But then why did he give her the cold shoulder at the church?

"…need your help, Nessa."

"I'm sorry, Mama, what did you say?"

"I said, 'I'm planning an extra nice meal and I'll need your help'. Ellie, you and Opal go wash the dishes. I want to talk with Nessa, alone."

"But, Mama. it's Nessa and Opal's turn!" Ellie gave Nessa a hostile look.

"Nessa will take your next turn."

Papa intervened in a mild voice. "Do as your mother says. I'll hear no more fussing today."

They ate the rest of the meal with the usual relating of the day's events. Mama rose when they finished and motioned to Nessa.

"Come to my room, Nessa, where we won't be disturbed."

Nessa sat beside her mother on the bed, wriggling her toes inside her shoes, and playing with her fingers.

"You'll be fifteen next month, Nessa." She smiled. "It seems like yesterday that I held you in my arms for the first time." She patted Nessa's knee. "And look at you, now. You're a young woman, and you must begin to put away childish acts and thoughts."

Mama continued despite Nessa's grimace. "It won't happen over night. I've noticed your confusion, but you mustn't be alarmed. Everyone goes through changes as they grow. You're torn between the security and lack of responsibility of childhood, and wanting to be treated like a young lady."

Why is Mama saying these things to me, now? Nessa gazed at her mother, perplexed.

"You know you can come to me, Nessa, when these thoughts overwhelm you." Rebecca frowned. "Perhaps I should have spoken to you before."

Nessa wrapped her arms around her mother and nestled her head on her breast. Tears threatened. "It's so hard, Mama. Especially for a girl. I'm not sure I want to grow up!"

Her mother's hand stroking her hair soothed her, but her next words caused Nessa to gasp and rise to her feet.

"I agree, it is difficult, but what choice do you have, dear?" Rebecca gave her daughter a questioning look.

Nessa stared at her mother for a few moments. "I never thought of it that way," she said slowly. Sadness battled with anticipation in her heart. "How did you manage it, Mama?"

Rebecca shook her head. "I wish I could tell you, but I really don't know. I cannot recall a day when I believed I was grown up at last. It happened over time. Perhaps it is more difficult for you because you have such a quick spirit, just like your grandmother." She smiled and caressed Nessa's hair. "One important rule to remember is to think before you speak. You have a good mind, and you know right from wrong. A woman must guard her emotions—not suffocate them, but let them show at the proper time." She lowered her gaze to the floor.

Nessa sank to her knees and dropped her head in Rebecca's lap. "I love you, Mama."

"I love you, too, daughter. You're my first child, and I so want you to be happy." She shifted slightly on the bed. "There's something else." She caressed Nessa's cheek, and smiled. "A few months ago, as you know since you were eavesdropping, Sam Jackson asked your father if he could begin courting you. You didn't hear all of their conversation. Knowing how young you were, Sam told your father he would proceed very slowly, and would wait as long as your father thought necessary before asking for your hand in marriage. Your father agreed. He told Sam he should wait until you were sixteen."

"I didn't know." Nessa's gaze locked on her mother's serious blue eyes.

"It's time for you to know. Nessa, tell me how you feel about Sam."

Nessa rose and sat beside her mother. "Sam's nice…terribly serious much of the time. Then he can be amusing the next minute. I know I feel safe when I'm around him, like nothing bad can happen when he's near." Her lips curved in a tiny smile and she faced her mother. "I had never thought of that until this very moment. How odd!" The smile disappeared and her eyes took on a dreamy shine. "I used to dream of being swept off my feet and carried away—like in the fairy tales you used to read to me." She straightened her shoulders and focused on her clasped hands. "Real life isn't like that, is it?"

Rebecca put an arm around her shoulders and drew her close. "No, dear. The characters in those stories didn't concern themselves with everyday living. Coping with having sufficient food and clothing, sick children, bad weather, and all the other adult problems. But another part of life makes it all worthwhile. When a man and woman truly love each other, the Bible says they become one." She released Nessa and shifted to face her. "It's difficult to explain, but the person you love is more important to you than your own desires, and he feels the same, if he truly loves you. Each one wants to please the other more than anything else. Then what happens is almost magical."

Nessa sat spellbound by her mother's shining eyes. "Tell me, Mama, I want to have what you have."

"I can't tell you how to obtain it, Nessa. It involves so much. Unselfish love, respect, serving. I can only pray you will experience it." She took Nessa's hands in hers. "Your father believes Sam is a good man—honest and hardworking. And he's already shown he is considerate of you."

"I didn't exactly feel giddy when Sam first spoke to me. But he caught my attention. There's something about him that makes me want to be near him. And I...I wasn't going to tell you this." She grimaced, but met her mother's gaze. "Last week at the church, Louise dragged him off to eat with her, and I felt angry. I told her to leave him alone."

Rebecca's lips lifted momentarily before reposing into their usual pleasant curve. "I would say he has made an impression already. You must allow your feelings time and room to grow; don't you think?"

Nessa smiled and nodded. "Thank you, Mama. I'll remember what you have told me. Perhaps growing up is not so terrible after all."

CHAPTER 9

❦

Darkness and mosquitoes drove Sam's thoughts into the background and his body into action. After completing his chores and cooking an uninspiring supper, which he ate without tasting, he hooked his lantern on the outside post and sat at the rough-hewn table which served as workshop, cooking space, and desk during warm weather. He placed a tattered piece of paper, from the supply his mother had sent with him for writing letters, on the table surface and drew a vertical line down its center with the stubby pencil he had honed to a sharp point with his pocket knife. On the left side of the line he printed *Why* and on the right side *Why Not*.

After a half hour of writing, scratching his head, rising to look at the stars, crossing out and rewriting, he tossed the pencil aside and read the resulting words aloud. *Why.* 1. Could marry Nessa in a year. 2. Wouldn't have to work on a ranch this winter. 3. Could add a room to the dugout. Two lines were crossed out. Why Not. 1. Good Book says owe no man anything. 2. Don't like being beholden to anybody. 3. Worst thing is to owe future father-in-law. 4. Nessa might think I can't take care of her. Number four had been crossed out, then rewritten.

He sighed, crumpled the paper and threw it on the dying fire. *Four against three. Guess that about settles it.* He grabbed the lantern from its hook and plodded down the steps of the dugout.

"Father," he prayed after dropping onto the bed, "I've decided this the best way I know how, and tried to do what's right. If You don't agree, please let me know."

He woke after a restless night to more turmoil and indecision than when he had fallen on his makeshift bed. Dreams of Nessa had filled the intervals between wakefulness. Remembrance of the vision of her riding beside him, sitting at the table with him, and…He slammed the door on his thoughts, dressed, and walked up into the troublesome dawn. *Maybe hard labor will clear the cobwebs from my wooden head.*

By noon the garden basked in the sun weed-free and a sack of fresh vegetables lay in the shade as a gift to Mrs. Long The barn and chicken coop were shoveled clean, with the mixture of straw and manure piled in a heap for future fertilizer. Sam drew a ladle of water from the well, drank deeply, and poured the remainder over his sweaty hair. His knees buckled slightly and a roar like rushing water swirled in his head. Then he remembered. He had neglected to eat breakfast.

An experimental kick at the ashes of last night's cookfire convinced him it had expired. A slab of two-day old cornbread and fresh picked tomatoes washed down with several cups of cool water replenished his strained muscles with energy and vaulted him into a surge of activity. He built up the fire, heated buckets of water which he poured into his battered wash tub, then scrubbed until every inch of his flesh tingled with energy. He dressed in his best jeans, smoothed the wrinkles as best he could from his Sunday shirt, and rubbed a mixture of charcoal and bacon fat on his old boots with a rag.

After hurrying through the evening chores, Sam brushed the dust from his clothes and boots, then saddled Gallatin. The sun flirted with the horizon by the time he urged the horse into a trot. A few hundred yards further he reined him in, only to urge the animal to a gallop five minutes later. Gallatin, apparently reacting to his master's indecisive actions, snorted and shook his head, up and down and from side to side, in protest.

"Whoa, boy. Take it easy. You're lucky to have someone to tell you what to do and when to do it. Me—right now, I think I'd rather be in your shoes." Gallatin neighed in seeming agreement and set his own stride. Sam took no further notice.

🍁   🍁   🍁

Mr. Long sat under the cottonwood tree in his rocker reading the Bible when Sam rode up. He rose to his feet as Sam approached.

"Glad you could make it, Sam. Have a seat over here and we'll talk. Supper'll be ready shortly."

Sam stepped to the vacant chair. His heart sank as he lowered his body, sat on the edge of the seat, and dropped the gift of vegetables on the ground beside him.

Mr. Long pursed his lips and formed his hands into a teepee. Sam straightened his shoulders and forced himself to meet the older man's steady gaze.

"You know, Sam, this is a great part of the country. Wide open, clean air—seems honest somehow. I've come to love it. It's growing and I expect we'll attain statehood within ten years. I'd like to think I have a part in its growth. Less than ten families had homesteaded around here when I started the store four years ago. Now there's more than thirty. It's a wonderful thing to watch a community grow. The church is almost finished and we'll build a proper school next spring."

Sam hands gripped his thighs, and he shuffled his feet. He didn't understand where this conversation was going and it made him more uneasy.

"You can be a part of this growth, too, Sam." Owen captured Sam's gaze with his own. "Actually you already are, with your farm doing so well, but you could play a bigger part. Folks around here are beginning to prosper." He shook his head. "I know the tornado set some back, but with help, they'll be on their feet in no time. What we need is outside influence, and you can help provide it. With regular deliveries of goods and mail, and the young ones getting more education, there'll be a demand for books and newspapers and catalogues. Folks can keep up with the rest of America—feel a part of the country, get interested in the government. This will be a great state someday. Do you understand what I'm trying to tell you, son?"

"I think so. Afraid I've been too busy to give it much thought."

Mr. Long nodded. "You're a hard worker, Sam, no doubt of that. And today's labor is important. The future's important, too. Think about your kids and grandkids—how can you help make life better for them?"

Sam scratched his head in bewilderment. What did this man want from him? Kids and grandkids! Right now he had all he could do to keep himself and a few animals fed. The future past next week, certainly past next winter, remained out of his range of vision. He frowned with concentration.

"Sorry, Sam, I didn't plan to make a speech, but you understand how important it is, don't you?"

"Yes, sir. I just don't know what all that has to do with me right now. What can I do about it?"

"One thing you can do is agree to the proposition I made you. Can't you see how it will affect people's lives in a positive way?"

Sam stood and paced a few steps, then stopped, placed his hands on his hips and looked at the dusky sky. Finally he turned to face his host who sat patiently in his chair. "I planned to tell you I couldn't accept your offer."

"Why, Sam?" Mr. Long's intelligent blue eyes looked puzzled.

Sam ducked his head and studied the prints his boots had made in the dust. "The Bible says to owe nothing to a man, and my pa taught me to be beholden to nobody."

Mr. Long sighed. "Sam, you won't owe me anything except your labor. I don't know what you mean."

"The mules and the wagon."

Owen frowned and nodded. "All right. If you wish, they'll belong to me until you earn them. You'll begin to pay for the mules by providing their feed. I told you their care would be your responsibility." He pulled on his earlobe. "Now, the wagon. I can hold two dollars out of your weekly commission until its paid for. Would you agree to that?"

"That seems fair enough." Sam sighed. "But, then there's Nessa."

"What about Nessa?"

"I want to be able to care for her on my own. It's not right for her pa…"

"Whoa—stop right there. You're right in thinking I had Nessa in mind when I offered this to you instead of another man. I have three daughters, who mean the world to me, and it's true I'll do anything I can to make them happy." Mr. Long stood and stepped in front of Sam and looked square into his eyes. "I'll be starting this freight run, Sam, hopefully with you, but if not, I'll find someone else."

Sam's felt the trouble in his face slide to the ground, as though tugged by gravity. He blinked and the grayness swirled away, clearing his vision. His lips tingled as they remembered how to curve upward.

Mr. Long smiled and held out his hand. "Are we agreed then?"

Sam nodded and vigorously shook the proffered hand.

"Very good. I'm sure you won't regret it. He gestured toward the house. Now let's find out what the womenfolk have prepared for supper."

Sam retrieved the sack of vegetables from the ground and followed Owen to the side door of the living quarters. Mrs. Long met them in the dining room with a smile.

"Welcome, Sam. I'm glad you could come. Supper is almost ready."

Sam removed his hat. "Thank you, ma'am; I'm looking forward to it. These things came from my garden. I thought you might could use them."

Rebecca took the bag and peeked at its contents. "How thoughtful of you, Sam. We never have too many tomatoes and I've not seen peppers like these. What are they called?"

"They're green chile peppers. I got the seed from a fellow trading out of Santa Fe. He told me to chop some up with summer squash and onions, mix them with cornmeal and fry them in bacon fat. They're spicy but not fiery hot."

"How very interesting. I will be sure to try your recipe." She turned to her husband. "Owen, you two just as well seat yourselves. The girls and I will dish up and be right with you."

Owen motioned Sam to the chair to the right of his own at the head of the table. Opal rushed in from outdoors and sat at her father's left. Rebecca, Nessa and Ellie entered, laden with bowls of steaming food. Nessa moved to the chair beside Sam. He nodded, and bent to pull the chair out, knocking his fork onto his lap. His ears warmed as he hastily retrieved it and set it back beside his plate. His gaze swept around the table. No one seemed to have noticed except Nessa who gave him a sly grin as she took her seat.

Despite his uncharacteristic nervousness, Sam enjoyed the meal. Owen and Rebecca kept a lively conversation going, periodically drawing Sam in with questions about his family in Tennessee. At the end of the meal, Rebecca poured coffee for the men, then politely excused herself and the girls to clean up the kitchen.

Sam pushed back his chair and rose to his feet. "I'd like to help, Mrs. Long. Least I can do for such a good supper." He grinned. "If you trust me with your good dishes, that is."

"Oh no, Sam. You're our guest. There's no need for you…" She paused and beamed a smile at him. "On the other hand, I am a little tired. I take you up on your offer. Nessa can wash and you can dry." She gazed at her husband and smiled. "I declare, Owen, close your mouth before you catch a fly."

Sam looked from one to the other in bewilderment. Nessa touched his sleeve. "Come on, Sam. I'll find you an apron."

At Nessa's direction, Sam poured hot water from a big kettle on the stove into a basin and Nessa worked up a sudsy brew with a cake of yellow lye soap. After scraping the plates and placing them in the water, she tossed an embroidered tea towel at Sam. "You've probably never done this many dishes before."

Sam snorted. "You're wrong there. I have three brothers and a little sister at home. Us boys took turns helping in the kitchen every night."

Nessa washed a dish, and dunked it into another basin of hot rinse water. Sam fished it out, shook it gently and wiped it dry, watching Nessa all the while. A gleam filtered into his brown eyes.

"Uh oh. This one isn't clean." Sam dumped it back into the soapy basin.

"Oh, sorry." Nessa scrubbed the plate's surface with her dishrag.

"Hmm, this has food on it, too."

"Oh no." Nessa frowned. "I don't under…"

"Yeah, and here's another one."

Nessa's hand grabbed at his arm as he attempted to slide the bowl into the dishwater. "Wait just a minute, Sam Jackson! Show me where the food is on that bowl!"

Sam peered at the dish in his hand. "I thought I saw something just a minute ago."

"Just as I thought! You—" She flicked her dripping fingers at his face.

Sam grinned and ducked. "Hey, hold up. You're getting water on my shirt, and look at the puddle on the floor."

"The mop's over there in the corner," Nessa said serenely and turned her attention back to the dish pan.

Sam mopped at the floor and chuckled. Nessa smiled and he felt his toes curl.

Nessa looked at Sam each time she slipped a dish into the rinse water, and Sam's smiling brown eyes held her gaze for long moments.

"What's taking you two so long to finish up in here?"

Sam jerked his head around and Nessa jumped at her mother's voice.

Nessa's cheeks turned pink."We're almost through, Mama." She fished the silver from the sudsy pan, tossed it into the rinse water, and grabbed the greasy skillet.

Sam concentrated on his drying chore. A few minutes later, he followed Nessa to the parlor.

When the clock's hands pointed to nine-thirty, Sam rose, thanked his hostess, nodded and smiled at Nessa, and stepped out to the porch, followed by Mr. Long. A half-moon was climbing to the milky way, and a warm breeze rustled the leaves of the cottonwood trees in rhythm to the melodic hoot of an owl and a chorus of crickets. Sam took a deep breath of the rose perfumed air.

"Beautiful night," Mr. Long walked to the steps and gazed at the stars. "I'll let you know as soon as I find some mules and a freight wagon for sale."

Sam shook his hand, then strode down the steps into the darkness, following the sound of Gallatin's low neigh.

CHAPTER 10

❀

Sam labored the next morning with renewed energy. His hands busied themselves with chores, hoeing, and carrying water to garden plants wilting in the hot sun, but his mind was consumed with calculating the cost of adding a room to the dugout next spring. Next summer he planned to construct a smoke house to preserve the meat from the calf and a pig or two. *And a windmill; a woman doesn't have the strength to use a hand pump on such a deep well.* He checked the field of towering sorghum, amazed at its growth spurt. Ironically, the same storm that destroyed his corn provided a boon to the crop a few yards away.

Saturday afternoon Hank dropped by.

"Ain't seen you all week," he said as he dismounted. "Thought you might like to go into town with me. Forget all your troubles."

Sam shook his head and smiled. "Not many troubles to forget and, anyway, I don't have extra money to throw around."

"What you saving it for? You said the thing with Nessa was all over. Let's have some fun, before old age get us." His blue eyes twinkled.

"I don't think you'll ever grow up, Hank. Don't you want to have a nice place someday? And a wife and young ones?"

Hank grunted. "Oh, sure, someday. But right now I just want to enjoy being single, handsome, and unfettered."

"Why don't you stay for supper and we'll play some dominoes. Then you could go to church with me tomorrow."

Hank tipped his hat back and stared at Sam. "You know, Sam, you're getting to be as dull as dishwater. Dominoes are okay in the winter, but church! What fun is that? Some friend you are!"

Sam's eyes widened then narrowed. "Now, just what do you mean by that, Hank?"

Hank studied the ground and shuffled his feet. "I don't know, Sam. We been friends for more than a year and I kept thinking you'd get tired of all this working around your place and let loose a little. I guess I was wrong. You're dead set on acting like an old grandpa." He strode to his horse and climbed into the saddle. "For the last time, are you coming or not?"

"No, Hank. I wish you'd stay here. You're going to get yourself in trouble one of these days."

"Forget it!" He whirled his horse around. A frown formed on Sam's forehead and sadness shadowed his eyes as his friend disappeared in a cloud of dust.

❦   ❦   ❦

Sam detoured by Hank's place on the way to church the next morning. Finding no one there, he decided Hank had stayed over in town and would be back by afternoon. He hurried on so not to be late, but planned to stop by again on his way home.

Panes of glass caught the sunlight while Sam was still some distance from the church and he mentally chastised himself for not volunteering his labor the past week.

His distress faded as he pulled Gallatin to a stop and saw Nessa walking up the church steps. She turned, gave him a sunny smile and a discreet wave, then spoke to her mother. Mrs. Long nodded and entered the church with her husband while Nessa stepped to the side and stood waiting.

Sam met Nessa's smile with one of his own, as he removed his hat. "You look mighty pretty this morning."

"Thank you, Sam," she said and adjusted her bonnet a fraction of an inch. "I was afraid you weren't coming."

"Well, I'm here. Shall we go in?" He offered his arm and led her inside.

As they entered, Louise, who stood near the door, glared at Nessa and flounced down the aisle. Sam gave Nessa a puzzled glance and saw the flame cover her cheeks. Then her chin lifted, and looking straight ahead, she marched to her parents' pew and took her seat. Sam followed and sat beside her.

After the service, Sam walked Nessa down the steps and drew her to one side. "I thought we might go for a walk or a ride this afternoon."

"I'd love to go walking, Sam. It's too hot to ride."

"What's the problem between you and Louise? I thought she was your best friend."

Sparks cannonaded from the deep blue eyes. "Was is right." Nessa searched for another subject of discussion. Louise stood a few yards away, sending inscrutable side-long glances toward her. Nessa frowned and looked at Sam. "You aren't interested in her, are you?"

Sam chuckled. "I'm only interested in one girl. She has dark curly hair, the bluest eyes I've ever seen, and I wish she wouldn't mess up her face with a frown like that."

Nessa brow smoothed and she gave him a big smile. "I just wanted to make sure. She's beautiful, and little, and cuddly, and…"

"Yeah. I reckon. I hadn't took much notice."

Nessa's smile grew. "I'll be waiting this afternoon."

Sam tipped his hat and walked toward his horse. He noticed Louise angling her way toward him and increased his pace. He slowed and turned at her voice.

"Sam. Wait a minute; you walk too fast."

"Morning, Miss Bagley."

"Louise." She smiled and lowered her eyes. "We haven't talked since we ate together at the church. I thought you might come out to the ranch one day."

Sam studied the dust on his boots. ""Look, Miss Bagley, I uh…I've got to go. Nice seeing you again."

For the second time in ten minutes, Sam witnessed eyes filled with female fury, this time directed at him. "Well, go on then. I don't know what you see in that little girl."

Sam watched her run toward her father's buggy and sighed. "Whew." He hurried toward an impatient Gallatin.

As he rode, he pondered the mystery of womanhood. The only women with whom he had experience were his mother, grandmother, a maiden aunt, his school teacher, and his ten year old sister. *They're a mysterious lot. Seem to be able to change moods as fast as a calf swishes its tail. How's a man to figure them out?*

His thoughts refocused when he neared Hank's place and saw an unfamiliar paint horse tied up in front of the dugout. He called out the customary, "Ha-l-l-o-o."

A slim figure emerged from behind the shed and waved. "You wouldn't be Sam, would you? I'm looking for a Sam Jackson."

"That's me, stranger." Sam halted his horse and studied the bearded young man.

"I'm Ben Miller; a friend of Hank Moran's. He sent me to find you. You weren't at your place, so I came back here to wait." He beckoned to Sam. "Could we sit over there in the shade and talk?"

Sam warily dismounted and followed the man to the lone cottonwood. "What's this all about, Mr. Miller?"

Miller grimaced. "Hank got himself into some trouble with the law. He said you might be willing to help him. I would if I could, but…I guess I better tell you the whole story. Hank and I were out on the town last night. A bunch of trail drivers—tough guys driving a herd from the railhead clear up to northern Kansas—well, they come in and…" He paused and took a deep breath. "I don't know exactly what happened first, but all of a sudden Hank took a swing at one of them and a big fight broke out. The sheriff came and threw us in jail. Most of us got out this morning, but Hank and a couple of the trail hands are being held until they pay their share of the damage."

"Look, Mister, there hasn't been a trail drive through here in several years." Sam's eyes narrowed.

"I know! But these guys had the cattle shipped from somewhere in South Texas by rail and they said they were herding them to some big ranch up north."

Sam rubbed his jaw. "So just what did Hank say to tell me?"

"He said you were good friends, and that…uh…maybe you'd loan him enough money to get out of jail. He said he'd pay you back as soon as he sold some of his corn, or if you wanted, you could take it out of his hide." He uttered a nervous chuckle and avoided Sam's gaze.

Sam smothered a faint grin. "Just how much damage did he do?"

"The judge said a hunnerd and five dollars all told. Hank's share amounts to thirty of that. Hank told me where he had ten dollars hid—all he has, he said. So he needs twenty more."

"His hide's not worth it," Sam said with a straight face, but his eyes twinkled. "I have to think on this some. I don't have twenty dollars, either." Sam removed his hat and flicked it against his leg. He thought of the twenty dollar gold piece his grandfather had given him on his eighteenth birthday. 'You keep this, Son,' he had told Sam, 'it's not to be spent unless there is no other way to either save your life or save your honor.' Sam shifted his feet. "They must have done a bit of fighting to cause that much damage."

"Yeah. Broke a window and tables and chairs—a mirror, I think, and some glasses."

"Hmm. How'd you say you escaped all that?"

Ben's cheeks flushed through the deep tan. "I'm no fighter. And there were a half dozen of those tough guys. I sort of backed out and went for the sheriff."

Sam's face hardened. "And how much are you helping your old friend Hank?"

"I ain't got…" Sam's stare drew Ben's head up and his gaze met the flint in Sam's penetrating brown eyes. Ben's gaze wavered. "I reckon I could pitch in five dollars," he said in a low voice.

"Good. Hank's lucky to have such a good friend," Sam said without smiling. "You run along back and tell Hank I'll be in directly. I'll try to scrape up the rest of the money." He nodded and walked toward his horse with his head bowed in thought.

He reached a decision at the same time he reached home. He retrieved the rusty coffee can from its hiding place and carefully counted out the few bills and coins it contained. Fourteen dollars and thirty-five cents. Eight month's savings toward fixing up the dugout. And still short by almost six bits. He sighed and dug into the front pockets of his jeans—a dollar and eight cents—all he had except his grandfather's gold piece and that he vowed not to touch.

He rubbed a hand through his hair and mentally calculated the supplies on hand. Animal feed was okay, flour, a bag of beans, some bacon, and the vegetables in the garden plus a couple of chickens. Low on coffee, but maybe I can trade a few eggs and tomatoes to Mr. Long. He stuffed the money in a small leather pouch and went outside to do his chores; it would be late by the time he got back from town.

His watch showed three o'clock when he mounted Gallatin and urged him to a trot. More than four miles down the dusty road he reined the horse in. *Nessa.* How could he have forgotten? His shoulders slumped but he flicked the reins and continued on. *Surely she will understand.* But doubt pained his heart. *Lord, it seems like I take one step forward and two back. Now, I know it's not your fault, but I sure could use a little help here with Nessa. Can you somehow let her know I had no choice? If you don't help a friend when he's in trouble, you're not much of a man, are you? That's what the parable in the Bible is about isn't it?* The heaviness in the pit of his stomach eased. *She'll agree I did the right thing.* He spoke to Gallatin in a low voice and the horse leapt to a gallop. "I hope."

By the time he reached the edge of town, his spirit exuded serenity, knowing he had made the right decision. The main street was almost empty and Sam couldn't spot Ben's horse, but the sound of children playing hide-and-go-seek behind the houses made him smile.

Sam introduced himself to the sheriff and stated his reason for being there. The sheriff shook his hand and pulled an official looking paper from the drawer of a battered desk which looked like it had fallen out of a wagon once or twice.

"Ben said you'd be along. Let's see, I've got fifteen dollars here which leaves Hank fifteen short. You willing to pay fifteen dollars to get that dumb kid out of jail?"

Sam smiled and pulled out the weathered pouch. "Here's the rest of his fine, Sheriff. Can I see him now?"

The sheriff counted the money Sam handed him and nodded. "Yeah, come on. I'll release him. If he's smart, he'll go home and stay there till he gets some sense."

Hank flinched and looked away when he saw Sam. The sheriff gave him a stern lecture ending with, "I don't want to see you in town for a month or so, Moran. You don't deserve a friend like Jackson, here, and he likely will come to that decision next time."

"Thanks, sheriff, sir. I'll keep that in mind." Hank limped outside.

Sam followed and stopped at the hitching rail to scrutinize the scrapes and bruises on Hank's face. "You look like you tangled with a wild cat, and he came out the winner."

"Look, Sam, don't start in on me now. I know I acted like a horse's rear end and I owe you big time. I just don't feel much like talking."

"Where's your horse?"

Hank grimaced and shook his head, then groaned with pain. He stumbled against the side of the building, and gave Sam a bleak look. "Danger's at the livery stable and I don't have a cent to pay his bill."

Sam fingered the two coins in his pocket. "Empty your pockets."

"What?" Hank stiffened and narrowed his eyes.

"Empty your pockets. Maybe you've got something you can trade."

"I ain't got nothing worth a plugged nickel," Hank said with a whine, but he obediently turned out his jean's pockets revealing a dirty handkerchief, a pocket knife, and three pennies. "See?"

"How about your shirt and jacket pockets?"

"Sam, I'm telling you…" Hank retrieved a moldy biscuit from one jacket pocket and a wrinkled scrap of paper from the other; his shirt pockets produced nothing. He shrugged and threw up his hands.

"I can't help you out, Hank." Sam rubbed his chin with one hand. "You can probably leave your saddle with the liveryman until you can pay the bill."

"And ride bareback?"

"I don't see as you have much choice."

Hank snorted and hobbled off toward the stable. Sam grabbed Gallatin's reins and followed.

The liveryman agreed to take the saddle as collateral, but only for two weeks. If it wasn't redeemed by then, he told Hank, he would sell it.

A tight-lipped Hank jumped on his horse's bare back and tore out of the stable.

Sam thanked the stableman, led Gallatin outside, mounted, and followed at a slower pace. He watched the swirl of dust enclosing Hank diminish and disappear as he trotted along into the glare of the setting sun. An hour later he drew up beside his friend who had stopped to let his horse rest. Hank sat on the ground beside the trail, with his chin on his chest. His clothes, as well as his mount, were soaked with sweat. Sam waited. Minutes passed, broken only by the soft neighs of the horses, the creaking of Sam's saddle when he shifted position, the mournful call of a dove, and the cheerful song of a curlew. Hank's gruff voice shattered the air like distant thunder.

"Well, aren't you going to say anything? Tell me what a no-good I am; how you warned me I was headed for trouble?"

"Nope. I figure you're thinking on all those things. No sense repeatin' 'em."

Hank snorted and hurled his hat with a snappy side-armed toss into the weeds on the other side of the trail. "Well, say something. I'm tired of hearing what's in my head."

"Okay. Get on your horse. It's past my supper time and I'm hungry. You're invited to join me if you'll clean up some first. You smell almost as bad as an old polecat."

Hank chuckled and got to his feet. "Sam, you're one of a kind." He limped across the rutted wagon trail to retrieve his hat.

They followed the starlit trail until Hank turned off at his place with a wave and, "See you shortly." Sam continued on.

Frying chicken sputtered in the skillet and biscuits browned in the make-shift Dutch oven by the time a scrubbed and muted Hank rode in. When only bones and crumbs were left, Sam poured cups of coffee and settled on one elbow by the fire. Hank paced in front of him.

"Thanks, Sam. You're a true friend—more than I deserve, like the sheriff said. I've been thinking on some of the things you've been telling me about settling down and being a man. And even some of the words you quoted from the Bible. My ma taught me right but I put her words out of my head years ago. When she died and left me to fend for myself, I decided to have fun, do things my way. Well, my way ain't so amusin' any more. I've been a fool, Sam, and I'm getting tired of it." He abruptly sat down. "What I'm meaning to say is, do you think it's too late for me to change?"

"It's never too late to change, Hank, if you really want to. I'm not saying it's easy, though."

"You think this is easy? Being beholden to you, owing the livery man, no saddle, and having three cents in my pocket? I may lose my place. Not that I've worked it like I should have." He got to his feet, stuck his hands in his front pockets, and contemplated the sky. "I'm between a rock and a hard place, ain't I?"

Sam chuckled. "Sometimes a man has to get in a rough spot before he'll pay attention. Hank, I'll help anyway I can. God knows I don't have all the answers." He shifted to a cross-legged sitting position, and tossed the grounds from his coffee cup into the darkness. "I'll help on one condition. You come to church with me Sunday. The preacher will be there and he can answer some questions that you need to ask. That's where your problem is, Hank, between you and the Lord."

"I knew you were going to bring that up." He waved an arm in Sam's direction. "Oh, I know you're right. I've been running from God for years and He just keeps following me. Well, maybe I'm getting tired of running."

"Good. I'll come by early next Sunday. Now get off home and let me get some sleep."

Hank grinned. "Right, Dad, thanks for the supper."

CHAPTER 11

❀

After watching Louise flounce away from Sam, Nessa skipped toward the buggy, lifting her skirts to avoid the muddy ruts.

"Sam's coming this afternoon," she said as Papa guided the team onto the road. "We're going for a walk. May I have some apple cake and buttermilk to take with us, Mama?"

Mama smiled and glanced at Papa. "I suppose so, if there's any cake left after our dinner."

Nessa anticipatory thoughts continued until they reached home. She hummed as she helped her mother prepare dinner, then ate little. Excusing herself, she fetched cool buttermilk from the well house and filled a quart jar, then wrapped a clean tea towel around the remainder of the cake to keep it moist. After brushing her hair and tying it back with a blue ribbon she sat on one of the old wooden chairs on the front porch to wait.

The store's ell shaded the porch from the sun, but also blocked the gentle breeze, and the heat penetrated Nessa's thin cotton bodice. The soft sound of her parents conversation drifted from the open parlor window. She nodded and her head drooped. The slam of the screen door jerked her upright.

"Sam not here yet?" asked Opal. "I'm going to play behind the barn with the new kittens."

Nessa blinked up at the sky. The sun had slid half way to the western horizon. She wiped her moist face with her fingertips and frowned. It must be four o'clock. After a moment of contemplation, she jumped to her feet and called through the open doorway.

"Mama, Sam's not here yet. I'm going to saddle Nellie and ride down the road."

"Your mother is taking a nap, Nessa; I'll tell her," said her father.

Out on the road, Nessa gradually urged Nellie to a gallop, relishing the force of the wind blowing her hair back and cooling her face.

Louise! She yanked on the reins, causing Nellie to stumble. By the time she had the startled horse under control, her thoughts had raced ahead. *I saw her stop Sam this morning; she probably heard our plans for this afternoon. She must have intercepted him somehow.* Her anger expanded, extinguishing all logic.

"I'll go to her house and have it out with her once and for all," she said to the wind and urged her horse to greater speed.

Forty minutes later, she approached the ranch and drew Nellie to a walk. No Gallatin stood tied in front of the house or in the corral. An ember of common sense kindled in her thoughts and she realized how impetuous she had been. The sun hung low in the sky and she bit at her lip, then rode Nellie toward the ranch house. Someone might have seen her; she was committed to stopping for a quick hello out of courtesy. Louise came to the door.

"Why, Nessa. What a surprise. Come in, you're just in time for tea." She held the door wide matching her smile. "Did you ride all the way over here by yourself? How daring of you!"

"I…I don't know why I came. I don't want to interrupt your family tea, and it's getting late."

"Nonsense." She gave Nessa a little hug. "We'll forget the tea and go to my room. It's been ages since we had a girl talk. Come in and say hello and I'll ask Mother to excuse us."

Nessa flushed with chagrin. The meeting was not turning out like she had envisioned. After stammering a greeting to Louise's parents, she followed her friend upstairs to a richly appointed blue and white bedroom.

"What a beautiful room, Louise, you must never want to leave it. The last time I was here your new house wasn't finished."

"Has it been that long? Shame on you! Well, I'm glad you're here now." She sat and patted the ruffled bedspread beside her. "Come on, sit down."

Nessa obeyed with reluctance. "I thought you were mad at me."

"Oh, that! Don't be silly. It was just a little game. I lost and you won."

Nessa felt her friend's probing gaze and continued studying the polished pine floor.

Louise frowned. "Now, Nessa, you didn't ride over here just to visit did you? Why did you come?"

Nessa swallowed hard to stem the tears forming behind her lids and clenched her hands in humiliation. "What does Sam Jackson mean to you?" she asked in one breath.

Louise drew back from the onslaught. "Is that what has upset you?" She smiled and shook her head. "Nessa, Sam's just a convenient man to have a little fun with, break the monotony around here." Nessa eyes widened as she listened and Louise's pretty mouth smirked. "You don't think I'd let myself get interested in him do you? Of course, I was annoyed that he appeared to prefer you over me. But really, Nessa, I assumed you would understand it's a game. Although, when you spoke to me at the church the other day…I should have guessed. You really care for him, don't you?"

Nessa nodded and a single tear circumvented its guard and slid down her cheek. She allowed Louise to pull her into her arms. "I'm sorry, Nessa; I really didn't know. We've been friends for a long time. I was so glad when your folks moved here; you were the only girl any where near my age. You're sort of like the little sister I wish I had."

Nessa withdrew from Louise's embrace and turned her face aside to brush the tears away. "I don't know what to say…I thought…" She jumped up. "Thanks, Louise. I must leave. It's late and Papa's going to have a conniption fit."

Louise moved to the window. "Nessa, it's almost dark. Maybe I should ask Father to take you home in the buggy."

"Oh, no! I couldn't do that. I've caused enough trouble all ready. Please apologize to your parents for my rudeness." She hurried out of the room, down the stairs and out the front door with Louise following. She grabbed Nellie's reins and hoisted herself to the saddle in one quick motion.

"I'll come over one afternoon this week, Nessa, early afternoon," Louise called from the front steps.

Nessa waved in acknowledgment and put her sure-footed pony to a gallop. She was almost home before she remembered Sam's perfidy. Annoyance replaced the joy of reconciling with her best friend. But, she quickly pushed that to the back of her thoughts, as well, in lieu of the pressing necessity of concocting a plausible explanation for being out so late and worrying her parents. As nothing sprang to mind, she cared for Nellie as best she could in the dark, and squared her shoulders as she walked toward the back door. The kitchen and dining room were dark. Muted voices drifted from the lighted parlor, and she paused in the doorway. Ellie saw her first.

"Nessa! Where have you been? You are in so much trouble!"

Her mother rose and cried, "Nessa! Oh, thank God. We were so worried." She rushed to Nessa and enfolded her in a bone-wrenching embrace.

Nessa struggled for enough breath to speak. "I'm sorry, Mama. I didn't realize how far I had ridden, and I stopped to see Louise, and we talked a while, and…"

"Good gracious! Look at your hair and where is your hat?" She sighed. "You must be exhausted and half-starved." She drew Nessa toward the kitchen and spoke over her shoulder to Ellie, "Take a lantern outside, hold it as high as you can and swing it in every direction. Maybe your father will see it and come home."

"Where is Papa?" Nessa sat, rested her elbows on the kitchen table, and cupped her chin in her hands.

"Mercy, Nessa! He's out looking for you." Rebecca stood at the range and gazed at Nessa over her shoulder. "He even considered the idea you and Sam had eloped, although I told him he was acting foolish." She sighed and turned back to her task. "I've never seen him so upset."

Nessa paled. "Oh, Mama. What am I going to do?"

"You're going to eat, take a bath, and go to bed. I'll speak with your father." Mama set plates of bread and butter in front of her daughter, took a bowl from the cabinet, and proceeded to fill it with stew. "But if you ever frighten us like this again, I'll paddle you, young lady, even if you are almost fifteen!" She emphasized her warning by shaking the ladle in the air. Nessa grimaced behind Mama's back, then smoothed her face when her mother brought the dish to her. Her stomach rumbled at the aroma and she picked up her spoon.

Mama filled two kettles with water and stoked the fire in the range. "This water will be hot enough for your bath by the time you finish eating."

Nessa, filled with misery, choked down a few bites of food. *How could I have been so inconsiderate and caused my family so much trouble. And just when I thought I was learning about being grown up. I guess I am still a baby.* Salty droplets ran down her cheeks and fell to her bowl.

"What's this?" asked her mother. "Nessa Lee Long, you stop crying this instant. The women in this family don't wallow in self-pity." She went to the range and picked up a kettle in each hand. "Get upstairs and get your night clothes. We'll discuss this further in the morning."

Nessa pushed back her chair, and Opal rushed in breathing heavily.

"Ellie said to tell you she thinks she sees the lantern Papa hung on the buggy. He's about a half mile to the west."

Rebecca nodded and sped into the washing room.

Nessa splashed the soothing warm water on her heated body, then quickly soaped and rinsed, stepped from the galvanized tub and slipped her nightgown over her head. When she stepped out of the tiny windowless room into the downstairs hall, she heard her father's loud voice followed by soothing tones from her mother. She sighed, quietly sped up the stairs to her room, and crawled between the covers. As she endeavored to relax, the aches in her body, from the lengthy ride and the trepidation of facing her father, drove all else from her mind. She closed her eyes, drew her knees up to her stomach, and took a few deep breaths.

❦   ❦   ❦

Nessa woke in the early light, dressed and tiptoed from the room without waking her sisters. Maybe she could get the confrontation with her father over with before breakfast. Her parents voices rose from the kitchen as she started down the steps.

Willing a smile on her face, she strolled in. Her mother stood at the stove and her father sat at the table. "Good morning, Mama, Papa."

Her mother turned and smiled."Well, you're up early, and looking a lot better than last night."

"Sit down, daughter," said her father, "we need to talk."

Nessa obeyed. "Papa, I apologize for causing you to worry. I selfishly thought only of myself yesterday. You keep telling me to control my emotions, and I've been trying. Actually, I thought I was doing pretty well. Until yesterday when everything you've said flew out the window. I was so angry at Sam. I'm really sorry, Papa." She lowered her head and peeked through her thick lashes.

Papa's stern look softened. "Now how am I supposed to scold you after a confession like that?" He slapped his legs with the palms of his hands. "I was all set to give you a tongue lashing for scaring us half to death. We've tried to teach you to be considerate of others and I came to the conclusion we had failed. Now, you admit you were thoughtless, and that's some consolation. Still, Nessa, who's to say you won't repeat the same mistake the next time something doesn't suit you?"

Nessa opened her mouth to reply but her father's upheld hand stopped her. "Let me finish. You say you're sorry and you'll try to control yourself. I'll take that as progress. I don't want you to smother your spiritedness—just direct it." He picked up his coffee cup and drank. "I won't say any more. You're safe, praise the Lord. But where did you go? I rode over to Sam's place last night looking for you."

"Oh, no, Papa!" She felt heat rise from her neck to her cheeks. "What did he say?"

"He wasn't there."

Nessa breathed a sigh of relief. At least she'd be spared that indignity. "I'm so ashamed, Papa. I've made so many mistakes, lately."

Her father rose, drew her to her feet and embraced her. "We all make mistakes, Nessa. The important thing is to not repeat them." He held her away from him. "Enough of this for now. Wipe your face. I think your Mama has breakfast ready."

Nessa turned to see her mother wipe her eyes with the edge of her apron. "Oh, Mama…"

"We'll speak no more of this." She spooned oatmeal into bowls.

"Thank you—both of you for being so wonderful." She grabbed plates and silverware from the cabinet drawer and began to set the table.

Later, while upstairs making beds, her father's words returned. "He wasn't there." *Where had Sam gone? What if something happened to him?* She slumped onto the bed. *Please, Father, let him be all right.*

She finished tidying the rooms in slow motion and headed for the stairs. Half-way down the hall, she heard Opal giggling and then Ellie's lilting voice.

"Nessa, someone's here to see you."

She hurried back to her room, tossed the broom against the wall, combed her fingers through her hair and smoothed the skirt of her faded work dress. Back at the top of the stairs, she stretched to her fullest height, willed her breathing to near-normal, and sauntered down into the room. Sam stood near the front door, shuffling his feet. Nessa ignored Ellie's smirk and Opal's grin.

"Hello, Sam. Won't you sit down?"

Sam nodded and walked toward her. "I saw these on the way and thought you might like them." He held out a bouquet of bluebells and wild daisies clutched in one work-worn hand.

Her gaze met his pleading brown eyes. She smiled and accepted the floral offering. "Thank you, Sam, no one ever…I mean they're very pretty." She bent her head.

"They don't smell, much. Not like your ma's roses."

"Oh, I don't mind; they're beautiful just the same." She gave her siblings an over-the-shoulder big-sister look. "Ellie, please put these in a vase of water.

Opal, you can help her." A sweet smile appeared as she turned to face Sam. "Let's sit on the front porch. It's a lovely morning."

They sat on the steps not speaking for a long moment. Nessa lightly tapped one foot and watched Sam study his fingernails. Finally, he cleared his throat and spoke.

"I apologize for not coming yesterday. Something came up and I had to go into town, and no way to let you know. I wouldn't blame you for being angry."

"I was angry, Sam, but I should have known you…that is, I know you wouldn't break your word if you could help it."

"I got home too late last night. I came as soon as I did my chores this morning to try and explain."

"I'm not angry now, so let's talk about something else. We could go for a walk."

Sam stood and faced her. "I'd like nothing better, Nessa, but I have an awful lot of work to do at home. Would it be all right if we waited till next Sunday afternoon? I thought we might have a picnic down by the creek. I can go ask your father for permission."

"Oh! You mustn't…I mean I don't know where he is right now." She placed her hand on his arm. "I'd love to go, and it will be all right I'm sure. I'll ask Papa at lunch time. You don't want to waste time when you have so much work waiting at home." She jerked her hand away and took a step back. "Thank you for the flowers, Sam, It was sweet of you. I'm glad you came this morning and a picnic will be fun." She smiled at the puzzled look in his eyes and her heart thumped as he nodded and turned toward the steps. She returned his wave as he rode off. Then she sighed and ran down the steps and toward the store.

"Papa?" she called when she entered the dimness of the interior.

"Back here, Nessa."

She scurried toward the desk where her father sat working on his accounts. "Papa. Will you promise me one thing."

Papa looked up and frowned. "Well, I can't very well promise something if I don't know what it is, daughter?"

Nessa fiddled with the ruffle on a sleeve of her dress. "Please, Papa, promise you won't tell Sam about last night. Don't tell him I rode out to Louise's, and don't tell him you went to his place." She leaned toward him and gazed into his eyes. "Please?"

Her father's frown deepened. "What's this all about, Nessa? You know very well that we do not discuss family affairs with outsiders."

"Yes, Papa, but I thought you might tell Sam you were out there, and he would wonder why, and…I simply couldn't bear it if he found out."

Mr. Long smiled and shook his head. "I don't really understand your problem, but I promise not to mention it to him."

Nessa reached to kiss his cheek. "Thank you, Papa. I love you." She danced a few steps, then turned back to catch her father's enigmatic smile, which she dismissed in her eagerness. "I almost forgot. Sam asked me to go on a picnic down at the creek next Sunday after church. He wanted to ask your permission himself, but I…that is, he had to hurry home. I told him I would ask and I was sure you would say yes. You will say yes won't you, Papa?"

Mr. Long folded his hands on top of the desk and Nessa winced at his piercing gaze. "You're not toying with that young man are you, Nessa?"

She flushed. "No, of course not. I like him." She lowered her eyes. "I like him very much, Papa."

"Very well. If your mother agrees, I have no objection to the picnic."

Nessa awarded him a beaming smile and swished into the living quarters.

"There you are, Nessa. We must get busy. Ellie and Opal should be about finished picking the string beans for canning. You can start by washing and sterilizing these jars. It's hard to get my hand inside them." Rebecca arranged several canning jars in the dishpan.

"All right, Mama, but I have something to tell you." Nessa snatched an apron from the hook by the range.

"I'm listening. But work while you talk."

Nessa plunged her hands into the hot soapy water and slid slender fingers inside a jar. "Sam wants to have a picnic Sunday after church." She reached for another jar. "Papa said it's all right with him, if you agree." She caught her mother's glance and smiled. "Please say yes."

"A picnic?" Nessa tensed as her mother bit her lip. "Well, if you're sure Papa approves, I guess…"

"Thank you, Mama!" Nessa grabbed her mother around the waist and swung her around the kitchen.

"Nessa! You're getting water everywhere!" Her mother wrenched free, but her smile belied her words. Then her face grew serious. "Nessa, do you care for this young man?"

Nessa grimaced. "That's just what Papa asked me." She looked into her mother's eyes, and without faltering, said, "Yes, Mama. I really do care for him."

"All right, child, I believe you do." She smiled and gave her daughter a playful swat. "Now, back to work."

Ellie and Opal came in with baskets of string beans, and Rebecca began Nessa's canning lesson.

After a quick dinner, the instruction continued. Nessa watched her mother lock the pressure cooker lid on the last batch of green beans, and stuck dated labels on the sides of the fourteen quarts cooling on the table. Mama brushed the skirt of her apron over her hot face "Do you think you can do this by yourself now?"

Nessa fanned the steamy air with one hand. "I'm not sure. I never knew canning could be so much work."

"Yes, but those beans will be delicious next winter." Rebecca checked the cooker's steam gauge and the big clock on the wall. "Twenty-five more minutes. Let's step outside for a breath of air."

"Well, aren't you the busy bees. Forgive me for just walking in, but I knocked and no one answered."

Nessa turned to see her friend dressed in a crisp, pink cotton dress. A matching, ruffled bonnet covered most of her shiny blonde curls. "Louise. I forgot you said you were coming this afternoon." She lifted both hands to shove damp strands of hair from her neck. "I look a fright." She glanced at her mother. "Mama?"

"Go on and visit with Louise, dear. I'll finish up here."

Nessa walked toward the door leading to the garden. "Let's go outside, it's hot upstairs. How do you look so cool after riding way over here?"

"I waited for a breeze. It's quite pleasant at a slow gait." She sat on the step beside Nessa, and removed her bonnet. "Now, tell me all about Sam; I want to hear every detail."

Nessa twisted her fingers. "There's really nothing to tell, except—" She gave Louise a self-satisfied smile. "He asked me to go on a picnic."

Louise's eyes widened and she smirked. "Oh, really! A picnic. And did Papa say yes to this little outing?"

"Of course, he did." She lifted her chin. "Why shouldn't he?"

"Well…I thought he would want more for his little girl." Louise drew her gloves from her soft white hands and studied her nails.

Nessa frowned. "What do you mean?"

"Look, Nessa. That's why I came over. To talk to you about Sam." She patted her curls, stared into the distance for a long moment, then faced Nessa. "Sam's nice, Nessa, and good looking, too, in a rough sort of way, but he's just a farmer. He has his little homestead, and that's about all he will ever have."

"But, almost everyone around here farms. The only ranchers are your dad and a couple families up north."

Louise sighed. "Yes I know. It makes it very difficult. Father wants to send me to school back east in the fall. I really don't want to stay with an aunt I've never met."

Nessa stared at her. "I don't understand what you're saying."

"Look, you little goose! The men around here will never amount to much, and that includes your precious Sam." She grasped Nessa's arm and shook her. "Do you want to live in a shack all your life and raise a swarm of babies and never have anything?"

Nessa's dream of the big house, the travel, the adoring husband returned. She blinked and her mouth gaped. *I thought I had buried my dream. But Louise is right. I'll never have much if I marry Sam. Do I want to give it up forever?*

Louise rose, and Nessa allowed herself to be pulled to her feet. "I have to go," said her friend. "Just remember what I said." She gave Nessa a brief hug and walked toward the front yard. Trance-like, Nessa followed. Louise mounted her horse and waved as she cantered off. Nessa stared down the road until horse and rider disappeared, then walked slowly into the house and up to her room. She stood gazing out the window at nothing.

"Nessa? Did I hear Louise leave?" Her mother's voice wakened Nessa from the nightmare in her heart and soul, but she continued to slump on the edge of her bed, and stare at a feathery crack in the wall.

"Nessa, are you upstairs? Are you all right?"

With a sigh of inevitability, Nessa forced sound to erupt from her mouth. "I'm fine, Mama."

Footsteps on the stairs confirmed her fear; her voice and words had been unconvincing. She rose and paced in a circle, not knowing what to say or how to say it.

"Nessa?" Her mother spoke softly from the doorway. "What is it, dear? Are you ill?"

"Ill? No, I…" *Ill—that would be a way out. But untrue. And I promised not to tell any more lies.* "Oh, Mama." She sobbed and flew into the sanctuary of her mother's arms.

After her mother's soothing words and caresses had calmed her, Nessa related what Louise had said.

"I see." Rebecca smoothed dark hair from Nessa's face, then cupped her hands around her daughter's chin. "I know you dreamed of a different life than we have here. When I was a young girl, I, too…" She cleared her throat. One should have dreams, but as one grows and faces the realities of life, the dreams usually change. They must reflect the possible, the things within our grasp. The childhood fairy tales fade and, when recalled, seem amusing. Perhaps even a bit embarrassing." She kissed Nessa's brow. "Do you understand what I'm trying to say?"

Nessa saw her own anguish reflected in her mother's blue eyes. "I think so, but I'm not sure I'm ready to give up my old dreams."

"You will dear, when something or someone else becomes more important than any dream."

Nessa's eyes widened. "Like Sam?"

"Like Sam," said Rebecca with a nod. "How do you feel about him? Do you think of him as a good man or 'just a dirt farmer'?"

Nessa squirmed from her mother's arms, stood, and walked to the window. "I never thought about it at all, until Louise…" She looked at the cottonwood trees in the yard, at the rustic barn and pasture beyond, all stark silhouettes against the flat green and gold fields extending to the clear blue horizon. A meadow lark's song reached her ears; the untiring wheel of the windmill caught her eye, and the fragrance of roses wafting through the open window tickled her nose. "I must think about this, Mama. It's a big decision and will affect the rest of my life." She turned from the window and smiled. "Thank you. I'll remember what you said." She reached out and gave her mother a hug. "I'll be all right, now."

Rebecca patted her shoulder. "Ask the Lord to help you, Nessa. Remember He's always there and He'll give you wisdom."

Nessa prayed and struggled the next few days. She took solitary walks in the early evening when the breeze cooled her turmoil, as well as her body. During the day, Mama taught her more and more about housekeeping. She quickly learned the basics of cooking, cleaning, washing clothes, and tending the garden. Now she began to learn how to preserve meat with salt, how to bake bread and maintain a continuous supply of yeast, how to make lye soap, and how to keep an even temperature in the wood-burning cook stove.

"You know, Mama, learning how all these plants can heal people is much more interesting than I thought." She stood at the cabinet grinding herbs with a mortar and pestle. "I wonder how people learned a smelly onion could cure an earache or peppermint tea brought down a fever?"

Rebecca paused from kneading bread, and brushed a stray tress from her eyes. "Some of the remedies are centuries old, I think, and we learned a lot about herbs from the Indians here in America. God put the plants here for our benefit, so it stands to reason He would show people how to use them."

"Why, yes, God made the plants for medicine! I'll never get it all straight, though, this for tea, that for a poultice, combine this and that for the flu." She dumped the ground feverfew into a glass jar and reached for a handful of dried chamomile.

Nessa had begun sewing at age six, and she felt confident in her embroidery, knitting, and crocheting skills. Mixed emotions consumed her when Mama helped her cut scraps of cloth for a wedding-ring quilt. Nessa chose the pattern, not only for its beauty, but also because it mostly consisted of one repetitive piece, and she expected to stitch it together quickly. But, by the time she had completed two blocks, sewing the short, straight seams bored her. She fidgeted, stuck her finger, yanked the thread out of the needle, and wished the pattern had more variety.

She tried to listen to the words Papa read aloud from the Bible after supper, but her thoughts wandered. She glanced around at her family. Mama busily mended socks, Ellie worked on her embroidery sampler, and Opal played with the lone, yellow offspring of their barn cat.

Papa finished reading the first chapter of Acts, closed the family Bible, and placed it on the shelf beside the fireplace. He picked up the month old Atlanta newspaper and settled back in his rocker. The near silence pricked at Nessa's consciousness. Her hands stilled as she listened to the creak of the rocking chair, the click of the knitting needles, the gasp when Ellie pricked her finger with a needle, the purr of the kitten, and the tick of the mantle clock. *Just everyday sounds on an ordinary evening. Why do they make me feel safe?* She studied her parents. *I hadn't noticed the gray in Papa's hair. And the little furrows between Mama's eyebrows.* She swallowed the lump in her throat, smoothed the quilting in her lap and continued to make the tiny, even stitches as her mother had taught her.

CHAPTER 12

✿

At nine o'clock, Sunday morning, Sam arrived at Hank's place planning to tell him about the Lord's saving grace, and to persuade him to go to church. Sam hadn't seen him all week which was puzzling. Hank usually dropped in for supper every evening or so. Sam reined in Gallatin at the top of the rise. Thin smoke filtered from the pipe on top of the dugout and Hank's horse grazed in the small pasture. He called out as he approached.

"Hank! It's Sam. You still asleep?" He swung from the saddle and knocked on the door.

Several minutes passed before he heard a footfall on the steps inside. The door opened and Hank peered out, blinking against the light. Sam's eyes narrowed as Hank slumped against the door jamb. He wore soiled and wrinkled jeans and a stained shirt, his hair looked like a derelict birdnest, and his face resembled an immature porcupine. He stood flexing his bare toes on the hard packed dirt step.

"Sam? What are you doing here?"

"How you been, Hank?" Sam tugged the door open wider and waited for an invitation to enter.

Hank scratched his head and ran a dirty hand over his beard. "Place ain't fittin' for company. Have a seat under the tree and I'll rustle up some coffee." He turned and went down the steps, followed by Sam's thoughtful gaze.

"Help me out here, Lord. I don't know what's going on." Sam walked to the circle of rocks outlining the campfire, toed the cold ashes with one boot, and shook his head. He arranged a couple of logs, struck a match and nursed a handful of dry grass into a blaze, then found a clean bucket, pumped water to its brim, and placed it on the fire. Hank emerged from the dugout and stumbled toward him. The only change in his appearance was the addition of mud encrusted boots on his feet.

"Where's your bathin' tub? And a cake of lye soap?"

"What? Now wait a minute, Sam."

"Don't rile me, Hank. You smell like a dead skunk, and your breath could start a fire. After you get cleaned up, we're gonna have a long talk." He fetched the tub and checked the temperature of the water. "Good enough. Now get those clothes off and try to scrub some sense into that muddle-head you carry on your shoulders."

Twenty minutes later Hank sat near the fire, dressed in clean clothes, cheeks smooth shaved, and hair combed. His steady fingers accepted the cup of coffee Sam thrust in front of him. He drank greedily and stared at the flickering embers.

"Now we talk." Sam settled himself on the other side of the fire. "When I left you last week, you were ripe to change your way of living. What happened?"

Hank slammed the cup to the ground, sloshed coffee on his hand, and cursed. "Now look, Sam, you're a good friend, but you got no right…"

"Save it." Sam's harsh voice caused a deep frown to appear on Hank's brow and his mouth hung open. "A friend wouldn't let a man step on a rattlesnake, or drown in a river, if he could stop it. And a friend wouldn't let a man kill himself with poison and wrong living, either." Sam's piercing gaze held Hank motionless. "I'm your friend, Hank, but listen good. We're going to talk this out right now or I'm going to get on my horse and ride off, and that'll be the end of our friendship." He rose, put his hands on his hips and stared at the stunned man. "Now, what's it going to be?"

Hank hung his head. "Ah, Sam, go ahead and leave; I'm just no good."

"Is that a fact. Did you come up with that smart idea all by yourself?"

Hank rubbed his nose and sniffed. "I don't know, Sam. After you left me last Sunday night I got to thinkin' and…"

Sam grinned and sat down. "Now that's a dangerous thing to do!"

Hank snorted, shook his head, looked at the sky, and chewed at his bottom lip. "My ole man always told me I wouldn't amount to much—I'd end up just like him." He looked at Sam. "He's been in and out of jail since I can remember, and my ma—she done the best she could for me and my sister."

Sam lowered his gaze when tears glistened in his friend's eyes, and said nothing as Hank continued. "She was a God-fearin' woman and she taught me right, but I always figured I was marked." He turned his face from Sam and swiped at his eyes. "I came out here hoping to get away from my pa's curse, but it's caught up to me."

"Listen, Hank. Your pa didn't put a curse on you. And the only thing you brought out here with you was your own fear. Every one of us has to face fear sometimes. What I don't understand is why you didn't come over. We could have talked this out."

"I planned to Sam, last night. But Ben came out and he brought a bottle and…Well you know the rest." Hank sighed and hid his face in his hands.

"I'm going to tell you about a Friend who'll never ride away no matter what you do. And He can lift that fear off you like you'd lift a burr from your horse's tail. If you're ready to listen."

Sam's earnest voice seemed to lift Hank's head. He straightened his shoulders and looked into Sam's warm brown eyes. "I'm listenin'."

"This Friend is Jesus, and He never gave up on you. He's been waiting a long time for you to call His name." Sam took his Bible from his coat pocket and read John 3:16 and the Twenty-third Psalm. When he finished, he looked into Hank's eyes.

"We can pray now if you're ready to ask Jesus into your heart."

Hank shifted position and toed the dust with his boots, without meeting Sam's gaze. "I don't know, Sam. I listened like I said I would, but I guess I need to think on this some." He gave a nervous chuckle. "Make sure I know what I'm gettin' into, you know?"

Sam sighed. "Don't wait too long, Hank. Who knows when you'll get the chance again." He rose to his feet. "But it's up to you to make the decision." He put his Bible in his pocket and strode toward his horse. "You are coming to church with me aren't you?"

"Yeah. I more or less promised, didn't I? And I'm a man of my word."

Sam turned and studied his friend. "Yes, I believe you are, Hank. Let's go then." He pulled out his watch. "We may be a little late, but it won't matter."

After church, Sam stood beside the Olsen buggy with Nessa by his side. He shifted his hat and scratched his ear while listening to Mr. Long.

"You know I trust you, Sam, or this picnic would be off. Now take good care of Nessa and bring her home before dusk."

Sam nodded and looked Owen straight in the eye. "Yes, sir. You can count on me."

Mr. Long smiled and flicked his riding whip at the fidgety horses. "I know I can. Have a nice outing."

Sam let out a long breath and took Nessa's arm. "The wagon's over here. I borrowed it from a neighbor."

Like an obedient child, Nessa silently followed him. He shook his head. *Now what!* He assisted her to the wagon seat, climbed up, and took the reins. The pair of gray mules strained against the harness and, obeying Sam's commands, trotted onto the road.

"There's some white daisies over there," Sam pointed out, "would you like to stop and pick some?"

"No, thank you." Nessa continued to gaze straight ahead.

Sam lifted his eyebrows and shifted to a more comfortable position on the bare wooden seat. "Would you like to grab the blanket in the back to sit on?"

Nessa gave him a quick glance and a smile. "This is fine."

"There's where the twister went through, and see the tip of the mountain over there?" Sam pointed with his index finger. "It's about a hundred miles from here. I plan to go deer hunting there this fall. Do you like venison?"

"It's all right. I haven't eaten it much."

Sam placed his foot lightly on the brake, tightened the reins, and turned the team into the downhill track toward the creek.

"Whoa Zack; whoa Zeke." He stopped the wagon under an old cottonwood tree a few yards from the water's edge.

"Not much water after this hot summer," he said to Nessa, who smiled and nodded.

After securing the reins and jumping to the ground, Sam sneaked a glance at Nessa as he walked around the mules. She sat straight and tall on the back-less seat holding a yellow, ruffled sunshade with a polished oak handle.

He raised his strong, stubby hands to her waist, swung her down beside him, and held her a moment, aware of her warmth beneath her flowered dress. She looked up into his smiling face and a tiny frown formed on her brow. His smile disappeared and his hands dropped to his side.

"I'll get the lunch basket." Puzzled thoughts roared through his mind. "Want to sit over there in the shade?"

Nessa slowly followed, arranged her skirts, and sat on one corner of the blanket he spread on the ground. Sam placed the basket beside her and went to unhitch the mules. He led them to the creek, and tethered them to a piece of driftwood after they drank. When he returned, Nessa had unpacked ham sandwiches, sweet pickles, a jug of buttermilk, and an apple pie.

"That sure looks good." Sam sat cross-legged beside her.

Nessa smiled. "I made it myself."

"That makes it even better." He took her hand and they bowed their heads. "Thank you Lord for the good food this woman has prepared for us. Amen."

Nessa placed two sandwiches and a pile of pickles on a tin plate and handed it to Sam. She poured buttermilk into tin cups and chose a sandwich for herself. When only crumbs remained, Sam yawned, then drew her to her feet.

"Let's walk awhile after that spread," he said with a grin. "It sure was good eatin' and I ate most of it."

He held her arm, guiding her around rocks and fallen logs as they strolled along the bank. She held her parasol in one hand and lifted her skirts with the other to avoid patches of thistles. The muscles in her upper arm rippled under his hand. *Her chin comes about to my shoulder—just right. She'll fit perfectly in my arms. And those blue eyes! They have a hint of mischief and passion when she smiles that I'd like to explore.* His pace faltered. *She's not quite herself today. Her eyes lack sunshine.* He shrugged slightly and dismissed the negative thought. *Her mouth reminds me of the cherries back home in Tennessee, and when I lifted her from the wagon…*Abruptly, he shook his head and broke the silence.

"What do you call that thing you're carrying; that sunshade thing?"

Nessa smiled up at him and dipped the parasol in front of his face.

"It's a parasol. Mama says a lady should never get browned by the sun."

"Fancy name. Anyway, it appears to work, your skin is near white except for the roses in your cheeks, and…" He drew his gaze from her red lips and looked at his nutty brown hand, calloused and streaked with scratches. He had scrubbed his nails and trimmed them with his knife, but the smudge of dirt under them had defied his efforts. His confidence wavered. Still, he had made up his mind. This would be the day, and he'd better get on with it.

"Let's sit a spell," he said and led her to a fallen tree trunk.

Sam waited while she adjusted her skirt, sat, and stared at the sandy patch of soil in front of her feet. Her cheeks flushed and her fingers tightened into a fist.

Sam took her hand and gently pressed her fingers until they molded into his. "Nessa, we've been stepping out for quite a spell now, and I…"

"It sure is hot!" Nessa shifted an inch or two away from him. "That water looks nice and cool."

Sam dropped her hand. He stood and looked down at her bowed head. Perplexity, anxiety, and confusion fought across his face. *This girl is going to be my wife, but she's sure going to be a handful.*

"Take your shoes off and we'll wade in the creek. That'll cool you off some."

"Oh, I couldn't!"

"Sure you can. There's no one around."

She shifted her gaze to the water sparkling in the sun. "All right. I'll do it, but don't you go telling anybody. And turn your back and don't look, either."

Sam walked a few yards away and faced the creek bank.

"All right. You can turn around, now."

Nessa was gingerly making her way through the weeds and sand. Sam watched with thoughtful eyes for a moment, then bent to remove his boots and roll up his pants legs. He placed his boots beside her button shoes and long black stockings and grinned as she used both hands to lift her skirt a few inches and dip one foot into the water. She giggled and took a couple of steps. When Sam joined her she glanced at him and laughed. He looked down at his pale shins covered with dark brown hair and echoed her laugh, then led her into the middle of the stream

"I can see your toes," he said with a grin. "Can you wiggle them like this?"

She curled and uncurled her toes in the cool water. "Oh! It's wonderful." Her smile sent a shiver down his spine. He kicked his feet and watched as the sun caught the drops of water, turning them into diamonds. He kicked harder.

"Oh, stop! You're getting my dress wet." She stepped backward, the stone under her foot turned and she swayed. Sam reached for her and missed. Nessa sat, hard. Her hands still clutched her skirt which floated around her legs like a sail. Water dripped from her chin onto the heaving bodice of her dress. "Oh…oh…you…"

Sam grabbed her up in his arms and strode toward the bank. Nessa beat on his chest with one fist. When he reached the grass, he set her on her feet, wrapped his arms around her and lowered his head to still the angry words he could see forming on her lips. He felt the tension leave her body and he held her mouth a moment longer. Then still embracing her, he gazed into her eyes. "Now are you ready to listen to what I have to ask you?"

He sighed with happiness as he watched a faint smile replace the shock on her face.

She tilted her head to one side and the gaiety returned to her eyes. "Yes," she said in a meek voice.

He nodded and led her back to the tree trunk.

When she was seated, he knelt beside her and took her hand. "Nessa, I love you. I don't have a lot to offer, but I promise I'll work hard to take care of you and make a good life for us. Will you be my wife?"

"Yes, Sam."

He drew her close to his heart. It's beat thundered in his ears, and after a moment he released her. "You won't be sorry, Nessa. I promise to make you happy." Her smile was all the reward he could handle for the moment. He reached into his jeans' pocket. "I don't have a proper engagement ring, Nessa. This brooch belonged to my ma, and her ma, and I guess further back than that. Ma gave it to me when I left home. Said I'd find the right one to give it to someday." He held out his palm revealing a circlet of garnets in a heavy gold setting. "Would you wear this as a token of our promises to each other until I can get you something more fittin'?"

Nessa smiled and took the brooch from his hand. "It's beautiful, Sam. I'd be proud to wear it." She released the catch in the back and pinned it on the left side of her bodice. "Over my heart, Sam. Thank you."

Sam gathered her into his arms and gently kissed her. "That seals it then. We're promised to each other. You understand?"

Nessa giggled. "Of course, I understand, you silly."

Sam grinned. "Well, I want to make sure there's no mistaking it."

Nessa wrinkled her nose at him. "I won't be forgetting and you better not either. No more talking to Louise, or any other girl.

"No talking?" Sam frowned. "Now, Nessa, you know I never started talking to Louise, but I couldn't just ignore her. Couldn't be rude."

Nessa's eyes twinkled. "That's what you say. But I'm giving you fair warning. No fooling around." She tucked her arm around his and laid her head on his shoulder.

Sam shivered despite the sun's heat, then chuckled, stood, and lifted Nessa to her feet. "All right, woman, anything you say. But I got to get you home like I promised."

Sam sat tall on the wagon seat with Nessa close by his side and spoke no urging sounds to the mules to move on as he had earlier in the afternoon.

"I promised your father I'd have you home before dusk, so we don't have to rush." He glanced at Nessa's slim hand clutching the sunshade on her lap. "Your hands and cheeks are kind of pink; I hope you didn't get too much sun when we were in the creek."

Nessa touched her face with her free hand. "Oh! Mama will take the skin off me." She hastily raised the parasol over her head.

Sam chuckled. "Well, don't worry on my account. I like a girl not to look so pale. Makes me think she's sickly."

Nessa glared up at him. "Oh. And did you think I looked sickly the first time you saw me?" Her voice carried a mixture of anger and amusement.

Now I stepped in it. He gritted his teeth and studied the twitching ears of the slow moving mules, then smiled when he spotted a patch of color off the trail.

He deftly tugged the left rein and the wagon veered and bumped over the grassy hillocks.

"What are you doing?" Nessa grabbed the edge of the seat on each side of her.

"You'll see." He pulled on the reins and when the mules stopped, he jumped from the wagon, and ran to a patch of bluebells. His knife made swift work of the tough stems and he filled his arms with blossoms. He walked back to the wagon and held the bouquet close to her face.

"This is what went through my mind the the first time I saw you: 'I always thought bluebells were the prettiest color I'd ever seen, but that little girl's eyes are so blue, they put the flowers to shame.'" His gaze moved from her eyes to the flowers. "Now I know I was right. And another thing, her lips are prettier than cherries, and her cheeks are prettier than apple blossoms, and her hair is prettier than…than…"

Nessa's smile grew and her cheeks turned even pinker. "Thank you, kind sir. I didn't know you were so poetic. Now, what about her hair?"

Sam grinned. "I can't think right now, but whatever it is, her hair is prettier than that." He caressed a tendril behind her ear and caught his breath as it curled around his finger. "Better get moving, old Mr. Sun is about to say good-bye for the day." He clambered up and cracked the reins. The mules broke into a trot and the wagon careened over the pasture and onto the trail, raising a cloud of dust. They wheeled up to the Long corral gate just as the last rays slid behind the horizon.

"Sam Jackson, that's the worst ride I've ever had. It nearly jarred my bones apart." Nessa jumped from the wagon and scolded him with a stern mouth, but Sam noticed the twinkle in her eyes and grinned.

"Likely, it toughened you up some. Got rid of a little bit of baby fat."

Nessa gasped audibly and raised her palm in a blur of motion.

Sam caught her hand an inch from his cheek. "Nothin' wrong with your come-back either." He took both hands in his and held her away from him. Then, he tilted his head to one side and studied her slim form from her dusty shoes to the stormy depths on either side of her nose. "Uhuh. Prettiest girl I've ever seen. Only thing is her temper. Can't take a bit of teasing. That's apt to happen to a girl with no brothers, but a thing I can remedy in time." He released one of her hands and gently lifted her chin. "I love you Nessa just the way you are. I was just funnin' you."

Her face softened and her mouth curved into a bow. "You have an odd way of giving compliments, Sam Jackson." She reached for the flowers strewn on the floor of the wagon bed. "Well, come on. Mama invited you for supper. And bring your manners with you."

He chuckled and watched her stride toward the steps, then fetched a bucket of water for the mules before following her to the house.

Sam joined in the common place discussion of crops, rain, and livestock which dominated the conversation during supper. The bouquet of bluebells, clustered in a cut glass vase, held the place of honor in the center of the table. After chewing his last bite of apple pie, Mr. Long rose.

"Delicious as always, Rebecca. Sam, come in the living room and we'll talk."

"Thank you for the supper, Mrs. Long. I sure enjoyed it." He glanced at her husband and back to her. "I'd like to repay you by helping with the clean up."

Rebecca smiled, and waved her fingers. "You and Owen go have your talk. We'll manage fine, Sam, but I appreciate the offer. We'll join you later."

❧ ❧ ❧

"Nessa," whispered Ellie, "what did you do this afternoon? Where did you get the brooch?"

Nessa picked up a stack of plates and headed for the kitchen. "We ate our picnic lunch and then we talked and then we came home."

"Is that all? Hmm, not very interesting."

"Well…"

Rebecca poured a kettle of hot water into the dishpan and added a few shavings of lye soap. "Stop twaddling, girls, and get the kitchen cleaned up. I thought Sam might enjoy some music tonight."

Nessa groaned. "Mama, please not tonight. I'm terribly tired."

"Nonsense. It's only seven-thirty. You and Ellie can sing at least one song and I'll play a few pieces on the piano. We should have some entertainment for our guest."

❧ ❧ ❧

Mr. Long sat in his rocker and motioned Sam to sit across from him on the horse-hair sofa. "I heard of a team of four mules for sale up north. They may be what we're looking for to pull the freight wagon. I'd like to send you up there to look them over, and if you're satisfied, buy them. Could you go next week?"

Sam pulled at an ear. *The sorghum is harvested. Hank will probably look after the animals.* "How far is this place?"

"About sixty miles, I guess. You should be back in three days."

"That'll be all right. I can make arrangements tonight and set off early in the morning. I'm helping a neighbor get his corn in this week and I need to go up in the foothills and get firewood for the winter."

Owen nodded. "A group of men are going after wood on Friday. You should be back then. It's mild for October, but winter's bound to get here soon."

"I'll plan on leaving in the morning then."

"Good, that's settled." He stood. "I have a letter of introduction for you to give to the owner of the team and the money we agreed on if the mules meet expectation. I'll get it for you now."

When Mr. Long left the room, Sam rose from the sofa and walked to the small bookshelf beside the fireplace. He scanned the top shelf—a dictionary, a book on medicinal herbs, a history of the United States and a biography of Thomas Jefferson. The second shelf was more interesting. A thin volume of Shakespeare's sonnets, a well-worn volume of English poetry. *What was the man's name—Lord something. It started with a B.* He took the book from the shelf, opened to the table of contents and ran a finger down the column. *Byron, that's it, Lord Byron.* He turned to the indicated page.

"You like to read, Sam? We only brought a few books from our old home in Georgia. Not much space, but I managed to squeeze in a few. You're welcome to borrow any you'd like."

"I don't have time to read much, except the Bible, but Nessa mentioned she liked verses and I don't know anything about poetry." He wistfully fingered the cloth cover, and placed it back on its shelf, carefully lining it up with its neighbors. "Maybe I'll take you up on your offer later. I'm pretty busy right now."

"Any time." He handed a sheet of paper to Sam. "Here's the letter I told you about. I wrote to the owner about my interest, and this will let him know I sent you to inspect the mules."

Sam took the paper, folded it and put it in his shirt pocket. "Are there any special instructions about what to look for?"

"No, use your good judgment; I trust you to know good animals when you see them." He gave Sam a small leather pouch. "There's money if you decide to buy. Offer what you think is fair and dicker some if you have to."

Sam tucked the pouch in his jeans pocket just as the women entered.

"Well," said Rebecca, "that's done. Are you gentlemen through talking business?"

Owen smiled and led his wife to her rocker. "All finished, dear."

Rebecca straightened her skirts. "Do you play a musical instrument, Sam?"

"No ma'am. Guess I'm the only one in the family who doesn't play. I used to do a little singing when we all got together."

"How wonderful! I thought some music would be nice to end the evening. I'll play and you and the girls can sing."

Sam turned red. "I don't know how to sing parts."

"Oh, we won't be fancy. Just sing—what are you, a tenor or a baritone? Tenor I would guess; surely not a bass. Well, it doesn't matter. We'll just enjoy ourselves." She went to the piano and began to play a few chords. "Owen, you choose the first song."

Mr. Long looked at Sam and shook his head. "I don't sing much. Rebecca says I have a rough baritone voice, but when she gets in the mood for music—" He rubbed his chin with his fingers and looked at the ceiling as though the title of a song might be written there. "How about *The Battle Hymn of the Republic?*"

Rebecca hit the opening chords with a smile and led in her clear soprano voice. Next, Nessa chose *Home on the Range*, and they followed with *We're Tenting Tonight*, and *My Old Kentucky Home*, interspersed with several hymns.

Owen called a halt at nine-thirty. "Sam has a long ride home and six comes early for me in the morning."

"Thank you, Mrs. Long, for the supper and the music. I sure enjoyed the evening." Sam went to Nessa and took her hand. "Thanks for today, Nessa. I'll see you when I get back from Colorado."

The stars lit his way as he maneuvered the cumbersome wagon over the trail ruts. He hummed and chuckled and hummed some more. It had been the most perfect day of his life.

CHAPTER 13

❁

Nessa watched Sam's broad shoulders disappear into the darkness. She stood on the porch listening until the chirping of the crickets transcended the crunch of the wagon wheels on the packed dirt trail. Contented, she smiled and marched into the house.

"…hope he can purchase the team. It will make a big difference to get supplies every week this winter." Her father stood speaking to her mother, who was putting sheets of music in the compartment of the piano bench.

"Mama, Papa, I have something to tell you." They turned their attention to her and she suddenly felt very small. Would they welcome her news?

Papa yawned. "Well, daughter, any time now would be fine."

"I—he—Sam asked me to marry him," she blurted in a single breath.

Her mother rushed to her and wrapped her in her arms. "Oh, Nessa, my little girl." Mama released her and looked into her eyes. Nessa's gaze followed the path of a tear as it slipped from her mother's eye, and made its way around the curve of her cheek to the corner of her mouth, before being whisked away by an abrupt swipe of her mother's hand. "I'm happy for you, child, and yet…" She sighed. "It doesn't seem possible. I guess I'm a little sad, too." She gave Nessa a teary smile.

Nessa glanced at her father as he moved to her side. He was smiling. "Well, what did you tell him?"

Nessa stared at him in surprise, then giggled. "I told him yes!"

"Good girl!" Her father guffawed and slapped her gently on the back.

"Owen," her mother said in a reproachful voice.

"Well, she did do good. I'm delighted she showed such good sense." He looked at Nessa. "He did tell you no wedding until you're sixteen, didn't he? I told him…"

"Owen!"

"What, Rebecca? Why do you keeping saying Owen? You know as well as I—"

Rebecca grabbed her husband's arm and rushed him toward the dining room. Nessa stood frozen and bewildered, her mouth gaping, until her mother returned a moment later.

"Nessa, it's wonderful news and I want to hear all the details, but it's late. You'd best go to bed now and we'll talk about everything in the morning." She smiled and gave Nessa a hug. "You're going to be a beautiful bride."

The sound of her sisters' muted whispers and giggles arrested Nessa's thoughts as she walked into the dark bedroom and realized she had no recollection of climbing the stairs. She undressed, slipped into her nightgown, placed the brooch under her pillow, and crawled between the sheets without reacting to Ellie's soft, "Nessa?"

She closed her eyes and mouthed routine prayers, then whispered with animation, "Thank you, Father God, for this day, and for helping me grow up. Help me to be a good wife to Sam. In Jesus' name, Amen." She turned her back on her sisters and watched the stars through the window. *I know you're there God. And I know you care about me. Thank you.*

❧   ❧   ❧

Nessa's eyes flew open at the sound of her mother's voice. "Nessa, rise and shine!" She sat up and blinked at the sun streaming into the empty room. "Oh my, it's late." She hurriedly dressed and combed her hair, then pinned Sam's brooch to her dress. She ran down the stairs, glancing at the mantle clock on her way to the kitchen. *Almost eight.*

"Mama, I'm sorry I overslept. I didn't hear you call."

Rebecca turned from the pan of dishwater. "It's all right, Nessa; I decided to let you sleep in." She smiled. "How do you feel this morning? Being an engaged lady?"

Nessa blushed and lowered her eyes. "I don't know. I haven't had time to think about it." She sat at the table and ran her index finger over the red embroidered daisies on the white cloth. "I'm different now, aren't I? I'll never be the same Nessa again, will I, Mama?" She gazed at her mother, and fought to banish the quiver in her lower lip.

"Sweetie!" The touch of her mother's hand on her shoulder, broke the restraint and Nessa burst into tears.

"Nessa, dear. You don't lose part of yourself as you grow; something is added. You're not quite the same because there's more to you—more knowledge, more character, more wisdom, and when your growth is straight, there's more love. You're the same Nessa with an enhancement." Nessa listened to the soothing voice and her agitation calmed under the ministering hands smoothing her hair. "You're the same Nessa who learned to walk and feed herself as an infant. The same Nessa who learned to read a few years later."

Nessa raised her head and wiped her damp face with the hem of her skirt. "I'm sorry, Mama. I don't know what came over me. I was so happy last night, and half of me is happy now, but..."

"It's normal to be a little mixed up. The unknown, which is what new experiences always start out as, is often frightening. Your father has convinced me that this relationship with Sam will be good, Nessa, and your father is a wise man." She rose and pulled Nessa upright. "Now go wash your face properly while I fix your breakfast and we'll talk more. I sent the girls to clean the chicken house so we could have a private time together."

Nessa smiled and hurried to the small room off the kitchen, stepped around the big copper bathing tub, and poured water from the flowered china pitcher into the matching basin. She avoided looking into the square framed mirror hanging above the white-painted pine dresser. If she was enhanced inside, might it show in her features as well? She uttered a nervous giggle and gasped when the splash of cold water met her face.

Back in the kitchen, she sniffed the smell of bacon and found herself ravenous. She sat and sipped the creamy coffee her mother placed before her. A plate of bacon and biscuits followed minutes later and her mother sat across from her. "Now, dear, tell me all about yesterday."

Nessa nodded and buttered a second biscuit. "I'm so hungry for some reason."

"Being nervous affects me that way, too."

"Mama, what did Papa mean last night about..."

"Oh, pay no mind to your father; he was just excited and happy for you."

"About getting one daughter off his hands," Nessa said in a playful voice.

Rebecca returned the grin. "He'll be more nervous than you on your wedding day. Just wait and see."

"My wedding day. I can't really imagine it."

"Well we have lots of work to do before it arrives. We'll get started on your hope chest in earnest, and a wedding will seem more real to you."

"Sam acted…I think he was nervous. I'd never seen him like that. And I felt scared and excited and I wanted to run away, and at the same time listen to him. I just knew I was going to burst into a fit of giggles." She stopped and laughed. "It's funny now, but…Anyway, he knelt down on the grass and, in this deep sober voice, said a bunch of things about taking care of me, and then he looked into my eyes and said: 'Nessa, will you be my wife?', and I could hardly breathe. All I could answer was 'Yes, Sam'. That's all I said. I felt so foolish later, but he didn't seem to notice. He just kept looking at me with a big smile on his face and I felt warm and safe, and I wanted him to never stop looking at me like that." She brushed a stray strand of hair behind her ear and searched her mother's face. "Is that the way it was with you and Papa?"

A smile lit her mother's face and her eyes seemed to take her far away. "Something like that, yes. And his look makes me feel warm and safe even after all these years." She took a deep breath and returned her gaze to the present. "It's a wonderful thing to love and be loved, Nessa. I believe it's a spiritual thing. We'll talk more about that later, but now it's time to get to work. I asked your father to bring over a bolt of muslin. It's on the dining table. You'll need sheets, and pillow cases, tea towels, and rag rugs, and quilts, and…" She paused and her face took on a serious and determined look. "So many things; I hope we have time. The sewing machine would make it so much easier." She shook her head and smiled. "Well, never mind; we'll have to do it the old-fashioned way."

"Oh! I almost forgot." Nessa unpinned the brooch from her bodice and held it out to her mother. "Sam didn't have a ring. He gave me his grandmother's pin as a token of our engagement."

"I wondered when you were going to mention it," said Rebecca with a smile, as she took the brooch. "It's beautiful, and very becoming with your dark hair. The setting is very fine."

Nessa followed her mother into the dining room and helped measure lengths for the needed linens. Then she fetched her sewing box and began hemming.

"Remember, Nessa, tiny, tiny stitches; it saves hours of mending later."

After supper, Nessa proudly showed her family the finished sheet with the even stitches, and the set of pillow slips marked out with a pattern of morning glories ready to be embroidered.

By the end of the week, two sets of bed linens were sewn with neat stitches, rinsed and pressed, and Nessa smiled with satisfaction as she placed them on top of her mother's sewing basket.

After breakfast the next morning, Rebecca invited Nessa to her bedroom and rummaged for a key in a small lacquered jewel box, then moved to a trunk sitting beside the bed.

"My mother gave me this trunk when I started my hope chest," Rebecca told Nessa. "I asked your father to bring it down from the attic this morning. Now, I'm happy to pass it on to you with the same love with which it came to me."

Nessa watched her mother caress the worn leather surface before lifting the camel-backed lid. The trunk had never been opened in her presence. She vaguely remembered a rare argument between her parents when they were packing to leave their old home. Her mother had insisted the trunk be included in the wagons. Now she gasped in delight when she saw the pink satin lining. Her mother removed several layers of newspaper before lifting a bulky muslin-wrapped item.

Nessa clasped her hands to her cheeks at the sight of the creamy satin and lace.

"This is my mother's wedding dress, and I wore it on my wedding day, too." Rebecca held the shimmering garment up, tilted her head and frowned. "You're a little taller and maybe a little fuller on top. I think we can fix it; skirts are shorter so it won't matter if your shoes show." She laid the gown across her bed and straightened the full skirt. "What do you think?"

"It's the most beautiful thing I've ever seen, Mama." Nessa caressed the gleaming fabric with nervous fingers, and looked at the portrait hanging over her mother's bureau. "It's much prettier than it looks in that painting of you and Papa."

Rebecca moved to the bureau, and Nessa watched her mother study the images. Nessa smiled at how young her parents looked on their wedding day. And although they sat stiff and formal, they seemed to be looking into the future with innocence and confidence. Her mother's blue eyes twinkled. "It isn't very good is it? Not professional by any means. Your grandfather had an artist friend paint this a week after our wedding. What he lacked in talent, he made up for in style." She laughed. "He had me sit on a velvet covered chair, and your father stood to the side and just behind me. We grew so tired of posing—it took many hours." She cupped one hand under her chin and tilted her head. "We look like an amateur copy of Louis the Sixteenth and Marie Antoinette, don't you think?"

Nessa grinned. "It's a terrible pose, isn't it? But I imagine it brings good memories to mind."

"Yes, I suppose it does." Rebecca abruptly turned from the painting and began to wrap the gown in it's muslin shield. "We have plenty of time to work on this. I just wanted you to see it, and let me know if you would like to wear it."

Nessa put an arm around her mother's waist. "I love it Mama, and thank you for allowing me to use it."

Rebecca placed the garment in the trunk, closed the lid, and locked it. "Okay, that's settled then. I'll ask your father to carry the trunk into your room." She handed the key to Nessa. "Now back to the present. Your birthday is next week, so the wedding is a year away. I've been wondering if we could celebrate your fifteenth birthday with more than a family dinner. Would you like to have a party with a few friends for square-dancing and supper after?"

"Oh, Mama! Could we? How many friends? Could we have a big cake and little sandwiches like those you've told me about, and…"

"Mercy, one thing at a time! I haven't spoken to your father yet. I think he will agree, but the party will have to be rather small. Maybe Sam and three couples, enough for a square?" Nessa beamed and nodded and Rebecca continued. "We might be able to manage a cake and roast beef sandwiches. I have a little white sugar, and if I sift the flour several times, it should be light enough." She smiled at Nessa. "I'll speak to your father tonight."

Nessa whirled around the room holding her skirts out with each hand, stopped in front of her mother, and executed a respectable curtsy."

Rebecca laughed. "Enough, now. Time to get busy."

❦　　　❦　　　❦

Sam fed his livestock before dawn with the aid of his lantern, and was on his way north by first light. He had driven the borrowed mules and wagon to Hank's place last evening and Hank had promised to return them to their neighbor. Hank also agreed to water Sam's garden and care for his animals until he returned.

"Guess I owe you a lot more than that, Sam. It's the least I can do; don't worry, I'll take care of your place."

"I didn't ask you because you owe me anything, Hank. You don't. I asked you because you're a friend and I trust you."

Hank looked startled and met Sam's clear gaze with puzzled eyes. "I—uh…"

"Never mind. I appreciate your help. See you Thursday or Friday." He turned his horse around and trotted off, yelling over his shoulder. "Thanks, Hank."

Now, as he urged Gallatin to a steady mile-eating gallop, Sam chuckled at the look on Hank's face. *The fellow is embarrassed to be caught doing a good deed for somebody. He don't know the good inside himself. But you do, don't you, Lord?"* He looked at the fading stars overhead and the dim glow in the east. "It's going to be another scorcher, Gallatin. We'll have to make good time while it's still cool."

By mid-morning, he reached the top of the mesa running east-west across the prairie and rising to the distant western mountains. From this perch he could see more than ten miles in every direction. He stopped to give Gallatin a breather, and admire the beauty of God's handiwork. Purple peaks rose to his left, pale prairie grass dotted with wild daisies, bluebells, buttercups, and orange paintbrush in front and to his right, with a square of emerald here and there, where a farmer had hacked out the sod and planted corn or sorghum, and overhead, the blue sky splotched with a dozen orphan clouds. He gulped in the clear air with pleasure. "You sure paint pretty pictures, Lord."

Just after one in the afternoon, he stopped at a streamlet, removed the roll of blankets and the provisions tied on Gallatin's back, hefted the saddle to the ground, and let the horse free to drink and munch on the tufts of grass along the bank. He rummaged in a flour sack for biscuits and bacon he had prepared for the journey, then walked upstream of the animal, dipped his cup in the cool running water, and settled against a cottonwood tree to eat his dinner. The hot sun filtered through the leaves, dappling the ground with a moving pattern of shadows from the light breeze. He removed his hat and rested his head against the rough bark, lifted his browned face to the cooled air, and closed his eyes.

A snort from Gallatin brought him upright to catch a glimpse of two does, with half-grown fawns beside them, leap over a fallen tree and disappear over the rise in front of him.

"Well, thanks ole pal for waking me." Sam looked at the sun overhead and pulled his watch from its pocket. Two-ten. He whistled softly, and Gallatin trotted toward him. Sam rubbed his nose and led him to the stream. "Drink hearty, boy, may be awhile before we get another chance." He filled his canteen, saddled the horse, tied the roll on behind, and mounted. Once out of the trees lining the stream, he searched the flat land before him. "Not much in the way of landmarks around here, Gallatin. He reined the horse with the sun over his left shoulder, and urged him to a canter.

Just before sunset, he turned slightly to the right and headed for a line of trees signaling running water in this semi-arid land, and proving to be a river several yards wide with ample depth for swimming if one was inclined.

"Whoa, Gallatin. We'll spend the night at this inn." He eyed the dead limbs scattered about and chose a level glade by the riverbank where the sandy soil appeared relatively free of rocks on which to spread his blanket. "All any man or beast could ask for—a soft bed and fuel for a fire to warm himself and cook his supper." Gallatin snorted and lifted his head in reply. He stood quietly while Sam unburdened his back, then kicked his heels and raced up and down the verge several times before stepping to the water and drinking deeply. Sam chuckled. "Hey, you're too old for such shenanigans. Act your age." By the time the moon showed itself over the tree tops, Sam had eaten a can of beans, heated on a small fire, and sprawled on one elbow sipping strong coffee. A half hour later, he built the fire up, rolled up in his blanket and slept, after thanking Jesus for a good day's journey.

Rider and horse, rested and refreshed, ate a quick breakfast and were on the way north at dawn. Sam located a shallow crossing a quarter mile down the river, and when they reached the other side, Sam gave Gallatin his head. The horse spurred into a rhythmic gallop, eating up the miles. They arrived at the small settlement of Springdale before noon and Sam asked the owner of the livery stable for directions. His destination was about two miles west. He splurged on a half bucket of oats for his mount, and strode down the street to the rooming house. He treated himself to a chicken and dumpling dinner, paid for with the expense money provided by Mr. Long.

Unaccustomed to the heavy noon meal, Sam yawned as he hauled himself into the saddle and turned onto the trail heading west. The clear blue of the sky, the heat of the sun, the uninterrupted repetition of the prairie, and the monotonous sway of Gallatin's gait lulled him, and he alternated between nodding and jerking himself upright.

Sam lifted his head, blinked, then stared without comprehension at the barbed wire fence a foot in front of Gallatin's nose, stretching north and south as far as he could see. The trail continued on the other side, but he saw no sign of a ranch house. He turned to study the narrow track behind him. A long moment passed before he noticed the gate. Then he dismounted, released the post from its wire loops, led the horse through, and re-fastened the gate. The distant slow-moving reddish-brown blots registered as cattle on his sluggish mind, and he shook his head at his folly.

"Gallatin, I'm sure glad one of us has some horse sense." He gave his companion a fond pat on the nose and swung into the saddle.

At the top of a rise, Sam reined in his mount. A shallow valley lay before him, cut diagonally by a winding tree-lined stream. A sprawl of structures surrounding a two-story log ranch house rose from the prairie near the center. Gallatin covered the remaining yards at a walk while Sam admired the view. Several men, working at various chores, looked up as he approached. He waved, stopped at the water tank near the corral, and dismounted. A tall weathered man, sandy-haired with creeping gray at the temples, and sporting a thin moustache, strode toward him, stopped a few paces away, and with hands on hips, asked, "Can I do something for you, stranger?"

Sam smiled and removed his hat. "Mr. Long, down in Oklahoma Territory sent me about some mules. My name is Sam Jackson." He took Mr. Long's letter from his jacket pocket and offered it to the man.

"Long, yes. I expected someone a couple weeks ago; thought he must have changed his mind." He took the letter with his left hand and held out the right. "I'm Brian Kilgore, owner of this spread."

Sam shook his hand. "Mighty nice place you have, Mr. Kilgore."

"Yes, we like it." He called to a worker to fetch the mules from the pasture, and invited Sam inside. "It'll take him a half hour to round them up. We'll take care of your horse; come have a drink before we talk business."

"Thanks, but I'm mighty dusty. Slept on the trail last night."

"Oh, don't worry about that. My wife will be glad to see you. We don't have many visitors out here."

Sam noticed the masses of roses and iris as they walked to the front yard, and the vineyard and orchard off to the right. "Flowers must be mighty pretty in the spring. What kind of fruit do you grow?"

Brian stopped and grinned at Sam. "You interested in flowers? My wife spends a lot of time in the yard. Nobody around here appreciates it much, I'm afraid. No good for eating." He laughed and looked toward the equally spaced fruit trees. "We have some apples, pears, and plums started. First year they've borne fruit. The grapes, now, I'm partial to them. They make a respectable wine. Concord vines, they are, hardy and prolific." Brian turned to study Sam and he noticed a speculative glint in the eyes of the older man.

"You a married man, Sam?"

Sam grinned and ducked his head. "Not yet, but I plan to get hitched up next summer."

Brian chuckled and slapped his shoulder. "Aha. You work for Mr. Long?"

"I got me a homestead last year and I'm proving it up as I can. Mr. Long wants to haul freight from the new south railhead to his store and he offered me the job. That's why he needs the mules."

"I see. So you're working your own place." He scratched his head, then tugged at his chin. "I got an idea. Would you like some cuttings from the vines, and some starts from the fruit trees? And Milly, my wife, she'd be delighted to give you some of her flowers, I reckon. It's a little late in the season, but if you shade them and give them plenty of water, they should do all right."

Sam inhaled deeply, then let the air pass slowly out between his lips. "Mr. Kilgore, that's sure generous of you, but I don't want to put you to no trouble."

"Ah, no trouble. Need something for my men to do, anyway." He called one of the hands and gave instructions. "Now, come on in and meet Milly."

Mr. Kilgore introduced Sam to a diminutive woman with merry brown eyes and thick auburn braids wound around the crown of her head. "Happy to meet you, Sam Jackson."

"Sam's come about the mules. He has a place in the Oklahoma Territory and is getting married soon," Brian told his wife.

"Well. Congratulations." Her smile transformed her rather plain face into one of uncommon beauty.

"Likes flowers, too. I told him you might give him some cuttings to take back."

Milly's smile broadened. "That rare creature, a man who loves flowers! I'd be delighted to share what I have as a wedding present for you and your young lady." She motioned to a leather chair. "Please sit. Would you like a cup of coffee or tea?"

"Now, Milly, Sam and I are going to have a drink and talk business." He walked to a cabinet and pulled a bottle from an inside shelf.

"If it's all the same to you, Mr. Kilgore, I'd rather have a cup of coffee." He turned his gaze on Mrs. Kilgore. "If it's no trouble ma'am."

Mr. Kilgore frowned and held the bottle out. "It's good whiskey, Sam, straight from Ireland. None better."

Sam smiled and nodded. "Thank you, sir. I'm sure it's the best." He felt the heat rise on his neck and studied his toes. "I just don't partake of spirits."

Brian's arm fell to his side. "A teetotaler? Well, I'll be a..."

"Brian!" Milly's voice cut in.

Mr. Kilgore's confused gaze flashed from Sam to his wife then to the bottle in his hand. "Well, each to his own. Milly, fetch out some coffee for our guest, but if you don't mind, Sam, I'll have a dram of this. Have a seat there." He whipped a glass from the cupboard, poured, and walked to a chair opposite the one where Sam sat on the edge of the seat. He chuckled and raised his glass. "Relax, son. I admire a man for his principles, even when I don't agree with them." He sipped his drink and leaned back with a smile.

Mrs. Kilgore set a tray laden with a steaming cup of coffee, a pitcher of cream, a bowl of sugar cubes, and a plate of gingerbread on the table beside Sam's chair, then left the room.

"Now, let's get down to business. The mules should be in the corral any minute. Providing they're what you're looking for, what are you prepared to offer?"

Sam took a deep breath. "Well, sir, Mr. Long is willing to pay top price for top animals." Ignoring the cream and sugar, he picked up the coffee cup and sipped the strong brew with pleasure, then continued. "There are some facts to consider, such as, you'll no longer have to feed animals you have no use for, and you won't have the expense of taking them to a new owner."

Brian slammed his glass on the side-table, slapped his knee, and guffawed. "Hot dingy, son, I like you. You must be carrying the blood of the Irish in you."

Sam mouth formed a doubtful grin. The appearance of a ranch hand at the door, spared him the effort of mustering a suitable response. He picked up a slice of gingerbread.

"Come on, Sam. Let's go look at these mules you're willing to take off my hands," said Brian with a twinkle in his grey eyes.

Sam stifled the quick intake of breath at the sight of the magnificent, matched dapple-grey, sixteen-hands-high animals in the corral, and noticed Mr. Kilgore eyeing him from beneath his bushy brows. "Well, Sam, do you think this team can pull a freight wagon over the flat land down south?" he asked in a solemn voice.

Sam chuckled. "Mr. Kilgore, I think they could pull a wagon over the Rocky Mountains. That is, if they had a mind to." He approached one of the mules and gingerly opened its mouth to inspect his teeth.

"They're about six years old," said Mr. Kilgore.

Sam nodded in agreement. A quarter hour of half-hearted haggling followed before Sam counted out the cash, received a bill of sale, and shook hands sealing the deal. "I thank you for your hospitality, Mr. Kilgore."

"It's been a pleasure doing business with you, Sam. You're welcome to stay the night. There's space in the bunk house, and Milly would be delighted to have company for supper."

"I better be gettin' back." He looked at the sun. "Should be able to make ten or twelve miles by nightfall." A ranchhand assisted Sam in securing ropes to the mules' halters, and another brought Gallatin, looking well-fed and ready to travel. Mr. Kilgore tied a burlap bag with tree sprouts sticking out the top and another filled with flower shoots on top of Sam's bedroll. "Quite a load you've got there, and trailing the mules, too."

"I'll manage. I can't thank you enough." Sam mounted and gathered up reins and ropes. "If you're ever down south, come by and see my place. I'll have an orchard started and flowers blooming in a year." He grinned.

Brian lifted his eyebrows and chuckled. "I might just do that."

"Sam, wait!" Mrs. Kilgore rushed from the house waving a small bag. "I made some sandwiches for you."

Sam doffed his hat. "Thank you, ma'am, for all your trouble. I won't forget your kindness." He slipped the tied ends of the bag over the saddle horn and turned Gallatin away from the lowering sun.

CHAPTER 14

Nessa stepped out on the porch after supper Wednesday. Venus shone brightly in the west and the moon gleamed overhead, but she saw no movement on the dark road running east. She knew it unlikely Sam would arrive tonight, but just in case, she wanted to be the first to see him. To her surprise, his absence had affected her more than she had expected. She laughed at the realization.

"Nessa? What are you laughing at out here all by yourself?" Ellie asked as she joined her.

"I was just reminded of how much a person can change in a few months." She lifted her head to breathe the fragrance on the cooling breeze.

"Nessa, will you not make fun of me if I ask you something?"

Nessa turned to survey her sister in the faint lamp light filtering through the open doorway. Her eyes widened. *Ellie has grown this summer. She's only an inch or two shorter than me, and she's filling out too.* She swallowed the giggle forming in her throat. *My little sister! I wonder if Mama knows?* She grimaced. *Well, of course she does, you ninny. You're so wrapped up in yourself these days, you haven't noticed.* She placed an arm around Ellie's shoulders. "I promise I won't make fun of you. What is your question?"

Ellie ducked her head, and spoke in a barely audible voice. "What does it feel like to fall in love?"

Nessa's arm dropped to her side as if Ellie's shoulders had suddenly become a blazing log, and she stood in stunned silence.

"Nessa? Are you angry with me?"

"No! No, Ellie. I'm just not sure how to answer your question. I'm trying to understand how being in love feels, and…well…It didn't happen all at once, at least not with me. It came over me like spring. It crept up on me before I knew what love really is. And now, looking back, I'm not even sure when it happened." She took a deep breath and gazed at the stars. "But I can tell you that at the sound of Sam's name, my heart seems to beat twice as fast, and at the sound of his footsteps—oh yes, I know they're his, something inside me leaps about. And, well, I feel safe and warm when he's near me." She slipped her arm around her sister's waist. "It's like coming inside during a snowstorm and smelling the hot cocoa Mama is making."

"Did Sam kiss you? What's it like to be kissed?"

"I…" Nessa frowned at Ellie. "Isn't it your bedtime? You mustn't make Papa come outside looking for you. Maybe we can talk more tomorrow." She hurried down the steps to the rock pathway, ignoring Ellie's groan of annoyance, and breathed a sigh of relief when her father's voice came from the doorway.

"Ellie, you out there? It's your bedtime."

"Coming, Papa."

"Nessa, about time for you to come in, too."

"Just a few more minutes, Papa, please."

"All right, but it's almost ten o'clock."

❧   ❧   ❧

Voices ascending from the kitchen woke Nessa. She raised her head and looked at the sunrise through the window. "Sam will surely be here today," she murmured and rose to dress quietly, not waking her sisters. She tiptoed down the stairs and heard her parents voices in the kitchen.

"What is the name of the man you bought the mules from?"

"Kilgore, Brian Kilgore."

"Kilgore. That's a good Irish name."

Nessa entered the room and greeted her parents who sat at the table drinking coffee.

"Well, you're up early, miss," said her mother. "Do you feel well?"

"Yes." Nessa stretched her arms above her head. "It's a beautiful day." She waltzed to the stove, poured coffee for herself, and sat at the table between her mother and father.

"By the way," Mr. Long said in a casual voice, "Sam left a message for you when he came through this morning."

Nessa frowned. "A message? This morning?"

"He arrived before dawn, Nessa. He wanted to get in last night, but it was too late, so he stopped for a few hours."

"Oh, I wanted to…" Her countenance fell and she sighed. "What was the message?"

"Sam said he wasn't fit to be seen by a certain young lady. He will return this evening, if there are no problems at his place. He also said he brought back your first wedding present. From the couple he bought the mules from. And you should see them, Nessa, the finest animals in the territory, and Sam got them for a good price—less than I expected." Papa chuckled and a satisfied smile filled his thin face. "Yeah, he did all right."

"Oh, mules!" Nessa battled the urge to thrust out her lower lip, and gazed at her father. "Did Sam say he'd be here for supper? You did invite him didn't you?"

"Of course, I did, but he wasn't sure if he could make it that early."

Nessa jumped up and ran to the window. The garden darkened as a low cloud passed in front of the sun.

Nessa spent the interminable hours at her mother's beck and call during the forenoon and fidgeted in the afternoon while her mother's flying fingers sewed the final seams of her yellow muslin dress. At the supper table, she sat like a dormant cocoon, heedless of the happy chatter surrounding her. She forked a morsel into her mouth now and again when she caught her mother's glance, chewed mechanically, and swallowed with difficulty. Ellie and Opal had kitchen clean-up, and Nessa excused herself to go to her room. She sat on her bed and stared at the rising gibbous moon.

"What is wrong with me, Jesus? I'm angry and I don't even know why. Sam acted like any sensible person would. I know it's childish to be mad at him, but I can't seem to help myself. I've been miserable all day." She bent toward the window at the sound of the soft "Whoa, boy" from the front of the house, jumped to her feet, and smoothed her hair with trembling fingers. She halted her speeding feet at the head of the stairs and took deep breaths, willing her body under control, and then stepped down in a deliberate fashion with her head high. Sam's stalwart shoulders appeared at the front entrance, and his gaze met hers.

She floated down the last few steps, and, oblivious of her parents, went to him. He smiled and took her hands in his. Fire raced down her spine and she trembled.

"Nessa. You look prettier than I remembered—like a butterfly."

"I'm glad you're back, Sam." Her cheeks pinkened.

"Well, Sam, our business can wait." Papa stood at the open front door. "You young folks want to sit on the porch or take a walk?"

Sam's smile turned sheepish. His head swivelled toward her father, then back to her.

"There's a big moon out there; how about it, Nessa?"

She sent a grateful glance to her father, then looked into Sam's luminous brown eyes. "I'd love to take a walk."

Sam took her elbow and led her outside. They turned left at the road, into the moonlight, walking in rhythm and silence. Sam's hand released her elbow and grasped her icy fingers. "You cold? You want to get a wrap?"

Nessa stopped and faced him. "I'm fine, Sam. A little nervous, I guess."

He took her other hand and cradled them both in his. "You? Nervous?" He laughed. "What about?"

"I don't know really. I've been flustered all day." She stared at his face, as though to memorize his features: the bushy brows, guileless eyes, slightly hooked nose, generous mouth, and firm chin. "Sam, you told me you loved me, but do you like me?"

Sam's smile disappeared and he dropped her hands. "Crikey, girl! What kind of question is that?"

"Well…what's your answer?" Her lips thinned.

"Of course I like you. I like you and I love you." He shrugged his shoulders and frowned.

Nessa sighed. "Never mind." She turned and resumed walking. "Where's my wedding present? Papa said you brought one."

Sam hurried to her side. "I don't have them with me. They're at my place. I got them all planted this morning before I helped Hank harvest his corn."

"Planted? The wedding present?"

Sam's roar of laughter caused Nessa to stop a second time. She placed her hands on her hips. "What's so funny, Sam Jackson? I don't like being made fun of and you always…"

Sam gulped and all traces of merriment vanished from his face. "Nessa, I wasn't laughing at you, but let's get something straight. You take everything you hear as though it's either for or against you, and you're way too serious. What I'm getting at is life is hard around here. I'd never hurt you on purpose, but if we can't share jokes and laugh at ourselves sometimes, well, we just have to, that's all, or we'll dry up like an old corncob." He caught her waist in his hands and pulled her close. "Don't you see, Nessa?"

His pleading voice stunned Nessa. Her mouth worked but no sound emerged. Sam thrust her at arms' length and shook her gently yet urgently.

"I…I guess I know what you mean, sort of. Like I heard Papa say, 'all work and no play makes you dull,' or something like that?"

Sam smiled. "Nessa, you're never dull, not for a moment." He brushed her nose with his lips. "That'll do for now." He linked an arm through hers and started walking. "Now, about this present. It came from the folks at the ranch where I bought the mules. We now have, my little wife-to-be, two more apple trees, two peach trees, two plum trees, and several grape vines. We also have a dozen or more iris bulbs, or whatever they're called, and three rose bushes. A mighty fine present, don't you think?"

Nessa smile became a giggle, her giggle rose to full fledged laughter, and Sam's hearty guffaw added harmony. Sam grabbed her hand, whirled her around and around until she collapsed against his chest. Her spine tingled at the fire in his eyes. She stood mesmerized in their depths until he raised his head to the sky. "Getting late. Got to get you home." He took her hand and began walking rapidly in the opposite direction.

Nessa struggled to keep up. "Slow down, Sam." She jerked her hand away from his. "I want to invite you to my birthday party."

"Your birthday? What day is it?"

"The twenty-sixth, Saturday. The party starts at four, but you're invited to come early if you can make it."

Shadows hid Sam's face now that the moon was behind them, and she was puzzled by his lack of response. "You will come won't you?"

"Oh, sure. I'll come, don't worry. I'll be there."

Nessa hugged herself, then spread her arms and danced around Sam. "It will be such fun, Sam, I can't wait." She stopped in front of him. "Oh, I almost forgot. Would you ask your friend Hank to come, too? That will make four couples and Mama says we can dance a few squares. Papa engaged two fiddlers and a caller." She grabbed Sam's hands and whirled him around. "Aren't you excited, Sam? I've never had a birthday party; just family celebrations." Sam's mouth curved in a smile, but the smile didn't reach his eyes.

"Saturday. Yeah, it sounds like fun."

❦   ❦   ❦

Sam hurried Nessa up the steps and into the living room, apologized to her parents for the late hour, took Nessa's hand and promised to see her soon, then hurried out the door. He climbed into the saddle and urged his horse into a dangerous gait on the dim trail. After a half mile, he slowed and patted his horse on the neck. "Sorry, Gallatin, but I got big trouble. Nessa's birthday is Saturday. I have no present and no money, and I don't know what I'm going to do."

Sam lay on his back on his cot and strove to banish the tumult of disastrous scenes floating in his head. His prayers were fervent but he received no release from anxiety. *Nessa will be so mad…she'll be hurt…she'll toss her head and flounce away.* A shiver ran down his spine. *She might even break our engagement.* He rolled to his side and squeezed his eyelids tight, but he could not rid himself of the images. Finally, exhaustion triumphed and he lapsed into fitful, dream-laden sleep. At five-thirty his internal clock dutifully woke him to remembered hopelessness.

Shoulders slumping, he completed necessary chores, then rode toward Hank's place to help with the corn harvest. The sunrise, symbol of the beauty of God's creation, failed to energize him. Hank greeted him with a cup of coffee and a smile that caused Sam to wince. Hank's new-found love of life brought him no pleasure this morning. And guilt piled on to gloom.

Sam attacked the corn field with vengeance, and soon strode yards ahead of Hank, stripping the golden ears from their stalks, and dropping them into the burlap bag hanging over his left shoulder. He tried in vain to stifle that still small voice, *Trust Me,* and worked with a vehemence that left him panting at the end of the row.

"Sam? What in the world is the matter with you? Wait up!" Sam ignored his friend's question, but out of the corner of an eye, he saw Hank slashing at the stalks with energy matching his own recent frenzy. He turned away, strode to the next row and began hacking with his machete. At the tug on his arm, he sighed and lowered his head.

"Sam! You'll be worn out before noon at this rate. You're the one who taught me to pace myself. What got into you?"

Sam raised his eyes and looked at his friend's frowning face. "I'm sorry, Hank. It's nothing to do with you. I've got a problem and no way to fix it." He put his gloved hand on Hank's shoulder, smiled and squeezed. "Let's get back to work."

"Sam, I'm your friend. Maybe I can help."

"I know you are, and I appreciate your offer, but…" He sighed and lifted the machete to the next stalk.

"All right, Sam. We'll forget it for now, but at dinner, we're going to talk."

When the sun reached its zenith, they stopped at the end of a row, drank greedily from the water jug, and headed for the dugout.

"Good morning's work." Hank slapped Sam on the back. "I've got chili beans and cold biscuits. Course they're not up to your standard, but they're filling."

Sam smiled. "Sounds good. I'm so hungry I could eat corn stalks. I didn't have breakfast."

They sat on weathered logs under the lone cottonwood tree and ate the cold repast with relish. Hank set his empty plate on the ground, rose with a muted grunt, and stretched his stiff muscles. "Okay, Sam, what's eatin' at you?"

Sam chewed his last bite of biscuit and looked up at his friend. He clawed at his hair, rubbed his chin, and sighed. "Like I told you, you can't help me any."

"Hey, I can listen, and what makes you so sure I can't help?" He grinned. "I'm a man of surprises."

Sam shook his head. "All right. Here's the fix I'm in. Nessa's birthday is tomorrow, she's having a party, and I have nothing to give her. No present and no money."

Hank snorted. "I might of known it had something to do with Nessa." He took a few steps and surveyed the horizon. "If you hadn't spent your last dime on me, you'd have money to buy her a nice present."

"Let's not get into that." He waved his hand. "You'll pay me back when you're able."

"Yeah. When I sell my corn. But that'll be next week, too late to do any good." Hank returned to his seat and sighed.

"No use crying over spilt milk. Anyway, getting you out of your trouble was more important than a birthday present. Look where you are now."

Hank grinned. "Yeah. I wouldn't have blamed you for giving up on me a long time ago, but I'm mighty grateful that you didn't."

"Wasn't me that changed you."

"Yeah, I know, but…" Hank bit his lip and looked away for a long moment, then cleared his throat. "I'm not much good at figurin' women. What does she like to do?"

"Oh, the usual things, I guess." Sam picked up a twig and dug circles in the dirt. "She sews. She rides her pony. She likes flowers, but the irises I brought back aren't blooming and the spring wild flowers are gone." He drew circles within the circles. "She likes to read poetry, some."

Hank's eyes narrowed as though in deep thought. "Hmm…I wonder. Be right back." He jumped to his feet and hurried to the dugout. Sam clasped his hands behind his head and watched the breeze teasing the crisp shiny leaves above his head, then pulled out his pocket knife and began whittling on the twig. *Come on, Hank, if we don't get back to work, we won't finish with the corn today.*

"I found it. I knew I'd put it away somewhere for safe keeping." Hank sped toward him waving a small packet in the air. He skidded to a stop in front of Sam, spraying dust, and placed the package on Sam's knee with a flourish. "One of Ma's ladies she did laundry for gave that to her. I threw it in my pack when Ma died and I was gettin' ready to leave town." He took a deep breath. "I don't why I kept it, but maybe it'll do for a present for Nessa."

Sam removed the layers of yellowed newspaper, revealing a thin leather-bound volume, and read the printed gilt letters. *"Poems of the Southland."* He lifted the cover. "Collected by the Ladies' Literary Society of Charleston, South Carolina, 1858." A smile spread across his face, and he looked at Hank who stood fidgeting. "It's better than anything I would have thought of, but are you sure you want to let go of it?"

Hank snorted. "I got no use for it, and Ma didn't 'specially prize it. It's yours if you want it."

Sam clambered to his feet, holding the little book clear of the dusty ground. "You just saved my skin, Hank." His face broke into a grin, then collapsed into dismay.

"What's the matter, now?"

"Hank, I'm sorry. I was so tied up in my own problem, I almost forgot. Nessa invited you to the party. It's at four o'clock, tomorrow."

"What? Invited me?" He scratched his head in disbelief, then stared at Sam. "Now, I'm the one with no gift."

Sam sighed and held the book out to Hank. "Here, you take this back."

"No, Sam. That's not the kind of gift for me to give her. Don't worry, I'll think of something." He squashed his grimy hat on his head and grinned. "Come on, let's get the rest of the corn picked. You've wasted enough of my time already."

At dusk, Sam, weary, sweaty, and elated, saddled Gallatin and started home. The precious parcel, in it's paper wrapping, nestled in the pocket of his flannel shirt near his heart.

CHAPTER 15

❀

Sam arrived at two Saturday afternoon and assisted Papa in setting up a rustic trestle table in the yard, and moving most of the furniture out of the parlor to make room for the square dancers. At four, a beaming Nessa stood at the front door, with Sam beside her, to greet her guests. Her new blue dress, copied, she told Sam, from the society page of the Atlanta newspaper, added depth and a hint of mystery to her eyes, and white roses tied with blue ribbon nestled in the waves of her upswept coiffure. Her heart thumped when she caught Sam's admiring glance. She felt grown-up at last. Louise arrived first and lifted her eyebrows as she advanced up the steps to kiss Nessa on both cheeks. Hank and the other guests followed within minutes with birthday wishes and gifts.

Nessa walked to the center of the room. "I'll choose the partners for the first square," she announced with a smile. "Joe and Ellie, Henry and Delia, and Hank and Louise. So, take your places." She clapped her hands, stepped back, took Sam's right hand and drew him into position.

"Bow to your lady," sang the caller, and the fiddlers drew their bows.

"I wonder where Hank went?" Sam asked Nessa during a breather. He dipped a cupful of spiced tea from the bowl on the dining table and handed it to her.

"He and Louise went outside when the music stopped."

Sam raised his eyebrows. "Oh? Louise? Are you sure?"

"And why not??"

He refilled his cup and drank before answering. "Well, Hank is...and Louise...I know she's your best friend, but she's sort of full of herself, don't you think?"

"I think no such thing! She just…Sam Jackson, that's a terrible thing to say!"

"I'm not shoutin' it to the world. But it just strikes me as purely odd for those two to disappear together."

"And why should you care? Louise can take care of herself."

"I know that." Sam frowned. "It's Hank I'm concerned about."

Nessa sucked in a breath and glared. "That's a fine way to talk about my best friend!" She slammed her cup on the table and whirled away.

❧   ❧   ❧

Sam sighed and dipped another cup of tea. When the fiddlers returned, Nessa pulled Joe into position beside her. Sam grimaced and asked Ellie to be his partner.

"Thanks for asking me, Sam. I'm not a very good dancer yet, and I think Joe's tired of covering my mistakes."

Sam smiled. He was surprised to notice how Nessa's younger sister had grown in the last few months. "You're doing fine. A little more practice and you'll be showing all of us up." At the do-si-do, he caught Nessa's glowering gaze and grinned, then frowned as he glimpsed the saucy smile Louise gave Hank. At the end of the square, he thanked Ellie. "I think I better get back to your sister." He took Nessa's hand and eased her aside. "I didn't mean to put your friend down, but Hank doesn't know how to handle a girl like her. Shucks, I don't either. She scares me spitless."

Nessa laughed. "You are so funny. You strike off to a wild land, with hardly more than the clothes on your back, you tame wild horses to get money to buy you a homestead, live out in the open for weeks till you dig a little room, deal with snakes and tornadoes and…" She paused to catch her breath. "And you tell me you're scared of a girl half your size?"

"I'm serious, Nessa. Louise will tear Hank into little pieces and then stomp on them. Can't you ask her to leave him be?"

Nessa straightened to her full height and put her hands on her hips. "I really don't want to talk about Louise. This is my birthday and I'm going to have fun! Do you want to dance or not?"

Sam chewed at his lower lip, stared at his boots for a long moment, and gave a slight shrug. He looked into Nessa's angry eyes and smiled. "Let's go. I'll dance your feet off."

Nessa rewarded him with a wide smile, grabbed his hand, and stepped into position as the caller raised his voice.

❖   ❖   ❖

At the end of the square, Mama announced supper was waiting in the back yard. Nessa led her guests to a table laden with platters of roast beef, potato salad, and homemade pickles. Then, with Sam in tow, she took her place at the end of the line.

Hank stood behind Louise, in the middle of the queue. "Don't eat too much, fellows, or you'll be stepping all over the ladies' feet."

"Ha! Speak for yourself, Hank," said Joe, as he forked a hefty slab of meat onto his plate.

Mama entered the yard from the kitchen, carrying a pitcher of milk in one hand and a plate of hot biscuits in the other. "Don't worry, Hank. There's more in the kitchen."

Hank's face flushed. "Mrs. Long, I didn't mean…"

Mama laughed and gave him a wide smile. "It's all right, Hank. I know what you meant."

After more laughter and giggles, Nessa filled her plate and, with Sam beside her, sat on a bench under the shelter of a silver maple tree. She balanced the dish on her knees, gave a contented sigh, and gazed at the sun's fading rays. "Look, Sam, the sky is all gold, and pink, and violet. God gave me a present, too."

Sam grinned. "I'd say His is the best of all." He turned to gaze at Nessa, took her hand and squeezed it. "Happy Birthday, Nessa."

Love seemed to flow from Sam's eyes into Nessa's soul. She felt slightly giddy as she whispered, "Thank you." Her eyes misted.

After eating, Sam excused himself to help the men return the furniture to the front room.

Nessa chatted with her feminine guests, while her mother and sisters cleared the food away.

Papa appeared at the backyard gate holding a lamp. "All right, ladies, come inside now."

Nessa sat in the center of the sofa, surrounded by gifts. She unwrapped Sam's first, and smiled with delight.

"Oh, it's lovely, so unusual! Wherever did you find it?"

Sam grinned. "That, I'll never tell."

She lifted the cover of the little book, and a light flush infused her cheeks as she silently read the inscription in Sam's bold handwriting. *To my wife-to-be, my Sweetheart, forever, August 26, 1898. Your Sam.* A lump rose in her throat and her lips quivered. She laid the little book beside her and grabbed the box from her parents.

"Fancy party shoes! Mama, Papa, they're beautiful. Look everyone." She held the shoes above her head, then placed them in her lap and ran a finger over the soft white leather. "I've only had black shoes before. And look at the little heels; they're perfect." She smiled at her mother. "Thank you. I love them." After a lingering touch across the toes, she set the shoes aside.

Hank's gift sparked hilarity from the assembled party, when Nessa held up the tiny pony hand-carved from cedar. Nessa fondled it with her fingers. "Hank, how thoughtful. I didn't know you could carve like this. You're a true artist."

Her attention moved from Hank to Louise, and she drew a quick breath at her friend's enigmatic study of the young man beside her. Nessa stole a side-wise glance at Sam. He was watching Louise and gnawing on his lower lip.

Nessa picked up a package and exclaimed over the set of embroidered tea towels from Ellie.

"How ever did you do these without my knowing?" She examined the hems. "Ellie, your stitches are more even than mine." She smiled at her sister and Ellie's face glowed. "Thank you."

She briefly modeled Louise's gift of a Sunday bonnet of deep-green velvet decorated with pink feathers. She unwrapped the last gift, a satin and lace sachet filled with dried lavender, and breathed in the heavenly scent.

"I didn't make it, Nessa, my mother did." Joe grinned and the guests roared with laughter. Joe's face turned scarlet.

"Thank you, Joe, and your mother. I love lavender." Nessa held the sachet to her nose.

When Mama entered with the birthday cake, piled high with sweetened whipped cream, Nessa rose and placed her gifts on the side table. Ellie led the guests in singing the *Birthday Song,* and Nessa responded with a nervous giggle.

Nessa sat beside Sam, nibbling at her lower lip in thoughtful silence, while Mama cut and Ellie served the cake. She eyed her guests. Louise sat next to Hank, seemingly absorbed in eating, but Hank appeared perplexed.

Joe got to his feet and surveyed the few lonely crumbs on the silver platter. "Sure was a tasty cake, Mrs. Long, and a great party."

Mama smiled. "Thank you Joe. I'm glad you enjoyed it."

Joe moved to stand in front of Nessa. "Happy Birthday, Nessa. Thanks for inviting me."

"Thank you, Joe. I'm glad you came, and thanks again for the sachet."

He nodded, waved at the others, and left.

After bidding good by to Delia, Joe, and Henry, Nessa, accompanied by Louise, followed Sam and Hank to the porch.

"Louise is spending the night," Nessa explained when she noticed Sam's puzzled look at her friend.

"Oh. Well, that's fine." A smile flickered across his face and he took Nessa's hand. "Will you walk a bit down the road with me?"

❦   ❦   ❦

Sam held Nessa's arm and led her away from the house. The star-filled moonless night encompassed them after a few steps, and Sam stopped. His arms encircled her waist. She raised her head and he lost himself in her luminous eyes. He cleared his throat.

"Nessa." He lowered his head and touched her smiling lips with his. He felt the quiver erupt and ripple down her back and his arms tightened. He marveled at her softness and moaned when her arms crept around his neck. After a moment, he released her, and struggled to control his ragged breathing.

"I love you, girl."

Nessa swayed and grasped his arm. "I love you, Sam."

He swallowed hard, took her hand, and turned to retrace their steps. "So, did you enjoy your birthday? Do you really like the book of poems?"

"It's the most wonderful birthday I've ever had." She squeezed his hand. "And I really do like the poetry book. I was so surprised you would give me something like that. Tell me where you got it?"

Sam grinned. "Can't do it, little girl. It's my secret. I was sort of surprised myself. Let's just leave it at that, all right?"

Nessa stopped. "Sam, how can you be so sweet one minute and so stubborn the next? Why is it a secret?" Her eyes twinkled and her lips curved. "You didn't steal it, did you?"

"Of course not!"

She laughed. "I was just teasing." She lifted an arm toward the heavens. "I don't want anything to spoil this day, but you are such a maddening man. You get my curiosity going, then you…Well here we are." She stopped by the steps where Hank waited with Louise beside him.

"Where you two been?" asked Hank. "We gotta go. Mr. Long has stepped out here twice and looked up and down the road."

"Uh oh. Goodnight, Nessa. See you at church tomorrow." Sam slapped Hank on the shoulder. "Okay. You could have saddled the horses, you know."

"You fuzzy-headed scalawag; they're waiting right there by the fence!"

❧   ❧   ❧

Nessa followed Louise into the front room to find Papa the sole occupant.

"Your mother and the girls went to bed," he said and yawned. "I suggest you two do the same."

"We'll make a pallet in here on the floor, Papa, so we can talk a while without bothering anyone. All right?"

Mr. Long yawned again. "I guess so. Don't stay awake too long. Church tomorrow."

Louise giggled and Nessa went to fetch blankets and pillows.

Nessa lay wide-eyed in the darkness. She and Louise had discussed the day in detail, from the dancing, to the gifts, to the cake.

"Louise? You awake?"

"Um-huh."

"I was surprised you danced with Hank so much. I paired you up with him as a sort of joke."

Nessa clutched at the sheet covering her, as it was flung to her feet, and Louise's triumphant voice announced, "Well, Miss Busybody, I had a good time with Hank, so the joke's on you!"

"You really mean that? You like Hank?"

Louise's sob brought Nessa upright. "What's wrong? What did I say? I don't understand you."

"Neither do I." Louise's weeping increased. "It's not possible, but if that's true, why am I so unhappy?"

Nessa slipped an arm around Louise's quivering shoulders. "What is it? Tell me."

"I guess…the joke's…on me…after all. Me. The smart one, the one who planned to have everything she wanted. Just having a little fun along the way. Now I'm caught in my own trap."

Tears fell on Nessa's bare arm, and Louise collapsed against her in shuddering sobs. "Ssh. I don't understand what's wrong, but I'm sure it will be better in the morning."

The sobbing ebbed and Louise pulled away. "Oh, Nessa! You're such a baby, but I love you anyway." Nessa stiffened and Louise patted her arm. "Never mind. I'm sorry I said that. You're a sweet friend." She sighed. "Let's get some sleep, my poor head is pounding."

❧   ❧   ❧

Sam rode beside Hank, rapt in the memory of Nessa's arms. *Another whole year. I don't think I can make it.* He sighed and stared into the beauty of the heavens. *Lord, I really need your help this time. It's more than mortal man can—*

"…believe it. Cat got your tongue?"

Furrows appeared in Sam's brow and he turned to see Hank staring at him. "What?"

Hank snorted. "Where you been, Sam? You haven't heard a word I said."

"Sorry, Hank. I been thinking. What were you talking about?"

"I was tellin' you how it appears I had that little gal all wrong. Thought she was too big for her britches, but when…"

"You talking about Louise?"

"Yeah. Who else?" Hank rubbed his chin and grinned. "She's all right, Sam. Yessiree, she's all right."

Sam pursed his lips. "And you learned all that in one evening of dancing?"

"Well, we had time to talk some. And can she talk! I hardly got a word in edgewise. She's awful smart, Sam."

"Oh? Is that a fact?"

"Now, don't take that tone! It wasn't so much the words she used, it was more the way she said them.

"She maybe made you feel big and strong, and she's just a little weakling, and you wanted to protect her from the big bad world?"

Hank's short laugh revealed his discomfiture. "It maybe started out kind of like that, but later…I think she really likes me." Sam didn't reply and he continued. "I know what you're thinkin'. The kind of women I've been around lately. Out for a good time, take what you can get. But that's all in the past. I don't want that kind of life any more."

When Hank pulled his horse to a stop, Sam reined in Gallatin and turned back.

Hank took a deep breath. "I watched you and Nessa tonight, and I want what you two got." He uttered a nervous laugh. "When your Jesus finally got hold of me, He really did a good job!"

"He's your Jesus, too, Hank."

"I know! That's what I'm trying to tell you. My head's been swimmin' in confusion for days, but I think I finally got it straightened out. I want to get my place all fixed up and get me a woman like you got. And I think maybe Louise is the woman for me."

"Hank, that little gal twisted you around and tied you up in a big knot. Believe me, she's not the kind of wife you want. Why, she probably won't remember your name the next time you see her. Nothing against you, but…"

Sam straightened in the saddle at the menace in Hank's deep-voiced words. "Now, just a minute, Sam. You're my best friend but I don't intend to listen to that kind of talk about the girl I hope to marry."

Sam sighed. "All right, Hank. Maybe I'm wrong about Louise. I hope I am. But watch your step, will you? And remember what you told me when I first met Nessa? Well, Louise is used to a lot more than Nessa has. Her pa is the most prominent man in the area. What's he going to say about his daughter hitching up with you? Now don't get riled, I'm in the same boat as you are. You know neither one of us has much."

Hank urged his horse to a walk. "Maybe not, but…Oh, you're probably right, but there must be some way. Look at you, Mr. Long thinks you're a white knight or something as far as his daughter's concerned. How did you bring that about, Sam?"

Sam grinned and shook his head. "Don't rightly know. Only thing I did was ask the Lord for help." He frowned and released a harsh breath of air. "He did, and I never thanked Him proper. I gotta straighten that out with Him tonight."

"You're telling me the Lord fixed things for you?"

"Only way it could've happened."

"Well, then." Hank grinned. "He'll do the same for me, too. Isn't that right? You said He was no respecter of persons, and a whole lot more stuff like that."

Sam chewed at his lower lip. "The Bible says that and I believe the Bible, but I don't think He always fixes things for one person the same way he does for another fellow. What I mean is, He does what He knows is best, and if…"

"Now don't you get off on that again! He'll think Louise is best for me just like I do."

Sam sighed. "I hope so, Hank. I really do."

CHAPTER 16

❀

The usual bustle of the Long family's Sunday morning preparation for church thwarted Nessa's desire to question Louise. Actually, it seemed Louise contrived to avoid her. Her friend looked pale and spoke only when spoken to at breakfast. She followed Nessa and her sisters upstairs to dress, but didn't join in the girlish chatter. Nessa tied Opal's hair ribbon, Ellie found her Bible, and then she and Opal ran downstairs to watch their father harness the team.

Louise stood before the bureau mirror arranging her blonde tresses. Nessa stepped behind her and sought eye contact. Louise's gaze lowered, but Nessa's remained on Louise's reflection.

"Louise, about last night—"

"What about last night?"

"Well, you admitted you were attracted by Hank."

Louise laughed, a bitter sound in Nessa's ear. "Attracted by Hank? Are you serious?"

Nessa frowned. "But you said…"

"You must have misunderstood, Nessa. How could I be attracted to Hank? He's just another homesteader. Oh, he's a passable dancer, and rather nice looking, if he'd get a decent haircut. He amused me for an evening, but that's all there was to it."

Nessa stamped one foot. "Louise Bagley! I don't understand you at all. Last night you were crying your eyes out."

"Yes, I did have a dreadful headache, didn't I? I feel like my usual self this morning." She lifted her chin and met Nessa's angry gaze. "Are you finished dressing? I think I'll wait on the front porch."

Nessa stood open-mouthed as Louise walked from the room. The sound of the screen door slamming jolted her from the catatonic shock of Louise's words. She sagged and sat on her bed. Her bosom rose and fell rhythmically as anger and disbelief ebbed and surged within her.

"Nessa? What's keeping you, dear?"

She rose at the sound of her mother's voice and purged her emotions with a painful swallow. "Coming, Mama."

The atypical quiet in the back seat of the buggy, even by the two younger girls, became apparent to Nessa when she saw her father question her mother with raised eyebrows, and her mother answer with a delicate shrug. Nessa tried and failed to think of an amusing story, then succumbed to black thoughts. *I thought Louise had changed, but Sam was right about her. How he'll gloat! No, I guess not. He'll be furious because of Hank. Poor Hank. But maybe he didn't like Louise anyway. But he did, I saw the way he watched her.* She shifted her body to escape the distress and glanced at Louise. *And she looked at him the same way. I know she did. And she cried because…Oh, I don't know. I wish I'd never invited Hank to my party.*

Nessa sighed when Papa guided the team to a stop in the churchyard, and she sighted Hank waiting beside Sam. Sam greeted her with a smile and helped her alight from the buggy. "You look mighty pretty this morning, Miss Long, and all grown up, too."

"Sam, I'm so glad to see you." She blushed at her foolish gushing, then became aware of how the touch of his strong, competent hands blasted her fears into oblivion, for a few precious moments. They rushed back at the chill in Louise's voice.

"Thank you, Mr. Moran, but I'm perfectly capable of descending from a buggy without your assistance."

Hank's face turned to putty and he stepped back in confusion. Nessa glanced at Sam and flinched at the fury in his eyes as he glared at Louise. He took a deep breath and turned to aid Ellie and Opal, then grasped Nessa's arm with authority and led her around the buggy to where Hank stood motionless, with his arms hanging as useless as broomsticks without their straw.

Sam slapped him on the shoulder. "Come on, Hank. You sit with Nessa and me today."

Hank walked in front of Sam, looking neither right nor left. Inside, Nessa ventured a glance about and saw Louise sitting like a finely chiseled marble statue between her parents. Sam touched Hank's arm and motioned him into the pew beside Ellie who gave him a wide smile and swept her skirt out of the way. Nessa followed and Sam took the aisle seat. He closed his eyes and Nessa saw his lips moving. She sighed with relief when the frown that distorted his face diminished and he opened his eyes to smile at her. Noting his release, she closed her eyes and pleaded. *Please, Father, let it be all right. Please, Father, let it be all right. Help Hank, Father. Please don't let Sam blame me.* She opened her eyes and sneaked a backward glance. *And, please help Louise, too, Father. Thank you.*

The service consisted of prayers, singing a half dozen hymns, and testimonies by one man and two women. Nessa sang and listened with minimum comprehension; her heart focused on her prayer words. After the last Amen, she followed Sam into the aisle, intent on drawing him aside, but her father circled around her and tapped Sam on the shoulder. "Sam, could I have a word with you outside?"

Her options closed, Nessa greeted friends, then followed her mother to the buggy. Sam stood beside Gallatin nodding now and then when her father stopped speaking to take a breath. Then the men shook hands, Sam climbed into the saddle without looking her way, and her father walked toward them with a big smile on his face. He climbed up beside her mother, spoke to the team, and they turned toward home. Nessa's gaze followed Sam as he joined Hank and they rode slowly down the track to the south. At the sound of her father's voice, she motioned her sisters to silence so she could hear her parents' conversation.

"…should work out fine. He'll leave in the morning and should be back by evening. We'll be all set and if everything goes well, you should have a sewing machine by All Saints Day." He patted Rebecca's knee. "I was told the wagon is sturdy enough to carry as many supplies as Sam can pile in it. The family that owns it moved to a place over in New Mexico Territory from somewhere in Kansas about a month ago. Carried all their household goods, including a piano, but they need a lighter weight wagon now to get around in, and will let it go at a reasonable price. The Lord is good, Rebecca. I had no idea where we could find a freight wagon. Thought we might have to get one from St. Louis, and that would have had to wait till spring."

Rebecca smiled, placed her hand on her husband's and squeezed it. "Just like Margaret Lukinbill's testimony today, 'He will supply all our needs if we just trust Him.' He has been so good to us, Owen."

Nessa strained to hear and understood little. *Why didn't I pay attention. It has something to do with the mules Sam bought.* She shook her head and wondered if God would answer her prayer as He apparently had done for her parents. *I'll try to catch Mama alone this afternoon and find out what this is all about.*

❦   ❦   ❦

When late afternoon breezes cooled the sultry air, Nessa noticed her mother picking up her gardening gloves and shears, and followed her into the backyard. Mama bent over a bed of zinnias and began clipping off the spent blooms. Nessa knelt beside her and yanked up an errant ragweed. "What is Sam doing for Papa tomorrow?"

"Your father plans to bring supplies from the new railhead down south twice a week instead of the hit-and-miss way people bring it to us when they happen to be going that way. Sam will make the trips. We'll have needed supplies for all our customers and we'll get mail regularly, too."

Nessa's impatience grew as she listened to her mother. "But why is Sam going over there in the morning?"

Rebecca sighed. "Nessa, we need a big sturdy wagon to haul all those supplies, and your father heard of one in New Mexico."

"And he'll be back tomorrow evening?"

"Your father thinks so."

"Will he bring the wagon here?"

"Probably. Your father will want to see it." Mama rubbed her back with her left hand. "Why do you ask?"

Nessa tossed a clump of chickweed over her shoulder. "I want to talk to him about something." She looked up at her mother. "Mama, what do you do when Papa is angry with you?"

"Well, I…" She frowned and reached for Nessa's arm. "Come sit here on the bench and tell me what this is all about."

Nessa sat beside her mother and hung her head. "I think Sam is angry with me. I did something at my party—for a joke. And now it's not funny, and I don't know what to do." A tear slipped down her cheek, and she swiped at it with a fist. "I paired Louise with Sam's friend Hank to tease Louise, and, it seems impossible, but they…Well, they sort of fell for each other. At least—" She blew her nose with fervor to thwart the sobs swelling in her throat.

"Mercy, Nessa, if they are attracted to each other, what is the problem?"

"Oh, Mama! Louise really liked Hank Saturday night. She talked and talked about him, then Sunday morning she…" Nessa sighed. "I guess she changed her mind. She just laughed when I mentioned his name and then at church, she treated him like an old dirty shoe. You should have seen Hank's face. And Sam—the look he gave Louise." Nessa shivered despite the heat. "I was stunned, and I know Sam blames me. Now Hank is miserable, Louise is miserable, and Sam is mad enough to bite nails. He didn't speak to me after church. He probably doesn't want to see me again." She succumbed to the turbulence inside her and fell into her mother's arms.

Minutes passed before the storm subsided and Nessa responded to her mother's gentle rocking and soothing voice.

"There, there, child, hush now. Sssh." Nessa raised her head and Rebecca handed her a handkerchief. "Nessa, you feel guilty because you wanted to embarrass Louise, which was unchristian, of course, but what happened between Louise and Hank is not your fault. You are not responsible for their feelings or actions. They will have to work this out themselves. You should be a friend to both of them, and pray they make the right decision."

Nessa wiped her hot swollen face and looked at her mother with watery blue eyes. "But Sam?" She closed her eyes and sniffed.

"Nessa, Sam still cares for you. Love doesn't come and go like the south wind, and Sam loves you." She sighed. "I hope your love for him grows and you understand this truth. Will you dismiss him when he does something you don't like?"

Nessa's eyes widened and her mouth gaped. "I wouldn't do that!"

"Of course you wouldn't and neither would he. So you see?" She smiled. "Did you tell Sam your motive for pairing Louise and Hank?"

"No, I haven't had a chance to talk to him."

"Tell him, Nessa. Honesty in any friendship is crucial. He will understand, and you will be building a fortress of trust in each other. And Sam is wise enough to realize Hank and Louise have to make their own way."

Nessa stared at the deepening blue of the sky and took a deep breath. "Mama, I don't think I'll ever be able to sort things out without your help."

Her mother laughed. "Don't fret, Nessa. You can do most anything you set your mind to, when you have to." She rose from the garden bench. "It's late and supper isn't ready. Can you imagine Papa disliking me for not having his meal ready?"

Nessa laughed, stood and took her mother's hand. "No, but he might give a subtle hint. 'Are we fasting tonight?' or 'Dinner was a long time ago.'"

❦   ❦   ❦

Sam turned Gallatin onto the trail and called, "Hank, wait up!" He shook his head as the sorrel in front of him lengthened its stride. He shifted his hand forward to loosen the reins. "Go, boy." After a run of a mile or more, he pulled along side Hank and shouted. "Pull up."

Hank reined in his mount and frowned at Sam. "I don't want to hear anything you say. You're the one got me into this. All this talk about Jesus and church and look what it got me! My old friends would never be as rude as your church-going folks."

"One folk, Hank, only one. Now be fair. And Jesus never promised you wouldn't get your feelings hurt. You're going to allow one snippety girl to destroy your faith? Didn't you hear the preacher this morning? Everything works out for our good if we believe."

"I guess I wasn't paying attention to the preacher. All I could think about was the look on Louise's face, 'Thank you Mr. Moran,' like she'd never seen me before!" He balled his right hand into a fist and struck the palm of his left hand, over and over, jerking the reins and causing Danger to snort. "And I'm supposed to believe that is for my good? Well, I don't see how, and I don't want to hear any more about Jesus caring for me and loving me, just a poor old sod farmer. Why should He care?"

Sam chewed on his lower lip. "You don't mean that. And you're not the sort of man I expected to wallow around in self-pity. When you're ready to talk, I'll be waiting." He tipped his hat, nudged Gallatin with his heels, and galloped away.

CHAPTER 17

❀

Sam performed his chores by lantern light, prepared a hearty breakfast of salt pork, eggs, and flapjacks smothered in butter and sorghum molasses, and packed a lunch of salt-pork-filled biscuits, and fresh tomatoes. The sun still hid behind the horizon, but the sky was pink and gold and gave sufficient light to harness the mules. A few minutes later he gathered the four pairs of reins in a gloved hand, mounted Gallatin, shouted hee-aw to the team, and they started off at a slow trot. Gallatin balked at setting his pace to that of the mules, but Sam held his head high and spoke. "Easy boy." So far as Sam knew, driving a team of harnessed mules while riding a horse had never been done, but the alternative was to walk behind the team all the way to New Mexico. He mulled the idea over Sunday night and decided to give the unorthodox method a try. After a mile, mules, horse, and rider settled into a steady trot.

Sam topped a low rise and eyed the sun. About ten-thirty he reckoned, and his destination was in sight. Two work horses and a milk cow were tethered on a grassy plot sloping to a creek bed carrying a sluggish trickle of water. A tiny adobe house brightened by a rose bush holding a remnant of faded yellow blossoms baked in the sun, and a rooster with flowing black tail feathers kept vigilance over a dozen bronze hens picking at the ground. A cumbersome wagon stood off to the side. Sam stopped a hundred yards from the house.

"Hello. Anybody home?"

A tiny young woman with yellow braids spiraling around her head, and inquiring gray eyes, appeared at the door at the same time a man about Sam's age strode from a shack beyond house, that Sam had not noticed earlier. The man waved and smiled. Sam urged his animals a little nearer.

"I'm Sam Jackson. Mr. Long over in Oklahoma Territory sent me about your wagon."

"Sure, and I remember," the man answered in an accent Sam didn't recognize. "I'm Clem Basetti. Give the reins over to me and I'll tie the mules to the tree. You, please, enter into the house."

Sam followed Clem through the door. Clem spread his arms wide. "My espousa, Katerina. Katerina, this be Mr. Jackson, our visitor from Mr. Long, who maybe has use for the wagon."

Sam removed his hat and nodded. "Ma'am." Mrs. Basetti gave him a dainty curtsy, and spoke with less accent. "Welcome to our home, Mr. Jackson."

"We'll talk a little business, Katerina. Maybe you bring Mr. Jackson coffee or milk. What you like, Mr. Jackson?"

"A glass of water would be welcome, if it's not too much trouble." Katerina smiled and disappeared through a door.

"Sure, and you sit here."

Sam took the proffered chair and Mr. Basetti sat on the opposite side of the small oak table. The tiny room also held a piano, an accordion, a wood stove, and two rocking chairs. A low table holding a chess board and pieces, such as Sam had never seen, caught his eye. The squares of light and dark wood were polished; a design of vine and leaves was carved on each side with a tiny cluster of grapes at the corners. The pieces of light and dark wood had a similar carved design.

Mrs. Basetti set two pottery cups in front of Sam, one filled with water and the other with buttermilk. Sam smiled and drank deeply of the water, then took a sip of the refreshing beverage from the second cup, while his host and hostess waited. "Thank you very much, Mrs. Basetti. That really hit the spot."

"Okay, now, let me and you talk the business."

Sam made the offer authorized by Mr. Long. Mr. Basetti, closed his eyes and nodded his head up and down. They soon reached an agreement and shook hands. Sam glanced at the little table. "I noticed your chess set, Mr. Basetti. I've never seen one like it."

Clem waved his arms and his pale blue eyes twinkled."Oh, and my great grandfather made it years ago in the old country." He smiled at Sam. "You play the chess?"

"I enjoy a game now and then."

"Good! You come back any time and we play." His voice descended to a whisper. "Katerina, she play with me a sometimes, but she say it big waste of time."

Sam grinned. "I'd like that. It would be a pleasure to play on such a beautiful board." He ran a finger over the intricacy of one corner. "What part of the old country are you from, Mr. Basetti?"

"Call me Clem. The chess players, they not so formal, eh?" When Sam nodded with a smile, he continued. "The old country, the Tyrol, some a times the Italian, and some a times the Austrian." He shook his head and waved his arms.

"Well, Clem, we'll have to have a game soon. And call me Sam." They shook hands in agreement. "How long you folks been here?"

Clem scratched his head. "Maybe two, three months. Mrs. Basetti and me marry in the spring and buy this land from a widow moving back to Santa Fe after her husband die." He looked at the bare wooden floor for a long moment. "Too late to plant much this year. I go back to coal mine in Kansas in few weeks for winter work. Katerina, she grow very big garden and stay here to care for animals. I come back in spring to start crops."

"You mean that little girl will be alone here this winter?"

"No choice. And she strong. She say we do this and then have good life." A shadow passed over his face. "I don't like that way, but she say yes, and I do what she wish."

Sam chewed on his lower lip. "Look, Clem. If it's any comfort to you, I'd be glad to keep an eye on her this winter. Have you met any of your neighbors?"

"Oh, the neighbors, they say hello when I go to village store, and we go to church, but they not come here yet." He looked at his feet. "We be the strangers. A little time needed to make the friends."

Sam shuffled his feet. "Well, Clem, I need to start back." He grabbed his hat from the floor, stuffed it on his head, and started for the door.

"Wait, Mr…Sam. You please stay for dinner."

Sam stopped and turned around. "I thank you for the offer, but I need to get home. I haven't driven that team with a wagon. I hope they don't give me any trouble." He smiled. "I'd like to come for supper some evening, though."

Clem nodded. "That a be good. We expect you." He grabbed his hat from a peg near the door. "I help get you hitched up."

Four hands made short work of maneuvering the mules to the wagon and securing the rigging. Sam tied Gallatin to the rear of the wagon, climbed up to the high wooden plank seat, and waved, before slapping the reins and directing the mules to move. "Tell Mrs. Basetti thanks for the buttermilk."

After a couple of miles, mules and driver hit their stride and Sam relaxed and turned his thoughts to the Basetti's. He was shaken by the thought of the young woman fending for herself. Yet, this couple had come to this land knowing they would have to sacrifice, and she appeared to be capable and determined. *They've probably survived worse.* He shook his head, thinking of the thousands who braved the crossing of an ocean to pursue a better life. He sighed and promised himself to visit Mrs. Basetti as often as possible during the winter. Around noon he stopped on a ridge and ate his lunch in the shade of the wagon, then pushed on, arriving at the general store in the early afternoon.

Owen inspected the wagon and smiled. "I'm pleased, Sam. This wagon is sturdy enough to haul any merchandise I order. Don't you agree?"

Sam nodded. "I think so, Mr. Long. And for all its bulk, it handles pretty good, even when empty."

"Good. And those mules should be able to pull it loaded without a problem."

Sam patted the off-side mule on the shoulder. "I think so. We're getting used to each other. They'll do the job."

"So. We're ready to begin our enterprise. I'll get an order written up for you to send on the train. And there should be some supplies waiting. Can you make a trip day after tomorrow?"

"Sure thing, Mr. Long." Sam tipped his hat and smiled.

"Sam? Could I speak to you now?"

Sam's smile grew at the sound of Nessa's voice and he turned to see her standing on the store steps. "Nessa. I was wondering where you were. Would you like to take a ride in the wagon?"

"Perhaps some other time. I'd rather walk today if you don't mind."

"Whatever you say."

"I'll get my bonnet." Nessa rushed inside and reappeared a moment later, tying the strings of a flowered cotton bonnet with a wide brim to shade her face from the sun. Sam took her arm and led her toward the road. He turned west so their return trip would be away from the lowering sun's rays.

"So, what did you want to talk about? You're wearing a mighty serious face."

❦   ❦   ❦

Nessa noticed the twinkle in his eyes when she looked up at him, and her courage faltered. He didn't appear angry. Maybe…No her mother said she must be honest. "Sam, I want to talk about Louise and Hank." She blanched as a frown displaced the playfulness in Sam's face.

"I really don't want to talk about it, Nessa. Hank—well, I don't feel at liberty to tell you."

"Sam, I have to tell you...I mean I have a confession to make." She withdrew her hand from his and studied the toes of her shoes. "I deliberately paired Louise with Hank as a joke on her. I never thought she would...I didn't mean for Hank to get hurt." She looked into his darkening brown eyes, shivered, and whispered. "I'm sorry, Sam. Please don't be angry with me." She held his gaze with her own, praying for a sign of forgiveness.

Sam grimaced and stood silent for a long moment. Then he sighed, and still unsmiling, reclaimed her hand. "I didn't know, but it makes no difference. They would have got together anyway. Louise fascinated Hank even before your party, and Louise..." Again, a hiss of breath erupted between his teeth. "Well you know Louise, she would have sensed his interest just like a dog smells a rabbit."

"Sam! Louise has her faults, but she doesn't prey on fellows." Nessa faced Sam with her arms akimbo.

Sam snorted. "You're saying I'm too hard on her? Not in my opinion. At any rate, it wasn't your fault that your little trick backfired. Louise is the one that needs to confess and apologize. Not much chance of that, I'm thinking!" He grasped Nessa's hand and resumed walking.

"Oh, Sam. You should have heard her that night. She talked and talked about Hank, how good-looking, such a good dancer, good manners, and on and on. And her voice sounded sort of dreamy when she spoke his name. She really liked him; I know she did. But the next morning, I didn't understand her at all. She looked pale and sick and she wouldn't speak to me. Then at the church...It was horrible."

"Huh. She probably figured out what you were up to and said those things to amuse herself."

"I don't think so. I think she likes him a lot and it scares her somehow." Nessa stopped, stared at her shoes, frowned, then gazed at the thoughtful look on Sam's face.

"Now, that is something to think about." He gave Nessa an odd smile. "Nessa, you may be right. Wouldn't that be something?" He laughed and pulled her into his arms. "Maybe the joke's on her after all."

Nessa pushed his arms away. "What do you mean? You're talking in riddles."

"Don't you see, Nessa? If Louise finally..."

Nessa glanced up the road. "Oh, dear! It's Louise. What shall we do?"

"You do what you want. I'm getting up on that wagon and going home."

"But what do I say to her?"

"Don't say anything. I don't imagine you'll get much chance, any way. Let her do the talking."

Nessa struggled to keep up with Sam's long strides as he hurried back toward the store. He stopped beside the wagon, tipped his hat toward Louise, who stood next to her horse watching them, kissed Nessa on the cheek, climbed up, spoke to the mules, and disappeared in a cloud of dust. Nessa stood open mouthed.

"What's wrong with him?"

Nessa turned to Louise. "I don't know. But never mind. Come in the house; it's hot out here." She wiped her brow with one hand, clasped Louise's arm with the other and started toward the porch."

Louise wrenched her arm free. "Wait a minute, Nessa. I can't stay but a minute. I just wanted to say goodby."

Nessa stopped and studied her friend. "Goodby?" She noticed the pale face, the slight redness in the eyes and the mouth that looked ready to pucker at any moment.

Louise flinched and looked down. "Yes, I'm leaving tomorrow. Mother and Father decided I should go away to school. In St. Louis." Her lips quivered.

"I don't believe it. You said you didn't want to go. Even though your mother thought you should, you said you could get your father on your side."

"I know. I changed my mind, that's all. Anyway, it's settled. Father will drive me to the train tomorrow and send a wire for my aunt to meet me. Aunt Emma wrote Mother about Miss…someone or other's…elegant finishing school."

Nessa heard the quaver in her voice and noticed the mist in her eyes. She took her fragile looking friend in her arms. "Oh, Louise. I'm so sorry. I don't want you to go. Please change your mind back again. I'll miss you so."

"I can't. It's for the best," said Louise in a muffled voice. "I have to get away. Don't you understand?"

I think she likes him a lot and it scares her somehow. Nessa's own words echoed in her head. "Oh! Louise, do you mean you…? Yes, you do care for Hank, don't you? But why do you have to leave?"

Louise laughed harshly, and extricated herself from Nessa's arms. "Oh, Nessa! You're such an innocent. Don't you understand that the daughter of the wealthiest man in these parts can't marry a sod-busting farmer? What would my father's friends say? They'd pity him and he couldn't stand it. Mother has chosen a man back in Virginia where she comes from. A third cousin or something. It's been settled for years I learned. My parents wanted to keep me with them until I was eighteen and then they planned to ship me off to marry someone I've never met." A dry sob wracked her body. She lifted her chin and gave Nessa a weak smile. "And, I really don't care about Hank anyway. He was just a passing fancy. It all will be over as soon as I board the train."

Nessa fought the threatened tears. "Won't you ever come back?"

"I don't know!" Louise fell into Nessa's arms. After a moment, Louise stepped back. "Goodby, Nessa. I'll always remember you as my best friend. I'll write if you'll answer my letters."

"Yes, of course I will. Please write. And come back, Louise, as soon as you can."

Louise gave her a wan smile and ran down the steps. She mounted her horse and galloped away without looking back at Nessa, who stood waving with tears running down her cheeks. When she could no longer see Louise, Nessa walked to the corral, saddled Nellie and rode off in the opposite direction.

She sat on a bed of weeds with her hands clasped around her knees and shouted. "God, how could you let this happen? Mama says it's not my fault, and Sam says the same thing. So who's to blame? Papa says you care about everything in our lives. What about Louise, God, and what about Hank? If you care about them, why didn't You stop it? They are hurting and so am I. Where are You? We need You to straighten this out and You're not here. Where are You?" She threw herself backwards on the ground, covered her face with her hands and wept bitterly. *Whom the Lord loveth He chasteneth.*

Nessa sat up, rubbed her eyes and peered into the darkness. Had she slept? Had she heard a voice, or dreamed it? *Whom the Lord loveth He chasteneth.* She remembered her father mentioning that verse. She stood and searched the heavens. A peace she didn't understand filled her being. *Forgive me Father. I know You are there and I'm sorry I doubted you.*

"Nessa, is that you?" Ellie's voice penetrated the darkness. Nessa turned to see her sister approaching, carrying a lantern.

"Papa sent me to find you. Opal saw you tearing up the road on Nellie hours ago. What are you doing out here alone in the dark?"

"I had to think. I guess I fell asleep."

Nessa reached for the reins of her faithful horse who grazed a few feet away. "Come climb on Nellie. I'm sorry you had to come looking for me. Is Papa angry?"

"More worried than anything, I think." She handed the lantern to Nessa and clambered behind the saddle.

"Oh dear. I've done it again," said Nessa in a low voice. "Will I never learn." She sighed and urged Nellie to a canter.

❦   ❦   ❦

Sam fed, watered, and brushed Gallatin and the mules, then milked Dolly, gathered the eggs and latched the chickens and the pig in their respective pens. He grabbed a slab of cold cornbread and drank a dipper of water on his way to the corral.

"Sorry, Gallatin, you're no doubt as tired as I am, but we need to check up on Hank. You can rest up tomorrow."

Horse and rider moved at a slow trot and Sam munched his cornbread. He topped the rise and slowed. The glowing embers of a dying fire revealed a shadowy figure sitting cross-legged with elbows on knees and head cradled in hands. Sam breathed a sigh of relief and walked Gallatin nearer. Leather creaked as he shifted his weight and Hank glanced up.

"Hope there's coffee in that pot." Sam dismounted and walked the few feet to stand on the other side of the fire."

"Howdy, Sam. Help yourself. It's probably thick as mud by now."

Sam took a tin cup, filled it, and squatted. "Was hoping to talk to you. Hoping you were home."

"Yeah. Not particularly by choice, I guess."

"What do you mean?"

Hank ducked his head and ran his fingers through his hair. "Ah, nothing. It don't make sense."

Sam studied his friend, who declined to look at him. "Well, why don't you tell me about it anyway. Lots of things don't make sense to me either."

Hank's eyes gleamed in the faint firelight. "Sam, you wouldn't believe what happened to me. I don't believe it myself." He paused, and swallowed. "Ah, Sam, you know me. I was so mad yesterday and I couldn't sleep and then all day I kept thinking about—Anyway, after supper I thought, who cares what she says? I'll go into town and forget all about her."

The dim light reflected his pale face, and his voice shook. "I saddled up ole Danger and…" He uttered a bitter laugh. "Even my horse is against me. Supposed to be my pal, and he ups and refuses to budge. Nothin' I could do. I even kicked him in the flanks—something I'd never done before. He didn't even twitch. Stood there like a statue while I yelled and kicked and slapped him with the reins." Hank got to his feet and kicked at a stone. "I reckoned maybe I was a dreamin' and I went to the horse tank and ducked my head. Thought that would wake me up for sure. And there ole Danger stood as still as before, saddled and everything. I was so shook I just put him back in the corral and I been sittin' here ever since. What do you suppose got into him?"

Sam let out a whoop.

Hank jerked to his feet, and rounded the fire with his fists up. "What's the matter with you? Here I am scared stiff and you think it's funny?"

Sam rose, still chuckling, and held up his hands, palms forward. "Listen, Hank. I'm not laughing at you. Just settle down and listen. Ole Danger just became Balaam's ass for a while."

"What are you talkin' about? Who's Balaam? What's he got to do with it?"

"Balaam was a man in the Bible and he had this donkey."

"Sam, don't you start throwin' 'spersions on my horse. I know I badmouthed him and called him a statue, but you got no right to call him a donkey. He's got good blood in him."

"Will you let me tell the story without getting all riled? I'm not casting aspersions on your horse. You'll see, if you sit down over there and listen. At least with one ear, all right?"

Hank's shoulders drooped. He dropped to the ground and hung his head. "Go ahead. If you can make sense of what's going on, I'll listen."

"Well to shorten the story—you can read up on it later in the book of Numbers—this fellow Balaam was going where he wasn't supposed to, and his ass stopped and wouldn't budge. Balaam yelled at him and beat on him, just like you did on Danger, and the animal just stood there."

Hank raised his head from between his knees and stared. "You're making that up. There's no such thing in the Bible."

"No, I didn't! Honest!. Like I said you can read it for yourself, tomorrow." Sam scratched his head. "Anyway, it turned out there was an angel standing there. The donkey could see him but Balaam couldn't."

"Ah, Sam!" Hank snorted and shook his head.

"It's true. I'd guess that an angel stood in front of old Danger and wouldn't get out of the way, and Danger had enough sense to stand there."

"But why would an angel do that?"

"I'm not sure, but I reckon God's got His hand on you."

"I don't know, don't seem likely." He shook his head. "And you're saying this angel wouldn't let Danger take me to town?"

"That's what I'm trying to tell you. Just like Balaam, you were fixing to go where you weren't supposed to."

Hank pursed his lips and looked at the stars. "So God didn't want me to go, and…Aw, He couldn't care where I went. I mean, why would He?"

"He cares, Hank. I've tried to tell you how much He loves you. He'll go a long mile to help you." Sam grinned. "You're just lucky Danger didn't talk back at you."

"What do you mean? I told you he didn't even nicker; just stood there like a stack of baby blocks."

"I know, but Balaam's animal talked back, asked Balaam why he was beating him. Finally, God allowed Balaam to see the angel standing there with a sword in his hand."

Hank shook his head and stood in front of Sam with his hands on his hips. "You better not be funnin' me Sam."

"Cross my heart."

Sam sat silent and unmoving while Hank strode around the fire twice, muttering to himself. He stopped behind Sam. "It makes sense, Sam, I guess, but I can't take it all in. You're sure He cares about a nobody like me?"

"You're a somebody to Him, Hank."

"Yeah. If you say so. Boggles the mind, don't it?" He squatted beside Sam. "Thanks, Sam, for coming over. I was beginning to wonder if I was losin' my mind or something." He slapped Sam on the back. "You know, Sam, I never had trouble with women before. But, Louise! Now if you could tell me a Bible story about that."

Sam grunted and got to his feet. "Sorry, Hank. I'm no expert, but I don't think there's a story in the Bible to help men know about women." He sighed and walked toward his horse. "As a matter of fact, I could use one myself." He uttered a wry chuckle. "Well, goodnight, Hank. See you Sunday, if not before. Get a good night's sleep and tomorrow morning, I'd go apologize to old Danger if I was you." He climbed into the saddle.

Hank lifted his hand in salute. "Yeah, I'll do that."

CHAPTER 18

The next morning, Sam finished hitching the mules to the freight wagon as the first golden light speared across the eastern sky. He climbed up and set the team on the thirty-five-mile, plodding trek south. His body shifted into a comfortable slump, and he relished the cool September air on his sunburned cheeks. The expanding light revealed a clear blue sky, and Sam knew the heat would be oppressive by mid-day.

The mules required little guidance and Sam searched the landscape for wildlife, as a game to banish the monotony of riding the bumps over the rutted track. Rabbit tracks teemed in the skirting of softer soil on either side, along with the spoor of antelope, coyote, quail, and, near the creek, wild turkey. He took pleasure in identifying each sign, then chuckled at his foolishness, causing the mules to prick up their ears and snort.

He stopped for lunch in a grove of ancient cottonwoods and allowed the mules to graze on the sparse vegetation. After drinking from his canteen, he forced himself to his feet, fighting the drowsiness brought on by the sun's rays, the meadow lark's melody, and a satisfied stomach.

A cooling breeze in late afternoon and the sight of train smoke in the distance straightened his shoulders. He urged the mules to a fast trot. They responded as though they smelled the forthcoming water and oats as reward for their day's work. Sam, too, anticipated a good meal.

The railway manager greeted Sam and they checked freight orders against the merchandise stored in the makeshift warehouse behind the station. After promising to load up at sunrise the next morning, Sam left the wagon and walked the mules to the stable.

The crisp fried slices of liver and browned onions served at the diner offered a welcome change from salt pork. While eating, he exchanged news with several patrons he had met previously, and teased the young widow, who served as cook and waitress, in a friendly manner.

Now he lay in his bedroll on the sagging, second floor of the station house, along with five other men who had paid twenty-five cents for the privilege of sleeping indoors. He prayed silently, then alternately stretched and flexed his legs and arms to discourage the threat of cramps caused by hours of sitting on a bouncing, unyielding wagon seat. The snorts and snores of his roommates thwarted his expectation of restful slumber.

The image of Nessa arose before his closed eyelids, and the noise around him faded. Her eyes challenged, her smile beckoned, and his body relaxed.

A breakfast of eggs, flapjacks, and sand plum jelly nestled warmly inside Sam when he arrived to load the freight cartons into the wagon. An hour later, he climbed up and whistled the mules into action.

"I'll most likely be back the end of the week," he told the station master.

"Be expectin' you then."

The return trip unfolded without incident, but seemed to take longer, and Sam shifted position with impatience. He was eager to see Nessa and learn about Louise's visit. He asked the Lord to forgive him for his distrust of Nessa's blonde friend. She seemed to travel with trouble surrounding her like fog. Anyone near her lost direction for a spell. Maybe he was wrong about her. He would try to be more charitable for Nessa's sake. But, look how she treated Hank. Cruel. Sam sighed and flicked the reins. The mules tossed their heads and sustained their pace. Hank had accepted the Lord with his words, but his heart needed assurance that only faith could provide. So far, Hank had little on which to base his faith. He needed an experience of the Lord's intervention on his behalf. Sam grinned. Hank's experience with his horse had left him more bewildered than inspired.

Noon came and went. Sam declined to stop and eat, choosing to wait for the expected invitation to supper from Mrs. Long. His industry was at last rewarded with sight of the general store in the haze of the late afternoon sun. He pulled his hat from his head and slapped it against his thigh to remove the dust, then wiped his face with a handkerchief. Mr. Long emerged from the side door as Sam called "Whoa" and the heavy wagon came to a halt.

"Good to see you, son." Owen's face rounded with a smile. "You made good time."

Sam climbed down and gestured toward the stacks of merchandise. "Appears to me you bought out those eastern stores."

"Hope folks will take it off my hands soon." He climbed onto the wagon. "Did you get a big crate marked for me personally?"

"Up at the front."

"Yes. That must be it. Early Christmas present for Mrs. Long, a sewing machine."

Sam nodded. "Bet she'll enjoy that."

"Sam!" Nessa ran from the open door to stand in front of Sam, then frowned at her father. "Why didn't you let me know he had arrived?"

"Well, he just now…"

Sam didn't hear the rest of Mr. Long's protest. He smiled at Nessa and took her hand. "Seems like more than a day since I saw you, Nessa. Could we go for a walk after I unload these crates? I need to get the kinks out of my legs." He squeezed her fingers. "I brought you a little present."

"I love presents!" She lowered her head and looked up at him through dark lashes. "Tell me what it is."

Sam felt heat rise on his neck. "Nothing to get excited about. Hardly anything at all. A little something I thought you might like." He studied the dust on his boots. "You probably already have one."

Nessa pursed her lips in a near pout. "Well, tell me what it is and I'll let you know if I have one or not."

"You'll find out when you open the package." He dropped her hand and grinned. "And if I stand here talking all day, I'll never get your father's goods unloaded."

"Oohh, all right." She waggled her fingers at him and strolled inside.

"You going to help with this, Sam?"

"Sorry, Mr. Long. I'm coming."

❧   ❧   ❧

Nessa's impish grin evaporated at the sight of Opal entering the storeroom.

"Hmm. That dreamy look on your face must mean Sam has arrived." Opal raised her eyebrows and smirked. "Guess I'll go say hello."

"Fine. You can help Papa put things away on the shelves." Nessa raised her head and gave her sister a haughty look as she strutted from the room. She swiped at her hair with fidgety fingers and raced up the stairs to freshen up, before returning to the kitchen to help her mother with the pickling.

A half-hour later, Rebecca removed her apron, sat at the kitchen table, and smiled at the five half-gallon jars filled with sweet pickles. "That's done. The last of the cucumbers."

Nessa savored a deep breath of the spicy air and hung her apron on a hook beside her mother's. "I'll go see if they've finished storing everything."

"All right, Nessa." She stretched her arms and arched her back. "Tell your father I'll be out to look at the new items in a few minutes."

"Would you like a cup of tea, Mama? The kettle is still hot."

Rebecca sighed. "Tea sounds wonderful. Thank you."

Nessa dumped leaves into the pot, poured hot water over them, and placed the pot, a cup and saucer, and spoon in front of her mother. "I'll run along now."

She found Sam watering the mules from a bucket. "Ready for our walk?"

"Ready for my present." She patted one of the mule's muzzles, and reached to scratch another one behind its ears. "Do you like these mules? I hear they can be hard to handle."

"I like them." Sam grinned. "They're easier to figure out than a woman."

Nessa whirled to face him. "What does that mean?"

Sam set the empty bucket down. "Just that I can pretty well predict what the mules will do, but you..." He repositioned his hat on his head and grinned. "Guess that's half the fun of it, though. Wondering what you'll say next."

"Sam Jackson, you're the most impossible man!" She stamped her foot and grimaced. "I never know when you're teasing."

He strolled to the wagon and recovered a parcel, wrapped in brown paper, from under the seat, stuck it in his back pocket, and returned to her side. "You want to go for a walk or not?"

Nessa stared into his eyes for a long moment, drank in their teasing warmth, then took his arm.

When they were some distance from the store, Sam flattened a patch of native grass with his boots. "Have a seat, my lady." He gave her a deep bow.

Nessa giggled and took the hand he extended. When she was ensconced on her soft cushion, he knelt on his haunches beside her. The contour of his lips and jaw stiffened.

"I have something to confess, Nessa." The muscle jumping in his left cheek fascinated Nessa. "I've been uncharitable to Louise, and I want you to know that's a thing of the past. I still think she treated Hank like a dog, but it was probably for the best, and I don't know her side of the story."

Nessa blanched as he spoke and a tear meandered down to the tip of her nose and fell on her tightly clasped hands. She sniffed. "Louise is gone, Sam. She's on her way to St. Louis to live with an aunt and go to school." Nessa took the proffered hanky and delicately blew her nose. "I probably won't see her for years, and I miss her already." Sam's hands touched her shoulders and she collapsed against his chest.

"I'm sorry, Nessa. Why did she leave so suddenly?"

Nessa sat back and wiped her face. "I think she was afraid. Of Hank, of her parents, maybe of herself."

Sam shook his head. "I don't think I understand."

"I don't either, really. Louise talked about her father wanting a son, and she had to think of the family line. Oh, Sam, I think she kind of fell for Hank. And because he's a—I mean, he hasn't much money and apparently no family, she, well, don't you see? She can't like him because of her folks."

"Hmm." He rubbed his jaw. "Explains a lot about the way she acts doesn't it?" He smiled and squeezed Nessa's hand. "Maybe she'll come back next summer."

Nessa gave him a watery smile. "If only she would."

"The only thing we can do, Nessa, is to pray for her, and for Hank, too. The Lord will work everything out for the best."

Nessa looked surprised. "You literally believe what that verse says?"

Sam frowned. "Sure. I believe what all the verses say. Don't you?"

Nessa tilted her head and looked at the horizon. "I'm not sure. I think Papa does."

"God wouldn't put lies in the Bible, Nessa."

"Oh! I don't mean that. It's just maybe some things in there are not for us."

"Read Acts chapter ten, verse thirty-four, and we'll talk about this another day." He drew her to her feet. "Did you forget about your present?"

She clasped her hands and smiled. "I did forget for a while. What is it?"

Sam retrieved the parcel from his pocket and handed it to her. "Like I said, it's nothing special."

Nessa undid the wrapping and lifted out a comb. "Ooh! I've never seen anything like this. It's lovely, Sam." She held it up to catch the light. "It looks like some sort of shell, and what is that embedded on the top?"

"It came from Santa Fe. The man at the railway store said it's made from a tortoise and the little greenish pieces stuck in it are turquoise."

"Turquoise." Her fingers stroked the bits of stone. "It's a beautiful color, isn't it?" She ran the comb through a long raven tress. "I love it, Sam. It's much more than something special. Thank you." The pleasure reflected in his face hurled icy tingles down her spine and her breath caught. She wriggled her toes and wrested her gaze from his.

"Oh, Sam! Look at the sunset. All orange and gold and pink. I wish flowers bloomed in those brilliant shades." Sam's arm encircled her waist and they stood entranced, watching the painted sky until it greyed.

"That's the end of God's show for today. Guess we better start back."

Nessa sighed. "Do you suppose He made that beautiful sky just for us?"

"Well, now, maybe He did."

Awed silence gripped Nessa as Sam turned her around to retrace their steps. He swung their entwined hands in rhythm with a gay, tuneless whistle, and Nessa focused on harmonizing with his long strides.

A hundred yards from the store, the whistling dwindled and Sam's steps faltered. Nessa took a deep breath and placed a hand over her racing heart.

"How would you like to visit the young couple I bought the freight wagon from? We could ride over there after church on Sunday, stay an hour or so and be back before dark."

"Give me a minute. I'm not accustomed to chasing wild turkeys through the woods of Tennessee."

"Why didn't you say something?" He took her hands in his. "Are you all right?"

Nessa wrinkled her nose at him. "I'm fine, but next time you want to go for a walk, I'm bringing Nellie along to take me back." She smiled and watched the concern disappear from his face. "What are these people like?"

"About our age. Just moved from the coal mine area in eastern Kansas. Only married a few months." He took her arm and they moseyed along the road. "I think you'll like the wife."

"Yes. I'd like to visit them Sunday. I'll pack a picnic lunch so we can leave right after church. It will be nice to talk to a young wife."

Rebecca appeared at the storage room door. "Nessa, we've waited supper for you. Sam, I hope you'll join us."

The aroma of beef stew assailed Sam's nostrils, and he sighed. "Thank you ma'am, but it's mighty late now, and I have hungry animals to tend to." He hoped she couldn't hear the protesting rumble from his empty stomach. "I better get off home."

Nessa helped Sam harness the mules to the wagon, and waved as they clumped off into the darkness.

When Nessa entered the house, the family sat at the dining table, waiting, and she hurriedly took her seat. At her father's Amen, following the blessing of the food, she caught her mother's gaze. "Mama, Sam has invited me to visit the young couple who sold him the freight wagon. He wants to ride over to their place Sunday after church. May I go?"

Rebecca frowned. "We don't know those people, Nessa. Did Sam tell you anything about them?"

"Only that they recently married and moved out here from Kansas. The man is about Sam's age and his wife is a little younger, he thought."

"I think it's a fine idea, Nessa." Owen nodded and buttered a second biscuit. "They no doubt have had little time to make friends. You can invite them to our church, if they haven't found one close by. It's only a couple of hours' ride."

Nessa smiled at her father, then looked to her mother for affirmation. Her parents seldom disagreed, but she felt her mother had been inclined to refuse permission. Mama glanced at Papa and sighed before meeting Nessa's questioning gaze. "I suppose you can go, since you'll be with Sam, although I'm a little uncomfortable about your visiting strange people."

Nessa gave her mother an encouraging smile. "Thank you, Mama. Sam says they seem very nice. And it will be fun to have a friend my own age to talk to, now that Louise is gone."

🍁   🍁   🍁

Sam breathed in the tangy coolness in the air when he walked outside the next morning. The mid-September air even smelled like autumn—a heady fragrance of harvest ready plants. His favorite time of year. He inhaled again, deeply, and surveyed the delicate hues of the dawn spreading across the cloudless sky. It would be hot by noon. He mentally spurred himself into movement. No time to take pleasure in God's handiwork. He must accomplish much before winter.

Chores and breakfast taken care of, he began staking out the ground for digging a second room. If the supplies sold as well as Mr. Long expected, two or three more trips would pay him enough to purchase the supplies for the roof. At dusk, Sam threw his spade aside, eased his protesting shoulders, climbed from the shadowy hole, and mentally measured his progress. A depth of about two feet in the eight by ten foot staked area. A fair start.

The next morning, he made a second trip to the railhead, stayed overnight, and returned the following day. Nessa helped him and Owen unload. He tramped to the side of the empty wagon and hesitated. Nessa joined him.

"Sam, can't you stay for supper?"

"I'd like to but I'm about tuckered out. Just enough left in me to get home, I reckon." He touched a strand of her hair with a calloused finger. "Sorry, little girl."

Nessa frowned and covered his hand with hers. "Why do you have to work so much? Why can't we do more things together?"

Sam chuckled. "I can't answer that." He removed his hat and scratched his head. "Maybe the good Lord handed me all these chores now so we'll have more time after we're married." He replaced his hat, pulled it low over his eyes, and squeezed her hand. "Gotta go, Nessa. Probably won't see you till Sunday."

She stamped one foot, and resisted his pulling his hand away from hers. "Three whole days! It isn't fair."

Sam sighed and squeezed her hand before releasing it. Then he climbed aboard, spoke to the impatient mules, and turned onto the homeward trail. "One thing for sure, I don't have time to get into trouble. And I thank you for that, Lord. Some things are harder than digging a big hole in the ground."

CHAPTER 19

❀

Nessa rubbed a pair of her father's trousers down the length of the scrub board, lifted them from the steaming tub, squeezed out the soapy water, and dumped them into the rinse water, where Opal prodded and pushed them around with a length of broomstick. Ellie twisted the garments to remove as much water as possible before carrying them to the clothesline.

Nessa wiped a sudsy forearm across her brow and stretched her shoulders. The weekly laundry was done and she hoped her mother would be satisfied with the result. She carried buckets of wash water to the few remaining plants in the garden, then went inside to start supper.

Mama sat in the dining room in front of her new sewing machine, and her feet danced on the treadle. She had delegated many household chores to her daughters the past week while she cut and sewed the family's winter wardrobe. Nessa patted the towering stack of folded garments on the table, and smiled at her mother's rapt expression as the needle raced up and down. Mama had promised to show her how to use the machine next week. An uncertain giggle escaped from Nessa's lips at the thought of stitching her fingers to the fabric and she hurried to the kitchen.

Her brow furrowed as she stuffed lengths of wood into the stove. Preparing three meals a day, baking bread, churning butter, not to mention laundry, ironing, sewing and mending—how tedious. She sighed and mentally shoved the rising rebellion to the back burner.

Anticipating the excursion with Sam on Sunday evoked more pleasurable thoughts, and she dwelt on them while browning pork chops and peeling potatoes.

"Fine dinner, daughter," her father told her after devouring two chops. "Guess you'll do all right in the kitchen."

"Mama's been teaching me." Nessa beamed and left to fetch the coffee pot.

Ellie and Opal did wash-up and Nessa sat in the parlor hemming one of the newly sewn dresses while her mother crafted buttonholes in a flannel shirt. Nessa swallowed yawns and nodded her head several times, before her father lowered his newspaper and looked at the clock.

"Nine-thirty. Seems later. Days are getting shorter and I'm getting older." He grinned at Rebecca. "At any rate, I'm ready for bed, how about you?"

Mama nodded, and Nessa gratefully put her sewing basket away and climbed the stairs. She undressed to the tune of her sisters' light breathing and slipped her spent body between the sheets. The cool fabric caressed her legs and she curled one hand under her cheek.

"Father God, thank you…"

"Nessa?"

Her eyes flew open at the whisper next to her ear. "Ellie, you startled me. What are you doing out of bed?"

"I couldn't sleep. Could I ask you something?"

Nessa yawned. "Can't it wait until tomorrow? We'll wake Opal."

"I suppose so." Ellie's dim form stepped away from Nessa. "But Opal won't hear us, she always sleeps like she's in hibernation."

"Oh, all right, Ellie." Nessa sat up and thrust a pillow behind her back. "I'm wide awake, now."

"Thanks, Nessa." Ellie plopped on the side of the bed.

Nessa threw the covers back and shifted her legs. "Climb in before you get your death on that cold linoleum."

Ellie clambered between the sheets and shivered. "Remember last spring when I asked Papa if I could go to school to train to be a teacher, and he said he couldn't afford it?"

Nessa sighed and wriggled her toes. "I remember."

"Well, since the supplies Sam's bringing in are selling well, Papa changed his mind." Ellie turned onto her side to face Nessa. "He and Mama decided if they could find a nice family for me to board with, they would consider it. I've missed a week or two, but Papa wrote to the school in town, and he got a reply yesterday. I can stay with the teacher and pay for part of my board and room by doing chores."

"Ellie, that's wonderful. You're the smart one in the family and I'm happy for you." She put an arm around her sister and hugged her. "But I don't understand why you couldn't tell me in the morning."

"Well…that's not what I wanted to ask you about. It is part of it, but…"

Nessa slid further under the quilt and took a deep breath. "It's getting awfully late, and I would like to go to sleep."

"You won't call me a baby, or anything like that, will you?" Ellie's whisper ended in a squeak.

"Ssh!" Nessa raised her head and searched the darkness for movement from Opal. "Just hurry and ask, and keep your voice down."

"I'm scared, Nessa." Her sister's muffled sob tore through Nessa's conscience. "Mama's been talking to me about growing up and doing exciting things. New horizons, she called it. But I'll miss her and Papa. You, too. And I don't know those people in town, and nothing will be the same, and I don't know if I want to go!"

Nessa sat up and pulled Ellie into her arms. "It will be all right. You'll make friends in no time." She rocked back and forth and patted her sister's back. "But, if you really don't want to go, of course, Mama and Papa won't force you."

"I want to be a teacher, but I don't want to leave." Ellie wailed aloud.

"Move over, Ellie," said Opal in a sleepy voice, and Nessa heard her mother's feet hit the floor across the hall.

"Ellie, be quiet." She pushed her sister down, laid beside her and pulled the covers over Ellie's head. She felt rather than saw her mother enter the bedroom and pause by Opal, then approach the other bed. Nessa tried to breathe normally; while, apparently, Ellie held her breath. Nessa fought the eerie desire to laugh as she tried to follow her mother's path. She heard the bedspring squeak in her parents' room.

"Ellie, let's ask God to take away your fears and then you go back to your bed. We'll talk more tomorrow."

She lay mystified after her sister left. A few months ago, she would have derided Ellie for her fears. And Ellie would never have come to her in the first place. *I must be growing up—at least a little!* A new found compassion welled up inside her and she smiled at the pleasure of it. "Thank you, Father. I know, now. You do care for me and for Ellie. And I love You, too." She rolled onto her stomach. Sam's face appeared behind her closed lids. One brown eye winked and she smiled and slept.

❉   ❉   ❉

By Saturday afternoon, Sam had scooped out another four feet of soil for the dugout addition. He stowed his shovel and filled water buckets to heat for a bath, as elongated shadows slanted across his field of vision. While scrubbing himself with a rough rag and a lump of lye soap, he wondered about Hank, whom he hadn't seen all week. He usually appeared at supper time every few days, and Sam decided to ride over after eating.

Hank's place crouched along the side of a shallow ravine and when Sam topped the hill, he saw an empty corral and no camp fire nurturing the evening meal. Sam slapped Gallatin on the rump to hurry the horse along. He had prayed Hank would not fall into his old ways, and chided himself for not checking on him earlier. A whooping holler brought no response from inside the dugout, and Hank's saddle and bridle were missing from the shed. Sam grimaced, swung into the saddle and headed for home. Dread crowded out the joy that had earlier filled his heart.

Sam hurried through his chores the next morning, and left early to ride by Hank's place on the way to church. Danger, saddled and reins dragging the ground, stood in the corral with lowered head. After caring for the horse, Sam pounded on the door with his fist.

"Hank! Drag your sorry carcass off that mattress. I'm coming down." By the time Sam reached the bottom step, Hank sat hunched over on the bed, moaning, and covering his ears with his hands.

"Do you have to make all that racket, Sam? I don't feel so good."

Sam stood in front of his friend. Disgust and sadness churned inside him. "Don't feel so good, huh? Look at yourself! Clothes filthy, still wearing your boots, and your breath would knock over a skunk." Sam's lips tightened as Hank wiped his mouth with trembling hands. "I ought to tan your hide." He grabbed Hank by the arm. "Come on." He dragged the stumbling Hank up the steps and to the corral where he shoved him into the horse tank.

When a sobering Hank was crouched before a fire, wrapped in a blanket, and sipping scalding coffee, Sam knelt on one knee on the other side of the flames and gazed at him with narrowed eyes. "I don't have time nor inclination to mollycoddle you, Hank. I'm going to church and then riding with Nessa."

Hank squirmed and hung his head. "Ain't nobody asking you to."

"Yeah, well, until you grow up enough to take care of yourself, somebody has to, and I'm the only one who appears to be around at the moment." Sam pursed his lips and stood. "Anyway, like I said, you're on your own for the rest of the day." He rose and kicked a stray ember into the fire. "You come to supper tomorrow and we'll thrash this out once and for all." His lips moved in silent prayer as he mounted Gallatin and rode away.

CHAPTER 20

❀

Nessa stood on the church steps watching for Sam. She waved when she spotted him riding up the trail and waited for him to loosen the cinch on Gallatin's saddle. When he walked toward her, she smiled and beckoned. "Hurry, Sam. Church is starting."

He took the steps two at a time, and she took his arm. She chose a pew near the rear, when she realized the congregation had already started singing the opening hymn.

After church, Nessa walked beside Sam to the Long buggy. He greeted her parents and sisters.

"I've made a picnic lunch, Sam. Is there a pretty spot where we can eat?" She took the hand he offered and stepped up into the spring seat and sat beside Opal.

"Sure, several." He grinned and squeezed her hand. "Depends on how hungry you are, more than anything, doesn't it?"

She wrinkled her nose. "Why don't you follow us home? I'll change and pick up our lunch basket."

Sam tipped his hat. "Sounds fine." He stepped back. "Mr. And Mrs. Long, young ladies." He tipped his hat again and sauntered toward his horse as Owen urged the team forward.

🍁   🍁   🍁

When Nessa went inside the house to change, Sam walked to the corral to saddle Nellie. By the time he led the mare to the front yard, Nessa stood beside Gallatin feeding him an apple. She wore the same hunter green, riding outfit, but now a little peaked green hat, with a rakish feather on one side, nestled atop the upswept curls, and the brooch gleamed as her bosom rose and fell with each breath.

Sam paused a few yards away. The vision of raven curls, rich green skirts, reddish horse, and midnight blue eyes against the sun-drenched sky took his breath away. Nessa lifted her head and smiled at him, and his heart thumped against his chest. He took a deep breath, returned her smile, and strode toward her, wondering why God blessed him so.

"Are we ready?" She picked up the saddle bag at her feet.

"Ready." He brushed her hand with his as he took the bag and then tied it behind the cantle.

Nessa led Nellie to the mounting block and Sam hurried to her side, encircled her waist with capable hands, and boosted her into the saddle. His gaze met hers, and he held her for a long moment, his purpose lost in the depths of her eyes. He uttered a nervous laugh, shoved his trembling fingers into the pockets of his jeans, wrenched Gallatin's reins from the post, and swung into the saddle.

They rode in companionable silence for almost an hour. Sam stole occasional glances at Nessa, and she, apparently sensing his gaze, turned and smiled. Sam drew her attention to a chipmunk scurrying across the trail ahead of them, a hawk riding the air currents high above, and a lone cottonwood tree poking its branches into the skyline. The landscape began to change. Scraggly brush, red cedars, and a few stunted pines appeared on either side of the trail, then sturdier evergreens as they moved into higher country. A tiny stream trickled through the rocks to their right.

"This looks like a good picnic place." Sam reined Gallatin toward a spongy area under the trees. He helped Nessa dismount, then led the animals to a pool of water while she spread a cloth on the layer of needles.

Sam studied the chicken bone in his hand for a last shred of meat, and finding none, tossed it into the brush. He drained the last drop of tea from his cup, then leaned back on his hands to watch Nessa gnawing at her piece of chicken. Her hearty appetite provoked a smile.

She looked up, ceased chewing, and frowned. "What are you grinning at, Sam Jackson?"

He chuckled. "Just watching you eat. Thinking I'm going to have to buy lots more chickens before we get married, and maybe another sow." He laughed, bent forward and drew his legs up to rise. A chicken bone bounced off his hat and a tin cup sailed by his ear. He stood and ducked as a red-faced Nessa threw the last of the biscuits in his direction.

"Whoa, there, girl!" He strode to where she sat, arm upraised, and snatched the pie she held balanced in one hand. "Not that. I'm mighty fond of apple pie." He laid the pan on the ground, grasped her wrists, pulled her to her feet, and kissed her nose. "Besides you might put a dent in your Mama's pie tin, and how would you explain that?"

She jerked her arms to free herself. "Leave me alone, Sam. I don't like to be laughed at." She stopped struggling and their gazes met. "Do you really think I'm fat?"

"Now, Nessa, you know I never said you was fat." He smiled, released her wrists, and wrapped his arms around her. "Fact is, I like to see a woman enjoying her dinner."

"Sometimes I'd like to kick you, then, other times..."

Sam captured her lips in a long, sweet kiss. He lifted his head, looked deeply into her eyes, and took a deep breath. "Actually, as long as I can get my arms around you, I guess I won't complain." He stepped back with his hands still clasped in the small of her back. "Looks like you got a little ways to go yet."

Nessa shoved his arms away and stood with her hands on her hips. "I wish I'd hit you with the pie." She lifted her arms, twined them around his neck, and smiled. "But this is even more fun."

Sam's eyes widened. He pulled her closer and kissed her again. Minutes later he dropped his arms and shoved his hands into his pockets. "It's getting late. If we're going to do any visiting, we better get going."

Nessa sighed, opened her eyes, and nodded. "I guess you're right." She began packing the remnants of their meal. "Do you want some pie, now?"

"Leave a piece out for me. I'll eat it on the way."

Less than an hour later, they topped a rise and Sam pointed out their destination.

❧   ❧   ❧

As they approached, Nessa noticed a man and woman sitting side by side on a log in the shade of the house. The man stood and waved.

Sam waved back. "Clem. It's Sam Jackson."

The man smiled and walked toward them. The woman rose, placed her Bible on the log, and eyed Nessa.

"Sam! Welcome back. Climb down." Clem sent a big smile Nessa's way. "And you bring a pretty lady, too."

Sam helped Nessa dismount and took her arm. "Nessa, this is Clem Basetti, and his wife, Katerina. Folks, meet the girl I'll be marrying next year, Nessa Long."

Clem's grin grew wider as he nodded his head in greeting.

Mrs. Basetti touched the crown of golden braids on top of her head and smiled at Nessa. "You must be tired and thirsty after your ride. Please come in and rest." She beckoned, and Nessa followed her toward the front door.

Inside, Katerina motioned her to a rocker, and Nessa sank onto the feather-filled cushion with a sigh of pleasure. "Thank you. I guess I am a little tired." She removed her hat and tidied her hair with her fingers. "I'm not used to riding so far."

"Would you like a glass of buttermilk? Or I can brew some coffee."

"Buttermilk would be very refreshing." She started to rise. "Let me help."

"Oh, no." Katerina stepped toward her. "Please, sit. I'm glad you came with Sam. We have so few visitors." She untied her apron and swept it off over her head. "Excuse me, I'll be back." She hurried through a door at the end of the room.

Nessa wriggled her toes inside her riding boots and surveyed her surroundings. A piano took up half the space on one wall, and an accordion in its case rested on the floor beside it. A small landscape in oils, hanging on the wall over the piano, depicting a tiny hamlet nestled at the base slopes of towering snow-covered peaks, caught her attention. Basetti—it sounded Italian, but the husband had brown hair and blue eyes, and Katerina's eyes were a soft gray. And the painting looked like the Swiss Alps. Nessa frowned, trying to remember her sketchy knowledge of geography.

"Here is a nice glass of buttermilk." Katerina set a small pewter tray on the table, picked up the glass and an embroidered linen napkin, and offered them to her guest.

Nessa smiled and swallowed a third of the refreshing liquid before resting the glass on the napkin on her knee. "It tastes wonderful, Mrs. Basetti. Thank you."

"No Mrs. Basetti, please. Call me Katerina." She sat in the rocker on Nessa's right. "You are Sam's intended. Sam is our friend."

"Katerina, then." Nessa smiled. "And I'm Nessa." She took a sip of her drink. "I noticed the painting on the wall. Is that your old home?"

"Yes." A sad smile drifted across her face. "It is very beautiful, is it not? I don't remember it well, so I like to keep the picture where I can look at it every day." She sighed. "Here there are not many trees, and only small hills."

"You would like to go back?"

Katerina frowned. "Oh, no. For a visit only. I love America."

Nessa studied the young woman's face. "How strange. I don't think I've ever heard anyone say that before." She grimaced. "People seem to take for granted what they've always had, don't they?"

Her hostess flushed and looked at the floor. "I'm sorry. I don't understand."

"I meant that because I've always lived in America, I may not appreciate it as much as you do."

"Oh." She nodded and smiled. "Would you like more buttermilk?"

Nessa shook her head. "No, thank you. It was very good." She looked around the room searching for a topic of conversation, and wondering what had happened to Sam. "Do you play the piano and the accordion?"

"My Clem makes very good music on the accordion." Katerina shook her head in a modest gesture. "The piano is a gift from my parents. I play a little. We sometimes amuse ourselves after supper."

Before Nessa could reply, Sam, followed by Clem, entered through the front door. Clem stepped to Katerina's side.

"We have something to serve our guests, yes?'

Katerina gazed at Sam, and dipped her head. "Would you like a glass of cool buttermilk, Mr. Jackson?"

Sam smiled. "Please call me Sam. And buttermilk suits me fine, if it's no trouble."

Katerina scurried toward the kitchen, and Sam raised his eyebrows and gazed at Nessa. She smiled and nodded. "Katerina and I have been getting acquainted."

"Good." He pointed to the chess set on the side table. "Did you see this?"

"Oh, the chess." Clem grinned and picked up a king. "You play, miss?"

Nessa chuckled. "Oh my no, but my father does once in a while." She rose and stood by Sam eying the beautiful workmanship of the board and pieces.

"Clem brought this from Italy." Sam grinned at his friend. "One of these days, we're going to find out if he can play."

Clem laughed and gestured toward the chair. "Good. We play now."

Katerina set glasses on the table, then put her hands on her hips. "Clem, you start to play that game and the afternoon will be finished."

Clem winked. "Maybe yes, maybe no." He centered a few pieces on their proper squares.

His wife sighed and shook her head, then gazed at Nessa. "Would you like to see the baby kittens?"

"I'd love to."

"Good. We'll leave the foolish men to their ridiculous game." She snatched a bonnet off a hook, gestured to Nessa, and strode toward the front door. Nessa pulled her hat over her curls and followed.

❦   ❦   ❦

Sam played prudently during the first game, probing for any weakness in Clem's strategy. When Clem clapped his hands and called "check-mate", Sam grimaced and shook his head. "Good moves." He began to replace the pieces. "One more game, then we'll have to be heading home." He grinned. "I'll take you this time."

"Oh, ho!" Clem's blue eyes glinted with purpose. He chuckled and studied the board before moving a pawn.

After almost an hour of intense concentration, Sam check-mated the white king. He ran his fingers through his hair and nodded at his opponent across the board. "Clem Basetti, I thought I knew quite a bit about this game, but I learned more from you today than I care to admit."

Clem chuckled and leaned back in his chair. "Maybe so we need to play another time. We learn from each other."

"I'll be looking forward to it." He stood and noticed Nessa sitting beside Katerina. Neither woman smiled. Sam cleared his throat. "Hmm, I think we're in trouble, Clem. Seems we've neglected the ladies."

Clem strolled over, took his wife's hand, and pulled her to her feet. "Now, Katy, I have not the chance to play since we leave Kansas." He lifted her chin with his fingers and gazed into her eyes. "You not going to be mad in front of our guests. I make it up to you." With his free hand, he sketched a cross on his chest and grinned.

Katerina swatted his fingers from her face. "Oh, go on with you." She turned to Nessa and winked, then smiled at Sam.

Sam raised his eyebrows in surprise, then chuckled. "Ma'am, it's been a right pleasant afternoon. I'm sorry I didn't get to spend time getting to know you better." He nodded toward Nessa. "We should be getting on toward home."

Nessa rose and turned her back on Sam. "Katerina, I had a wonderful time. Thank you for inviting me and for the buttermilk. I hope you will allow me to come again."

Katerina's blue eyes sparkled and a smile creased her face. "You are welcome any time."

Sam gave Clem a nod and a knowing smile, then held out his hand. "Hope to see you again soon." He picked up his hat from the floor. "Mrs. Basetti, I apologize for any discourtesy, and thank you for your hospitality."

She acknowledged him with a nod and a shy smile.

Sam placed his hand under Nessa's elbow and led her outside. While she chatted with Katerina, Sam tightened the cinches on the saddles, then assisted Nessa up on her mount. He climbed up on Gallatin, gave a final wave and turned against the setting sun. It would be dark before he had Nessa home. He bit his lip and tried to remember how bright the moon would be. What a fool he had been. He shook his head, and glanced at the tight-lipped girl beside him. She sat upright in her saddle, with her nose elevated, and looked straight ahead. He sighed, glanced behind him at the glowing sky, and touched his heels to Gallatin's flank.

❧   ❧   ❧

Nessa held the reins loosely in her left hand. Nellie would keep pace with Sam's horse without instruction from her rider. She glanced at Sam out of the corner of one eye, and saw him shake his head. *Why?* She hadn't done anything wrong. She hadn't ignored him and spent the entire afternoon staring at wooden figures and alternately grunting and grimacing.

Nellie's gait increased and Nessa realized Sam had pulled slightly ahead. She shoved her hat firmly on her head and took the reins in both hands. The whisper of cool air that had brushed her cheeks became a cold blast stinging her face. The trail and landscape ahead lost its golden luster and turned a lonely gray. She shivered and ducked her head. Three miles or more fell behind her, and her icy hands seemed permanently attached to the pulsing reins as Nellie galloped forward.

The sudden slackening of speed caught her by surprise and the saddle horn dug into her mid-section causing her to gasp. When she recovered, she raised her head to peer from under the brim of her hat, and her gaze met Sam's frowning face.

"You okay, Nessa?" He wheeled Gallatin to her side and touched her arm.

"Soon as I catch my breath." She pushed her hat back into position. "What made you stop so sudden like that?"

"Sorry." He rubbed his chin. "I was mulling over this afternoon, and I think we need to talk, even if I am late getting you home." He pursed his lips. "I hope your father will understand."

"What's there to talk about, Sam Jackson? How you invited me to visit your friends then paid no attention to me at all for hours? What's important about that?" She flicked the reins to start Nellie moving.

Sam moved Gallatin to block her progress. "Whoa Nellie." The little mare raised her head and snorted. Sam petted her nose, then looked at Nessa.

"I want to tell you I'm sorry about this afternoon." He shook his head. "I don't know what came over me. Clem showed me the chess set the first time I was there, and I've been thinking about a game for weeks." Nessa softened at the stark plea in his evident in his voice. "I haven't had a chance to play chess since I left home two years ago." He shook his head. "Still, that's not a good reason. You're right to be upset." He moved Gallatin to her side and took her hand. "I promise I won't do anything like that again."

Nessa gazed into his liquid eyes. They appeared almost black in the dusk, and she sighed, allowing her annoyance to leave her heart as her breath erupted between her lips. She moved her fingers to grasp his hand. "I understand, Sam. It's all right." She smiled. "I was put out at first, but to be truthful, I enjoyed the afternoon as much as you obviously did. Katerina is a sweet woman and I hope we can be friends. Thank you for taking me to her."

Sam squeezed her fingers and grinned. "Thanks, Nessa. You're a wonderful girl, and becoming a fine woman, yourself." He straightened in the saddle. "But, I knew that the first time I saw you, when you were still a snippet of a little girl."

Nessa snatched her hand away and laughed. "And I thought you were too old for me."

"What? You never told me that."

"Sam, you don't know everything about me." She smiled.

"No, and probably never will." His eyes narrowed. "Guess the good Lord planned it that way for a reason." He looked at the dusky sky and grimaced. "If we don't get moving, I'm going to have a lot of explaining to do to your father, and I'm not sure he'll be as forgiving as you." He turned his mount around and smiled at Nessa. "You ready to ride? Only a couple miles to go." And without waiting for her answer, he nudged Gallatin ahead.

Nessa grinned, loosened the reins in her hand, and followed him.

They arrived at the Long corral breathless and chilled. Sam helped her dismount and held her waist in firm hands, as she turned to face him.

"I'll go in and talk to your father." He lightly kissed the tip of her nose. "I'd face a hundred angry fathers just to see that look in your eyes."

"We'll explain together." Nessa stepped away, and grasped the fingers of his hand in hers. "Let's get it over with, then."

Owen stood in the middle of the living room, facing the young couple, and listened to Sam's explanation.

"It's my fault, Mr. Long. I got caught up playing chess and the afternoon got away me."

He twisted his hat in his hands. "I promised you I'd take good care of your daughter, and always have her home on time. I feel like I let you down." He took a deep breath and opened his mouth.

Owen raised a hand to stop him. "Look, Sam, you needn't feel so guilty about it." He grinned and gripped Sam's left arm. "I know you pretty well by now and I wasn't worried about Nessa. I knew she was in good hands." He smiled at his daughter. "Now, supper is still warm, and I imagine you two are hungry. Your mother is in the kitchen, why don't you get washed up and go help her, while I take care of Nellie, and give Sam's horse some hay."

Nessa smiled and reached up to kiss her father on the cheek. "Thank you, Papa." She tossed her hat and jacket on a chair and walked through to the kitchen.

❧   ❧   ❧

After devouring a second helping of Rebecca's apple pie, Sam pushed away from the table. "That's the best eatin' I've had since I was here last time. Thank you ma'am." He patted his stomach, then sighed. "Guess I better get home. Still have hungry animals to feed when I get there." He turned to Owen. "I'll be making a trip to pick up freight early in the morning. Is there mail or packages to take with me?"

Owen took a sip of coffee and rose from the table. "Come into my office. There's a bag of mail."

Sam looked at Nessa, grinned and winked. "See you when I get back."

Nessa smiled and gave her mother a side-long glance. Rebecca seemed to be stifling a smile.

Sam took the bag of mail, secured it to the back of his saddle, mounted Gallatin and headed him toward home. The memory of Nessa's smile filled his thoughts and he hummed.

Half way home he remembered that he had invited Hank to supper. He pressed Gallatin to a gallop along the starlit trail and berated himself. How could he have forgotten? He had selfishly indulged himself all afternoon without a thought of the friend who needed him. He yanked on the reins in front of the dugout and jumped from the saddle. Hank's horse stood tied at the corral.

"Hank? Where are you?" He raced toward the post where he kept his lantern and noticed a glow beyond the dugout door. With cautious steps, he drew near. An eerie keening noise and scraping sounds punctuated by periodic thuds came out of the darkness. He stopped, raised his eyebrows, and grinned. His lantern stood on a mound of dirt in the half-dug hole of the addition to his house. Hank scooped up a shovelful of soil and tossed it up and over the side. His voice kept rhythm with his labor. "Where–the–cold–wind–blows–and the—"

"Grasses wave," sang Sam.

Shovel and clods of dirt flew into the air and Hank whirled around and peered up into the darkness. "Sam? Is that you?"

"Howdy, Hank. What are you doing down there at this time of night?"

"Well, what do you think?" He held the lantern up to Sam and climbed out of the hole. "Thought I might as well make myself useful till supper was ready." He playfully punched Sam's arm. "Did you have to scare me out of ten years of my life?" Hank stomped his feet and brushed dirt from his trouser legs. "Where you been any how?"

"Sorry about being late, Hank. I near forgot I invited you for supper." Sam shook his head. "Come on over here and sit, and I'll rustle something up to eat." He walked to the post and hung the lantern. "You didn't need to go digging down there, but thanks a lot." He brushed ashes to one side exposing a few feeble embers from his morning fire. After a minute of careful tending, he added small branches to the flames and soon had a blaze. When the left-over coffee was hot, he carried a cup to Hank and put a skillet on to heat. While he fried salt bacon, sliced potatoes, and eggs, he told Hank about his afternoon.

"So, I've had quite a day." Sam filled a plate and handed it to his friend. "Sorry there's no biscuits." Hank gave an appraising sniff and shifted to balance the plate on his legs. Sam fetched a cup of coffee and squatted facing his friend. "And what did you do today, other than dig? I really appreciate that by the way. Thanks, again."

Hank waved his fork and swallowed. "Oddest thing. I was so mad after you left last night I couldn't sleep. I wandered around the place, kicking rocks and muttering curses at you." He took another bite of bacon. "Then I stomped off down the track leading north. After a while I looked up and the stars were shining and the air felt warm in my hair." He grinned. "I didn't even have my hat!" He took a bite, chewed, swallowed, and sipped coffee.

"And I just kept walking. Before I knew it, I had walked clear to the church." He shook his head and sighed. "There it stood in the dark, but somehow there was light around it. Maybe the moon had come up and I didn't notice." He glanced up and looked into Sam's eyes. "And all of a sudden I felt sort of weak, and I stopped and sat down in the middle of the track and stared at that little old building with the cross on top." His gaze wavered and he gave a nervous chuckle. "I can't explain it, Sam. I don't know what happened exactly, but the next thing I knew I was on my knees and telling God all kinds of things I never told nobody before. And I just kept talking and talking, and then I just laid down on the ground. I was so tired I couldn't move. Then, it was like something just lifted off me. I felt light as a feather, and I wasn't mad at you, or anybody else in the world. I wasn't mad at my dad any more either."

Hank rubbed his chin and looked at his plate. "You got any more of this? I sure am hungry."

Sam rose without a word, filled the plate, and handed it to Hank, then sat cross-legged and waited.

After taking several bites, Hank laid his fork in his plate and gazed at Sam. "I woke up when the sun came up, and there I was afoot and miles from home. I sat there a while thinking, then got up and started walking." He drained the coffee from his cup and held it out to Sam. Sam grinned and carried it to the fire for a refill. Hank speared the last morsel of potato with his fork and set the empty plate on the ground. "I was really draggin' when I got home, so I did the chores and fell into bed. Woke up late this afternoon and came over to talk to you. Figured you'd show up any minute, so after awhile I got restless and decided to shovel dirt."

Sam rubbed his chin with his fingers. "That's quite a story, Hank. I'm sort of struck dumb. The Lord keeps doing things that throw me like a lassoed calf." He grinned and shook his head. "I sure am glad He's in charge." Sam leaned forward and gazed into Hank's eyes. "I guess I have a question, though. What did all this mean to you?"

Hank grimaced. "I was afraid you were going to ask that." He bit at his lip and looked up at the sky. "To be truthful, Sam, I'm not sure I know. I mean, I believe what happened last night came from the Lord, and I sure am glad to be free of all that junk I've been carrying around inside me. I told the Lord I sure was grateful for that. But I'm not sure I'm ready for Someone to take over my life.

"What do you mean by that? Are you saying you aren't ready to give up carousing in town every Saturday night?"

"No, I'm giving that up." He snorted. "All that gets me is a headache. I finally seen the light there."

"Then what are you afraid of?"

"I don't rightly know if I can put it in words." He scratched his head. "I been on my own pretty much since I was eleven years old, and I like to do things my way."

"Do you think your way is better than the One that made that sky up there, and the stars and everything else you can see?"

Hank frowned. "I'd be a fool to think that, it's just...Well, since you put it that way, maybe I am a fool." His shoulders slumped. He looked at one of his boots and picked at a scuffed place on the toe. "All right, Sam, I'm ready. If the Lord can fix me up, I reckon he has more power than I can resist."

"You're speaking from your heart, now?"

"Yeah, from my heart."

They knelt in the dust and Sam led his penitent friend in a simple sinner's prayer. When they got to their feet, Sam slapped Hank on the shoulder. "Congratulations. Now we're brothers as well as friends.

"Yeah. Ain't that something?"

Sam silently thanked Jesus when he saw Hank's smile filled with Sonshine.

"Thank you Sam. I feel like I a new man." Hank held out his hand.

Sam gripped it in his own. "You are, my friend, you are."

Hank strode toward the corral whistling off-key.

CHAPTER 21

Nessa moaned as she climbed out of bed the next morning after her mother's call. She gingerly stood and flexed the sore muscles in her legs, arms, abdomen, buttocks, and back. Even her neck felt stiff. "Some cowgirl you are," she said to the mirror, as she struggled to brush her hair without flexing her wrists. "One afternoon's ride and you can barely move."

She held her breath and lurched down the stairs. Upon reaching the kitchen, she straightened her back and forced the normal spring into her step before greeting her mother, who stood in front of the range.

"Good morning, Mama. Looks like a beautiful day."

Rebecca turned her head and smiled. "Good morning, dear." She tilted her head and eyed her daughter. "Your cheeks look like roses. You must have had a good time yesterday. Tell me all about your visit while you set the table."

Nessa took plates from the cupboard. "I met the nicest couple. They've only been married a year and the wife, her name is Katerina, is only a little older than me."

"Katerina? What kind of name is that?"

"Oh, I forgot to mention. They're both from northern Italy. They came to America a few years ago. Katerina speaks English very well. Clem doesn't speak it quite as well, but he is so nice, and he…"

Rebecca turned from the stove holding her stirring spoon. Gravy dribbled onto the floor and Nessa's mouth gaped. She pointed. "Mama, you're getting drips all over the floor."

Rebecca stood as though frozen. "Nessa, you mean Sam took you to a house of foreigners?"

"I don't understand, Mama." Nessa grabbed a dishrag and bent to wipe up the mess.

Rebecca wheeled back to the stove and stirred vigorously, in rhythm with her staccato words. "You're an impressionable young girl. I never thought he would do such a thing." She lifted the skillet and poured the contents into a bowl scraping the bottom and sides as though her life depended on getting every smidgeon of gravy. "Your father will just have to speak to him."

"Speak to whom about what?" Papa came through the outside door carrying a pail of fresh milk.

"Owen, do you know what Sam did yesterday?"

Papa's head jerked to meet Nessa's gaze. "What?"

"No, Papa…" Nessa scurried to a corner.

"Oh, Owen, listen! Those people he took Nessa out to meet aren't even American."

"Rebecca, what are you talking about?"

Mama stood with her hands on her hips glaring at her husband. "I told you, the couple Nessa met yesterday are from…"

"I heard that. What I don't understand is why you're so upset."

"Oh, Owen, don't you see?" Mama lifted her apron to her face and burst into tears.

Owen rushed to her and took her in his arms. "Rebecca, dear. This isn't like you, at all." He pulled the apron from her fists and cupped her face in his hands. "Sit down at the table and tell me what the problem is."

Mama allowed Papa to lead her to a chair. She sat and pushed her damp hair from her forehead. "You know I only want what's best for Nessa. And out here in this forsaken land, and now different people coming around, and…Owen they may have been in some kind of trouble back in the old country."

Papa frowned. "Rebecca, what a thing to say!"

"Well, you know perfectly well it can happen." She raised her head to gaze at Owen and her mouth tightened. "You know, yourself, that many of the people in Georgia had ancestors who had been in jail in England."

Owen snorted. "Dear, that was a hundred years ago! And most of them were in debtor's prison through no fault of their own. But what it has to do with this young couple escapes me." He sighed and took his wife's hand. "Rebecca, most Americans come from European stock, including you and me." He smiled and lifted her chin to gaze into her eyes. "The only one around with native blood that I know of is Sam. Surely you don't think he looks on us as being foreigners, do you?"

Rebecca gasped. "Of course not. But…"

"No buts, Rebecca." He looked up and met Nessa's gaze. "Nessa, go wake your sisters, while I talk to your mother."

"But, Papa…"

"Go on, now." He gestured toward the doorway. "I'll speak with you later."

"Yes, Papa." With tears streaming down her face, Nessa hurried from the room and raced up the stairs. On the landing, she stopped, took a deep breath, and struggled for composure. A creak of the bedsprings prompted her to open the bedroom door and enter, averting her ravaged face.

"Okay, lazy-bones. Time to get up. Breakfast is ready." She marched to the chest, poured water from the pitcher into the basin, splashed it on her face, and tidied her hair. She took no part in the girlish chatter between her sisters. Steps on the stairs drew her attention and she moved nearer the closed door. Her father's words brought a frown to her brow.

"Just rest an hour or so, Rebecca. The girls and I can manage. I'll bring you some tea later."

When she heard him close the door and his retreating footsteps, she hushed her sisters. "Ssh. Be quiet. Mama is resting. Finish dressing and come down-stairs."

Nessa hurried to the kitchen door and peeked in. Her father sat with his elbows on the table and his face covered by his hands. Fear raced through Nessa. She had never heard her parents quarrel and she had never seen her father so distraught. To her, he was invincible and all wise. What had she done to cause this family rift? "Papa?" Her voice trembled, and her feet seemed shackled as she took a few steps and sat across from him.

He raised his head and smiled at her. "Ah, Nessa. Think you can handle the household this morning? Your mother needs to rest."

"Of course, Papa. But what is wrong with Mama?" Tears filled her eyes. "I didn't mean to make her ill. What did I do wrong?"

Papa sighed and reached across the table to pat Nessa's arm. "It was none of your doing, daughter. Don't fret about that." He rubbed his chin and leaned back in the chair. "Your mother had to cope with harsh realities when she was a child. She was born just before the war ended, into a world of chaotic unrest. Her family suffered, as most did in the south." He sighed. "I think she feels cheated of her heritage. Your grandmother was a wonderful woman, but I don't think she ever recovered from the family losses. She filled your mother with stories of how it would be when things got back to the way they were. Of course, they never did and never will."

He gazed into Nessa's tear-filled eyes. "When we had to leave and move out here, your mother's dreams collapsed." He blinked several times and grimaced. "I've tried to make it up to her, but people who come to this new land have no time nor energy for pomp and splendor. They're very forthright and honest with themselves as well as with others."

He sighed and rose from his seat. "I shouldn't have placed this burden on you, Nessa." He walked to her side and caressed the curls on top of her head. "Just remember that your mother wants the best for you. She didn't mean what her words implied this morning. She's just frightened for you." His hand fell to his side and Nessa looked up to see the deep lines in his face. "I don't like asking this of you, but perhaps it would be better if you didn't visit that young couple again right away."

Nessa gasped. "But Papa, I said I would come again, and I left the impression that I would like them to visit us here."

Papa's shoulders slumped. "I see. Maybe you can delay your visit a few weeks. Your mother will come around, Nessa, but it may take some time."

"What do I tell Sam?"

Owen patted her shoulder. "One thing you must always do, daughter, is be honest with Sam. You'll have to tell him the truth. You may be surprised at his understanding." Owen walked toward the door to the store. "We'll talk more later if you wish. I think I have a customer."

Nessa leaned her arms on the table and clenched her fists. She wished she hadn't gone yesterday. She wished Sam hadn't met that couple. Footsteps racing down the stairs brought her to her feet. She straightened her shoulders, picked up two plates, and strode to the stove to get food for her sisters' breakfasts. *Jesus, please help me get through this day.*

After Ellie and Opal's prayer of thanks, Nessa poured hot water over the used plates in the dish pan and prepared to clean the kitchen.

"Tomorrow is the big day, Opal," Ellie said. "I don't know whether I'm happy or sad."

"I'm going to miss you, Ellie."

"I'll be home for holidays, and it will be nice not to do chores in the snow." She grinned. "And I can sleep later. I think I'm going to like going away to school."

Nessa dropped the silver into the sudsy water and sighed. She had forgotten Ellie would be leaving tomorrow to attend school in town.

"I wonder what's wrong with Mama. She was fine last night." Nessa heard a tinge of fear in Opal's voice.

"Mama will be fine, Opal. She's just a little tired."

Ellie, caught up in the excitement of her adventure, appeared unconcerned. "Oh, that's right. Since Mama is sick, Nessa, will you help me pack?"

"We'll start as soon as you two finish your chores."

"Will I have to do your chores, now, too?" asked Opal.

"I'm sure I don't know," Ellie said in an off-hand manner. "You'll have to ask Mama."

"That wouldn't be fair, would it Nessa? For me to do Ellie's chores?"

"Don't worry, Opal. We'll work it out between the two of us." Nessa tried to control her impatience with her sisters' trivial matters. She had a momentous problem to solve, and who could help her? Sam would return tomorrow night and she must have the answer then.

By the time she had supper on the table, she was exhausted, and ate only a few bites. Ellie chattered throughout the meal, as she had all day, while Opal's face grew longer and more solemn. Papa ate quickly then went to be with Mama. He had taken tea up twice, as well as a tray at noon.

"Your mother is better," he told Nessa when he came downstairs after delivering the light supper Nessa had prepared. "But she won't be down this evening. Maybe by morning..." His voice died away and Nessa sighed. She had hoped the three of them could talk and come to a solution that would please her mother as well as herself.

Now she lifted her body from the chair. "I have to make up the bread dough to rise over night." She looked at Ellie and Opal. "When you finish eating, please clear the table and do the dishes."

"Do I have to?" Ellie's lips turned down in a pout. "Opal and I wanted to talk about things."

Opal snorted. "You mean you want to talk. You've hardly let me say a word all day."

"Never mind that," Nessa said in a firm voice. "You can talk while you work."

❧　　　❧　　　❧

By the following mid-morning, Ellie was ensconced on the back seat of a neighbor's buggy. The couple were driving to town, and agreed to see Ellie settled at the home of the teacher, who had contracted with Papa to care for her.

Mama stood on the porch, after holding Ellie close for a long moment. Papa had helped her mother down the stairs a few minutes before the neighbors' arrival, and Nessa stood in shocked silence at the sight of her ashen face, her sunken eyes, and her feigned smile.

Nessa sighed and turned her attention back to Ellie. A bright colored quilt covered her to the chin, emphasizing her pallor and forlorn countenance. Nessa blinked away imminent tears and gave her sister an encouraging smile. All their petty childhood disagreements faded into oblivion. She had been much closer to Ellie since their middle of the night talk a few weeks ago, and Nessa's heart wrenched when she realized how much she would miss her sister.

After last minute instructions to his daughter, Owen backed away from the buggy, and with a final tentative wave, Ellie disappeared from sight.

Even her father appeared unusually somber when he turned and gazed at his wife. He went to Mama and led her inside. Nessa heard his soft voice murmuring as he half-carried her mother up the stairs. What was happening to her family? Her parents had provided a solid, seemingly invincible foundation in her life, and she stood watching in horror as widening cracks threatened the security she had taken for granted.

She trembled at the touch on her arm, and turned to find Opal at her side.

"Nessa?" Her little sister's voice quavered. "Is everything going to be all right?"

"Of course it is, silly." Nessa sighed and gave Opal a hug. "We'll miss Ellie, but she'll make a fine teacher one day, so we must be happy for her."

Opal bit her lip and a tear slid down one cheek. "And Mama? She didn't even notice me this morning."

Nessa sat in a porch chair and took her little sister on her lap as she had years ago. "Don't you worry. Mama will be fine. She needs some rest and we'll make sure she gets it, all right?" She wiped the child's face with the hem of her apron. "And don't think Mama didn't see you. She's just a little sad at Ellie's leaving, like we are." Nessa cupped her hand around Opal's chin. "If I don't see a smile, I'm going to tickle you."

Opal giggled and wrapped her arms around Nessa's neck. "You won't go away, too, will you?"

"I'll be here as long as you need me, Opal." Nessa swallowed hard, and her heart thumped against her breast.

❧   ❧   ❧

Nessa paced up and down the porch, anxiously awaiting and dreading to hear the sounds of an approaching wagon. The piercing orange rays of the setting sun prevented her from searching the trail to the west. She clenched and unclenched her hands and her lips moved. She had not prayed for the Lord's guidance before, but now she asked Him to give her the right words. Still she agonized, unsure if He would answer.

At last the clink of harness and creak of wheels reached her ears. She raced down the porch steps and around the side to the storage room. When Sam reined in the mules, she darted in front of them and waited. Sam climbed down and she threw herself into his arms. "Oh, Sam. I'm so glad you're here."

His arms closed around her and she clung to him. She heard his gasp, sighed, and tightened her hold. If only she could stay here forever where she felt safe and cherished.

"Nessa? If I'd known I'd get this kind of welcome, I would have driven those mules faster." He grasped her arms and held her away to gaze into her eyes. "Are you crying?"

"Ho, Sam. Thought I heard your wagon. Let me get a light and we'll unload."

Sam frowned. "Sure thing, Mr. Long." He wiped a tear from Nessa's cheek. "What's wrong, little girl?"

"It will have to wait, Sam." Nessa wrenched her body away. "Until you finish unloading and have some supper." She sniffed and turned toward the house. "I'll be inside."

She heard his harsh sigh as she went through the kitchen door.

Habit carried her through preparing supper, and fixing a tray for her mother. She carried it to her parents' room and set it on the table beside the bed.

"Thank you, dear," Mama spoke just above a whisper. "I'll eat in a little while. You needn't stay."

Nessa sighed and tiptoed out of the room. Back in the kitchen, Opal hopped around, setting the table and wondering aloud if Sam had brought her a present.

"Don't you dare ask him, Opal."

"I wouldn't," she answered in an injured tone.

"I'm sorry." Nessa sighed. "Of course you wouldn't."

When the men came in to wash, Nessa set bowls of steaming food on the table and retreated to the kitchen. How could she sit there and carry on a normal conversation? But her absence would only make things worse. Somehow she must carry through until after the meal. *Please help me, Jesus.* She straightened her shoulders and took her place across from Sam, avoiding his gaze.

Her father drew Sam into a discussion of the new merchandise, and no one appeared to notice when Nessa pushed most of her food to one side and covered it with a piece of bread. She served the apple pie in silence, then returned to the kitchen and stood facing the window. A few minutes later she heard Sam's footsteps.

"Nessa? Do I learn what's wrong, now?" He stopped behind her and touched her hair. "Your father said to find you, that we needed to talk."

She turned and grabbed his hand. "Let's sit under the trees."

When they were seated side by side on a bench, Nessa took a deep breath. "I don't know where to start, Sam. I've thought for two days about how to say this, but there's no easy way."

He reached for her hand. "Please don't. Not until I finish." She clenched her hands and welcomed the distraction of the pain when her nails dug into her palms. "Ellie left this morning to go to school in town."

"Yes. You told me about that last week. Is that why you're upset?"

"No, not really. It just adds to the rest."

"Please, Nessa, talk to me." He slipped his arm around her waist. "I can't help if I don't know what the trouble is."

"That's just it! You can't help at all." She met his gaze. "Oh, Sam, everything has gone wrong and I think we'd better not see each other—at least for a while." Her gaze fell. "Probably a long while. I'm sorry, Sam." She started to rise.

Sam snorted and pulled her down beside him. "What are you talking about? You can't just tell me we can't see each other and walk off." He stood and hovered over her. "Now I want some answers. Why can't we see each other? Have you changed your mind about me?"

"No!" She clenched her eyelids and swallowed hard. "I can't do this. I simply can't do it!"

Sam knelt beside her and took her hands in his. "Nessa, please don't. I can't stand to see you like this." He brushed a lock of hair from her face. "I promise you, nothing will stand in our way as long as you still love me. Do you hear me, girl?"

Tears streamed down her face. "You don't understand. Mama is ill and I'm to blame, and Papa is upset, and Opal needs me, and you can't do anything about any of it."

"Whoa! Let's take that one at a time." His grip on her hands tightened. "What's wrong with your mother? I noticed she wasn't at supper, but no one said anything, and I didn't want to be nosey."

Nessa took a deep breath. "Mama is upset because I visited your friends and they—well, she says they're foreigners."

Sam dropped her hands and stood. "She's upset because they weren't born in the United States? But that can't be right. Lots of people in America came from another country."

"I know, Sam. I don't agree with her, and neither does Papa, but she got real sick when I told her about our visit, and Papa is worried. He asked me not to go back there for a while until she's better." She sobbed. "She looks awfully bad and I don't think she's getting better. She went to bed yesterday, and only got up for a few minutes this morning when Ellie left." She gave Sam a pleading look. "If only I hadn't gone with you!"

Sam plopped down on the bench and allowed his arms to droop towards the ground. "I never expected anything like this."

"Sam?" Nessa bent to peer into his face. Their gazes met, and Sam gave her a weak smile.

"Just give me a minute. I feel sort of like I've been stomped on by an old mule." He raised one arm and cupped her face in his hand. "One thing for sure, darlin', you aren't getting rid of me."

"Oh, Sam." Nessa rested her head against his arm and wept.

Sam lifted her, set her on his lap, and held her close. "I don't have any answer for you, Nessa. Not right off. But there's got to be one, and I'll find it, with the good Lord's help." He rose and set her on her feet. "I promise, Nessa, I promise."

He kissed her trembling lips, and she snuggled closer in his arms. Then he released her and sighed. "You better get in the house." He lifted her chin with his fingers and their gazes met. "I need a smile to carry me home."

Her face beamed through the tears. He wiped her cheeks, then turned her toward the house. "Go on with you, little girl. I'll be back as soon as I can." She forced her feet to move away from him. When she reached the porch, she turned to see him standing on the walkway. He waved and disappeared around the corner of the store. She stood peering into the darkness until she could no longer hear mules or wagon.

❧   ❧   ❧

The creaks and bounces of the empty wagon over the rutted road caused Sam to grit his teeth. They roiled his already chaotic thoughts into further confusion. "Why God? And what am I to do?" He shouted into the darkness, and the startled mules broke into a gallop. Sam ducked his head into the wind and gripped the reins tighter. After a careening ride of more than a mile, the animals snorted and slowed to a fast trot. Sam took a deep breath and chuckled. "Okay, Lord. You got my attention. I'm listening now." Peace descended.

Upon arriving home, Sam fed his animals, milked the cow, gathered eggs, and secured pen doors by lantern light. He groaned when he sat on the edge of his bed, and realized he was exhausted. After removing his shoes and outer clothing, he fell into bed and pulled the quilts up around his ears.

Before eating breakfast the next morning, Sam again praised the Lord that Hank had at last seen the Light, and for his good night's sleep. He still had no idea how to solve his and Nessa's problem, but he trusted the One who had the answer. When the time was right, he would have it, too. He only hoped Nessa had the assurance he did.

With jaunty steps, he clambered down into the unfinished dugout, picked up his shovel, and began to whistle. A few hours later, Hank appeared above him.

"How you getting along, Sam? Got another shovel?"

Sam leaned against the wall. "Hank, you're just in time. I thought I'd take a breather and heat up the coffee. What brings you over here this morning?"

Hank shrugged. "Not much to do at my place this time of year. I ain't got a young lady to plan for." He lowered one hand to Sam and heaved him from the pit. "If you promise me lunch, I'll be glad to help you down there."

Sam chuckled. "You're a glutton for punishment aren't you? Diggin' isn't my favorite job."

"Depends on who you're diggin' with, maybe." He grinned and followed Sam to the fire.

By mid-day, the new room had straight walls and a level, hard-packed floor. After a cold lunch, they started on the roof, overlaying cross beams with planks, then mounding the soil from the hole to cover it.

Sam rested on his upright shovel and grinned at Hank. "That about does it. I'll cut a doorway into the new part later." He took a deep breath and glanced at the sinking sun. "Just in time, too. Let's get washed up and find something to eat."

Hank carried the shovels to the barn, and fed the animals while Sam milked, then squatted near the fire and watched his friend fry corn cakes. When the first batch were crispy brown, Sam scooped one from the skillet and tossed it to his friend. "That'll maybe hold you till everything's ready." Hank grinned and passed it from one hand to the other until it cooled enough to eat.

The stack of cakes in a warming pan near the edge of the fire grew to a dozen or more and Sam spooned the last of the batter into the pan. While it cooked, he fetched the pail of molasses, a bowl of butter, and plates and forks. He ladled bacon-flavored beans that had been cooking since morning onto the plates, balanced a handful of cakes on the side of each, and passed one to Hank. After slathering the bread with butter and molasses, they sat cross-legged on the ground near the fire. A chilly breeze from the north had strengthened when the sun went down, and Sam rose and tossed more branches on the blaze, while Hank replenished both plates. When their stomachs felt comfortable, they donned jackets, and sat watching the wind play with the flames and shadows.

"I sure appreciate your help today, Hank. Don't know why, but it seems two fellows can do more in one day, than one can in two days."

"Sure. That's because they don't want the other one to outdo them."

Sam chuckled. "I think I understand what you just said. Guess it makes sense, too." He leaned back with his hands on the ground behind him, and stretched his upper body. "Ever wonder why fellows try to outdo one another?"

Hank snorted. "What are you? One of those philosophegers or something?"

Again Sam chuckled. "I think it's philosopher." He bent forward and scraped mud from his boots with a twig. "No, I'm not one of them. At least I don't think so. But when you spend so much time with yourself, you do get to thinking about things. Like, why some people act one way in a situation and another acts the opposite."

Hank frowned at Sam. "Never thought about it. Mostly I just think about gettin' through with what I'm doin' so I can do somethin' else."

"Yeah. Keeping your mind on your work is the best thing. I just get to wondering sometimes."

"Well, I'm wonderin' how cold I'm gonna get goin' home." Hank rose and stretched his arms high above his head. "I'll leave all that heavy thinkin' to you. Thanks for the supper."

"Thanks for the help. Let me know when I can do something for you."

"Sam, what you've done for me couldn't be paid back in a life time."

Sam got to his feet, groaning at the stiffness in his legs and held out his hand. "Friends help when there's a need. Nothing unusual about that."

Hank gripped his hand in his. "Yeah, sure, but I've only known one. Thanks, friend." He gave a nervous laugh and strode toward his horse.

Sam smiled and waved as Hank rode away. The smile remained while he tidied up and clumped down the steps to his bed.

CHAPTER 22

❀

Nessa set the plate of eggs and bacon on the table in front of her father, then sat across the table from him, wincing at the furrows in his brow. Papa raised his head and gave her an unconvincing smile.

"Thanks, Nessa. The food looks good, but I'm not very hungry this morning."

"You look tired, Papa. Didn't you get any sleep?"

Papa ran his hand over his bristly chin and rubbed his eyes. "I'm all right. It's your mother I'm worried about."

Nessa bit her lip. As long as she could remember, Papa had never come to breakfast unshaven. "Do you want me to milk Sally for you?"

Owen shook his head. "Thanks, daughter. I finished the chores an hour ago. Got up at dawn." He sighed, steadied his elbows on the table, and picked up his coffee cup.

Nessa squeezed her hands together in her lap and took a deep breath. "How is Mama this morning?"

The chair squeaked as Papa leaned back and gazed at her. "I've been studying on how to tell you, or whether to tell you at all just yet." His gaze wandered to the ceiling and he sat motionless.

Nessa reached out and placed her hand on his. "Papa?"

He turned his palm up and grasped her fingers. "You're so young, Nessa. And you and Sam…I want you to have a good life together." He sighed. "I'm just gabbling to delay." He took a deep breath. "Nessa, you shouldn't have to deal with this problem, but…Your mother is in the family way."

"Wh-a-t?" Nessa jerked upright, knocking her chair to the floor. "Papa! You can't mean?"

"Yes, I'm afraid I do." He walked to her side and took her hands in his. "She's not happy about it, Nessa. That's what brought on all this trouble." He sighed. "She's distraught, even afraid, I believe." His eyes moistened and he blinked. "She blames me, even you, but most of all herself." His arms dropped to his side and he bent his head forward. "I don't know what to do. I've never felt so helpless."

Trance-like, Nessa pulled the overturned chair upright and sat, staring at emptiness.

"I'm trying to understand." Papa's voice broke. "Rebecca is so beautiful, and usually strong." He shook his head. "She's always been defensive about her ancestors. They came to Georgia from an English debtors' prison."

Nessa gasped and her father looked up at her. "I'm sorry, Nessa. I have to tell you all this. She wouldn't want you to know, but I need your help and you must know why this affected her so." His eyes pleaded for understanding. "Her people worked hard and her great-grandfather managed to acquire a large property as payment for a gambling debt. Her grandfather became a wealthy plantation owner. By the time your mother was born, shortly after the war-between-the-states, the family had lost most everything. Her grandfather died at Shiloh, and her father, wounded at Vicksburg, returned to his ravaged home a beaten man. He died when your mother was three, and she was raised by her grandmother and mother. The women sold item after item to buy food. Finally, they were forced off the land. A distant cousin, who had made a modest fortune during the war settled them in a small house in Savannah."

Papa cleared his throat and carried his cup to the range for more coffee. Nessa sat as though ice had filled her veins. Her father sipped the hot liquid, set the cup on a cabinet, clenched his hands behind his back, and paced around the small kitchen. "Rebecca was raised on grand stories of the past. She always thought the family would regain what they had lost, and the past would come to life for her." He stopped and took a deep breath.

"You see, Nessa, I am the son of that distant cousin, and I've loved your mother since she was twelve years old." Papa sniffed and wiped his eyes with one fist. "That's why I tried so hard to make a living in Georgia. But I had to give up, and move out here." He sat in the chair with his elbows on his knees, covered his face with his hands and wept.

Nessa brushed a tear from her cheek, stood, and went to him. She placed her hands on his shoulders and pressed her cheek to his thinning hair. "Please don't, Papa. I know you did the best you could. Mama knows that, too. She can't blame you for what happened because of the war."

"I don't know. She seemed to be happy here this last year. But you growing up and getting married soon, and Ellie leaving, and finding out about the baby was the last straw."

"It will be all right, Papa." She patted his arm. "I'll help you, and Jesus will too. Mama will be all right."

"Nessa? Aren't you going to wake me for breakfast?"

"Opal! My goodness child." She summoned up a smile for her little sister. "Anyway, it appears you woke yourself up. Sit down and I'll fix you a plate."

"Good morning, Papa. Did you sleep late, too?"

Her father rose from his chair and hugged his youngest child. "Morning, Opal. Things have been a little out of kilter today." He pulled out his pocket watch as she sat at the table. "I must get moving. Hope a customer hasn't been waiting. Enjoy your breakfast." He patted Opal's tousled curls and strode toward the door which connected the kitchen to the store. "Nessa, we'll talk more later."

❧   ❧   ❧

After taking a tray of tea and buttered bread to her mother, who pretended to be asleep, Nessa sent Opal to feed the chickens. Then she churned butter, cleaned up the kitchen, formed loaves from the dough she had set to rise the night before, and made the beds. Opal fetched a dish of left-over stew from the well-house, and Nessa built up the fire in the range, popped the loaves of bread into the oven, and set the stew to heat for the mid-day meal. She sat at the kitchen table with a tepid cup of tea and stretched her legs out in front of her.

"Aren't you going to finish this, Nessa? I want a glass of buttermilk." Opal stood in front of the churn and licked her lips.

Nessa sighed. "Just give me a minute, Opal." She gulped down her tea and moved to the cabinet. She placed a clean white cloth over a bowl and poured the contents of the churn into it. Then, holding the edges of the cloth, she squeezed the excess whey from the butter globules and dumped the butter into a bowl. Opal fetched a ladle and filled her glass while Nessa molded the creamy yellow particles into a ball with a wooden paddle.

During supper, Nessa had marveled that Papa had drawn strength during the day. He teased Opal and complimented Nessa on the meal. At nine, he sent Opal to bed and asked Nessa to join him in the parlor. He took her arm, led her to the sofa, and smiled. "I'd like us to pray together, Nessa. The Word says if two agree on what they ask, God will do it. That promise spun around in my head all day. I believe the Lord wants us to pray, as one, for your mother." He searched Nessa's face. "Will you agree with me?"

Nessa placed her palms on his chest and kissed his cheek. "Yes, Papa."

They knelt in front of the sofa, and Papa opened his Bible to Matthew 18:19. "Lord, I believe your Word, and Nessa and I come before you in agreement to ask that Rebecca be returned to us as wife and mother, in health. We praise You and thank You for hearing us, and for answering our prayers. In the name of Jesus, Amen."

"Amen."

Papa turned to Nessa and gave her a broad smile. "Trust Him, Nessa, to do what He says." He rose, then assisted her to her feet. "I'm proud of the way you handled everything today. You are a blessing, daughter."

Nessa's eyes moistened. "Thank you, Papa. I did the best I could."

"You did fine." He stifled a yawn. "I imagine you're as tired as I am." He patted her arm. "You go on up, now. I'll put the lamp out."

Nessa smiled. "Goodnight, Papa. Sleep well."

Her weary legs carried her up the stairs, assisted by her hand clasping the bannister. When she reached the top, she remembered that today was Monday—wash day. Her shoulders slumped lower. How could she have forgotten? Tomorrow she must do the wash, as well as the ironing, with only Opal to help. She sighed, undressed in the dim moonlight, and sank into the soft feather mattress.

For the first time since she could remember, she didn't wash her face. "I'm sorry, Mama, for breaking your rule, but surely it can't do too much harm this once. I don't have the energy to pour the water in the basin." She rolled to her side. When she closed her eyes, it felt as though she had been in a sandstorm. She blinked several times, then breathed a deep sigh and burrowed her head deeper into the pillow. For all Papa's compliments, she knew she couldn't take care of him and Opal like her mother would. A tear slipped from one eye and ran across her nose. "Help me, Jesus." She sniffed and tightly scrunched her eyelids together. *Lean on me.* The tautness in her face softened.

❦   ❦   ❦

Rebecca sat in the rocker, wrapped in a quilt, staring out the window when Nessa carried in a breakfast tray.

"Mama? I brought your tea and a soft-boiled egg. Would you like me to move the table over by the window?"

Rebecca waved one hand in her direction. "Just set it somewhere. I can't keep it down and I'm not hungry, anyway."

Nessa sighed and bit her lip. "You must eat something to keep up your strength. I don't know what you'd like. Tell me and I'll go fix it for you. Please?"

Rebecca sat unmoving except for one slipper-shod foot that shot out from under the quilt and tapped the floor in an agitated way.

"Mama? Were you sad like this before I was born?" Nessa set the tray on the table and plopped on the edge of the unmade bed. "You once told me that a baby was a gift from God."

Her mother bowed her head and her shoulders shook.

Nessa jumped up, went to her, and put her arm around her. "I'm sorry, Mama. I'm sorry. I didn't mean to upset you."

Rebecca reached out a shaky hand and clutched Nessa's skirt, then raised her head. Nessa gasped as tears rained down her mother's face and fell on her heaving breast.

"Please, Mama, stop crying." Nessa fell to her knees and wept.

Several minutes went by. At last Rebecca's tears abated, and she took the handkerchief Nessa provided from a dresser drawer. After wiping her face, she squeezed her daughter's hand and gazed into her eyes.

"Thank you for reminding me." A wan smile flickered on her lips. "A baby is a gift of God, and no, I wasn't sad when I knew you were on the way, nor when your sisters were expected. My heart sang with joy." Nessa's hand throbbed under her mother's grip.

"Everything will be all right now, Nessa. I don't know what happened to me the last few days." Rebecca released Nessa's hand then picked up the damp handkerchief, made a final swipe at her eyes, and took a deep breath. "Please bring my Bible from the bureau. And I'll have the tray here. You're very thoughtful." Her lips formed into the old familiar curve. "Would you ask your father to come see me after he finishes his dinner, if he has time? Thank you Nessa, and don't worry."

Nessa scurried to obey, then left the room. After gently closing the door, she leaned her back against it, and covered her mouth with her hand to mute her ragged breathing and pulsing heartbeat. In the past few days, her emotions had leaped around like a grasshopper in tall grass. Her eyes teared and her lips curved at the same time. A sound somewhat like a cackling hen erupted from her throat, and she hurried down the stairs so her mother wouldn't hear.

Opal stood in the kitchen doorway when she burst around the corner and into the dining room. She frowned. "Nessa, are you all right? You look funny."

Nessa swept her arms around her sister and danced a circle around the dining table. "I'm fine, you're fine, everything's fine." When Nessa reached the kitchen doorway, she released Opal, waltzed to the back door, and began gathering up the pillow slips filled with soiled laundry lying on the floor next to the outside door. "Help me get this wash going, Opal. We're getting a late start." She glanced over her shoulder and beckoned to her sister.

Opal stood in the middle of the kitchen, wide-eyed and biting at her lip. "Nessa, are you a grown-up now?"

Nessa stood motionless pondering. "I think, maybe, I'm about half way there."

❦   ❦   ❦

The next morning, Papa entered the kitchen after doing his chores and handed Nessa a pail of cool milk from the well-house. "We have extra milk with Ellie gone. I thought you might make a custard pudding today if you have time." He beamed a smile at her. "Your mother is fond of custard."

Nessa nodded. "I'll try, Papa. I've never made it all by myself before."

Papa sniffed the aroma of frying bacon. "You're turning into quite a good cook, Nessa. Is breakfast ready?"

"Almost. I'm starting the eggs. They should be ready by the time Opal gets back from feeding the chickens and the cats."

"Good. I'll wash up." Nessa watched him disappear into the wash room. Papa's steps seemed confident, and she felt lighter, as though a yoke had been lifted from her shoulders.

Opal came in blowing on her fingers. "Brr. It's cold out this morning."

"Where are your mittens?"

"I forgot them. And anyway it's hard to scoop up the feed with them on."

"Then don't complain. Get washed and finish setting the table. Breakfast is almost ready."

Nessa poured coffee for papa and herself, then sat across from Opal. Her eyes widened when her father entered the kitchen supporting his wife on one arm and beaming a big smile at his daughters. Dusky smudges under Rebecca's eyes marred her thin face, but Nessa noticed a delicate blush in her cheeks, and her lips curved as her husband deposited her in the usual place at the table.

"Good morning, girls. It's nice to see you all this morning, and the smell of that bacon just may tempt my appetite."

Nessa jumped to her feet. "I'll set you a plate, Mama. Would you like some oatmeal, an egg, and a biscuit, too?" She quickly poured a cup of coffee and placed it front of her mother.

Rebecca curled her fingers around Nessa's wrist, smiled and shook her head. "Just a small dish of oatmeal, please, dear. The aroma is tempting, but I'll have to work up to bacon and eggs."

After Owen's prayer, Rebecca ate a few spoonsful of cereal, then pushed her bowl aside. "I believe I owe you girls an explanation, and perhaps an apology." She gazed at Owen, and a smile lit her face. "Your father received his early this morning." Her smile faded and she lowered her eyelids. "This is harder than I thought it would be." She lifted her head and gazed at her youngest daughter. "Opal, I'm not sure what your father or Nessa has told you, but you know I have not been myself for several days. I'm sorry I have neglected you, and I assure you, I didn't intend to. And it won't happen again." She took a deep breath and smiled. "What would you say to a new brother or sister in a few months?"

Opal dropped her fork in her plate and gaped at her mother. "A brother?" She blinked, a frown creased her young brow, then softened into a look of bewilderment. "You mean? Mama!" She jumped up, knocking her chair backwards and rushed to give her mother a hug. "Oh, Mama."

Nessa's gaze locked with Rebecca's across the table for a moment. Nessa smiled and nodded, then Mama clasped Opal to her breast, and sighed. "I'm afraid I got befuddled for a while there. I feared the news of the baby would upset everyone."

Opal moved to set her chair upright and returned to her place. "It's wonderful, Mama. Just what I've always wanted. I hope it's a boy. We have enough girls in this family. I'm going to ask Jesus for a brother." She set her mouth in a determined line, gave an emphatic nod and picked up her fork.

Rebecca giggled and looked at her husband. "I guess that's settled. But you know, Opal, Jesus may have a different plan than yours. Let's just wait and see, okay?"

Opal shook her head. "No, I don't think so. I'm going to have a brother."

Mama caught Nessa's glance. "Thank you Nessa for helping me find myself yesterday." Rebecca swayed and clutched the edge of the table. "Owen, perhaps you better help me back upstairs. I guess I'm not as strong yet as I thought."

Owen tenderly lifted her in his arms. "You'll be fine after a little nap." At the kitchen doorway, he spoke over his shoulder. "Nessa, make sure your mother gets a soft boiled egg and some sweet tea about mid-morning."

Nessa rose from her seat. "Yes, Papa. Is there anything else I can do?"

"I'll let you know."

Opal jumped up and began dancing about the room."Is it really so, Nessa? I can hardly believe it. A little brother. And Mama will be all right, won't she? It must be true. Mama knows for sure, doesn't she? She wouldn't say so if she wasn't sure. What shall we name him? Nessa, a little baby in our house. And I'll be the big sister, and I can take care of him, and he'll have to do what I say, and we'll have so much fun."

Nessa laughed when Opal gasped for breath. "It's all true, Opal. But it will be sometime yet, and it might not be a boy. You won't be disappointed if it's a girl will you?"

Opal stopped, placed her hands on her hips's, and faced her sister. "I won't be disappointed at all, Nessa. I'm going to have a baby brother." She grabbed her coat and hat off the peg and ran out the kitchen door to the garden.

Nessa raised her eyebrows at her little sister's adamance, then shook her head and went to close the door.

CHAPTER 23

❁

Nessa built up the fire in the range and reached for the skillet. There had been no opportunity to speak with Papa the day before, and Nessa had tossed in her bed all night, visualizing the worst and best outcomes of her questions about Mama. Mostly questions about Sam and their future. She determined to speak to Papa before breakfast.

A few minutes later her father brought in a pail of milk.

"Morning, Nessa. Awful cold this morning. We may be in for a hard winter." He removed his coat and hat and hung them on the peg by the door.

"Morning, Papa. The eggs are almost done." She arranged slices of bacon on a plate and dished up a generous mound of scrambled eggs, then took a deep breath and carried the food to the table where her father sat, bowed in prayer.

When he raised his head and smiled, she asked, "Papa, is Mama really going to be all right?"

"She'll be fine, Nessa, as soon as she gets over this morning thing. It has left her weak in her body, but her spirit and mind are now as clear as ever."

Nessa bit her lip and gazed into her father's eyes. "And, Sam. Is she still angry with him and with me?"

Papa forked eggs into his mouth and shook his head. "No, Nessa. She allowed her fears for this new little one to overwhelm her, and she felt threatened by anyone or anything that interfered with her finding her way through the fog engulfing her. Well, praise the Lord, she did find her way out. You and Sam proceed with your plans."

"Then, would you invite Sam for dinner?"

Papa grinned. "Aha. Slipped that one in didn't you?" His voice turned deep and formal. "I'd be honored to pass your invitation along."

Nessa kissed Papa's cheek and overran his cup with coffee, filling the saucer.

Now, more than an hour later, after cleaning the kitchen and tidying the parlor, Nessa poured a cup of coffee and sat at the kitchen table, waiting for the water to boil for her mother's tea. Papa and Opal were at church. Mama had not felt strong enough to venture out into the cold air and Nessa had offered to stay with her. She glanced at the clock. Time for a short visit with her mother before beginning preparations for dinner. She wanted today's meal to be perfect.

She rose, rinsed her cup, arranged the tea tray, and carried it upstairs.

"Good morning, Mama. I brought tea and toasted bread with butter. Does that sound good to you?"

Rebecca sat up in the bed and reached for her robe. "Thank you Nessa. The tea is welcome, and perhaps a bite of bread." She slipped into the robe and slippers and walked toward the rocker by the window. "I'll sit here and you can bring the stool over and keep me company."

Nessa poured tea and handed the cup to Rebecca, then sat at her side and smiled. "You seem to be feeling better this morning."

"A little better." Mama sighed. "I hope this morning discomfort doesn't last long. It troubled me for over a month with Opal."

"Is there anything I can do to help?" She offered the plate of bread and her mother took a portion and bit into it.

Mama chewed and sipped her tea. "There's nothing to be done that I know of. Just grit my teeth and hope it's of short duration." She smiled and patted Nessa's arm. "This is tasty."

"I asked Papa to invite Sam for dinner. I hope you don't mind, and that you'll feel up to joining us."

Rebecca smiled and nodded. "We'll see. One thing I know, I'm getting tired of being in this room." She selected another morsel of bread. "What are you cooking?"

"Papa brought me a chicken. I'll have to leave in a few minutes to clean it." She played with her fingers and bit at her lip. "Mama. Everything is all right now, isn't it? I mean for Sam and me and our plans?"

"Nessa, dear, I'm so sorry about last week." Rebecca frowned and took Nessa's hand in hers. "Everything seemed to overwhelm me at once." She sighed. "You and Sam continue as you were. He's a fine young man and I'm very fond of him." She squeezed Nessa's fingers, took a sip of tea, and handed the cup to Nessa. "Go on now and prepare your dinner."

Nessa smiled and kissed her mother's cheek. "Thank you, Mama." She picked up the tray, balancing it in one hand, hurried out and down the stairs, and danced into the kitchen humming.

An hour later, Nessa stood, with her chin resting on her clasped hands, surveying the table. Her grandmother's china, silver, and cut-glass goblets gleamed against the embroidered cloth. The cinnamon-colored seed pods she had picked from roadside weeds, golden leaves, a small pumpkin, and russet apples spilling from a wicker cornucopia, rested in the center.

The sound of the carriage sent her flying to the front door. She halted before opening it, raced to the mirror across from the fireplace, patted her hair, pinched color into her cheeks, and sauntered to the door and out on the porch.

Sam assisted Opal to the ground, took her arm and started up the path. He raised his head and met Nessa's smile. He grinned and took her outstretched hand in his.

"I'm so happy you came, Sam. I thought you might not." She paused and bit her lip. "Not come, that is."

Sam drew her nearer and she blushed under his scrutiny. "You're even prettier than I remembered. I reckon this was the longest week I ever went through."

Nessa ducked her head. "Me too, Sam."

He took her other hand and squeezed them together in his. "If your pa hadn't invited me, I'd a come this afternoon anyway."

Nessa giggled. "Oh, Sam." Her gaze wavered and she noticed Opal watching, with her head tilted as though she was taking notes. Nessa wrenched her hands from Sam's. "My goodness, Opal. Go inside and take your coat and hat off. Dinner's almost ready." She shivered and opened the door. "Sam, you'll get chilled standing out here. What must you think of me? Come in and warm yourself by the fire." Sam chuckled and sidled into the parlor.

"Hang your things on the coatrack," Nessa told him and noticed Opal dawdling on the stairs. "I have to check something in the kitchen." She fled from the room.

❦   ❦   ❦

Mama, dressed in her Sunday frock, entered the dining room on Papa's arm, welcomed Sam with a smile, and complimented Nessa on the table setting. After saying grace, Papa carved the roast chicken. He and Mama took turns commenting on the tender meat, the nicely browned potatoes, the buttery mashed turnips, and the fluffy biscuits. Although Sam said little about the food, he winked when his gaze frequently met Nessa's across the table, and he asked for seconds.

Nessa toyed with her food, bounced up to get more biscuits, and finally excused herself to see to the dessert. Her hands shook as she arranged thick squares of plum cobbler on the small plates. She took a deep breath and chided herself. The interminable meal would be over soon, then she and Sam could take a walk. His nearness made it difficult to swallow, even breathe. She had so much to tell him, but how could she talk about her mother's condition in an appropriate way? Would her mother approve? What would Sam think of her for blurting out such intimate news? *Please, Jesus give me the words*. She sighed and carried the dessert tray to the table.

At last Papa pushed his chair away from the table. "Good dinner, Nessa." His gaze circled the table, pausing for a moment on each person, then returned to Rebecca. "Dear, do you feel up to joining me in the parlor?" At Rebecca's smile and nod, he turned his attention to Opal. "Opal, if you'll scrape the dishes and stack them in the kitchen, you and Nessa can wash them later." He smiled at his eldest daughter. "I imagine you and Sam have some catching up to do." Papa assisted Mama from her chair and lead her to the next room. Opal rose and began banging plates one on top of the other.

Sam slid his chair into place, went around the table to Nessa, and bowed. "Miss Long, would you do me the honor of accompanying me on a walk?"

Nessa giggled, rose from her chair and curtsied. "It would be my pleasure, Mr. Jackson."

Opal snorted and stalked into the kitchen with a stack of dishes in her hands. Sam chuckled and lead Nessa to the parlor where they donned warm coats and hats. He nodded to Nessa's parents, and opened the outside door.

The north wind bit at Nessa's face when they left the shelter of the house, and she gasped. "Brr, it's gotten much colder." Sam stepped to the windward side and drew her closer. "Some of the old timers are predicting a hard winter." He searched the gray clouds forming west and north. "Maybe we'll have snow before Christmas."

"Let's walk to the barn. It will be warmer there and we can talk." She strode to the side door and struggled to open it against the wind. Sam held it for her to enter and she stood rubbing her chilled fingers for a moment before leading the way to a mound of hay. "We can sit here."

Nessa sat and spread her skirt over her legs. Sam sat cross legged beside her, and stared at his boots. The wind whistled through the gaps in the walls, and

Nessa shivered and hugged her arms in front of her. Sam picked up a piece of straw, stuck it between his teeth and chewed.

The silence grew awkward, but Nessa's tongue seemed paralyzed. At last, Sam tossed the straw over his shoulder and turned to meet Nessa's gaze. "Your mother isn't still mad at me, is she?"

"Oh, Sam! It's been a terrible week." Nessa lowered her gaze to her lap. "Mama was so ill, and I've never seen Papa so upset. And Ellie's gone, and I couldn't talk to Opal, and I've been so scared." Her voice quavered. "And trying to cook and wash and take care of Mama, and she wouldn't eat." She swiped at the runnels of tears on her cheeks with her gloved hand. "I wished you would come. I thought you could make it all right, somehow." Sam took her hand in his and she gave him a watery smile, and took a deep breath. "Then Papa told me…He said…I'm going to have a baby brother or sister, Sam. That's why Mama acted so strange. She was afraid. Then day before yesterday I asked her…Well, we had a talk, and she cried and told me everything would be all right."

Sam frowned and squeezed Nessa's hand more tightly. "I don't know what to say, Nessa. I wish I had been here when you needed me, but I thought it best if I stayed away for a few days. When your father invited me this morning after church, I wanted to jump on Gallatin and race over here as fast as I could. It's been a bad week for me, too. Nothing like yours, but the not knowing almost drove me crazy." Their gazes locked. "So, congratulations on the baby brother or sister." His eyes narrowed. "Everything is all right, isn't it?"

Nessa blinked several times and smiled. "Yes. Papa, and Mama too, said we should get on with our plans."

Sam drew her into his arms and kissed her lightly. "I missed you Nessa, and I knew I wouldn't allow anything to take you from me, but I wasn't sure what I was fightin'." He heaved a big sigh. "I guess I better get on home. I have to leave early in the morning to pick up freight, and your father said there might be two loads this week. Folks have ordered a lot of extra goods for Christmas. I'll see you when I get back."

"I'll be waiting, Sam." She walked toward the door, and Sam hurried to hold it for her. "Oh, would you like to visit Mrs. Basetti next Sunday? It's likely the last chance we'll get before the holidays."

She lowered her hand from the latch and her shoulders slumped as she stared at Sam. Her mouth opened and closed, and furrows appeared in her brow. "Sam. I forgot to talk to Papa about that. I'm sorry. With everything else, I—"

Sam frowned. "You forgot? But I thought that was the problem, and you said everything was all right."

Nessa shook her head and looked at her feet. "I know, Sam. It was much more than the Basettis. Can't we just forget about them for a while?"

Sam leaned against the wall. "I can't forget. I promised. Clem has probably gone to work in the coal mines in Kansas by now, and Katerina is all alone. I promised I would check on her as often as I could." He took a deep breath and pushed bits of hay around with the toe of his boot. "I guess I can go alone, but I sure wanted to take you with me."

Nessa gasped. "You mean you'd go visit a woman you barely know all by yourself?"

Sam's eyes widened. "What are you getting at? She's the wife of a friend and I said I'd make sure she's all right this winter."

She drew herself to her full height, and shifted from one foot to another. "Fine. If you'd rather spend time with her, you go right ahead, Mr. Jackson. Nobody is stopping you." She pushed against the door, slipped through the opening, and stalked toward the house.

Sam raced to her side. "Nessa, stop. This is silly. You know how much I want to be with you, but I promised."

She stomped on down the path. "So now I'm silly!"

"Nessa will you stop and listen?" He stepped in front of her and held out his hands.

She circled around him and walked faster. "We'll discuss this later, if you have time after gallivanting around the countryside." She clambered up the steps to the porch and turned to face Sam. "I'll tell Mama and Papa goodby for you." She whirled around, opened the door, and went inside, shutting out Sam's voice calling her name.

"Nessa? Where's Sam?" Nessa bit her lip and lowered her head. "He had to leave, Papa." She shivered. "The wind is getting stronger." She removed her outer clothing and hung them on the rack. "I told him I would say goodby to you and Mama for him. He plans to leave in the morning to pick up freight."

"How odd," said Rebecca. "That's not like Sam."

"Sometimes I think I don't know him at all." Nessa started for the kitchen. "I'll go wash the dishes. Opal needn't bother to help."

❦   ❦   ❦

For two long days, Nessa kept busy, too busy to allow her thoughts to surface. Except at night. Those hours she spent in self-condemnation, self-indignation, tears, and prayer, mercifully followed by deep sleep.

Tuesday evening, when Sam was expected to return with a wagon load of freight, strained her composure. She burned the dinner biscuits, broke a dish, and seared her arm on the skillet. Every sound seemed to reverberate in her head. Rebecca, who was improving daily, and now came downstairs without assistance and performed light chores, entered the kitchen as Nessa dropped the baked potato she was taking from the oven.

"Nessa, dear." Her mother stooped to pick up the offending tuber. "Are you all right? Did you burn yourself?"

Nessa grimaced to squelch the burning tears. "I'm fine, Mama. Supper is almost ready. If Opal would get the table set. She's disappeared, it seems."

"Sit down for a minute. You're all flushed." She slipped her arm around Nessa's waist and led her to a chair. "I'll find Opal and dish up. Where is your Papa?"

"I think he's in the storage shed making room for the new supplies."

"I'll be right back." Nessa sat at the table, buried her head in her arms, and listened to her mother's receding footsteps. "Please, God, let us finish supper before Sam gets here. I can't face him tonight." She raised her head and smoothed her hair at the sound of Opal's voice.

"…but I was just helping, Papa."

"I know, Opal, but Nessa needs you right now. Wash your hands and set the table."

Mama gave her a smile. "There. Papa will be in to eat in a minute or two." She moved to the range. "The pork chops look delicious, Nessa. And we needn't mention the potato's mishap. Why don't you hand me your apron and go wash your face?"

Nessa untied the strings from around her waist and went to the tiny room next to the kitchen which held the tin bathtub. She poured a small amount of water from the pitcher into the basin on the cabinet and moistened a cloth. The touch of the cold wetness on her hot cheeks caused her to gasp. She finished quickly, then grabbed a comb and ran it through the damp tendrils. The image in the tiny warped mirror barely resembled the one she saw every morning. This Nessa's face had red and white blotches, and dark smudges under her lusterless eyes. She sighed and turned her back on the unfamiliar reflection. After drying her hands, she lifted her head, and marched to the dining room and her waiting family.

The creaking of the heavy freight wagon, and Sam's voice calling orders to the mules, penetrated the dining room as Nessa poured coffee for her parents. Her hand shook, and the hot liquid dripped onto the saucer, but her father didn't notice. He grinned and pushed back his chair.

"Save that until we unload, Nessa." He turned at the kitchen doorway. "You might keep something hot for Sam. Likely he hasn't eaten much since break-fast."

"Opal and I will take care of the dishes tonight, Nessa." Rebecca smiled and waved her hand at Nessa. "You go on and greet Sam."

"But, Mama!"

"Ssh. No arguing. Get out there and see your young man."

Nessa moved on heavy feet through the kitchen and onto the narrow walk-way that led to the storage shed.

"…and I was beginning to wonder if you'd had trouble."

"No trouble, Mr. Long. Just a heavy load and had to slow down some to give the mules a breathing spell."

"Well, guess we better get started. Hang this lantern on the wagon post. It'll most likely take us an hour to move all this."

Nessa stood in the shadows of the walk and listened to unintelligible sylla-bles punctuated by periodic grunts as the men heaved box after box from the wagon to the shelves.

During an apparent short rest, she heard her father's voice.

"You looking around for Nessa? I don't know where she is. Thought she was right behind me."

"I just wondered."

Papa chuckled. "She's probably fixing up some special food for you."

"Uh, maybe, but I doubt it." Sam's voice sounded depressed.

"You two didn't have a falling out the other night, did you? Come to think of it, Nessa acted strange when she came in."

"Ah, well." Nessa heard a huge sigh. "Better get back to work, I guess." Then the sound of footsteps fading into silence.

Nessa sniffed and shivered in the cool air. What should she do? Where could she go to avoid meeting Sam? Papa would be looking for her. Mama would be looking for her. She darted to the corner of the house and into the garden. The barn loomed in front of her. She unlatched the door, stared into the gloom at the stacks of hay on the floor, and burst into tears. Her chosen sanctuary was the very site where all her sorrows had begun. She threw herself face down and pounded the yielding straw with her fists. Some time passed before her fingers relaxed and her sobs subsided.

A cold draft filtering through the cracks between the wood planks of the barn walls brought her to her knees. She flicked bits of hay from her face and hair, and clambered to her feet. At the open barn door, she shivered and clasped her arms in front of her. The wind whistled through the bare limbs of the trees and an owl gave a triumphant hoot. Nessa closed the door behind her and raced through the garden to the kitchen door. She paused to peer through the glass and saw only darkness. She slipped inside and tiptoed to the dining room. The faint light from a lamp and muted voices coming from the parlor drew her steps forward. She stood motionless in the doorway for a moment, then recoiled at Mama's voice.

"Nessa, dear! Where have you been?"

Papa looked up from his newspaper and frowned. "What's going on, young lady? You didn't even say hello to Sam."

"Sam? Where is he?"

"Sam left, Nessa. It's late and he had to get home. He said to tell you…"

"Sam's gone?" Her voice rose and broke. She raised her hands to her cheeks and her eyes widened. "Oh, no!" She raced to the stairs and up to her room, where, for the second time in two hours, she flung herself face down, this time on her bed, and sobbed.

CHAPTER 24

Sam pushed the mules as fast as he dared in the darkness. His body ached, his heart throbbed, his thoughts pained his soul, and his soul pleaded for peace. The cold wind at his back added to his misery, and he yelled at the animals carrying him away from his dreams, from Nessa. Reaching home at last, he performed the necessary chores in the dark by habit, then made his way down the dugout steps, removed his boots and fell on his bed, not bothering to light the lantern. Sounds of protest erupted from his stomach, but he ignored them, pulled the quilts over his head, and prayed. "Jesus. I'm too tired and discouraged to talk to You tonight. Please forgive me and let me have a night of rest. I'll see You in the morning. Amen." He closed his eyes and forced his mind to invoke images of his childhood. Fishing in the river with a cane pole, playing games with his brothers—

He awoke in a tangle of bedcovers, sat up, rubbed his eyes, and began a new, but troubling, day. By the time he poured a second cup of coffee and huddled against the opening to the dugout for warmth, he had decided. Today, he would visit Mrs. Basetti. He would keep his promise to Clem. After chores, he found an old knapsack and filled it with dried beans, some dried apples, a slab of bacon, and a tin of tea.

Dressed in his warmest clothes, with an old shawl wrapped around his neck and chin, leaving only his eyes visible beneath the down-turned brim of his hat, he urged Gallatin into the wind. The sun shone, with a few puffy clouds here and there, but the stiff breeze from the north hinted at snow.

Smoke billowing from the fireplace chimney brought a grin to his face, when he topped the rise and viewed the lonely homestead below. He rode Gallatin to the corral and removed his saddle and bridle. Then he picked up the knapsack, ambled to the little adobe house, and knocked on the door.

A white-faced Katerina peeked around the edge of the lace curtain, then disappeared. The door opened and her smile brightened her thin cheeks.

"Mr. Jackson. How nice of you to call." She stood to the side of the door and beckoned him inside.

Sam smiled, removed his hat, and entered. "Thought I'd drop by and make sure you were doing all right, Mrs. Basetti." She turned to close the door and Sam's breath became ragged and his eyes widened, as he noticed the change in her tiny figure. He frowned. How should he handle his knowledge? Ignore it? *Help me, Lord.*

"Would you like some coffee, and a bowl of chicken soup?" Katerina started toward the kitchen, speaking over her shoulder. "I am ready to have a meal."

Sam grinned in relief. "Chicken soup sounds mighty fine. Let me help you."

Katerina stopped and looked back at him with a frown. "Oh, no. You sit at the table and I will bring the food."

Sam sat, dropped his sack of food on the floor, and ran his hands through his hair. *Clem, do you know about this? What would you have me do? When are you coming home?*

"Here is hot soup and bread." Katerina set a steaming bowl and plate in front of him. "Fresh coffee will appear soon." She left and returned with a small dish and sat opposite him. "Your young lady, she is all right?"

Sam struggled to hide his emotions. "Oh, yes. Nessa is fine. She's pretty busy with Christmas coming. Maybe she will come later."

Katerina nodded and bowed her head. "You will say the blessing on the food?"

Sam prayed, then ate in silence, wondering what to say. From time to time he noticed Katerina shyly peeked up at him from under her eyelashes.

"The soup is very good, and sure hits the spot after being out in the cold."

She smiled. "You would like more?"

Sam shook his head. "No, thanks. That was plenty." She left the room and returned with two cups. Sam sipped and nodded. "Good." He felt foolish when he couldn't seem to form his tongue into words. *If only Nessa was here. She could handle this situation.* He sighed and noticed the sack laying beside his chair. "I brought a few supplies I thought you might be able to use." He brought out each item and set them on the table.

Katerina's eyes widened. "But, no…I…You must not…"

"Oh, it's nothin' much. Not near worth what that soup meant to me." He grinned and lifted his coffee cup.

Katerina sat, looking thoughtful, then nodded and smiled. "Thank you, Mr. Jackson, and you're welcome, too." She picked up the offering and carried it to the kitchen. In a moment she returned with a blue enameled coffee pot and a plate of cookies.

Sam watched her refill his cup then selected one of the plump sugary rounds. His eyes widened in surprise as he bit into it. He held it up for inspection. "What's inside, chopped raisins?"

Katerina smiled and nodded. "You like them? I will send them with you. I made a big batch from raisins Mama sent. You give some to your young lady, Nessa. All right?"

Before Sam could protest, she sped to the kitchen and brought out two packages wrapped in sugar sacks. Sam accepted them with thanks, then shuffled his feet under the table and sighed.

"When do you expect Clem to get back?"

Katerina smiled but her eyes seemed sad. "Soon now. March maybe."

Sam tried to hide his concern. "March. Well, the time will pass faster than you think." He rose and studied her upturned face. "I have to go, now, but I'll be back soon." He walked to the rocker where his coat and hat lay. A frown creased his brow. He slipped on his coat, picked up his hat and turned back to her. "Is there anything I can do for you? Anything you need? Wood chopped or anything at all?"

"Thank you, no." She smiled and brushed one delicate hand across the front of her skirt. "I have all I need. I do fine."

Sam opened the door. "Take care of yourself, then. I'll try to come by next week."

"Yes. Very good. Perhaps Miss Nessa will come."

"Perhaps." Sam closed the door and strode toward the corral. Although the sun still shone, the wind seemed colder and dark clouds appeared on the distant northern horizon. He saddled Gallatin and started home with a troubled heart. When he turned south to travel the last four miles home, the sun seemed to have lost the last of its heat. He turned up the collar on his coat and hunched his head lower into its warmth. Home, at last, he built a fire in the old range and sat in front of the oven toasting his toes and mulling ideas over in his mind.

A half hour later, when he had no answers to his questions, he sighed and fixed a hearty supper of potatoes, beans and corn cakes. After eating, he did the outside chores, then sat near the fire reading his Bible until bedtime. The Word of God filled his heart with tranquility, and he thanked his Lord and climbed into bed.

Before sunrise the next morning, he drove the mules and wagon down the trail toward the railroad for another load of freight. Ice had covered the animals' water trough in the corral, during the night, and Sam had broken it up with a shovel, before adding more water from the well. Hank had promised to check on his animals this evening and tomorrow morning. Sam asked the Lord to protect them during his absence, then turned his attention to handling the powerful team tugging at the reins.

He arrived at the depot in late afternoon and had the wagon loaded by suppertime. As he walked toward the little rooming house, he glanced at the growing mushroom of clouds to the north. Talk at the table centered on the approaching storm. A couple of old-timers related tales of past December blizzards.

"Nope, we usually get only a smatterin' of snow before the middle of January, but I remember more'n twenty years ago." The old man waved his fork at those around him. "Just before Christmas it was, and a storm came out of nowhere. Caught people by surprise." His eyes narrowed and the fork clattered to his plate. He shook his grizzled head. "Was a bad year." He nodded, scooted back his chair, stood, and walked to the stairs leading to the sleeping rooms. Silence filled the room until the old man's footsteps faded, then there was a collective sigh, before anyone resumed eating. Sam sat quietly eating and listening as other stories unfolded.

When Sam entered the upstairs room with his bedroll over his shoulder, the dim light of the lantern in the hall pinpointed the storyteller, sitting on a blanket in one corner. He drank from the bottle in his hand, then stared at the floor.

"God keep you, mister," Sam said and carried his bedding to a far corner. He slept fitfully. Other men arrived at intervals, some on tiptoe, some boisterous. At the gray light of dawn, Sam rose and went downstairs. The owner's wife greeted him with a smile, poured him a hot cup of coffee, and went to cook his breakfast. Sam carried it to the single window facing south and peered into the morning. The weeds across the road stood upright, so apparently the wind had abated overnight. A good sign. His stomach growled at the smell of frying bacon, and he rubbed his belly and smiled in anticipation.

After finishing the generous portions of bacon, eggs, potatoes, and flapjacks, he dawdled a few minutes over a second cup of coffee, then thanked the lady, paid his bill, and left. He smiled at the pink and gold of the eastern sky and strode toward the freight office. By the time he turned the mules onto the road outside of town, a sliver of orange was sending feeble rays of promised warmth his way, but the sky in front of him loomed as black as coal.

He crossed the second creek about ten o'clock, according to his sun-reckoning. More than a third of the way home. A mile farther on, he brushed a flake of snow from his cheek by rubbing his face against his shoulder, then another, and then there were too many to dislodge. They melted, chilling his face, and dripping onto his legs. His skin cooled, and the snowflakes collected on the exposed area between his hat and muffler. The wind strengthened, and he turned his head to the side to breathe. The mules slowed.

Sam squinted into the whiteness around him, searching for a place of shelter. Nothing was visible more than ten yards away, and he could see no familiar landmark. How far had he come since crossing the creek? He didn't know. Time, as well as sight, seemed to be suspended in whiteness. One of the animals stumbled and cried out. Sam pulled on the reins and turned off the trail. Almost immediately ghostly shapes appeared in front and to the side. Sam stood on stiffened legs and yelled. "Thank you, Lord." He reined the mules in further and maneuvered them and the heavy wagon downhill amidst the grove of trees. If he could get close to the creek, the far bank would provide some shelter.

He could go no farther. Huge cottonwoods surrounded the wagon. Sam jumped down, unhitched the mules and tied them with long ropes. Then he gathered wood and built a fire on the lee side of a huge trunk. He hunkered in front of it, willing his body to inhale it's warmth, and contemplated his survival.

He watched the animals turn their backs to the wind-driven snow, and stand almost touching each other. By God-given instinct, they would take advantage of each other's body heat. There seemed no practical way for him to join them. He frowned and mentally searched the inventory in the supplies in the wagon. All sorts of foodstuffs, so he wouldn't starve. His frown turned to a grim smile.

He stamped his feet and left his meager shelter. Immediately snow filtered down his neck. He hunched his shoulders and strode to the back of the wagon. In a few minutes he had unloaded several wooden crates of supplies and stacked them two-high in a u-shape under the wagon. His throat and lungs ached from breathing the frigid air, his eye-lids were ice-encrusted, and his nose, hands and feet felt numb. Squinting into the eerie light, he stumbled once more to the wagon, and removed a piece of canvas and an armload of blankets.

Inside the structure under the wagon, he scraped snow to the sides, positioned half of the canvas on the ground, and placed several folded blankets in the center. Then he removed his hat and boots, sat on the blankets, unfolded three more, and wrapped them around his body, pulled the surplus canvas over his head, tucked it in, and prepared to wait out the storm.

❦   ❦   ❦

Tuesday morning Nessa took a deep breath before entering the kitchen, stretched her lips into a wide smile, and waltzed in to greet her parents.

"Morning, Mama, Papa." She paused by each of their chairs, in turn, and dropped kisses on their cheeks. "Mm, that coffee smells good and I'm hungry."

"Nessa, what—?"

"Don't bother, Mama. I'll fix my own breakfast." She moved to the range, humming a tune. "It's so good to see you up, Mama. Did you have a good night? How about you, Papa, did you sleep well?"

"We're fine, Nessa. What did you mean—?"

"Oh, I guess I better wake Opal. That little sleepyhead would stay in bed till noon." She started toward the dining room, avoiding looking at her parents. "Don't wait for us, I'll take care of our food in a little while."

She stopped at the foot of the steps, blinked her eyes and sniffed. Papa should have gone to the store by the time she returned, but evading her mother's questions would be much more difficult. She slowly climbed the stairs. Sam rarely came on Tuesday, and Wednesday he would go for more supplies. At best he would be back late Thursday. A sob escaped from between the thin line of her lips. *Almost three days. I can't stand it. I can't.*

The strain of appearing cheerful to her family exhausted her. Mama had sent questioning looks her way at intervals all day, but Nessa had ignored them. At supper, Papa had kept the conversation light, teasing Opal, and relating news from customers.

Opal chattered during the kitchen cleanup and seemed satisfied with an occasional sound of agreement from her sister.

"That's fine, Opal. I'll finish the rest." Nessa took the tea towel and hung it on the rack.

"Thanks, Nessa." Opal beamed her a smile and hurried from the kitchen as though Nessa might change her mind, bringing a faint smile to Nessa's face.

Oh, to be a child again, without a care in the world. She sighed and began to scrub the top of the range with vigor.

She hung her apron on a hook, walked into the parlor, and covered her forehead with the palm of one hand. "I'm going to bed now to try to get rid myself of this headache. Goodnight, Mama, Papa, Opal. See you in the morning."

Mama frowned. "Headache? Would you like some hot tea, dear, or warm milk?"

"No thank you, Mama. I'll just sleep it away." She mounted the stairs, made her way to her room, and undressed in the dark. After slipping between the chilly sheets with a shiver, she wrapped her feet in the long tail of her gown, folded her hands under her chin, and prayed.

"Jesus, please show me the way to make things right with Sam. Why do I keep doing things wrong? Hurting myself and those I love? I didn't mean those words I said to Sam. Please forgive me and please let Sam forgive me, too. I love him, Jesus." She paused to wipe her eyes with a fist. "I love You, too. Please help me to show it. Please. Amen."

Wednesday duplicated Tuesday even to the headache in the early evening. Nessa noticed the concerned looks on her parents' faces, but felt she couldn't confide in them until she had faced Sam and found forgiveness in his eyes.

Wind, whistling through the half-inch opening of her window, woke her at dawn on Thursday. She crept out of bed onto the icy floor, closed and latched the window, and peered out into the darkness. A few flakes of snow spit against the glass. She shivered and returned to her warm bed.

Two hours later she stood at the kitchen door staring at the snow encrusted glass pane. She turned the knob and tugged. When the door creaked open, globs of snow fell onto the floor. The screen looked like it had been covered with cotton wool. She pushed against it. It didn't budge, but the dislodged snow let her view the foot-high drift on the steps. *Oh, Sam. Where are you?* She grabbed the broom and swept snow from the floor over the threshold, then closed the door and stood with her back to it. She lifted her hands to her mouth in supplication, and closed her eyes. "Please, Father, let Sam be safe at the railway depot."

Papa closed the store at noon and struggled back and forth between the wood pile and the kitchen bringing in armload after armload of firewood. Opal and Nessa stacked it neatly against the wall on a scrap of canvas and swept snow down the passageway to the storage shed and outside. Rebecca handed Papa cups of hot coffee between trips. They toiled more than an hour.

Supper time came and the blizzard raged on. Rebecca closed off the rest of the house from the kitchen, to conserve heat and fuel. They sat, huddled at the table and shrouded in shawls. Papa asked the Lord to bless the food and added a prayer of protection on all the families in the path of the storm. He petitioned Jesus to help any travelers who had been caught outside shelter, specifically naming Sam Jackson.

After eating a dish of hearty chicken stew, Papa took a lantern to inspect the rooms upstairs. Mama sighed and rose to clear the table.

"It's my turn to wash," said Opal. She jumped up, grabbed glasses and headed for the dishpan.

Nessa's mouth gaped. "No, it isn't Opal. It's my turn."

"It would be, but I owe you a turn. You took mine when I fell and twisted my ankle last month. I'll pay it back tonight."

Nessa looked at her mother. Mama's lips quivered and her eyes twinkled. "Make sure you use hot water, Opal."

"Oh, I will, Mama." She emptied the kettle of water into the pan, then held her hands over the steam and smiled. "Ah, that feels good. Too bad I can't get my feet up here."

Nessa laughed. "Why you little schemer!"

Opal performed a little dance, causing her braids to swing, and plunged her hands into the soapy water.

"I think we'd better sleep down here tonight." Papa set the lantern on the table and walked toward the range, rubbing his hands. "Snow has blown through the cracks around the north windows, and drifted inside." He gazed at Rebecca. "Can you manage on the floor if I bring a mattress down?"

"Mercy, Owen. Of course, I can. You needn't carry down a mattress. I'll just get all the quilts off the beds and in the closet. We'll make one huge pallet for all of us. We'll be warmer that way."

Papa frowned. "Are you sure, Rebecca? You have to take care of yourself." He went to her side and took her hands in his.

Mama smiled up at Papa. "I'll be fine. It won't be the first time I've slept on the floor."

"Well…" His gaze held hers and he rubbed his chin. "All right. You stay here. Nessa can help me get the bedding."

"But who's going to dry the dishes?" Opal turned to face the others with her mouth in full pout.

Mama shook her head. "I'll dry, Opal." She lifted the stack of plates in front of her, and carried them to the cabinet. "Better get started on these before the water gets cold."

The pile of quilts covered most of the open space in the kitchen. Mama heated flatirons on the range, wrapped them in blankets, and stuffed them between the covers. Papa waited in the dining room while the girls removed their outer garments, donned flannel gowns warmed in front of the fire, and slipped into the makeshift bed, tucking the quilts under their chins. Papa returned, blew out the lantern, and joined his family on the far side of Rebecca. Nessa yawned and watched the light from the flames inside the range flicker across the room, and cast eerie shadows on the walls. Then she closed her eyes and thought of Sam.

The sound of papa stoking the fire woke Nessa. She thrust her arms against the heavy covers and sat up.

"What time is it, Papa?" She kept her voice low so not to wake Opal and Mama, who still slept beyond her, with only the crowns of their heads visible.

Papa turned his head and peered toward her in the dim light. "Nessa? Sorry I woke you. It's a little after five." He added another stick of wood to the firebox.

"Is it still snowing?"

"Appears to be, but I think the wind's died down a little. I could only open the storage door a few inches. There are drifts out there more than ten feet high. I hope the chicken house isn't completely covered."

At Nessa's deep intake of breath, Papa stepped away from the stove and faced her. "Are you all right?"

"Yes, Papa. I was just thinking of Sam." Her voice broke into a sob.

"Oh, well, Sam Jackson is a man who knows how to take care of himself. You can bet he's at the railway depot swapping stories with the other guests, or holed up somewhere waiting out the storm. Besides, we asked the Lord to watch over him." He smiled, and pointed his index finger toward the ceiling. "You have to have faith, Nessa."

Nessa sniffed. "Yes. You have to have faith." Did she have enough?

After breakfast, Papa managed to clear a narrow path to the chicken house. Nessa, wrapped in several layers, followed, awkwardly tramping the remaining snow into a fairly level surface with her boots. A snow mountain filled half the space from the roof in the back, to within a few inches of the door. The red rooster and his dozen hens huddled together on the near roost and cocked beady eyes their way when Papa wrenched open the door.

"They seem to be all right. Likely the tips of their combs are frozen, though." He scraped at the snow, and swung the door wider. "Can you bring them a little water from the kitchen? I can't get into the well-house yet." He wiped snow from his moustache and picked up his spade. "Their feed will have to wait until I get to the barn."

Nessa nodded and turned back toward the house. Snow still fell heavily, but the force of the wind had lessened somewhat. The flakes were driven in a more slanted pattern now rather than horizontally.

By noon, the animals had been cared for, and fresh water carried to the house. Nessa brought a basket of frozen and cracked eggs to her mother. "Papa wondered if you could use these."

Mama rinsed some of the eggs, put them in a pan of water, and set them on the fire. "Guess we'll have hard-boiled eggs for a day or so, and perhaps I'll make custard with the rest. The hens probably won't lay again for a week or more." She went to Nessa and placed her palms on her daughter's red cheeks. "Mercy, you're half frozen, child! Get those wet things off and stand by the fire." She poured a cup of coffee. "Drink this. When is your Papa coming inside?"

Nessa struggled out of her boots and mittens. "He told me to come in. Said he'd be right along."

Mama sighed. "I've not seen such a storm in all the years we've been here."

"Papa says it's weakening. Still snowing, but the wind has dropped."

"Your father won't be able to fetch Ellie home for Christmas. The roads are too bad." Rebecca wiped at her eyes with the corner of her apron. "We've never been separated at Christmas time. And she'll be with strangers."

Nessa put her arms around her mother. "I know. I'll miss her, too. But at least we know she's safe."

Mama stiffened, then hugged Nessa. "Sam will be all right, too, dear. God will answer our prayers."

Nessa spent the afternoon helping her mother, reading, and making periodic trips to the window in the parlor. She would lift the heavy curtain, scrape frost from the glass with her handkerchief, and peer into the white world, searching for a team of mules and a wagon. At dusk her faith plummeted and the welling tears cascaded down her cheeks. Several minutes passed before the chill in the unheated room forced her to dab at her face, and return to her family in the kitchen.

CHAPTER 25

Sam jerked his head up and blinked rapidly. He must have nodded off. He shifted his cramped legs to one side and drew out his pocket watch. Two o'clock, must be early Friday morning, though inside his canvas cocoon there was no difference between day and night. His ears caught the whistle of wind. Apparently the blizzard's fury continued.

He stretched in the confinement of his blankets. "You have to stay awake, Sam. Your business isn't finished. There's Nessa and Mrs. Basetti, too. You owe them." A sardonic grin split his lips and he shook his head. "If anyone could see me right now. Sitting underneath a wagon, wrapped up like a mummy, and talking to myself." Sounds of protest erupted from his stomach, and he sighed. "Guess I'd rather listen to my own voice than that." He rubbed his belly. "Go back to sleep. I'll try to find something to satisfy you as soon as it's light."

His thoughts returned to Nessa. For the tenth time, he tried to visualize their next conversation. He would apologize and reassure her that she came first. She would…what? Once she had been eager to apologize after one of their misunderstandings. Another time, she had interrupted him with a laugh and said it wasn't important. Then, again, she might poke her impish little nose into the air and refuse to listen to him. He sighed. *Will I ever know the way her mind works? Probably not.* He licked his chapped lips. *Better to think about something else.*

Mrs. Basetti. Did she have enough firewood in this storm? The thought of her struggling through the snow, in her condition, to care for her chickens and cow, sent a chill down his spine. He bowed his head. "God, I can't help her right now. Sort of need some help from You, myself. So, will You keep a close eye on her for a day or two? I'll get there as soon as I can."

He clenched and unclenched his hands and wriggled his numb toes to boost his blood circulation. "And, if You're not too busy, Lord, maybe You could put a thought in Nessa's head to go with me. You know Mrs. Basetti needs a woman to talk to. Nessa's young, but she has a kind and generous heart. It's the best idea I can come up with right now, and Nessa may need a little prodding from You to agree to it. Course, You may have a better plan." He frowned. "If You do, could You let me in on it? It's been plaguing me all night."

He checked his watch. Seven o-clock. "Okay, Sam. You better get out there and check on the mules." He pulled on his boots, released a corner of the canvas, and crawled through the breach between the crates. He brushed drifted snow to the side, and wormed his way out from under the wagon. On his feet, he squinted against the curtain of undulating white, and barely discerned four dark forms standing motionless by a tree. His sigh of relief created a circle of fog in front of his face.

"Thank you, Lord, for these sturdy mules." He stomped through and over drifts that reached his knees, and arrived at the tree breathing heavily. Ice encased the animals' bridles, and their long eyelashes were frozen to the hair below their eyes, blinding them. He moaned and touched two of the frosty noses with either hand. "Hang in there, old friends."

After several tries, Sam coaxed a handful of dried grass to ignite in a hollow he scraped in the snow. Then he fed twigs, one by one, to the feeble flame, and finally placed branches atop the tiny heap in a teepee fashion. When the bark caught and flared, he smiled, and went to get the mules. They lived up to the name "stubborn", resisting his efforts to pull them near the fire. Minutes passed and Sam's strength waned as he struggled against the snow and wind. At last he succeeding in dragging the four animals near the fire. He took a rag from his coat pocket, warmed it at the fire, and gently massaged the area under one of the mule's eyes. Several applications melted the ice and he grinned at the intelligent brown eye staring at him. After restoring the mules sight, Sam melted snow in a bucket, satisfied his thirst, then gave the rest to the animals.

By mid-afternoon, the wind had lessened and snow fell sporadically. Sam climbed aboard one of the mules, grabbed the reins of the others in his free hand and headed north. He would see Nessa before nightfall.

Progress proved slow. First Sam forded the treacherous frozen creek, then out on the trail, he met the full force of the wind, forcing him to turn his head to the side to breathe. He allowed the mule he was riding to pick it's own way, always turning it back into the wind after detouring around one of the huge drifts that frequently obliterated the trail.

Sam's body slumped low on the mule's neck. His right hand gripped the reins loosely, and he no longer cared where the animal took him. The sight of his left hand clutching additional reins seemed foreign to him. He blinked his eyes trying to remember. It didn't matter. His head sank lower.

Nessa seemed to be standing in front of him, beckoning. When he reached for her, she slipped farther away. He tried to call to her, but no sound came from his throat. The abrupt suspension of rhythmic motion underneath him jolted his body to the side, and he felt himself falling. An eerie braying sound disintegrated into nothingness.

❦   ❦   ❦

Owen sat in his rocker in the parlor re-reading a month old newspaper. He nestled further into the shawl around his shoulders, then glanced at the fire he had built. Flames licked at the stacked logs and gradually overcame the chill of the room. He smiled at the chatter of Rebecca and the girls cleaning up the kitchen. This evening, they would be able to have their usual family time in the parlor.

He rose to his feet, went to the front door, and stepped out on the porch. A frown furrowed his brow at the sight of the frozen landscape. The snow had ceased, but the wind moaned through the bare branches of the trees. A quarter moon and myriads of stars pierced the frosty air. *Where was Sam?* Owen had felt sure he would appear by dusk. He stiffened at the sound of a muted shriek, and peered toward the barn, but saw only shadows from the trees. He shook his head.

"What's wrong, Papa?" He turned at the sound of Nessa's voice.

"I was just checking the weather. A cold clear night." He stepped inside and started to close the door. "Thought I heard something, though. Strange." He stood undecided.

"What did you think you heard, Papa?"

Owen shook his head and pursed his lips. "I don't know. Could have been a screech owl, I guess, but…" He wrenched his coat off the rack, pulled a woolen cap over his head, and jerked the door wide. "It could have been a mule." He turned back from the open door to his daughter. "Nessa, get a lantern and bring it to the barn."

Nessa stood staring at her father, with her mouth gaping.

"Hurry, child." Owen went through the opening, slammed the door and raced down the steps. The cold seemed to steal the heat from his body by the time he turned the corner towards the corral. He slowed and took several ragged breaths. The sight of the mules lengthened his stride, and icy dread filled his heart. He spotted the dark mound on the ground and hurried even faster.

"Sam! Is that you?" He knelt beside the motionless body lying face down, grabbed an arm and pulled. Sam's ashen face caught the faint moonlight and Owen gasped.

"Papa?"

"Over here, Nessa. Hurry."

Nessa appeared by his side and the glare of the lantern revealed the accumulation of ice particles around Sam's nose and mouth. His eyes were closed. The lantern crashed to the ground and Nessa moaned, and covered her face with her hands.

Owen gently shook her by the arms. "Help me get him to the house, Nessa."

She lifted Sam's torso while Owen knelt in front of him and heaved him onto his shoulder. Nessa retrieved the lantern and led the way to the house.

She opened the door and screamed. "Mama! Come quickly. It's Sam. He's..." Her voice broke into a sob. "I think he's dead!"

Rebecca rushed into the room just as Owen draped Sam's body on the sofa, and stood catching his breath. She touched Sam's face and her face puckered. She took a deep breath and turned to her daughter.

"Nessa, close the door, and take off your coat. We must work quickly." She started toward the stairs. "Fetch a basin of warm water with a rag. Tell Opal to make strong tea with lots of sugar and put the irons on to heat. Owen see if you can get his boots and coat off."

Rebecca returned with an armload of blankets. Owen helped her wrap them around Sam's inert body.

"Rub his feet, Owen, gently. Especially the toes." She cupped one of Sam's hands in hers and moved them in a circular motion over the stiff fingers. When a white-faced Nessa returned with a steaming pan, Rebecca set her to massaging his other hand. Then she wrung out the cloth and began to wipe Sam's face with the same gentle motion.

After fifteen minutes of loving ministration Sam's eyes flickered and his lips moved in a low moan. Owen heaved a big sigh and Rebecca gave him a tiny smile. Nessa let go of his hand and fell across his chest clutching at his arms. "Sam! Oh, thank God!" Tears streamed down her face.

Owen drew her to her feet. "He needs rest, Nessa."

"Go see about the tea, Nessa." Rebecca lifted the mound of blankets and touched Sam's feet and ankles. "I don't think anything is frozen. I'll go get the irons."

Owen reached for his coat and cap. "You seem to have everything under control. I need to go take care of the mules." He made his way to the corral, opened the gate and led the animals inside. After fetching a pail of water and holding it while they drank, he put them in the barn and forked hay into a trough. They chewed energetically as he watched, and he smiled. They seemed to be recovering from their ordeal.

When he re-entered the house, Nessa was holding a dish of tea while her mother forced a few spoonfuls into Sam's slack mouth. Owen removed his heavy outer clothing and blew on his hands. When they had warmed, he arranged blanket-wrapped hot irons near Sam's feet and on either side of his legs. Opal appeared and stood a few feet from the sofa, moaning and wringing her hands.

"Opal, dear." Rebecca smiled at her youngest daughter. "Go to bed, now. Sam should be better by morning."

Opal sniffed and in a teary voice, said, "Goodnight Mama. Goodnight Papa and Nessa."

Rebecca rose from her kneeling position and stretched her shoulders and neck. "You two should go to bed, too. I'll stay with Sam. Owen, would you bring my rocker near the sofa?"

Owen took Mama in his arms and kissed her tired-looking face."Rebecca, you must get your rest. I'll stay. Just tell me what to do."

"No, Mama and Papa." Nessa set the tea on the side table and faced her parents with her hands on her hips. "I'm staying. Please don't try to dissuade me."

Owen's eyes widened at the determination in his daughter's eyes. Then he smiled. "I guess that would be best." He gazed into his wife's eyes. "Don't you think so?"

Rebecca hesitated and Owen winked. "I...perhaps so." She turned to Nessa. "Make sure he stays covered and try to get more tea into him every hour." She frowned in thought. "You'll need to reheat the irons before morning."

Nessa nodded. "Yes, Mama."

Rebecca gazed at her daughter and nipped at her lower lip with her teeth. "Are you sure you're up to staying awake all night?"

"Yes, Mama. I'm sure." Nessa low voice echoed the determination of her stance.

"All right, dear. Remember to come wake me if you need me." She sighed, rubbed her hand against her cheeks and gazed at her husband. "Mercy, I am a little tired."

Owen took her arm and led her up the stairs. Half-way up, he turned to meet Nessa's gaze and gave her a nod and a smile.

❧   ❧   ❧

Nessa clutched one of Sam's limp hands in her right hand, and bit the fingernails on her left hand to the quick. She stared at Sam's pale face ringed by dark hair and bristly whiskers. He lay so still with a barely perceptible rise and fall of his breast. The occasional pop of the logs in the fireplace were the only sound, and a bitter bile of fear rose in her throat. *Father, please make him well. I love him. Please don't take him from me.*

Sam moved his head side to side and moaned. Nessa dipped a spoonful of tea and hoped a few drops made it inside his mouth. She watched his Adam's apple bob up and down as he swallowed and sighed with relief. Thus encouraged, she forced the spoon between his lips and teeth again and again, then renewed her lonely vigil.

A chilly draft brought her to her feet. She glanced at the dying fire, hastily added more logs, and stoked the embers into a blaze. She arched her back, then pushed stray wisps of hair from her face. A frown narrowed her eyes, and she ran her fingers the length of her dark tresses. They felt oily and lank. She glanced at Sam. He would surely wake in the morning. He mustn't see her with dirty hair. She moved to the sofa and gazed down at him. She gnawed at her bottom lip, then raced to the kitchen.

She stoked the fire in the range, filled the kettle and put it on to heat, then hurried back to the parlor. Sam appeared to be the same. Could she safely leave him for a few minutes? She hesitated a moment before rushing back to the kitchen. When the side of the kettle felt warm to her touch, she poured water into a basin, removed the pins from her hair, and made a lather with the lye soap. After rinsing and drying her hair. She took an old cloth from a drawer and tore it into narrow strips.

Back in the parlor, she adjusted the blankets, then sat beside Sam. She combed strands of hair, twisted them with strips of cloth and tied the ends. By morning, her hair would be shining and curly.

Sam stirred and she trickled more tea into his mouth. She wiped his chin with a cloth and looked up to find his brown eyes gazing at her. She smiled. His mouth moved and she bent lower to hear.

"You…court…jester…picture…book…?"

Nessa raised her head and shook her head. *What did he mean? Court jester?* She frowned. Was he delirious? Should she call her mother. She peered at Sam's closed eyes and blinked. Had she imagined he had opened his eyes and spoke? She took his hand in hers and felt a faint quiver in his fingers. She searched his face. His cheeks seemed to have a tinge of pink, not that deathly gray. A tiny laugh emerged from deep inside her, and she whispered, "Sam. Do you hear me? It's Nessa." Her shoulders slumped when he didn't respond and she plopped down in her chair.

"Nessa, dear? Are you awake?" Mama's voice entered Nessa's consciousness and she opened her eyes and raised her head.

"Oh, Mama. I must have dozed off." Her gaze shifted to Sam's face. "I think Sam's better, Mama. His breathing seems easier and last night he opened his eyes and spoke." She frowned and gazed into her mother's concerned eyes. "At least I think he did."

Mama raised her eyebrows. "You're not sure?"

Nessa sighed. "I don't know. It seemed so real, but he said something about a court jester…Do you think he was delirious?"

Mama laughed softly. "When did you wash your hair, Nessa?"

Nessa lifted her hands to her head, and grinned. "I didn't want Sam to see my dirty hair."

"Go look in the mirror, Nessa. And imagine yourself being ill and half-awake."

Puzzled, Nessa rushed to the washing room and peered into the little mirror. A shaft of light, from the candle she held, illuminated the rag-wrapped coils encircling her head. She gasped and hurried back to the parlor. "Mama, you won't tell him, will you? What I look like?'

Rebecca smiled. "Mercy, child, I doubt he'll remember, but if he does, you may have to explain." She picked up the dish from the table. "I'll get some hot soup and take over now. You go upstairs and change clothes and fix your hair. Papa will be down soon."

Nessa dressed in a fresh pink cotton dress, and brushed her curls after releasing them from their wrappings. Back downstairs, she watched Mama coax soup into Sam's mouth, then went to the kitchen to start breakfast. She felt ravenous. Joy lifted her feet in a little dance and her heart sang. Sam was here. She would apologize and everything would be all right again. She nibbled on a slice of bread and butter while sipping coffee, and devoured the first piece of crisp bacon from the skillet.

When her parents began to eat, she returned to the parlor, and sat holding one of Sam's hands, willing his eyes to open. She turned his hand palm up and ran her fingers over the callouses, thinking how hard he worked so they could marry. She blinked to staunch the welling tears, then stared without comprehension as Sam's fingers curled around hers. Her gaze darted to his face to meet his warm brown eyes.

"Sam!" She threw herself across his chest and sobbed.

"Nessa. Little girl. I came back to you."

CHAPTER 26

Bundled in a quilt, and sitting on the sofa, Sam fidgeted at the unaccustomed attention. Nessa perched on a low stool at his feet and the rest of the family stood in a half-circle displaying varying emotions as he related his adventures of the last three days. When he finished speaking, he leaned his head back and closed his eyes as weariness overcame him.

"I'm afraid this has been too much for Sam." Rebecca's voice sounded far away. "Owen help him to lie down. Nessa plump the pillows. He needs rest now."

Reluctantly, Sam submitted to Owen's ministrations and sighed when his head sank into the down-filled pillow.

"Sam, if you're up to it, just tell me about how many miles away you left the wagon. I'll get some help and see if we can bring it home."

He opened one eye and peered up at Owen. "Just on the south side of the second creek in the stand of trees to the west of the road. About fifteen miles, I reckon."

Owen nodded and patted Sam on the shoulder. "Good enough. You sleep now."

※   ※   ※

Sam breathed in the cold air through his nose, and tried to wiggle his numb toes. He rubbed a gloved hand across his frosted eyebrows and lashes and squinted into the darkness. The snow hid all identifying landmarks, but he felt certain he was near the general store. The mules apparently felt so, too, for they quickened their pace. "Just a little longer. I gotta' hold out. Gotta get to Nessa…"

"Sam? You awake?"

Sam forced his eyes open.

"Partner, am I glad to see you!" Hank squatted beside the sofa and gripped Sam's right arm. "You near scared the life out of me."

"Howdy, Hank. What are you doing here?" Sam forced his cracked lips into a smile.

"What am I...? I been looking for you all day. Searched the road down several miles, then came up here to find out if Mr. Long had any news." He shook his head. "What am I doing? What do you think, when you didn't make it home?"

"Yeah, well, I didn't do too good. Had to leave the wagon."

Hank snorted, then gazed into Sam's bloodshot eyes and smiled. "Guess you did real good, Sam. You brought yourself in."

Sam closed his eyes and swallowed hard.

Hank punched him lightly in the upper arm. "You rest. I'm going with Mr. Long to get the wagon. See you later."

"Hank? My animals?"

"Oh, they're all fine. When that storm hit, I high-tailed it over to your place and stayed there for two days. Got the livestock penned with plenty food. Had some chore getting the pump to work yesterday, but finally got water. And ole Gallatin, he misses you somethin' terrible. On the way back, I'll ride over and fetch him up here for you, if you want."

"Thanks, Hank." He rolled onto his side and closed his eyes

❧   ❧   ❧

A soft touch on his hand woke Sam. He opened his eyes and gazed into Nessa's smiling face.

"How are you feeling? Would you like to come to the table to eat your dinner?"

Sam raised his head and started to swing his legs over the side of the sofa, then thrust them back under the quilt.

"Where are my pants?"

Nessa felt heat rise in her cheeks, and she gasped. "Oh! I'll go ask Mama. Be right back."

Sam grinned. He felt good. And hungry. Hank came in with his clothes slung over one arm. "Mrs. Long said you might need these." He held them up at arm's length. "You feel like wrestling for 'em?"

Sam sat up and slid his legs to the floor. "Nope, but if you don't give 'em over, I'll take you on tomorrow."

Hank chuckled and threw the pants and shirt into Sam's lap. "Guess you're about fit—gettin' ornery."

Sam stood and slipped into his pants. "You and Mr. Long brought the wagon in? And Gallatin?"

"Yeah. That horse don't like to be led much. He's about as ornery as you."

Sam smiled and nodded. "What about the supplies? Did a lot of stuff get ruined?"

"Didn't appear so. We unloaded everything and Mr. Long said he'd go through the boxes tomorrow."

Sam tucked in his shirt and smoothed his hair with one hand. "Reckon I'm ready. At least my stomach is."

After dispatching a second plateful of ham and sweet potatoes, Sam leaned back in his chair and thanked Mrs. Long for the excellent meal.

"It's good to see you enjoying the food, Sam." She gazed around the table. "Is everyone ready for dessert? I made a custard with some of the eggs that froze during the storm." She rose and went to the kitchen and Nessa began to clear the table.

"Custard isn't a very appropriate dessert for Christmas Eve, but I spooned some rhubarb jam on top to make it more festive." Mrs. Long set dishes in front of everyone. Sam frowned.

Hank plunged his spoon into the custard. "Christmas Eve! I plumb forgot."

"Sam? You do like custard, don't you?" He lifted his gaze to Rebecca and picked up his spoon. "Sorry. Is it really Christmas Eve? I must have lost track of the days."

"Well, no wonder, with what you went through. It really is Christmas Eve, but don't fret. I almost forgot, too. Can you imagine not remembering such a special time?" Rebecca smiled and shook her head. "So, I have to make hay while the sun doesn't shine, and do a little baking for tomorrow, if we're to have a decent Christmas dinner." She gazed at Nessa then Sam. "If you don't mind too much, Sam, I could use Nessa's help for an hour, then I promise to send her to keep you company."

Sam ducked his head and shifted in his chair. "Thank you, ma'am."

Hank chuckled and slapped his thigh.

"Come Nessa, and you, too, Opal." She and her daughters collected the used dishes and left the room.

Owen pushed his chair back a few inches. "Well, now that the ladies have left us, we can talk business."

"Mr. Long, before we do, I have a question. Did you find a package under the wagon seat?"

Owen grinned. "As a matter of fact, I did find a package. Wondered about that. Wasn't anything in it I ordered."

"No sir. I bought that, personal." Sam leaned across the table to gaze into Owen's eyes. "Was it…uh…?"

"None of the items were damaged, Sam. I'll get the package for you in a little while. Right now I want to tell you how happy I am you're recovering, and let you know that most of the supplies came through the storm in good condition. I may lose a little feed that got wet, but, Son, the way you stacked and covered them saved about everything." Owen blinked several times and took a deep breath. "When I think of you out there for nearly two days, I…well, I just want to say thanks." He took out his handkerchief and blew his nose, then cleared his throat and looked at Hank. "And I want to thank you, Hank, for your help today. I doubt I could have done it by myself—moving all those crates from under the wagon and getting it all back here through the drifts. I know you said you couldn't accept payment, but I wish you'd reconsider."

Hank gave him a sheepish grin. "Shucks, Mr. Long, I just went along to help a little, but mostly to see how deep the snow was. Never seen anything like it before. Do you know some of them drifts were higher than my head?"

Sam nodded. "Appears I'm beholden to this rapscallion too, Mr. Long. If he hadn't cared for my animals, I'd likely have none to go home to. You see, sir, Hank sort of has a problem accepting that anything he does is purely out of the goodness of his heart, so he makes a joke of it."

Owen raised his eyebrows and studied Hank's red face. "Is that so? Afraid we'll think he's not so tough, eh? Well, I'll just say, Hank, that I think you're the sort of rugged man we need to build this country, and if I can ever be of help to you, you let me know. I owe you."

Sam grinned. "That goes for me too, friend."

Hank squirmed under their scrutiny. "Thanks Mr. Long, Sam." He shuffled to his feet. "Guess I better get on home. I'll check on your livestock, Sam, but I know they're all right. I gave them water and more feed when I fetched Gallatin."

"Now settle down, young fellow." Owen rose and placed a hand on Hank's arm. "No need for you to go out in this cold tonight. You stay here. That is, if you don't mind bunking on the floor with Sam."

Hank's gaze darted from Mr. Long to Sam and back to his host. He sighed. "Thank you Mr. Long. I was sorta dreadin' that long ride. Guess I can put up with your other house guest one night."

"Good. That's settled." Owen strode toward the kitchen. "I'll get your package now, Sam."

As soon as he left, Hank turned on Sam. "Why'd you want to tell him all that stuff for?"

"What are you talking about? I only told the truth."

Hank sputtered. "Truth! You know me better than anybody and I'm no…"

"No good? Is that so? Well, sit down, Hank, and let me tell you something. You're good enough for Mr. Long to invite to his table, you're good enough to be my best friend, and most of all, you're good enough for Jesus. Now that's the truth whether you like it or not."

Hank sat glaring at Sam for a full minute, then his eyes twinkled. He leaned back in his chair, grinning from ear to ear.

"Here you are, Sam." Owen entered and placed a parcel on the table.

Sam carefully untied the string and undid the wrapping, peeked inside, then refolded the paper, and uttered a sigh of relief. "Thanks, Mr. Long."

Nessa entered with cups in one hand and the coffeepot in the other. "Anyone like fresh coffee?" They nodded and she filled the cups and passed them around, then gazed at Sam and smiled. "Mama says she can do without me for a while, and Papa, she said if you and Hank will come into the kitchen, you might get to sample the sugar cookies she just took out of the oven."

Owen laughed. "Come on, Hank, let's see what's cooking."

"Sure thing, Mr. Long."

Nessa watched them leave, then smiled at Sam. "Do you want to go into the parlor?"

"Reckon I do." Sam rose, picked up his parcel, and followed her.

❧   ❧   ❧

Sometime in the night, Sam awoke and rearranged the quilts over himself and Hank who lay beside him, snoring gently. He closed his eyes, but something nagged at his thoughts. *Katerina! How could I have forgotten about her?* He frowned and turned on his side. *I wonder if she had enough firewood to get through the storm. If she had to go outside—.* His heart thumped. *Please, Lord, watch over her. I'm sorry I didn't check on her today. I'll go first thing in the morning. Just keep her safe, please. Amen.* He rolled onto his back and stared into the darkness.

❦   ❦   ❦

"Merry Christmas, Sam, Hank."

Sam sat up at Mrs. Long's words and rubbed his eyes. "Merry Christmas, ma'am." He poked Hank in the ribs and Hank groaned and pulled the quilts over his head.

"Breakfast will be ready in half an hour, then we'll open gifts." Mrs. Long crossed to the entrance to the dining room and disappeared.

Sam scrambled from the covers and hurriedly donned his pants and shirt, then sat on the make-shift bed to put on socks and boots. He shook the hump he assumed was Hank's shoulder. "Rise and shine, Hank. It's Christmas morning." He received a grunt in response, and began pulling off quilts and folding them.

"Hey! Leave off, man, it's still dark."

"Yeah, and two little girls are going to come down those stairs any minute, and you'll have to stay under there all day."

"Hmmph. Very funny."

"Merry Christmas to you, too."

Hank grumbled and reached for his pants.

❦   ❦   ❦

Nessa sat at the table, pushed her food around her plate with her fork, and stole glances at Sam. Her thoughts focused on wondering what present Sam had for her. He must be excited, too, for he hardly spoke, and ate quickly. How could any of them eat? Opal sat opposite her fidgeting. Papa and Hank talked about the storm between swallows and asking for more biscuits, butter, and jelly. She sighed.

Rebecca rose from her chair. "I thought we'd sing a few carols as soon as everyone's finished. I'll go find the music and get my fingers warmed up."

Nessa's shoulders slumped and she wondered at Sam's frown. She loved singing the Christmas songs, but once her mother started playing—

Sam laid his fork down and cleared his throat. "I'm sorry, ma'am, but I have to go do something. I'll try not to be more than a couple hours."

Mama stopped in mid-stride. Nessa gasped. "A couple…Sam, what do you mean?"

"Yes, Sam. I think you had better explain." Papa stared at Sam.

Sam's gaze swept from Mama to Papa and settled on Nessa. His brown eyes seemed to plead. "I have to check on somebody. Make sure they made it through the storm." He ducked his head and stood. "I'll be back as soon as I can. I'm sorry."

"You're going to see her, aren't you?" She pushed her chair back and faced him. "How could you? On Christmas!" She covered her mouth with one hand and ran toward the parlor. At the entrance, she turned around. "Well, go ahead, Sam Jackson. I don't care if you come back at all!"

"Nessa!" She ignored her mother's voice and stomped toward the stairs. She heard Hank say, "Can I help, Sam?" just before she entered her bedroom and slammed the door.

After a few minutes of lying sprawled across her bed in the unheated room and no sound of her mother coming to comfort her, Nessa moaned and sat up. A still small voice inside her pricked her conscience and she felt compelled to analyze her grievance. Were her actions impulsive? What had Sam actually done to hurt her? What had he said? "I have to check on somebody. Make sure they made it through the storm."

The memory of the slight blonde woman telling her about the alpine painting hanging in her home brought Nessa to her feet. She paced the small room, hugging her arms about her. The image of Katerina, alone, and the wind-driven snow penetrating the cracks under the door and windows, prompted a shudder throughout her body. Mist filled her blue eyes. She had given no thought to Katerina. But Sam had. Nessa sniffed and swiped at her eyes with a clenched fist. She slipped to her knees by the bed. "Father, forgive me for my selfishness, and please let Sam forgive me, too." Tears warmed her cold cheeks. "And please let Katerina be all right." She rested her head on the bedcover and felt the Lord's love envelop her. Feeling cleansed, she rose, wiped her face, and left the room.

The sound of her parents' laughter, and the spicy scent of mince pies, led her to the kitchen. Mama sat at the table paring potatoes, and Papa sat across from her slicing turnips.

"Nessa, dear. Are you all right? We thought it best to allow you to sort out your feelings without interference."

Nessa made a wry face. "I'm all right, Mama." She straightened her back and strode to the center of the kitchen, gazing first at one parent and then the other. "I want to apologize for my inexcusable behavior earlier. I'll apologize to Sam when he gets back." She pursed her lips and looked at her feet. "You didn't know, but Katerina's husband went back to work in the coal mines this winter. They needed the money to put in crops in the spring. She's been all alone and Sam promised Clem he would keep an eye on her." Her face crumpled and she licked at the tear that trickled to the corner of her mouth. "I didn't even think about her. All I cared about was finding out what Sam got me for Christmas. I'm sorry."

Mama lifted her burgeoning body from the chair, stepped to Nessa's side, and took her in her arms. "Everything will be all right, dear." She released her daughter and sighed. "I need to apologize, too. I'm at least as responsible as you are. My uncharitable words and actions weeks ago were uncivil and unchristian."

Nessa smiled through her tears, then hugged her mother.

Papa came and wrapped an arm around each of them. "Sam didn't want to tell us where he was going for fear of upsetting your mother, but he felt he had no choice. We straightened everything out. Your mother apologized to Sam, and sent Christmas greetings as well as some chicken soup and other things, to Katerina."

Mama backed away and her shining eyes blinked rapidly. "There's more, dear, that you don't know. Sam feels sure that Mrs. Basetti will have a child in a few months. That's another reason he was so concerned."

Nessa's mouth formed a big oval, then her eyes crinkled and a grin split her face. "How wonderful, and what a surprise for her husband when he gets home."

Papa returned to the bowl of turnips. "Sam and Hank should be back in an hour or so."

"Yes, and I need to have supper ready." Mama carried the pan of potatoes to the range. "They'll be hungry after their long ride."

"Mama, let me finish the potatoes." She looked at the trio of pies on the cabinet, and sighed. "You've been working while I lolled upstairs acting like a spoiled egg."

CHAPTER 27

Sam rode silently alongside Hank and squinted at the brilliance of the snowy landscape in the sunlight. His troubled thoughts darted from Nessa to Katrina and back again. His brow furrowed. He felt trapped in a snare between the two young women, owing to no fault of his own.

He glanced at his partner. Hank rode with his eyes nearly closed, and whistled tunelessly through his teeth. Nothing seemed to bother him for long. Troubles just slid off him like rain off the old slicker tied behind his saddle. *Maybe he has it right, and I'm wrong.* Sam shook his head. *No, that's not my way.* He sighed and urged Gallatin to greater effort.

Topping the hill, Sam reined his horse to a halt, and heaved a great sigh at sight of the spiral of smoke curling into the sky from the little structure below. He looked at Hank and smiled. "This is the place. Looks like she's all right. There's a fire."

Hank nodded and followed Sam. They tied their mounts to a post and strode up to the walk. Sam knocked.

A wary face peeped from behind the curtain of the window to their right. Sam tipped his hat and smiled. A moment later, Katerina opened the door. She wore a bulky shawl wrapped around her shoulders.

"Mr. Jackson! Merry Christmas." She eyed Hank. "And you brought a friend?"

"Yes, ma'am. This is Hank Moran. He homesteads just next to me."

Katerina acknowledged Hank's nod with a smile, and drew the door fully open. "Please, both of you. Welcome."

The men stepped inside. Sam removed his hat and held it chest high, fiddling with the brim with calloused fingers. "Guess Clem hasn't got back, yet?"

A shadow seemed to pass over Katerina's face, then the smile reappeared. "Not today." She gestured toward chairs. "Please make yourselves seated. I will brew the coffee." She hurried toward the kitchen.

Hank looked around the room, then walked to the table holding the chess set. "So this is the chess set you told me about." He picked up the white king and studied the workmanship. "Mighty fine work. Better'n anything I can do."

Sam nodded and frowned at the small stack of firewood next to the fireplace. "Be right back." He centered his hat on his head, strode toward the door, and went outside. He tramped through the snow to the side of the house, and around to the back. A chopping block lay on the wood-chip covered ground. An axe stood leaning against three or four uncut logs. He sighed, shrugged out of his coat, and picked up the axe.

"Sam? What the dickens are you doin'? Leavin' me to entertain a woman I don't know."

Sam straightened his back and rested his weight on the handle of the upright axe. "Thought you needed to brush up on your manners around a nice lady."

Hank snorted. "Give me that axe. She is a nice lady, and you go visit with her. I'll finish this little chore."

Sam loaded his arms with newly cut logs and headed for the front of the house. Inside, he stacked the logs then placed one on the feeble flames in the fireplace. Katerina entered the room and stood gaping at him. "Mr. Jackson! What you are doing? I can cut the wood."

Sam grinned. "No doubt you can, at least as good as me, but I needed a little exercise."

Katerina laughed. "You joke. But thank you. Now please, sit, and I bring hot coffee."

Sam sipped the fragrant liquid she set in front of him, and took a cookie from the plate she held out. "More of your raisin-filled cookies. They're about the best I've ever eaten."

"Thank you. It is an old family recipe." She placed the dish in front of him. "Please take another."

"Don't mind if I do." He munched and drank. "You had no trouble in the storm? Your animals are all right?"

"Oh, yes. The good Lord watches over me. I see snow flakes and put animals in pens and give more feed." She shuddered. "The wind, it was bad. And no water for one day, but now all is well."

"Seems the brunt of the storm missed you here. A lot more snow a few miles east." He drained his cup and got to his feet. "I almost forgot. Excuse me." He went outside and retrieved the bags lashed behind Gallatin's saddle. Back inside, he handed one to Katerina. "Mrs. Long, Nessa's mother, sent a few things. Said it was a little Christmas present from her family to you."

Katerina paled and held her arms stiffly at her sides. "But I have…"

"Mrs. Long said she sure would like to have some of the wild plums next summer from that thicket alongside the pasture, if you can spare some."

Color returned to Katerina's face and she accepted the bag. "Very good for pies and jelly. Please tell Mrs. Long thank you and she is welcome to as many plums as she like."

"She'll be grateful." He shifted his feet, rubbed his chin and set the other bag on the table. Uh…I hope you won't be offended, Mrs. Basetti. I brought a few other things I thought you might could use."

Katerina smiled uncertainly, and untied the string, then reached inside and slid the contents out on the table. She gasped, and covered her mouth with the thin fingers of both hands. "You know!"

Sam looked at his feet. "Yes, ma'am. Since last time I visited." He took a step backward. "If you feel I've overstepped in manners, I apologize. Out here we…sometimes we…and Nessa couldn't come today."

Katerina plopped into a chair and fingered the yards of white flannel and pastel muslin, and the hanks of knitting wool. A tear escaped and ran down her cheek. "Mr. Jackson. This is the nicest thing a person ever did for me. Clem does not know. I did not know how to get word to him, quickly." She shook her head. "I wanted no stranger to tell him." She rested her head on her arms and softly sobbed.

Sam released a noisy breath of air, sat across from her, and looked at the ceiling. After a few moments, Katerina lifted her head, drew a handkerchief from her pocket, and wiped her eyes. "Please to forgive me." She gazed into Sam's eyes. "Thank you, Mr. Jackson. I promise to repay you for your kindness."

"Oh, whoa, now. This is just a little gift for your little one." He uttered a nervous chuckle. "Like a welcome to a new neighbor."

She nodded and smiled. "Thank you from the bottom of my heart. Clem thanks you too, as soon as he knows." She stood and picked up his cup. "We need more coffee, yes? I will drink some, too."

She disappeared into the kitchen and Hank stuck his head inside the front door. "Sam, should I bring more wood in?"

"Another armload will do."

"You about ready to leave? It's the middle of the afternoon."

"Yeah we better get going."

Hank nodded and shut the door, reappearing a minute later with arms laden. Sam opened the door for him and helped stack the logs.

"Please, I can do that." Katerina stood by the table holding a plate replenished with cookies.

"All done." Sam went to the table and sat, followed by Hank. "If there's nothing else we can do for you, ma'am, we'll be on our way. I'll check your animals before I go."

Katerina wrung her hands. "I do not know how I can thank you."

"It was a pleasure, ma'am." Sam drained his cup, got to his feet and placed his hat on his head. "I'll be back in a few days to make sure you're doing all right." He moved toward the door.

Katerina followed behind Hank. "There is one thing…"

Sam turned and waited. Katerina looked at the floor and bit her bottom lip. "I would be pleased if you would now call me Katerina. I think we are friends, yes?"

Sam smiled and nodded. "I'd be honored, Katerina. I'm your friend, Sam."

She nodded. "Sam, yes."

The men tipped their hats, walked outside and toward the little barn. The cow stood at one end munching hay, several chickens scratched for corn on the floor, and buckets of water sat nearby.

Hank grinned and shook his head. "Quite a little lady. I got the notion she can pretty much take care of herself.

Sam chuckled. "I think you're right. Did you notice the shotgun standing behind the door?"

Hank nodded and they strode toward their horses. "I gave Gallatin and Danger a drink afore I brought the wood in."

Sam nodded and mounted. They rode swiftly and silently as the sun sank behind them. Sam's thoughts of Katerina lightened his heart. She would be fine until Clem came home. As he neared the Long place, a heaviness settled in his middle. How would Nessa greet him? Were they destined to always misunderstand each other?

Sam removed Gallatin's saddle and bridle, and walked toward the corral gate, ahead of Hank. His steps slowed and he sighed. One more fence to climb before he could rest.

Hank trotted to his side. "Come on, man. I'm starvin' and I bet Mrs. Long's got a feast waitin' in there."

"Yeah."

"Now don't you worry none about Nessa. Her mama and papa will have set her straight on things." He tugged on Sam's arm.

Sam sighed and stepped onto the porch. A whirl-wind shaped Nessa raced out the front door and straight into Sam's arms.

"I'm so glad you're back, Sam. I've been waiting and waiting. Is Katerina all right? Next time I'll go with you, if you like. I'm sorry I acted so hastily this morning. Mama told me everything. I'm so happy for Katerina."

Sam twined his arms around her waist and stared at her in amazement. "Nessa." He gazed into her eyes and shook his head. "I love you, girl, but I don't imagine I'll ever figure out what to expect from you."

Nessa smiled, stepped back and took his hand. "You don't need to, Sam. I'll tell you everything you need to know."

❧   ❧   ❧

After eating all they could hold, Mama suggested they retire to the parlor. "We're a little late with our celebration, but Owen can read the Christmas story, and perhaps we can sing carols after our dinner has settled." She smiled at Sam and Hank. "We opened family gifts this morning after you all rode off, but I found a few packages left over and I think they are meant for you."

She gathered brown-paper wrapped parcels from an end table and laid them in the young men's laps.

Hank flushed, and tried to hand his package back to Mama. "I can't accept a gift. I brought nothing for any of you."

Mama ignored his outstretched hand. "Mercy, Hank! You helped Owen with the wagon and wouldn't take payment. That little old token doesn't begin to repay you." She sat in her chair and smiled. "If you'd rather not open them now, that's all right."

Hank smiled. "No ma'am." He ripped the paper away to disclose a jar of sugar cookies and a second bundle held a slab of salt pork." Hank's eyes twinkled. "Nothin' I like better than bacon and sweet bread for breakfast. Thank you ma'am, and you, too, Mr. Long. I'll be thinkin' of you folks every time I eat next week."

Sam balanced his parcel on one knee, and picked up the bag he had retrieved from the storage room before entering the parlor. "Opal, here's a little gift for you."

The child rushed to take the little bag from him, and squealed with delight when she saw the contents. "Peppermint drops! Thank you, Sam. They're my favorite."

Sam's gift, of a lacy handkerchief, to Mama, caused her to gasp with pleasure. Papa's face took on a warm glow when he uncovered the watch chain. Then, Sam unwrapped the gray wool muffler Mama had knitted, and folded it around his neck. The hair brush from Papa, brought a speculative twinkle to his eyes.

Finally, while Nessa held her breath, Sam reached into the white cotton sack and brought out a small package wrapped in a pink scarf. He gave Nessa a nervous smile, and placed his gift in her hands. "I hope you'll like it."

She smiled and handed him the package she had concealed in her pocket. "And here's yours, Sam."

Nessa's fingers fumbled on the string, while her family watched in rapt silence. She lifted the wrapping, and held up a golden-hued hand-mirror with a painting of a Victorian lady on the back. "Oh! It's the prettiest thing I've ever seen." She turned it over and peered at her face, warmed with excitement, then lowered the glass, caught Sam's gaze and smiled. "Thank you."

Sam grinned and lifted the final layer of paper from his gift, revealing a miniature oval tin box painted in shades of brown and green. He held it between his thumb and forefinger, then turned it over and inspected the back.

Nessa nudged him with her elbow. "Aren't you going to open it?"

Sam exhaled and gently lifted the lid. Inside lay a curl of raven black hair tied with a tiny pink ribbon. Sam touched it with one stubby finger and shifted in his seat. "Thanks, Nessa." He slipped the box into this shirt pocket. "I'll carry it with me every where I go." He lifted his head and their gazes met.

Nessa felt almost giddy, as she looked into brown eyes that seemed to encompass her entire world. The sound of Papa clearing his throat caused her to blink. She sighed and shifted her gaze.

Papa took the Bible from the shelf and read the account of Jesus' birth. Then, Mama went to the piano, and everyone gathered around to sing the familiar old carols.

Sam gestured to Nessa, and she followed him to the dining room. "I wish I didn't have to go." He took both her hands in his, and sighed. "But, I've been away from home too long. I'll be back tomorrow to get the mules and wagon."

She smiled and reached up to lightly kiss his cheek. "Be careful, Sam, and come back early."

He squeezed her hands and went to get his coat and hat. "Sir, ma'am, thank you for the best Christmas I've had in many a year." He winked at Opal. "Don't eat all those at once and get a tummy ache."

Hank donned his coat and added his thanks. Papa lit a lantern so they could see to saddle the horses, then the three men walked outside.

Mama shut the front door and shivered, then turned toward her daughters. "Merry Christmas, girls. Now we have to go clean up the kitchen."

Nessa followed her mother out of the room. Even unwashed dishes couldn't tarnish the joy in her heart.

CHAPTER 28

❀

Nessa shoved her quilt aside, stretched her shoulders, and walked to the kitchen to make a cup for tea. She paused by the window and sighed. Fluffy white flakes drifted down shutting out the view. Two months into the new year and yet more snow. Not so severe as the blizzard before Christmas, but she longed to walk in the sunshine. It had been weeks since she had seen the bare ground.

She put the kettle on the fire and stirred the pot of soup simmering on the back burner. The eerie quiet of the house and the dimness of the room caused a shiver to race down her spine. She laughed at her foolishness. Mama would be waking from her nap any minute, and her sister, no doubt, was in the store with Papa. She carried a steaming cup to the table, sat, and drew the letter from Louise from her pocket. Sam had delivered it last evening with the supplies, and she had read it twice, but it baffled her. She read it again, searching between the lines.

ᐭ

My dear Nessa,

Forgive me for not writing sooner. I hope your holidays were gay.

You would be amazed at the celebration here. I attended several parties between Christmas Eve and the new year. Aunt Edna provided me with a new costume for each one. You should have seen how elegant I looked.

School is proceeding, but it interests me less than an old tumbleweed. Still, I must carry through with my parents' wishes and hope for better days.

How I long to gallop my mare across the pastures. Carriage rides about the avenues on Sunday afternoon pale in comparison.

I have met a few young men whom my aunt considers suitable, but they do not amuse me.

Please give your family my best wishes, and write when you can. I long to hear about you and Sam.

Your friend always,
Louise

Nessa sighed, rinsed her cup and returned to her quilting. *So many changes in my life the past year. Meeting and falling in love with Sam, Ellie going to school in town, Louise leaving, Mama expecting a baby.*

"How is the quilt coming along, Nessa?"

"Ouch!" Nessa frowned at the ooze of blood on her index finger and stuck it in her mouth.

"Mercy, child. What is it?"

Nessa jerked her finger from between her teeth and grimaced. "Just a little prick, Mama. I didn't hear you come downstairs."

Mama frowned. "If you are sure you are all right, I must get back to hemming diapers." She sat at the sewing machine. "Only five more. Then I can begin to sew the gowns. It's a pity I didn't save any of Opal's baby clothes. Who would have imagined I would need them again?" She smiled. "At least they will be useful when you need them, Nessa."

Nessa blushed. "Mama! I'm still toiling over underclothes for myself, not to mention this quilt."

Mama gave her a mysterious smile before bending her head to the square of white flannel, and moving her feet on the treadle.

Nessa's breath caught in her throat. The thought of a baby had not occurred to her. She knew Sam wanted a family, but they had not really discussed it. She wanted children, too. Some day, far in the future. Her breath erupted from her mouth, and she stared at her mother's swollen body. She must speak with Sam. Find out what he expected of her. She tossed the quilt aside, stood, and ran her palms over her flat stomach.

"I'll check on the soup, now, Mama, and stir up some cornbread for supper."

"All right, dear. That will be very nice." Her mother nodded but did not look up from her task.

Nessa scurried to the kitchen.

❦   ❦   ❦

Sam eyed the little pot-bellied stove with satisfaction, then slapped Hank on the shoulder. "Thanks for your help getting that stovepipe set up. Nessa will be warm next winter." He gazed around at the addition to the dugout. The high window on the south brought light into the room, even on a snowy day. "It is well-worth the cost."

"If you say so. Me, I'd just as soon prop my feet up near the oven on my cook stove." He tilted his head and grinned. "Course, I don't have a two-room mansion like yours."

Sam chuckled. "Well, it's better than it was a year ago, but a far cry from what I'd like to have for my wife." He sighed. "Maybe when Nessa puts some rag rugs on the floor, and hangs some quilts or something on the wall, it won't be too bad."

"Now, Sam, stop frettin' yourself. Your place is nicer than most around here."

"It'll have to do for now." He walked to the other room, up the steps, and peered outside. "You'd better stay the night, Hank. It's still snowin'." He retraced his steps and reached for his coat. "I'll get the chores done, then see what I can scare up for supper. Maybe, we can have a game or two of dominoes after."

"A'right, since you twisted my arm." Hank thrust his arms into his coat and grabbed his hat. "I'll help with the chores. And, I been working on my game strategy."

"Oh, yeah? Well, we'll see."

By the time the chores were finished, darkness had set in. A smattering of lazy snowflakes drifted down, and a few stars gave out a feeble light in the southwest.

"Appears to be clearing. I have to go for supplies, tomorrow. Maybe, I can get back before another storm hits." Sam carried a pail of fresh milk downstairs and set it on the table.

Hank snorted, sat in a kitchen chair, and pulled off his boots. "Worst winter I ever saw. Ain't thawed in weeks. I should a bought snowshoes instead of new boots."

"Did you grease them up with hog fat?"

"Sure, I did, but I guess it's all worn off." He sighed and removed his socks. "Got a spot to hang these to dry?"

"Drape them over the back of the chair next to the stove."

After setting a skillet on the burner, and adding bacon fat, Sam began to peel potatoes.

"I'll do that, if you'll mix up some biscuits." Hank held out his hand for the knife.

Sam nodded and brought a bowl from the shelf.

"Who's going to do the cookin' after you Nessa get married?"

"I reckon Nessa will. She's getting to be a good cook, according to her father."

"A shame to waste all your talent."

Sam chuckled. "Cooking's all right, I guess, but I'll be happy to hand it over to Nessa. I hope to have something besides potatoes and beans all the time."

"Yeah, I've near forgot what steak and pie tastes like." He sliced potatoes into the smoking skillet. "Think you'll get your smokehouse ready by fall?"

"Hope so." Sam shook his head. "Got to get a washhouse built first."

"Humph. Seems like one thing leads to another when you take on a wife."

Sam slid a pan of biscuits into the oven, then sliced onions into the skillet. Hank took the dish of butter from the shelf, and placed forks and knives on the table.

After two helpings of potatoes and beans, and four biscuits, Hank shoved his plate aside, and heaved a happy sigh. "Now let's get down to this game I'm plannin' to win."

"Let's get on with it, then." Sam dumped the dominoes on the table.

After losing two games to one, Hank frowned and leaned back in his chair. "Maybe I need to take up that chess game you play with that fella Clem."

"I'd be happy to teach you, if I had the pieces."

"Yeah, I bet you would." He grinned. "Just like you taught me how to play dominoes." He poured the remaining coffee into their cups, then stood looking about the room. "You know, Sam, you've got quite a cozy place here, with the new shelves, the stove in the other room, and all." He yawned. "I don't know where you're gonna put the kids, though. You gonna dig out another room?"

"What kids?"

"Why, your kids. You are plannin' to have kids, aren't you?"

Sam frowned and stared at the dominoes he had placed in their can. "Sure we're plannin' to have kids." *But I've never talked it over with Nessa. Does she want kids?* He sighed and eyed his friend. "You know, Hank, you have a habit of bringing things to my attention that I've neglected to take care of. Nessa and I haven't talked about kids. I reckoned she would want a big family like I do, but she never said so." He grimaced and shook his head. "I'm obliged to you for bringing the subject up. I'll talk to Nessa when I get back. What do you think she'll say?"

Hank chuckled and shook his head. "Don't ask me. I'm the one who can't figure out anything about women, remember?"

"Well, nothing to be done about it, tonight, but you sure gave me a lot to think about on the trail." He rose and put the tin of dominoes on the shelf, then banked the fire. "Let's turn in. I got to sleep on the problem."

❧   ❧   ❧

Sam turned the mules into the snow-packed trail in the clear, frosty dawn. He shifted to a more comfortable position on the old blanket covering the wooden seat, and let his thoughts ramble. Last night's sleep had been fitful, and he yawned, releasing a fog that obscured his vision for a moment. The bleak landscape offered nothing to stir his drowsiness. Nothing but shadowy white cold on all sides. He welcomed the streaks of pink and gold forming to his left. A jack rabbit crossed the trail, spooking the lead mules, and causing the wagon to sway. By the time Sam had the team under control, the sun's rays had turned the ice and snow into glittering lights that, though beautiful, pained his eyes. He pulled the brim of his old hat down and squinted, viewing the trail between the ears of the lead mules.

By the time Sam reached the railway, late in the afternoon, his head pounded, and furrows raked his forehead. He gladly turned the care of the mules over the liveryman, and clumped into the rooming house. After downing several cups of strong coffee and a dinner of chicken and dumplings, he carried his bedroll upstairs and settled in a corner of the communal room.

Next morning, Sam eyed the high white clouds hiding the stars, and nodded with satisfaction. No storm threatened, and the sun would be less blinding.

He pushed the mules as much as he dared, and brought them to a halt beside the store a little after nightfall.

Owen appeared out of the darkness carrying a lantern. "Glad to see you, Sam. Any trouble on the trail?"

Evenin', Mr. Long. No problems this trip." He climbed down and stamped his feet. "Still cold, though."

"Go get a cup of coffee and warm up a bit. I'll start unloading."

"Thank you for the offer, but I'd rather finish the job, first."

Owen met Sam's determined eyes. "All right, Sam, if that's the way you want it."

Sam nodded and moved to the rear of the wagon, while Owen hung the lantern on a post by the supply room door.

The freezing wind increased, and Sam gritted his teeth and pushed his body to work faster.

"Whew." Owen leaned against the wall, and took a deep breath. "Couldn't seem to keep up with you, tonight, Sam. Let's get some food and water for the mules, and take a rest."

Sam grinned. "Sounds all right. I'm give out, too."

❦   ❦   ❦

Nessa greeted Sam with a radiant smile and a steaming bowl of soup, when he trudged through the door ahead of her father.

"Sit down, Sam, and have some hot soup. You look like you're about done in." She eyed her father's gray face. "You sit, too, Papa. Do you want more to eat?"

"Thank you, Nessa. I'll just take a cup of coffee and join your mother in the parlor."

Nessa poured coffee, and handed a cup to Papa, He smiled his thanks and walked out of the room.

Nessa placed a steaming cup in front of Sam, then sat across from him.

Sam swallowed a spoonful of soup and buttered a slice of bread. "This sure hits the spot, little girl. Warms me inside and out."

"I'm relieved to see that sparkle back in your eyes."

"That sparkle, as you call it, comes on every time I see your smile."

"Why, Sam! What a pretty turn of speech. Thank you."

"You're welcome." He swallowed the last of the soup. "Nessa, we need to talk about something that had purely slipped my mind all these months."

Nessa bit her lip. "I want to discuss a matter with you, too."

"All right. You want to go first?"

"No. You go ahead."

Sam nodded, took a deep breath, and gazed into her eyes. "Nessa, how do you feel about a family? Our family, I mean. We've never talked about it, and I need to know."

Nessa gasped. "That's what I wanted to ask you."

Sam uttered a nervous laugh. "Well, what do you know." His mouth formed a thin line, and his eyes seemed to pierce her soul. "So, what's your answer?"

She smiled, then looked at Sam's hands clasping hers. "I certainly want a family some day, Sam. I hadn't given it much thought until Mama mentioned it this week. Perhaps two children, a boy and a girl. It would be nice if the boy came first so the little girl would have a brother to defend her at school. I always wished I had one." She grinned. "Of course, that's not up to us, is it?"

"Only two? I kind of had plans for several sons and two or three daughters."

"Sam! That many?" She chewed at her bottom lip. *All those diapers, and cooking meals, and washing and ironing their clothes.* "I don't know, if I can take care of them. Would you mind if I think about it? We could start with two, couldn't we?"

Sam laughed. "We'll probably start with one, and that won't be for a couple years, till I can get a house built." He squeezed her hand and got to his feet. "Just wanted to make sure you wanted a family as much as I do."

He drew her to her feet and into his arms. "Only a few more months, darlin', and I'll never have to say goodby to you. I'll just say goodnight."

His eyes darkened and Nessa raised her lips to his. His arms tightened, and his mouth held hers in a long, sweet kiss, then released her with a sigh. "A few long months."

CHAPTER 29

❀

Nessa gulped a breath of fragrant air and smiled at the blanket of green covering the ground in all directions. Nellie's ears flickered and a rabbit family scurried across the road in front of them. Nessa tightened her hand on the reins and laughed.

"Spring is sprung, and none too soon, either. I'm weary of winter. Even this mud is better than the snow pack we rode through the last two or three trips."

Sam nodded and pointed. "See the purple over there on the hill? Early wild flowers." He glanced up. "Even the color of the sky says it's spring."

They rode side by side down the side of the ridge and stopped at the Bassetti corral.

A smiling sandy-haired figure bounded from the barn, with arms outstretched. "Sam. I wondered when you come again."

Sam dismounted and grinned. "Clem. Glad to see you're home." Nessa smiled as the men shook hands and smacked each other on the shoulder, then she slipped from Nellie's back, tied both horses to the fence, and strolled to Sam's side.

Clem's blue eyes twinkled. "Miss Long. Katerina speaks of your many kindness to her this winter." He took Nessa proffered hand in his and shook it vigorously. "I thank you and anything I can do for you in all time, please allow me."

Nessa gave him a wide smile and a nod.

"How is Katerina, Clem?" Sam glanced toward the house.

"Ah, come, you see." He took Sam's arm. "She most happy to see you."

Clem opened the front door and ushered Nessa and Sam inside. "Katy! See who comes. Our good friends Sam and Miss Long."

A petite Katerina appeared in the kitchen doorway, smiling. "Welcome. Please sit and I'll bring coffee." She glanced at Sam and her smile widened. "And raisin cookies, Sam?"

"I'd like nothing better." Sam removed his hat and bowed.

Katerina's skirts whirled and she returned to the kitchen.

"Please to sit." Clem gestured toward the table. Nessa removed her hat and gloves and sat in the chair Clem pulled out for her.

Sam took the seat beside her and grinned at Clem. "So, what's new?"

Clem looked puzzled. "New?" His gaze darted around the room then a light appeared in his eyes. "New! Excusa me." He rushed through a side doorway, and returned a moment later awkwardly balancing a squirming, blanket-swathed bundle in his hands. He stopped in front of his guests, and held out his arms. A little face, framed with curly blond hair, blinked bright blue eyes. "Here is first son, Thomas Jefferson Bassetti." He lowered the baby into Nessa's arms. "What you think, huh?"

Nessa cuddled the warm body close to her bosom, and touched a chubby cheek with one finger. Thomas Jefferson rewarded her attention with a bright-eyed look and the tiny lips curved into a smile. Nessa hugged him closer. "The little darling. Sam, look. He smiled at me." She glanced up, and the sight of Sam gazing at the baby with a silly grin on his face, caused her heart to skip a beat.

Katrina returned with cups of coffee and a plate of cookies on a pewter tray. She set the tray on the table and gave Nessa a shy smile.

"He's beautiful, Katerina. I'm so happy for you and your husband."

Katerina nodded and lifted the baby from Nessa. "Thank you."

"How old is he? We were here only two weeks ago."

Clem laughed and slapped his thigh. "The good God, He plan everything." He shook his head. "Who can know His ways? I mean to work in coal mine to end of month. But big snows all winter, then rains. Mine has too much water. It must close for some weeks, so I come home. Two whole weeks work lost and I not happy. Want more wage to bring to wife." He gazed at Katerina holding the child. "I come in house to tell her I sorry not to bring more. Then I see her. I not know before." Clem grinned at Sam. "You and Miss Long here early in that day. I come at time sun goes down." He swallowed hard and blinked. "She tell me bambino comes now. I go to village and find Senora Hernandez. She put Katy to bed and I wait. I tell God I sorry for anger about losing wage, and beg Him to please watch over wife and little one. I filled with happiness and fear all at the same time." He gazed at the wall behind Nessa with moist eyes, and shook his head. "He hear me." A smile lit his face. "Senora call me into bedroom, and there is my Katy, smiling and holding *bambino*."

Sam rose and patted Clem on the shoulder. "Congratulations. He's a fine boy, and you gave him a fine name, too."

Clem grinned. "Katy and me, we learn of great man, Thomas Jefferson, when study to be citizens of United States of America. We want son to be all-American boy, so give him all-American name."

Sam nodded. "I think Mr. Jefferson would be proud."

"Now, eat. Coffee gets cold." Clem pulled out a chair for his wife, then sat beside her across from Sam and Nessa.

Nessa bit into a cookie. "These cookies are delicious, Katerina. Sam told me about them. I keep forgetting to ask if you would you give me the recipe."

"I am happy to. I write it out for you for next time you come." She smiled up at her husband. "They are Clem's favorites."

Clem gazed at Sam then at Nessa. "You having wedding soon, Sam?"

"In the summer. We'll let you know the date."

"You'll come, won't you Katerina?" Nessa asked. "I'd truly like you and Mr. Bassetti to be there."

Katerina smiled and nodded. "Thank you. We would like to see you and Sam marry." Her hand rested on the table beside her coffee cup, and Clem put his hand over hers. "We wish you the same happiness we have." She gave her husband a dazzling smile.

Nessa nibbled at her lip. "Katerina, would you play the piano at my wedding? And Mr. Bassetti could do a special song. When I was very young, I heard a man in Savannah playing the accordion and I loved it. I haven't had a chance to hear you play, Mr. Bassetti, but I would be so pleased if you would agree to perform when Sam and I get married." She cast a smile toward each of them. "Please, say yes."

Katerina gave her husband a surprised look, then gazed at Nessa. "I do not play well, but I know the wedding march. Clem knows many songs, and he can play anything after hearing it once." She gave him a fond glance. "I must have the notes written down."

"Perfect!" Nessa grinned. "Mama has some music books you can borrow, Katerina, and Mr. Bassetti can play two songs he thinks are appropriate." Nessa clasped her hands together. "It's just the thing our wedding needs." She looked at Sam. "Don't you agree, Sam?"

"Sure do. I think it's a great idea."

Clem grinned at his wife, then bowed toward Nessa. "We accept the honor with pleasure."

Sam drained the last drop from his second cup of coffee, and got to his feet. "It's been a very enjoyable afternoon, and I hate to leave, but I guess we better start back home. Lots of work to do tomorrow." He pulled Nessa's chair back. "You need anything to get your crops in, Clem?"

Clem laughed. "Fields all ready to plant. Seed waiting in sacks. And have good wife to push me out the door early in the morning. I have need of nothing more."

Sam chuckled. "Good. We'll expect to see rows of green next time we stop by." He slapped his hat on his head. "Thank you, Katerina. Those cookies are still the best I've ever eaten."

Nessa hugged her hostess and kissed the baby's curly head. "See you soon, Katerina." She went through the door Sam held open for her and walked toward the horses. Clem boosted her up into the saddle, and Katerina stood in the open doorway holding the baby. Sam turned Gallatin toward home and Nessa positioned Nellie beside him.

Clem waved one arm in the air. "We come to wedding. I promise."

Sam tipped his hat and Gallatin took to the trail. Nessa waved, then touched her boots to Nellie's flanks and followed.

❦   ❦   ❦

Sam paused at the end of the newly plowed field, dropped his hoe, and let the sack of seed corn slip from his shoulder to the ground. He reached for the jug of water, drank greedily, then removed his hat and poured cool liquid over his head. After wiping his face with his handkerchief, and slapping his hat back on, he gazed at the shiny wheel turning in the breeze next to the dugout. The windmill had been pulling up all the water he needed for almost two weeks, but it still brought a grin to Sam's face every time he watched it doing his labor. He stretched his arms high above his head, then moved to the next row.

By the time the May sun sent long shadows over the field, Sam had planted corn in more than half the field. He slung the hoe over his shoulder, picked up the bag of seed and his empty water jug and trudged toward the house. After milking, feeding, and bedding his animals, he trod toward the dugout carrying a basket of nine fresh eggs. Enough for supper, breakfast, and tomorrow's lunch.

When the biscuits began to brown in his makeshift Dutch oven, Sam chopped a green onion, and a handful of turnip greens from his garden, and dumped them into the bowl of beaten eggs, ready to scramble. He squinted toward the dusky east, looking in vain for a dust cloud heralding Hank's arrival.

"Hmm. Wonder what's he's been up to." He poured a cup of freshly brewed coffee and sat in the old wooden chair he had brought outside when the weather warmed. His eyes closed, and the vision of rows stretching to the horizon, appeared to be painted on the backside of his eyelids. He sighed, relaxed his shoulders, and stretched out his legs.

"Well, if you ain't the picture of a hard-working man."

Sam's eyes jerked open and he sat up. "Hank, where have you been? Supper time was an hour ago."

Hank dismounted and grinned. "I guess some of your energy rubbed off on me. I've been plantin' corn all day, and I'm hungrier a bear." He peered toward the fire where the Dutch oven sat on the edge of the coals along with the coffee pot. "Don't appear to be nothin' to eat. Did I come on the wrong night?"

Sam chuckled and got to his feet. "We've got a treat tonight. Scrambled eggs and biscuits with sorghum." He set the skillet on the embers and added some bacon drippings.

"Sounds good. I ain't had eggs in months. Sure get tired of salt pork and water gravy three times a day."

"Don't complain to me. I told you I'd give you a couple hens and some seeds to start a garden."

"Hmmph. I been thinkin' on it." He tossed his hat on the ground and sat cross-legged near the fire. "Never thought I'd see the day, but I have to admit you sure live a lot better'n I do."

Sam stirred the egg mixture again, then scooped it onto plates, added biscuits and handed one to Hank. "Forks and sorghum in the usual place. Help yourself."

When they were seated facing each other on the ground, Sam asked the Lord to bless the food.

Hank picked up his fork, then hesitated and peered at his plate. "What's that green stuff in there?'

"Turnip greens. They'll keep you from getting scurvy." Sam speared a healthy bite, put it in his mouth and chewed.

Hank looked at Sam, at his plate, and again at Sam. "What's scurvy?"

"Disease that makes your teeth fall out." Sam sopped up sorghum with half a biscuit.

Hank forked eggs into his mouth. "Doesn't taste too bad, but that yarn about making your teeth fall out. I ain't that dumb."

Sam chuckled. "It's the honest truth." He sipped at his coffee. "Cows eat lots of green stuff. You ever seen a cow with no teeth? But, you take a dog now, they eat meat and I know you've seen dogs with bad teeth and some missing."

Hank studied Sam's face in the faint light from the fire, swallowed, and looked thoughtful. Then shook his head and took another bite. "Sometimes I think half the stuff you tell me you made up yourself." He rose to get more biscuits. "And what's worse, after you explain it, it makes some kind of sense. So how's a man to know?" He seated himself and balanced the plate on his thigh.

Sam shook his head and grinned. "Faith, Hank, you got to have faith. I wouldn't steer you wrong." He rose and scraped the crumbs from his plate into the fire. "You want to lose a game of dominoes tonight?"

"Ha! That'll be the day." Hank stuck the last half biscuit in his mouth and got to his feet. "You set up the game and I'll pour more coffee."

"It'll have to be just one game, though. I have to leave early in the morning to get a load of freight."

They sat cross-legged on either side of the strip of canvas and began to play.

"Did you know I can see the top of your windmill from the rise behind my corral? Must be nice not to have to work that pump. Hope I can get one next year."

"Greatest thing ever invented for this country. I dug some furrows so I can water the garden row by row by directing the water and damming up the other rows."

"You'll be gettin' plumb lazy." Hank frowned and studied the dominoes in front of him.

"You going to play one of those, or just stare holes in 'em?"

"Keep your shirt on. I'm working out my strategy."

Sam chuckled. "I hope it's better than the last one."

"Right now, my strategy is to beat you at this man's game." Hank added a domino to those aligned on the canvas in front of him. "So, have you and Nessa set a date yet?"

"Sometime in August, after her birthday." Sam shook his head. "Seems like a long time."

"Think of it this way." Hank chuckled. "Compared with being married for the rest of your life, it's no time at all."

Sam made a wry face. "One of these days, Hank, you'll know what I'm talking about."

"I don't think so. I've sworn off women forever."

"Uhuh. I doubt that will last till the end of summer."

"I'm serious. Women are nothin' but trouble. Believe me, I found that out the hard way."

"What you found out is that you don't know how to pick the right one."

"Harumph."

Sam studied his friend and grinned. "Been meaning to ask you if you'll stand up with me at the wedding."

"What do you mean?"

"Be my best man. Carry the ring and…" He explored the inside of his cheek with his tongue. "I think that's about all, nowadays. Guess the best man used to have to negotiate with the bride's family and protect the groom from his enemies on the wedding day, but I don't think you'll have to worry about that."

Hank gave him a wary glance. "Good thing. I'd be no good at all trying to convince Mr. Long you were the man for his daughter." He drew two dominoes from the reserve pile. "But I guess I can carry a ring and stand in front of everybody at the church."

"Good. That's settled. You'll need a decent shirt and a tie."

"A tie! Don't own one."

Sam laughed. "I'll see what I can do. Actually, I have to get one for myself." He placed his final domino on the make-shift board. "Your turn."

Hank picked up his three remaining dominoes and tossed them aside. "Can't play none of them."

"Sorry, old friend, better luck next time."

Hank uncrossed his feet and stood. "I'll see you when you get back with the freight. At least the weather's warm now."

Sam rose and stretched. "Worst winter I ever saw, but at least there's plenty of moisture for the corn. I should have it in the ground by Saturday. Only making one trip to the railway this week."

"Good luck. I'll probably finish plantin' Wednesday." He walked toward Danger and mounted. "Much obliged for the chow. I might take you up on some vegetable seed if I can get a plot cleared."

"Any time. I'll give you some direction in planting. It's a bit different than tossing corn seed in the ground and covering it up."

"I might a known." He turned his horse, waved, and rode into the darkness.

Sam grinned, poured hot water into a tin basin, and began to wash the dishes.

❦   ❦   ❦

Nessa stuffed the letter from Louise in her pocket and strode to the corral to saddle Nellie. She wondered what news her friend had to relate. In her last message, over two months ago, Louise had seemed dissatisfied with city living, almost homesick. Nessa trotted Nellie down the road toward the church, then urged her to a full gallop, relishing the wind blowing through her hair. She slowed when she approached the solitary cottonwood tree marking an abandoned homestead, then reined Nellie to a stop and dismounted. She sat on a fallen log and opened the letter. Her smile widened as she read.

It's difficult for me to admit, but I no longer enjoy the pleasantries of the city. I long for the sight of prairie grass, fields, even cows. And I desperately miss the sunsets. I've prevailed on Father to allow me to come home at the end of May. I will probably arrive only days after you receive this letter. I can hardly wait to see you. Your friend, as always, Louise.

Nessa jumped to her feet, flung her hat to the ground, stretched her arms upward, and gazed at the heavens. Louise could be her maid-of-honor. She whirled around and around, stirring up little puffs of dust with her boots. The sun's rays bathed her face. She closed her eyes and drank in its warmth, while her feet ceased their movement, and her lips moved in silent praise to her heavenly Father for His goodness.

"What are you doing, pretending to be a corn stalk?"

Nessa's eyes flew open and she blinked rapidly, unsure whether the sight of Louise sitting on her horse in the road was real or apparition. She lowered her arms and walked forward. Louise dismounted and ran toward her, smiling.

After embracing her friend and giggling like a school girl, Nessa stepped back, took a deep breath, and expelled it with a happy sigh. "I just now read your letter. I'm so happy you're back. I've missed you so."

Louise's azure eyes twinkled. "No more than I've missed you, as well as this country." She wrinkled her nose. "I never expected to hear those words come from my mouth." She grinned and kissed Nessa's cheek. "That old adage about not appreciating what you've got until you lose it holds some truth."

Nessa laughed. "Well, you're back, now, and that's all that counts."

Louise breathed in the spring air, then gazed at Nessa's mussed hair. "What were you doing out here?"

"We've had the most terrible winter." Nessa sighed. "Some days when it snowed I felt I would climb the walls if I couldn't get out of the house." She smiled and gazed around her. "Nothing could keep me inside on this golden morning, so I decided to go for a ride, and then read your letter without interruption." Her gaze focused on Louise's riding clothes. "And look at you, so stylish and all." She touched the sleeve of the royal blue jacket, edged with lace, then looked up. "And your hat matches perfectly. What kind of feather is that?"

"Gracious! I don't know. Just an old black feather." Louise tilted her head and stood tall. "Do you really like it?"

"You look like the ladies I've seen on the society page of the Atlanta newspaper." Nessa swallowed the envy that roiled inside. "Well, what are we standing here for? Come home with me. Mama will be surprised to see you."

After dismounting at the corral, and tying Nellie to a post, Nessa ran up the path and burst through the kitchen door. "Mama, guess who's here. It's Louise. She's come home."

Rebecca stood at the range holding a large serving spoon. "Mercy, Nessa. Slow down and close the door." She resumed stirring the stew. "I didn't understand a word you said."

Nessa took a deep breath and opened the door wide for Louise to enter. "We have a guest, Mama."

Rebecca lifted her left hand to smooth her hair, placed the ladle on the side cabinet and turned. "Louise! How nice to see you. When did you get home?"

"Hello, Mrs. Long. I arrived yesterday." She gave a miniature curtsy and smiled. "I wanted to see Nessa right away."

"Well, welcome back. I'm sure you girls have a lot to talk about."

"I want to show Louise my hope chest and wedding clothes that we've finished."

"Very well. We'll have dinner in less than an hour. Louise, you'll stay won't you?"

"Thank you. I'd love to."

Nessa grasped Louise's hand and led her up to her room. She placed a finger to her lips and closed the door. "I don't want to share you with Opal right now." She went to the chest at the foot of her bed and opened the lid. "Mama gave me this trunk, and I get to wear the wedding gown that she and my Grandmother wore." She lovingly lifted the muslin-wrapped dress, spread it on the bed and unwound the protective layers.

"It's the most beautiful dress I've ever seen, Nessa." Louise's eyes sparkled, and she fingered the delicate satin and lace.

Nessa smiled and held it up to herself. "I helped Mama alter it. It fits perfectly." She replaced the gown on the bed and took another wrapping from the chest. "And this was Mama's veil." She arranged the length of lace on her head. "I'll pin it on the sides with flowers." She pirouetted in front of her friend.

Louise adjusted the folds, then tilted her head and studied the effect. "What kind of flowers?"

"I don't know." She sighed and removed the veil. "All the pretty garden flowers will have faded. Mostly what we have in August is sunflowers!"

Louise giggled. "That would be different!"

A full-fledged pout swelled Nessa's lower lip, and she flounced on the bed. "It's impossible! If only Papa would let me get married in June, I could use pink roses."

"Have you asked him?" Louise sat on the edge of the bed.

"No. The baby's due in a week or two." She covered her cheeks with her hand. "Oh, did I write you that I'm going to have a new brother or sister?"

Louise smiled. "Yes, isn't it exciting?" She took one of Nessa's hands in hers. "You are so lucky not to be an only child. I wish I had…"

"You always say that, but you don't know how hard it is sometimes."

"Well, there's nothing either of us can do about it." Louise sighed, rose, walked to the mirror and fussed with her hair. "So, you're not happy about the new baby?"

Nessa jumped up. "Oh, no, I didn't say that. I think it's wonderful, but you see why I haven't asked Papa about getting married earlier."

"There must be an answer to the problem of the flowers." Louise pursed her lips.

"I almost forgot the most important thing!" Nessa grabbed Louise's hands and swung her around. "You can be my maid-of-honor." She stopped and gazed at her friend. "You will, won't you?"

Louise smiled and squeezed Nessa's fingers. "Of course, I will."

"Thank you. Now everything is perfect—except the flowers." She sighed.

"I'm happy for you, Nessa." Louise hugged Nessa to her. "I hope you'll forget what I said about Sam. I'm sure he'll take good care of you, and you'll be very happy."

"I know he will, Louise. He's the most wonderful man in the whole world."

When Louise stepped back, Nessa saw the horror in her friend's face. "What's wrong? Are you in pain?"

Nessa could barely hear Louise's whispered words. "Nessa, who will be Sam's best-man?"

She laughed. "Well, who do you think? Hank of course." She sucked in her breath at the look on her friend's face. "Oh, Louise!"

CHAPTER 30

❀

Sam pulled hard on the reins to bring the mules and wagon to a stop beside the storage room door, and hopped to the ground.

Mr. Long emerged and walked around the team. "Sam. You made good time."

"Nice weather." Sam removed his hat and wiped his brow. "And the supplies weren't quite so heavy as usual."

"Good. We'll get this lot unloaded and have supper." Owen climbed into the wagon and began untying the tarp. Sam went to the rear, grabbed two sacks of flour and carried them inside.

A half hour later, Owen took a deep breath and leaned his weight against the side of the empty wagon. "Those fifty-pound sacks seem to get heavier every week." He chuckled and swatted Sam on the back. "Don't seem to slow you down, though." He looked up at the starry sky. "Let's go wash up and see what Rebecca and Nessa have cooked up for us. They've been in the kitchen since the middle of the afternoon."

Sam's gaze met Nessa's as soon as he walked into the room. His smile echoed hers, a lover's smile, laden with promise. He removed his hat and turned to greet Mrs. Long, whose swollen body could no longer be concealed by the shawl draped around her shoulders. She gave Sam a tired smile.

"Ma'am. I hope my being here hasn't caused you too much trouble."

"Of course not, Sam. Hurry and wash. Supper's ready."

"Rebecca, you go sit down." Owen went to his wife, took the serving bowl from her hands and led her toward the dining room. "I'll help Nessa just as soon as I clean up."

Sam relaxed against the door frame and watched Nessa. "Your cheeks are all pink from the fire. Sure look pretty."

Nessa fluttered her eyelashes. "Thank you, kind sir."

Sam grinned. "Smells good. What are you cooking?"

Nessa scooped potatoes into a bowl. "The last of the beef steak until this fall. Mama wanted a nice supper tonight. I guess she expected someone special." Her blue eyes twinkled. "Made strawberry shortcake, too."

Sam's grin widened. "Sounds great. Were you expecting someone special?"

"Oh, I thought some drifter might drop in with an empty stomach."

Sam's face reddened as guttural sounds erupted from his belly, and Nessa giggled. "Guess I was right." She forked steaks onto a platter, and her voice grew serious. "Sam, we need to talk later."

A frown creased Sam's brow. Surely their problems were behind them. "What's the matter now?"

Mr. Long entered and finished unrolling his shirt sleeves."Okay, Sam. The washroom's all yours."

After washing and smoothing his hair with his fingers, Sam joined the family in the dining room. "Why, Ellie! I didn't know you were here. Good to see you."

Ellie smiled. "I got home about an hour ago." She lowered her eyes. "Good to see you, too, Sam."

Mr. Long said a blessing, then passed the meat platter to Sam. "Eat up, son. Looks like the womenfolk cooked enough for a half dozen hungry men."

Sam forked a steak onto his plate and held the serving dish for Nessa. After taking servings of potatoes, gravy, green beans, and biscuits, Sam cut into the juicy meat, forked a morsel into his mouth, and chewed with relish.

Mr. Long asked about Sam's crops between bites, then turned to Ellie. "So, Miss, tell us what you've been studying all winter."

"School is wonderful, Papa. I want to learn all I can and then teach others." Her face glowed. "I never knew so many books existed. There must be at least a hundred in the school, and another twenty at the teacher's house. One tells about how people in China live, and another one about our presidents, and..."

"You haven't neglected your Bible reading, have you?"

Ellie turned to smile at her mother. "Not at all, Mama, we have devotions every morning after breakfast." She gasped. "Mama! What's wrong?"

Mrs. Long's face contorted and she placed her hand under her breast. Owen pushed his chair back. "Rebecca?"

She nodded to her husband. "Yes, Owen, it's time."

He rushed to her side and helped her to her feet. "Can you make it upstairs?"

She nodded again, and with Owen's support, took slow steps toward the staircase. The girls sat as though frozen. Opal looked terrified, Ellie confused, and Nessa's once-pink cheeks were ashen.

Sam rubbed his chin. "Now, everything will be all right. Let's get the table cleared up so we can do whatever your father needs done when he comes down." He stood and began to stack plates. Nessa swallowed hard and rose to her feet. "Ellie and Opal, you help Sam. I'll go upstairs and see if I can help."

Opal grabbed her arm. "Nessa, I'm scared."

Nessa smiled and patted her sister's hand. "You do like I told you. You should have that little brother by morning."

Nessa met her father at the bottom of the steps. "Good girl, Nessa. Go to your mother. I'll fetch Mrs. Allen down the road. She promised to help."

Owen stood looking around the room, running his fingers through his hair. Sam set the dirty dishes on the table, stepped to Owen's side, and placed his hand on the older man's shoulder. "Sir. Let me go for the lady. Mrs. Long needs you.

Owen nodded several times. "Okay. Take the buggy." He gazed into Sam's eyes. "And hurry, Sam, please hurry."

Sam smiled encouragingly. "Don't worry. I'll be back before you know it." He went through the kitchen, picked up his hat, and strode out the back door.

❧   ❧   ❧

Nessa stopped just inside her parents' room. The candle, on the table by the bed, spread a yellow cast over Mama's face. The multi-colored quilt covering her body, rose and fell with the harsh breaths issuing rhythmically from her half-open mouth. Nessa flinched then moved to the bedside.

"Mama? Papa's gone for Mrs. Allen." She took one of her mother's hands in hers. "What can I do until she gets here?"

Rebecca closed her eyes and managed a weak smile. "Hot water, dear, in the two kettles." Mama moaned, closed her eyes, and squeezed Nessa's hand until it throbbed. Several moments passed, then Mama took a deep breath and gazed at Nessa. "First, get the stack of sheets I told you about last week, and put a little blanket in the cradle. Also, heat the flatirons. We might need them."

Nessa released her hand from her mother's grip and nodded. "Yes, Mama. I'll be back in a few minutes. Would you like Ellie to be with you while I'm gone?"

Mama uttered a weak giggle. "Mercy, child. I don't think I can look after her right now."

Nessa echoed her mother's laugh, and went to do as she was bidden, then hurried down stairs.

Owen was pacing up and down in the dining room. "Papa? I thought you went to get Mrs. Allen."

Papa gave her a confused stare. "Sam said he would go. He left some time ago." Papa ran his fingers through his hair, stalked to the parlor window, and peered into the night. "They should be back by now."

"They'll be here, Papa." Nessa touched his arm. "Come into the kitchen and I'll fix you some hot milk."

Papa sighed, thrust his hands into his pants' pockets, and followed her.

While the milk heated, Nessa filled the kettles and placed them on the hottest part of the range. After settling her father at the kitchen table with a steaming bowl of milk, she raced back upstairs.

"Are you doing all right, Mama?"

Rebecca smiled, then grimaced. She gripped Nessa's hand until the spasm of pain subsided. When Mama released her fingers, Nessa stacked sheets on a chair near her mother's bed, then arranged soft coverings in the wooden cradle that had held her and her sisters, as well as Mama. On her way out of the bedroom, to check on the hot water, Nessa heard her father greet Mrs. Allen at the front door, and sighed with relief.

Papa and Mrs. Allen nodded to Nessa as they reached the top of the stairs, then they went into Mama's room. Nessa entered the kitchen as Sam came in the back door. Ellie continued to vigorously scrub cabinet tops, and Opal stood wide-eyed, holding a tea towel in fluttering hands. Sam removed his hat and gazed at Nessa.

"What can I do now?"

"Everything seems to be under control." Nessa smiled and took a deep breath. "I don't think any of us can be of help now. It's up to Mama and Mrs. Allen."

Sam nodded. "She seems able enough. Has four youngsters of her own." He sat at the kitchen table. "Is there any coffee left? I could use a cup. Then, I guess I better get home."

After pouring two cups of coffee, Nessa sat across from him. "I'm glad you were here. Papa runs from one place to another, muttering and scratching his head."

"Just new father nerves. He'll be fine once the baby arrives." He swallowed coffee then laid a big hand over Nessa's slim one. "What did you want to talk about, Nessa?"

Nessa heaved a sigh and her shoulders slumped. "I had forgotten, but it can wait. This isn't the time." She gazed into his brown eyes. "Or maybe I should mention it. It doesn't seem so important now."

Sam's gaze was steady. "I'd like to know what it is. Otherwise, it'll worry at me till I see you again."

"All right." She lowered her gaze to the table top. "Sam, you did ask Hank to be your best man, didn't you?"

"I sure did, and he accepted. We're all set."

She could hear the smile in his voice and she nibbled at her lip. "Louise came back this week. I was so happy to see her." She grimaced and lifted her gaze to meet his. "Sam, I asked her to be my maid of honor."

His lips lengthened into a thin line and his hand tightened over hers. "I see."

Nessa frowned. "She said she would love to, then her face turned pale. She asked me who would stand up with you, and I laughed and said, Hank, and she burst into tears." Nessa drew her hand from Sam's, pulled a handkerchief from her pocket and wiped her eyes. "I didn't know what to do. She just jumped up and ran out of the room. By the time I caught up with her, she had reached her horse. She got in the saddle and raced off without a word, even though I kept calling her name. I don't know what to do now."

Sam rose, went around the table, and touched his lips to the curls on top of her head. "I'll have to work this out. We don't have to come to a decision tonight. There's plenty of time, so don't worry." He slipped his hat on. "I'll be off home. See you Sunday. If you need anything before then, send Ellie to fetch me."

She stood looking up at him. He smiled, drew her into his arms and lightly kissed her trembling lips. "Just keep thinking about being my wife." He shook his head. "Only a couple more months, but it seems forever." He abruptly released her and stalked to the door, opened it and waved. Then he was gone, and Nessa slumped back into the chair, and rested her head on her folded arms on the table top.

"Nessa? Do we have any hot water?"

Nessa started at her father's voice and jumped up. "Papa, is everything all right?" She moved toward the steaming kettles. "There's plenty of hot water. Shall I take it up now?"

Papa blinked and rubbed his chin. "I'll take one now, I guess. Mrs. Allen didn't say how much she needed." He gave his daughter a nervous grin. "She says it's almost time." He snatched up a pot holder, grabbed a kettle, and rushed out. Nessa followed slowly to the stairs and stood looking up wondering what she could do now, except wait. She turned back to the dining room.

"Nessa, what's happening?"

Opal sat across the table from Ellie. A checker board lay between them. Both girls looked at Nessa with wide, curious eyes.

Nessa stopped beside her youngest sister and patted her arm. "It's okay, Opal. These things just take time. Papa will let us know. He thinks it won't be long." She smiled at each girl. "Who's winning?"

Ellie looked at the board and frowned. "I don't know. We forgot whose turn it is."

Nessa laughed. "That's okay. You haven't gotten very far. Why don't you start over?" She rearranged the red and black pieces. "We'll probably hear from Papa before you finish one game." She took her sewing basket from the sideboard and sat at the end of the table. "I might as well hem my new night dress while we wait."

A half hour later, they heard clumping sounds on the stairs, and Papa entered the room wearing a wide grin. "Opal! You were right, you have a baby brother." He pulled back a chair and fell into it. "A boy; a son." He shook his head and ran his fingers through his hair. His gaze darted from daughter to daughter. "A little son, and he's got a great voice. I'm surprised you didn't hear him. And Mrs. Allen says your Mama is fine."

Opal clasped her hands under her chin. "I knew it. I told you it would be a little brother."

She jumped up and rushed to her father. Ellie and Nessa followed wearing broad smiles.

"Papa, that's wonderful." Nessa squeezed her father's lower arm.

Opal plopped into his lap and hugged him. "Take me up to see him."

"What shall we name him, Papa?" asked Ellie.

"Does Mama need anything?"

"Whoa, girls. Let me catch my breath." He patted Opal's head. "You can see him as soon as Mrs. Allen says we can go up." He leaned back in his chair, grinning. "Mama's in good hands, Nessa, you can relax now." He shook his head.

"Mama wants to name him after me, but I don't want my son to be called junior. I think we'll give him my middle name, Patrick. Patrick something. Anyone have an idea?"

Nessa glanced at the furrowed brows and pursed mouths of her sisters. No name came to her mind. She felt slightly giddy. After waiting all these months, suddenly a new little person had arrived in their midst. It seemed like a miracle. It was a miracle.

Papa got to his feet. "You can think about a name later. Right now, I want to thank the Lord." They made a circle, holding hands and bowed their heads. "Lord, thank You for taking care of my wife tonight. Thank You for giving wisdom to Mrs. Allen, and bless her for helping us. Thank you for my son, Father. You alone know how much he means to me. And thank you for my three fine daughters. Help me to be a good father to all of them. You've brought great joy to my wife and me." Papa's voice faltered. "Thank You, in the name of your Son, Jesus. Amen."

Nessa sneaked a glance at her father through her eyelashes, and watched a salty tear course its way to the tip of his nose. He sniffed, then raised his head and took a deep breath. "God is so good." He reached for his handkerchief and blew, then smiled at his daughters.

"Would you like a cup of coffee, Papa?"

"Yes, Nessa. I could do with one."

She returned from the kitchen, and set a steaming cup on the table. "It's pretty strong, been at the back of the stove since supper. I added extra milk."

Papa sat and sipped. "Tastes fine, Nessa. Thank you."

"Papa, I thought of a name. I read it in a book at school. How does this sound? Patrick Horatio Long."

A miniature stream of coffee erupted from Papa's mouth and landed on the white tablecloth. He coughed and wiped his mouth with a finger. "That's a fine name, Ellie, but awful big for such a tiny boy. I'll keep it in mind, though."

"I never heard of that name, but one of the boys in my class is named Butch. I think that's a fine name, don't you Papa? He's a nice boy, and cute, too. He has red hair and brown eyes.

Papa's lips twitched. "I'll think about that name, too, Opal." He gazed at Nessa. "Don't you have a suggestion?"

Nessa grinned. "I thought of Aaron. Patrick Aaron has a good sound, and it's a name from the Bible."

Papa nodded. "I'll see what your mother says." She turned at the sound of footsteps on the stairs and watched Mrs. Allen enter carrying a blanket.

She smiled at the family. "Your wife is asleep, Mr. Long, so I brought the baby down for you to see." She gently laid the blanket on the table and pulled the top layer aside.

Nessa's breath caught at the sight of the little body, with curly dark hair, and blue eyes that blinked, and seemed to stare at her father.

"He's a fine big boy, Mr. Long. More than seven pounds I think."

Papa wore a foolish grin that Nessa remembered seeing when Opal was born. He nodded. "I'll weigh him on the scale in the store tomorrow."

Opal laughed when the baby's fingers curled around her finger. "I'm happy to meet you, Patrick Butch. We're going to have great times together. I'll teach you everything I know."

Mrs. Allen smothered a chuckle and wrapped the blanket around the baby. "I'll take him back upstairs so he'll keep warm." She picked him up and turned to Papa. "I'll stay the night, if you don't mind, just to make sure Rebecca is okay."

Papa nodded. "Thank you for coming, Mrs. Allen. We would have been hard pressed without you. Would you like something to eat or drink?"

"A cup of tea would be nice, if it's no trouble."

"Not at all. Nessa will bring it up and get you a quilt and a pillow. I'll make do on the sofa the rest of the night."

Nessa went to the kitchen to put on the kettle. When she returned with the tea, her father was arranging quilts in the parlor.

"I sent Ellie and Opal to bed. You join them as soon as you deliver the tea." He yawned and stretched his arms high above his head. "I'm about done in. It's almost three in the morning."

Nessa smiled. "Good night, Papa. Sweet dreams."

She quietly opened the door to her mother's room and tiptoed to the figure lounging in the chair by the bed. "Here's your tea, Mrs. Allen." At her whisper the lady raised her head and smiled. "Thank you, dear."

"Is there anything else I can do for you?"

"No. Your father brought what I need. I'll see you in the morning."

"Good night, Mrs. Allen."

Nessa undressed in the dark and slipped her nightdress over her head. She slipped into bed, breathed a happy sigh and closed her eyes.

❦   ❦   ❦

Sam snapped the reins to encourage the plodding mules to pick up their pace. His shoulders slumped and he fought to keep his eyes on the moonlit road. Elation at the birth of a baby skimmed through his mind, followed by Nessa's words. "I laughed and said, Hank, and she burst into tears." What should he do? He yawned, and concentrated on the team's progress.

At home, he unhitched the mules, pitched them some hay, greeted Gallatin with an apple, pumped water, checked on the new calf, gathered eggs, latched the chicken house, and stumbled down the steps to his bed. He removed his boots and outer clothing and flopped on the bed, pulling the quilts up to his chin. *Nessa looked like a sunrise wearing that yellow dress, and her cheeks all pink.* He smiled.

Next morning, when the sun peeked over the distant horizon, Sam leaned on his hoe and admired the view. It reminded him of Nessa, and he gazed at the sky until the round orange ball was fully exposed, then turned back to his labor. By the time all the roots of the pesky weeds lay exposed and drying in the heat, and the garden plants stood strong and unmolested in soldierly rows, he had made up his mind. After supper, he would visit Hank.

The remaining daylight hours went quickly as Sam watered the garden, hoed several rows of corn, washed his few clothes in a tub by the fire and hung them on the corral fence, then heated water and washed himself in the same tub. He dried beside the fire, donned sun-fragrant clothes and cooked his supper.

The quarter moon had risen above the top of the cottonwood tree by the time he saddled a frisky Gallatin. The horse had not been ridden in three days and strained at the bit, when Sam turned toward Hank's place, so Sam loosened the reins. They arrived in full gallop and Gallatin slid to a dusty halt in front of the corral. Sam dismounted and turned to meet a red-faced Hank, carrying a rifle in one hand.

"What the dickens do you mean riding up here like a band of outlaws?" Hank removed his hat, wiped his brow on his shirt sleeve, and glared at Sam. "It's a wonder I didn't shoot you!"

Hiding a grin, Sam tied the reins to the fence. "Gallatin needed some exercise, and I didn't want to find you half asleep. Need to talk something out with you."

Hank frowned. "Humph. Scare a man out of his few remainin' wits, risk gettin' a hole in his hat, and he needs to talk somethin' out!" He stalked to his dugout, hid the rifle behind a stack of wood, and threw a log onto the dying fire. He gestured to a stool. "Okay, then, sit and talk. I'm listenin'."

"Got any coffee? I didn't take time to make any at home." Sam sighed, and eased his body to the low seat

"Now the man wants coffee, too." Hank grinned, picked up the blackened pot resting at the edge of the fire, and shook it. "A little left, but it's likely thick as mud." He poured, not quite filling a tin cup, and handed it to Sam.

Sam peered at the thick liquid. "Want to share it with me?"

Hank chuckled. "Not on your life. You'll probably be awake all night."

Sam grinned and took a sip. "Tastes fine." He wiped his mouth with his hand. "Good weather today. Just right for hoeing in the field."

Hank pursed his lips. "Yep, and tomorrow promises to be another fine day." He sat on a stool facing his friend. "Now that we've discussed the weather, how about telling me what you came for."

"Mrs. Long probably had her baby last night." Sam set his cup on the ground and rolled his shoulders to get the kinks out. "I fetched Mrs. Allen to attend her before I came home."

"Umm. That's good news."

"Opal has said all along it would be a boy. I wonder if she was right?"

Hank heaved a sigh. "Sam, you alerted me just fine, but now you're about to put me to sleep. I never knowed you to beat around the bush before."

Sam threw his hat on the ground and ran his fingers through his thick hair. "Yeah, I know." He gazed at his friend. "You remember the other day when I asked you to stand up with me at my wedding, and you said you would?"

"Yeah, and you offered to throw in a shirt and tie."

"Well, I'm giving you the chance to back out, if you want to, but I'm hoping you won't."

Hank frowned. "Do I get to know the reason, or are we playing some new guessing game?"

Sam grinned and rubbed his chin. "I'm getting there. It's not easy." He placed his hands on his knees and leaned toward Hank. "Louise is back from St. Louis, and Nessa asked her to be her maid-of-honor. That means you'll have to stand at the altar with her, and then walk her down the aisle behind Nessa and me after the ceremony. At least, I think that's what Nessa told me. I've never been to a wedding this fancy before."

Hank bent to pick up a stick and drew circles in the dirt. An owl hooted, a horse neighed, then silence filled the night. Sam waited, breathing in shallow gulps of air through his mouth.

"Sam, I figure you saved my life. God knows you're the best friend I've ever had." Hank tossed the stick onto the fire and met Sam's gaze. "I'll do it for you. Probably wouldn't for another soul on this earth. But…" He shook his head. "I doubt Miss-High-Tone-From-St. Louis will agree to it."

"Thanks, Hank." Sam sighed. "I appreciate it and I owe you." He got to his feet. "And you may be right about Louise. Nessa will have to handle that." He strolled toward his horse. "Sorry I scared you, Hank. Watch that trigger finger."

Gallatin took him home at a more leisurely pace, while he pondered.

CHAPTER 31

❀

Nessa balanced the laden tray on one arm, tapped on the door and entered her mother's bedroom. Rebecca lay propped up on pillows nursing baby Patrick.

"Here's your breakfast, Mama." She set the tray beside the bed and smiled at mother and child. "May I hold him while you eat?"

"He's about to fall asleep. You can rock him." She caressed the small fuzzy head. "He's such a good baby, slept until two this morning." She laid him beside her and Nessa placed the tray on Rebecca's lap.

Nessa sat in the old squeaky rocker holding Patrick on her shoulder. "Have you and Papa decided on Patrick's middle name?"

Her mother swallowed a bite of biscuit and giggled. "Not definitely. Papa told me the names suggested by Opal and Ellie." She spooned oatmeal into her mouth and chewed. "I like the name Andrew and your father wants James. That Scots-Irish blood of his. We'll decide before Sunday. I want Papa to take you and Opal to church, and he can let our neighbors know the baby and I are fine. Ellie can stay with me for that short time."

Nessa laughed. "I'm sure all our neighbors know all the details by now. Many people have been in the store, and Papa is so proud. He acts like Patrick is his first child."

Rebecca nodded and smiled. "He acted the same when each of you girls were born. Of course, he'd given up hope of having a son. I had, too." She blinked several times. "God has been so good to us."

"Patrick is sound asleep, but I want to keep rocking him."

"I know, but we mustn't spoil him. It's not so much fun at four in the morning."

"I suppose not." Nessa's finger traced the curve of a tiny pink ear. "He's so innocent and sweet. It's a pity babies have to grow up."

"Perhaps." Mama sipped the last of her tea and set the tray on the chair beside the bed. "Innocent. Yes, he is. But God has a plan for him, just as He has for each of us." She settled against the pillows and her face became thoughtful. "I wonder what Patrick will do with his life? Will he make his part of the world a better place? Surely, he'll have trials, and I hope they won't be too harsh. I hope he'll find happiness and know love. Most importantly, I pray he learns how much God loves him."

Her mother's words held Nessa spellbound. Her mouth gaped and she stopped rocking so not to miss a syllable.

"You see, Nessa, Patrick is not just a baby, he's a person, a soul in a tiny body." Rebecca gazed at her eldest daughter and gave her a wistful smile. "He isn't really mine, you know. God is only lending him to me for a time."

"Oh, Mama." Nessa breathed hard. "I never thought of any of those things."

"A baby is God's gift, but it's a gift you have to give back in a few years." Mama's eyes misted. "The time is almost here for me to give you up, Nessa. A time of happiness touched with sadness." She wiped her cheeks with her hand-kerchief. "And I walk through the years since you were born and wonder. Did I teach you well? Did I prepare you for whatever you will face in the future? Did I love you enough?"

Nessa gasped, rose, and placed the baby in his cradle, then knelt beside her mother's bed.

"You're the best mother a daughter could have." Tears streamed down her face. "I'm sorry I didn't always listen and obey you. Forgive me for being stubborn and causing you pain." She laid her head on her mother's bosom. "I didn't know. I didn't understand."

Rebecca's hand smoothed Nessa's hair. "You've been a joy since I first saw you, and I'm proud of the young woman you've become."

When Nessa raised her head, Mama smiled and placed her handkerchief in her daughter's hand. After blowing her nose and wiping her eyes, Nessa bent to kiss her mother's cheek. "I love you, Mama."

"I love you, too, child."

Nessa picked up the tray. "I guess I'd better go get dinner started." She smiled. "Thank you for telling me these things."

❧   ❧   ❧

Sam halted Gallatin in the dusty yard and noticed Danger, saddled and waiting, outside the corral. "Hank! You ready? We're running a little late."

Hank stumbled out the door of the dugout. "You go on, Sam. I'm feelin' poorly and guess I'll have to miss church today."

Sam urged his horse to Hank's side. "What's the matter with you? You were fine last night."

Hank hung his head and toed the dirt with one boot. "I don't know, Sam. I came over all peculiar just before you got here."

"Humph." Sam pursed his lips. "You aren't going to let a certain little yellow haired girl keep you penned up at home all summer are you?"

Hank's head jerked up and he stared at Sam. "What are you talkin' about? I'm sick I tell you."

"Yeah, and I'm rich as Solomon." He gazed into clouded blue eyes. "Hank, you're going to have to face her or leave the country, and I'll sure miss you."

Hank's shoulders slumped and he sighed. "I ain't no coward, Sam, you know that, but I'd as soon face a hungry bear as that little gal."

Sam grimaced. "Just what do you think she's going to do to you? You're too tough to chew on, and she probably won't get close enough to kick you." He bent and slapped Hank on the back. "Come on, Hank. She'll probably turn up her nose at both of us and not speak. Nothing we can't handle together."

A wry grin spread across Hank's face. "You do have a way of speakin' plain, Sam. You should a been a preacher." He stuffed his hat on his head and sauntered toward his horse.

❧   ❧   ❧

Nessa sighed with relief. Only one buggy stood in the churchyard. Now if only Louise would arrive soon, they would have time to talk before the service began. Papa stopped the team, jumped from the buggy, and offered a hand to Nessa and Opal. Opal rushed to the side of the church where fall planted irises sported purple blooms, and Nessa walked to the edge of the road. She smiled when she spotted the Bagley's matched Arab team trotting toward her, then, in an off-hand manner, opened her Bible and pretended to read. She lifted her head when the buggy stopped beside her and smiled.

"Hello, Mr. Bagley, Mrs. Bagley. You're early, too."

Mrs. Bagley smiled. "Good morning, Nessa. Tell your mother how happy we are about the baby, and I plan to visit her very soon."

"Thank you, Mrs. Bagley. I'll be sure and tell her." She nipped at her upper lip and gazed at her friend. "Louise, why don't we stay out here for a few minutes and enjoy the sunshine?"

Aided by her father, Louise alighted and gazed at her friend. "If you wish. The day is lovely."

Louise's parents greeted Nessa, then strolled toward the church steps. "What do you want, Nessa?"

Nessa opened her mouth to protest, then grimaced. "Let's don't quarrel, Louise. I missed you."

Louise sighed. "I'm sorry, Nessa. I missed you, too. It's just..." She played with her fingers. "I want to be your maid-of-honor, but I'm not sure I can get through it." She bit at her lower lip. "Me, the one who pretended interest in every fellow I met. It's only fitting I got trapped in my own foolish game." Her eyes misted.

"I'm so sorry. Maybe..." Nessa squeezed Louise's arm.

"No! Don't say it. Don't even think about it." She lifted her head and gazed into Nessa's eyes. "I'll be your attendant, Nessa, on one condition. I will not take Hank's arm. He is not to touch me. Do you understand?"

Nessa gulped in air and swallowed. "If..." The look in Louise's eyes silenced her, and she sighed. "All right. I'll tell Sam. Thank you, Louise." She glanced up and gasped. "Hurry inside. There's Sam, and Hank is with him." She grabbed Louise's hand and they rushed toward the church.

Nessa took her seat beside Papa and smiled at Sam when he appeared beside her and sat down. Louise sat across the aisle with her parents, looking straight ahead. Nessa could not see Hank and assumed he had taken his usual seat in the back pew. *Please, Father, keep them apart today.* Sam and Papa exchanged nods and the pianist began the opening hymn.

Without enthusiasm, Nessa sang, half-listened to the preacher's message, and sighed when the final prayer ended. She turned to Sam.

"Mama invited you for dinner."

"Nessa, how is your mother? Did the baby arrive safely?"

Nessa laughed and covered her mouth with one gloved hand. "I forgot you didn't know. I'm sorry. Yes, Mama's fine, and it's a boy, named Patrick."

Sam grinned and glanced at Papa. "Congratulations, Mr. Long." He looked from Nessa to her father. "Are you sure Mrs. Long wants company? I don't want to put her to any trouble."

Papa grinned. "Nessa and I got dinner started this morning and Ellie can handle the rest. Rebecca especially wanted you to come. She wants to show off her son."

Sam laughed. "In that case, it's my pleasure."

"You're welcome to ride in the buggy. We can tie your horse to the rear."

Nessa trembled when Sam's fingers brushed her hand.

When they reached the church steps, Hank's horse was gone, and Nessa could hear Louise's voice behind her. *Thank You, Father.* She clambered into the buggy and sat beside Opal, while Sam brought Gallatin, tied him, and climbed in front with Papa.

A quarter of a mile from home, she tapped her father on the shoulder. "Papa, would it be all right if Sam and I walked the rest of the way?"

Papa brought the team to a halt and smiled at Sam. "Don't dawdle too much. Dinner will be ready soon."

"We'll be right along, sir." He jumped down and assisted Nessa to the ground.

The buggy pulled away and Sam took Nessa's hand. She skipped to match Sam's pace, and he grinned, squeezed her hand and slowed his pace.

"Sorry. My thoughts have been running all over the place this morning, and I guess my feet tried to keep up."

Nessa smiled and swung their arms in rhythm with their steps. "I know. I've been preoccupied, too. That's why I wanted time to talk without my family." Her steps faltered and she stopped. "Sam, I talked with Louise before church. She'll be my maid-of-honor, but with one condition." She chewed on her lip. "It's rather silly, but she says she'll do it only if Hank doesn't touch her, doesn't take her arm." She gazed at Sam's face. A muscle in his cheek twitched and his lips hardened into a thin line.

"The little trouble-maker." His eyes looked thoughtful. "But it will be all right. I think." He grasped Nessa's arms and pulled her close. "Hank will be best man for my sake, but he's none too happy about it."

Nessa pulled away. "Sam, is our wedding going to be ruined because of our best friends?"

"We won't let that happen. We're going to have the best wedding in the territory." A tear meandered down her cheek and he brushed at it with his little finger.

She smiled and wiped her eyes. "You promise?"

He grinned and kissed her nose. "Promise." He took her hand and began walking. "Reminds me, I promised your father we wouldn't be long."

Nessa sighed and nodded.

Papa looked up from his chair at the head of the table, when Nessa rushed into the dining room. "About time you two got here." He smiled at Sam.

"Sorry, Papa." Nessa took her seat. Sam tossed his hat in the corner and sat beside her.

After the blessing of the food, and the serving dishes had gone around, Sam looked at Mama's empty chair. "Is Mrs. Long all right?"

Papa grinned. "She's fine, Sam. Just not up and about yet. As soon as we finish dinner, I'll take you upstairs to see her and our son."

Sam returned the grin and picked up his fork.

Nessa paid little attention to the sporadic conversation, mostly between Ellie and Opal. She ate with pleasure, for the first time since Louise had jumped on her horse and galloped down the road.

🍁   🍁   🍁

Owen wiped his mouth with his napkin and pushed back his chair. "Ellie, you did a good job of getting dinner together. Your school teacher must have taught you a bit about cooking as well. You and Nessa will rival your mother in the kitchen one day." He beamed at his daughters. "Opal, you'll be learning soon." He rose. "Well, let's go see Mama and Patrick."

Sam followed the family up the stairs and into the bedroom where Mrs. Long lay propped up on pillows, cuddling her son. Owen kissed his wife's cheek, then took the baby in his arms. He grinned and ambled toward Sam.

"Here he is, Sam. Look at that hair, and he's going to be taller than me, too. Mrs. Allen measured him at twenty-one inches and he weighed just under eight pounds on my scale."

Sam chuckled and eyed the tiny face fringed with dark hair. As he watched, Patrick opened deep blue eyes, wrinkled his nose, and began to cry. Owen deftly lifted him to his shoulder and patted him on the back. "Now Patrick, that's no way to act when someone comes to see you." Owen winked at Sam and returned the baby to Rebecca.

"He's a mighty fine looking boy, Mr. Long. Congratulations. And to you, too, ma'am."

Rebecca smiled. "I want to thank you for fetching Mrs. Allen the other night."

Sam shook his head in embarrassment. "Least I could do."

"Papa," Opal tugged at her father's arm. "What is Patrick's other name? Nessa said you would decide today." The little girl sat on the edge of the bed and played with the baby's delicate fingers.

Owen looked at his wife and raised his eyebrows. "Rebecca, you tell them."

She grimaced, shook her head, and straightened the ribbon on one of Opal's braids. "Your father and I almost always agree on everything. You wouldn't think a middle name for a baby would cause such a fuss. Papa didn't care for the name I chose, and I wasn't happy with his choice. And even the suggestions you girls made didn't seem quite right." She grinned and wrinkled her nose at her husband, much as her little son had done a few minutes earlier. "After much to-do, we have finally agreed, or perhaps compromised."

Opal fidgeted and sighed. "Please, Mama, just tell us what it is. We don't care about all that."

Mr. Long bristled. "Young lady, don't…"

Rebecca raised her hand. "Mercy, it's all right, Owen. Your brother's name is Patrick Robert Long." She cupped Opal's face with one hand and kissed the tip of her nose. "Do you like it?"

Opal smiled. "It has a nice sound." She frowned. "If it couldn't be Butch, I think Robert is the next best."

Sam chuckled and glanced at Nessa. She smiled and spoke in a low voice. "I'll tell you later."

Patrick began to howl, and Rebecca's ministrations seemed to have no effect. "I'm sorry, I think he's hungry."

Owen nodded. "We'll clear out." He again kissed Rebecca, then ushered Sam and the girls out and downstairs.

In the living room, Sam sat on the couch, at Mr. Long's invitation. "You have a nice family. The little boy rounds it out just right."

Owen shook his head. "I can hardly believe the Lord gave him to us. I never expected to have a son." He grinned. "Although I had hopes of three strong sons-in-law to help me out when I needed them in my old age."

Sam laughed. "Well, I'll be glad to be one of them." He rose as Nessa sauntered in.

"Would you like to ride awhile, Sam? Ellie and Opal agreed to clean the kitchen, if I do their chores for two days." She stopped in front of Sam, touched his arm, and smiled. "I thought it was worth it."

Sam grinned, got to his feet, and glanced at Mr. Long out of the corner of one eye. "I'd like to take you riding, if it's all right with your father."

Nessa turned her smile on her father. "All right, Papa?"

"Go on and enjoy yourselves. I might have a little nap there on the sofa."

❧   ❧   ❧

Nessa climbed onto Nellie's back and breathed in the fragrant spring air, then loosened the reins and nudged Nellie's flanks. "Let's go toward the church, then we can watch the sunset on our way back."

Sam nodded, turned Gallatin, and looked up. "Not a cloud to be seen. Good corn growing weather." He moved to Nessa's side and set a slow pace.

"Corn! Is that all you can think about on such a magnificent day?"

Sam chuckled. "Well, I was thinking that pretty as the sky is, it doesn't match the blue of your eyes."

Nessa gave him a sidelong glance and a smile. "Thank you, kind sir. That's much better."

As they ambled along in companionable silence, Nessa's thoughts turned to the future. She marveled at how they seemed to communicate without words, and prayed it would ever be like this. She could share his nearness and strength, bask in his love, and yet feel free. The thought of the dreamy, self-centered girl of a year ago caused her to wince. She could hardly wait to be Sam's wife. Her happiness erupted in a giggle, and she glanced up at Sam, who looked puzzled.

"What's so funny? You look like a little girl who just got her first peppermint stick."

Nessa beamed at him. "Well, maybe I did, in a way, only this will last a lot longer than a piece of candy."

He shook his head. "I don't know what you're talking about. But whatever makes you happy is fine with me."

"Oh, Sam, I love you." Sam pulled on the reins and Nessa shifted in the saddle to look back. He looked stunned. "What's wrong?"

Sam gaped at her for a long moment. "Nothing wrong. Your saying that just jolted me all of a sudden, like a kick from a mule."

Nessa turned her horse alongside Sam, facing him. "You mean it hurt you?"

"No! It sort of knocked the wind out of me for a minute." He grinned. "But it felt good."

"Well, thank goodness!" She laughed and touched his hand with her gloved one. "I don't think I've ever seen you in a flap about anything, not even when Mama's baby was coming." She gazed into his merry brown eyes. "I like it—if it's just for me." She grinned and moved her face closer. "I love you, Sam."

Sam sighed, grasped her arm, bent his head, and kissed her. Gallatin shook his head and Nellie stepped back. Nessa glanced at Sam's dark eyes, grinned and turned her horse around.

"Race you to the churchyard!" Nessa loosened the reins and kneed Nellie. She heard Sam chuckle, followed by Gallatin's pounding hoofs.

At the church, she pulled Nellie to a sliding halt and jumped from the saddle. Gallatin stopped just behind her. "Where you been, slow poke?"

She watched Sam's lips split into a wide grin, before he dismounted and tied the horses to a post. Then he captured Nessa's hand and led her to the steps.

Nessa swiped at the dust with a glove, then sat with her feet on the path. "Sam, you haven't taken me to visit your place. Tell me about it."

He frowned and removed his hat. "I've been working to make it as nice as I could for you, but it's not what you're used to, Nessa." He sighed and wiped his brow. "You know what a dugout is like. Mine has two rooms and the new one is built up so there's a little window on each side, but they're too high for you to see out. It's a fair size, so there's room for your things, I hope. The other room has a cookstove, a table, cabinet, and some chairs. The floors are dirt, but I laid down some canvas, and I thought you might put some rugs on it. I tried to whitewash the walls, but they don't look like much." He gazed at Nessa, and she caught her breath at the distress in his eyes.

She swallowed hard. "Sounds warm and cozy." She squeezed his hand. "I think Mama has a couple of extra rag rugs and I can make more." She chewed at her lip. "I have an old quilt Grandmother gave me that we could hang on the wall."

Sam released her hand, put an arm around her shoulders and pressed her against his chest. "Thanks, Nessa. I've been afraid to tell you, but I knew I had to before…" His arms went slack and he stood looking down at her. His eyes glistened. "Anyway, I got the windmill so you'll have all the fresh water you need and the garden is in, some flowers are blooming, and we have seventeen baby chicks, a new calf, and eight piglets. I plan to get you a dog for company."

"We'll do fine, Sam, and I'd love to have a puppy."

He blinked, and his eyes searched her face. "I'll make it better as fast as I can, Nessa. You'll have a proper house, and everything I can get to make it easier for you."

"I believe you." The lump in her throat hurt as she swallowed.

Sam shifted his gaze to the horizon and sighed. "Look at that sun, way over there." He pulled her to her feet.

Nessa stood beside him, looking toward the west. "My goodness! All gold and pink and lavender." She gazed at Sam and smiled. "Just like our life will be, Sam, filled with the glow of heaven."

Sam smiled and led her toward the horses.

CHAPTER 32

❀

Nessa opened her mother's door, tiptoed toward the bed, and set the breakfast tray on the chest. "Good morning, Nessa. I'm wide awake, and I want to have breakfast sitting in the chair."

"Morning, Mama. Do you think you should be up, yet?"

Rebecca sighed. "Mercy, yes. I intend to be downstairs for supper. One more day in this bed and I'll be weak as a kitten."

Nessa giggled, brought her mother's robe, and helped her to the chair by the window. After placing the tray on her lap, she knelt by the cradle. Patrick's long lashes lay fringed against his pink cheeks. "Could anything be so beautiful?" She touched one curled fist, then rose and sat on the edge of the bed.

"He is truly a gift from God." Mama bit off a piece of toast and gazed at her daughter. "But children bring responsibility along with joy."

"I know, Mama." Nessa played with her fingers. "That's kind of what I'd like to talk about. Responsibility and all."

Mama raised her eyebrows. "We had several talks about marriage and being a wife. Did I not make things clear?"

Nessa smiled. "I understand all that. This is a little different. Sam told me about his house the other afternoon." She sighed. "Mama, I love Sam, and I want to be his wife, but I'm afraid he'll be disappointed in me. I don't know how to live in a dugout, being unable to see outside, taking care of Sam and a garden and animals, all by myself. You've taught me well, but there's so much to do, and I want to make Sam proud of me." Tears ran down her face. "I'm a little scared, Mama."

Rebecca set the tray on the chest, and Nessa flew into her outstretched arms. "It will be all right, Nessa. You'll make Sam a fine wife, and it's all right to be nervous." She caressed the top of Nessa's head. "After all, your life completely changes in one short day. Sam is a good man and a hard worker." She cupped Nessa's face in her hands and looked into her eyes. "I can't promise you happiness. You have to make that decision for yourself." She frowned. "I almost forgot that myself several months ago. I lost my way and turned from all the good things I had. God, your father, you girls." She sighed. "I don't know how I could have been so foolish, but your words one morning made me get on my knees to thank the Lord for His goodness, for my husband and my children, and now I'm so happy to be who I am." Her eyes glistened and she blinked rapidly.

Nessa wiped her eyes and slipped to her knees beside her mother's chair. "Oh, Mama. I didn't mean to make you cry."

Mama smiled. "Mercy! Look at the two of us. Silly women acting like children, and crying because we're loved."

Nessa got to her feet and handed the cup of tepid coffee to her mother. "Maybe this will help if it's not too cold."

Rebecca sipped and nodded. "It will do."

Nessa returned to her perch on the bed. "I think I understand what you've said." She bit at her lip. "Will you give me some help in making our house more cheerful?"

Rebecca smiled. "Of course I will. And I'm quite good at it, too." She grimaced "When we could only afford to heat two rooms in Grandmother's house years ago, my mother vowed she would never allow us to live in desperation. She made those rooms into a home filled with warmth and comfort." Mama set her cup aside and looked thoughtful. "But, most importantly, filled with love."

Nessa kissed her mother's cheek and picked up the tray. "Thank you, Mama. I'll set the table for five tonight."

❦   ❦   ❦

Sam juggled a pail of foamy fresh milk and a basket of eggs, and, with an elbow, pushed down the latch on the chicken coop door. He breathed in fragrant evening air and surveyed his domain. The addition on the barn, to accommodate Nellie, picked up the waning rays of sun, Daisy lay chewing her cud with her growing calf beside her, and the sow and piglets snuggled in their pen. Lush green filled the garden rows, and fields of corn and sorghum. The ripening wheat rippling in the breeze reminded Sam of a picture of the waves of the ocean he had once seen in a geography book. The windmill whirred, bringing gallons of water from underground, and the horse-drawn plow that had enabled him to clear an additional ten acres for spring planting, rested beneath a cottonwood tree. The fruit trees had grown to more than five feet, and one or two sported a few blossoms, and the young irises and rose bushes thrived along side the dugout.

He took another breath, grinned, and headed for the house. Before reaching the door, he paused at the sound of approaching hoofbeats, and smiled as Hank halted in the yard.

"Hank. What are you doing out so late during the week?"

"Howdy, Sam. Been worrying on somethin' since Sunday and decided to come over and talk to you."

"Climb on down. You had your supper? I just finished the chores. Let me put this stuff up and I'll get the fire going." Sam strained the milk through a cloth into a gallon jar and carried the eggs inside. When he returned, Hank had a blaze going and was filling the coffee pot with water.

Sam kept the conversation on crops, while he fried potatoes with onions to go with the warmed over pinto beans and cornbread. They ate mostly in silence, then Sam poured more cups of coffee. "What's on your mind, Hank?"

Hank shook his head. "Now that I'm here, I don't know how to say it."

"Well, the best way is just to say it right out." He raised his eyebrows. "You got a beef against me?"

Hank grimaced. "No! Nothin' you did. More the other way 'round, sort of." He sipped coffee and gazed into the embers of the fire. "Sam, weddings are important, especially to the womenfolk involved. Don't you think?"

"I'd say so." Sam frowned. "Don't quite know what you're getting at."

"Yeah, that's the trouble." He sighed. "Nessa's gonna be mighty hurt if anything goes wrong at her wedding, ain't she? Well, I think Louise and me, walkin' down to the front of the church stiff as broomsticks is gonna ruin the whole thing." He sighed again and drew designs in the dirt with a twig. "Thing is, I don't know what to do. If I try to talk to Louise, she'll likely just walk off, but if you want, I'll give it a try."

Sam sat quietly, chewing on his bottom lip and gazing over Hank's shoulder into the night.

"What I thought, Sam, was maybe you'd rather get somebody else to stand with you, seeing as how I'm the one…"

Sam waved his arm. "Hold on. Let's not get hasty. The wedding isn't for several weeks and things have a way of working themselves out." He reached over and grasped Hank's forearm. "I don't plan on having anybody else, Hank." He stared at the starry sky. "Let's pray about this and let the Lord work at making it right."

Hank met his gaze. "You honestly think God has time to fuss with marriage plans?"

"I think He cares what happens to us. Are you ready to agree with my prayer?" At Hank's nod, Sam bowed his head. "Lord we know You have lots of things to take care of, and our problem doesn't amount to much except to us, but I read in your Book that when we ask You hear and You answer. So, Lord, we're asking that You fix this problem between Louise and Hank. It don't seem right that my best friend and Nessa's best friend don't get along. I guess that's all I've got to say, Lord. I just leave it in Your hands. Amen."

Sam raised his head and grinned at Hank. "We turned the problem over to Someone who has the power to do something about it, so let's don't worry our feeble brains any more."

Hank chuckled. "It seems so easy, but I'm not used to praying like that. Just have to pinch myself to believe that God cares that much. I can't figure out why He bothers."

Sam smiled and swatted Hank on the back. "I know what you mean, but believe it, God cares. Even for two ole farmers like us."

"Yeah." Hank stood and headed for his horse. "Thanks Sam. I'll be sleepin' better tonight."

❦   ❦   ❦

Nessa finished weeding the third row of string beans, now covered with white blossoms, and looked at the sky. If she hurried, she could finish the rows of beets and turnips and sew the lace on the second of her new petticoats before dinner. Her trousseau was almost complete. Mama had insisted on four new sets of underthings and Nessa enjoyed plying her needle on the soft cotton. She smiled, wiped her brow with one hand, then lifted the hoe to chop a nettle.

"Well, aren't you the busy little bee. Your mother said I'd find you out here."

Nessa raised her head and gave Louise a wry smile. "You would visit when I'm all hot and dusty." She leaned her weight on the hoe handle. "I'm almost through. Would you like to sit on the bench for a few minutes?"

Louise brushed imaginary dust from her riding skirt and peered at the log seat set against the fence. "I'll admire your mother's flowers. The roses smell heavenly."

Nessa nodded and began hacking at the weeds as quickly as she could. She was eager to show Louise her new clothes.

She propped the hoe against a fence post and joined her friend, who was bending over a clump of fragrant lavender. "Come inside and we'll have some cool tea. I'm so thirsty." She led the way into the kitchen. "Sit at the table while I wash up. Be right back." She washed her face and hands in the adjoining washroom, then poured tea, sat across from her guest and took a sip. "It isn't very cool, is it? I can get cold water from the well house."

Louise removed her hat and gloves, lifted her glass, and drank. "Don't bother. It's refreshing." She set the glass on the table and gazed at the wall.

A slight frown marred Louise's face. "You're out riding early in the day. Did you come for a special reason?"

Louise bit her lower lip, and craned her neck to look toward the dining room.

"Let's go to my room." Nessa rose. "Ellie will need the kitchen to fix dinner soon, and I want to show you some new bridal things."

Nessa sat on her bed and patted the space beside her. "We can talk here."

"I've been thinking about your wedding, and being maid-of-honor. Perhaps you should ask someone else." She sat beside Nessa. "Why not Ellie?"

Nessa gaped, then gulped. "But I thought you were my best friend. I've always planned for you to be beside me. I thought we had decided."

Louise sighed and studied her fingernails. "Nessa, I don't want to ruin your big day, and I don't want to walk with Hank. I don't know what to do." She squeezed her eyes shut and a sob shook her body.

Nessa put an arm around Louise's shoulders, and blinked rapidly. "It's all right. Don't cry." She pulled Louise close and swallowed hard. "I'm sorry, I didn't realize how much you were hurting." Louise's body convulsed against hers and tears dampened her bodice. She silently rocked back and forth, and patted her friend on the back.

Louise raised her head and sniffed. "I thought I could do it for the sake of our friendship, but...I don't think I can go through with it. I'm so sorry." A fresh torrent streamed down her face.

Nessa went to her chest and brought a handkerchief to Louise. "I'll ask Ellie tonight. She'll be delighted." She heaved a sigh and forced a smile on her numb face. "You will come to the wedding, won't you?"

Louise gasped. "Of course! I wouldn't miss seeing you get married." She wiped her eyes and blew her nose. "Thank you, Nessa, for understanding." She went to the mirror and gazed at her reflection. "I look terrible."

"You can wash your face and you'll be fine." Nessa poured a little water into the wash basin, dampened a cloth, and handed it to Louise.

Louise scrubbed at the red blotches, and grimaced at the resulting bright pink of her cheeks. "I'd better go. I don't want to be rude, but I'd rather not meet your mother or your sisters right now."

Nessa went to the door and listened to the sounds from downstairs. "Mama is in the kitchen with Ellie, and Opal is outside playing. You can slip out the front door if you hurry."

Louise nodded. "I left my hat and gloves in the kitchen. You can bring them to church on Sunday."

They tiptoed down the stairs. At the front door, Nessa kissed Louise on the cheek. "Be careful riding. I'll see you Sunday, and don't worry, everything will work out." She watched her friend step to the mounting block, climb into the saddle, and wave, before turning toward home. She shut the door, leaned against it, and closed her eyes.

"Nessa? Are you upstairs? Ellie could use some help, and I must feed Patrick."

She took a deep breath. "Coming, Mama."

CHAPTER 33

❀

Sam poured a second bucket of hot water into the wash tub, and strode to the fire to get the third. He smiled as he carried it toward the crude well house he had finished last week. *At least now, Nessa will have a private place to bathe without having to carry heavy buckets down the dugout steps. As long as the weather was warm.* He sighed. *Winter will arrive in a few months, and what can I do to make it easier for Nessa, then?* He dumped the bucket's contents and removed his clothes. *Don't borrow trouble before it finds you, Sam. You'll think of something before it snows. Today is your wedding day. In a few hours, all your dreams will come true. Nessa will be your wife.* He grabbed the cake of lye soap and stepped into the water.

After scrubbing his body to a rosy glow, paying particular attention to his fingernails, he stropped his straight razor on a strip of leather. He propped a foggy mirror on the bench, and stooped to study his bearded cheeks. He frowned at the image of his shaking fingers clasping the razor, and breathed deeply to steady his surging heart. After finishing without mishap, he dumped a measure of baking soda in his palm, and cleaned his teeth with an index finger. Finally, he dressed carefully in his new black pants, white shirt, and black tie, plastered his thick hair to his scalp with a brush, and stepped outside.

He raised his face to the August sun, glowing overhead in the clear blue sky. A gentle breeze teased the leaves on the cottonwood trees and ruffled Sam's damp hair. The brown and white mongrel puppy, that Sam had chosen a couple of weeks ago from a litter at a neighbor's farm, raced toward him. The puppy, named for Nessa's favorite poet, bounded to Sam's side and scratched at his legs.

"Down, Byron!" Sam brushed at his pants. "Look at what you've done. You just wait till your mistress gets here. She'll teach you some manners."

Byron barked and sat on his haunches. Sam laughed. "I don't have a treat in my pockets right now. Besides you had a good breakfast." He bent to ruffle the puppy's ears. "Now you behave yourself while I'm gone. You're supposed to guard the place and keep the jack rabbits out of the garden."

Byron gazed at Sam with solemn brown eyes and barked. Sam chuckled and strode toward the corral where Gallatin stood saddled and ready. Sam mounted and set a slow pace so not to work up a sweat.

At Hank's place, Sam dismounted, tossed Gallatin's reins at the post and rapped on the door leading to the dugout. "Hank. You ready to go? I don't want to be late."

A moment later, the door opened and Hank's smiling face appeared. "You got more'n two hours, Sam. What's the hurry? You'll just stand around at the church gettin' nervous and bothered." Hank's gaze shifted to Sam's hands. "Well look at that. A little shaky today, aren't you?" Sam frowned and backed away, and Hank chuckled, stepped out and closed the door. "Now, I'm a tenderfoot at this best man business. What am I supposed to do when the groom's got a bad case of the fidgets?"

Sam stuck his hands in his pockets. "Hush, Hank. I'm fine."

"Oh, yeah? Well you could a fooled me."

Sam ignored him and walked toward his horse.

"Wait a minute, Sam! You gotta help me with this blasted tie. I got no idea how it works. Never had one before."

Sam turned and grinned at his friend. "You're looking mighty citified, Hank. You going to a wedding or something?" He retraced his steps and stood in front of Hank who held out a strip of black cloth. "Let me see that thing." Sam removed his hat, snatched the tie, and wrapped it around his neck. "Tell you the truth, I'm not too good at this myself. Mr. Long showed me the other day, and I hope I did mine right." He slowly twisted the cloth over, under and through. "I think this is the way it goes." He slipped the loop off his head and onto Hank's. "Now we tighten it like this, and…"

"Hey! You tryin' to choke me?" Hank yanked the tie ends from Sam, adjusted it around his neck, and muttered. "No wonder they call a hangin' a necktie party. This thing is pure torture."

Sam grinned, and eyed his friend from sandy hair to polished boots. "You'll do, I guess, til something better comes along." He slapped his hat back on his head and turned toward Gallatin. "I see ole Danger's ready to go. Let's get this show on the road."

❧   ❧   ❧

Nessa frowned at the image in her mirror. Face too pale, cheeks too pink, and blue eyes clouded with uncertainty. Even her hair seemed unfamiliar. Rolled and held high with tiny combs that clung to her head like burrs. She closed her eyes and placed a palm under her rib cage where the breakfast her mother had insisted she eat roiled and knotted. *Please, God, don't let me throw up.* She took a deep breath.

"Nessa, are you ready for your petticoat?" Ellie's smiling face appeared to be floating in a cloud of yards of ruffled, lace-edged cotton.

Nessa sighed, and turned to face her sister, bent her neck to protect her hairdo, and held her arms out. Ellie lifted the layers over her sister's head and tugged them into place.

"You look beautiful already, Nessa. I can't wait to be a bride." Her gaze met Nessa's. "Are you all right? You look awfully pale. Should I call Mama?"

"No! Don't call Mama. I'm fine, just all the excitement." She forced her lips into a curve.

"I'm not surprised. I'm a little nervous myself. Mama says all brides are that way before the wedding." Ellie smoothed the skirt of her pastel blue dress. "Just think, Nessa, in a few hours you'll be Mrs. Samuel Butler Jackson, and in the morning…"

"Will you stop chattering, and help me with my dress? I still have to put on my shoes, and fix my veil, and it must be getting late."

"Oh, sorry." Ellie raced to the bed, picked up the wedding gown, and held the skirts high. Nessa slipped her arms into the long sleeves and ducked her head as the heavy satin slid down her body. She turned her back, and Ellie giggled as she fumbled with the dozen tiny satin-covered buttons. "I'm glad we don't wear dresses like this every day. We'd barely be dressed by dinner time."

Opal entered the bedroom, stepping carefully so not to trip over the long skirts of her pink gown. "Papa says we should leave in ten minutes. The buggy is waiting out front." She gaped at Nessa. "You look like the fairy princess in my book."

Nessa smiled. "You look mighty pretty, yourself." Her gaze flitted from Opal to Ellie and back to Opal. "Both of you." She blinked rapidly. "I'm going to miss seeing you every day. I know sometimes I haven't been a very good big sister, and I'm sorry, but I love you both very much."

"Love you, too, but you better hurry or Papa will be up here." Opal walked out, closing the door, and Nessa heard her knocking across the hall. "Mama, are you ready?"

Nessa grinned at Ellie and shook her head. "I don't think anything will ever make Opal nervous." She pinned Sam's brooch over her heart, as she had done every day since he gave it to her, then sat on the bed and lifted one foot. "I guess I'm ready for the shoes. I hope they fit. It seems years since I got them for my birthday."

"Almost a year ago. Thursday you'll be sixteen." Ellie knelt to hook the the shiny white buttons on Nessa's shoes. "Mama is planning a family birthday dinner for you next Saturday." Ellie gazed up at her sister. "Everything will be so different now with you gone and just coming over to visit. It's almost like you're not my sister any more."

"Silly goose." Nessa smiled and touched Ellie's face with her fingers. "I'll always be your sister, and you can come visit me, too. Besides you'll be going back to school in town in a few weeks."

"I want to go to school." Ellie sighed. "At least I think so, but everything is changing too fast. Why did we have to grow up so quickly?"

Nessa shook her head, remembering her adolescent pain of a year ago. "It happens, Ellie. You should have a long talk with Mama before you leave. She'll help you understand."

"Rebecca? Girls?" We should be leaving now. Sam's going to think he's been stood up."

Nessa gasped as her father's voice echoed up the stairs. "Ellie, help me with the veil. I hope my hair is okay, and where are my gloves?"

Ellie snatched up the veil and arranged it over Nessa's curls. "Be still! It's halfway over one eye." She sighed. "You fix it and I'll get your gloves. They're right here on the chest."

With shaky fingers, Nessa straightened the net. "Oh, no! Where are the flowers and my bouquet?"

Ellie took Nessa's arm and headed toward the door. "Mama has the altar flowers wrapped in a damp cloth in a basket. We'll arrange them at the church. And Louise is bringing your bouquet, remember?"

"Oh, Ellie, I'm too nervous to remember my own name." She grabbed at her skirts as Ellie pulled her down the stairs.

Nessa allowed herself to be ushered out the door and lifted the layers of skirts to manage the stairs.

❧   ❧   ❧

Nessa stood on the steps of the church. One hand held the ends of her veil, and her bouquet of white Shasta daisies, from Mrs. Bagley's garden, against the rising breeze. She clutched her father's arm with the other. Her stomach churned, and she prayed the rumbling would not be audible to anyone but herself. Ellie stood just in front of her grasping her skirts. Piano music drifted through the half-open church door and Nessa bit her lip, waiting for Katerina to begin the wedding march. A few minutes more in the wind and her veil would be snatched away, her hair would tumble down, and she would probably fall off the steps.

"Papa, can't you hurry them up?"

Her father gave her a smile and patted her hand. "Any minute now. Sam and Hank just took their places." As he spoke, the melody changed, Clem swung the door wide, and Ellie took a measured step forward. Nessa's feet followed her father's lead, while her gaze centered on the man waiting for her at the flower bedecked altar. His brown eyes gleamed with the promise of her future. An air of serenity, safety, and love surrounded her, seeping into her heart. Her lips curved and her steps grew steady.

Papa stopped and placed her hand in Sam's. Papa spoke in a low voice. "I give Nessa to you, Sam. Take good care of her."

Sam's gaze moved from Nessa to Papa. "I will, sir." Then he again looked into her eyes and drew her forward to stand beside him facing the preacher.

"Folks, we're gathered today to join this couple in holy matrimony, in the presence of God. If anyone has a reason why this marriage should not take place, let him speak now or forever hold his peace."

Nessa's heart thumped as the preacher recited the love verses from First Corinthians thirteen, followed by his instructions for building a marriage under God. Then she relinquished her bouquet to Ellie and faced Sam who took both her hands in his.

She gazed into his eyes as he spoke. "I, Sam, take thee, Nessa, to be my wedded wife, and promise to be a loving and faithful husband, as long as we both shall live."

Nessa swallowed and took a deep breath. "I, Nessa, take thee, Sam, to be my wedded husband, and promise to be a loving and faithful wife, as long as we both shall live." Her gaze held his.

Clem took his place to the side of the wedding party and played a medley of lilting Italian love songs. Nessa could barely restrain the joy bubbling inside her, as the music lifted her soul. When the last note faded into silence, she took a deep breath and smiled at Sam, surrendering herself to the love in his eyes.

Brother Langtry's voice interrupted the intimate communion."Sam, do you have the ring?"

Sam accepted the circlet of gold from Hank's outstretched hand, then repeated after the preacher. "With this ring I thee wed. I pledge my loyalty, my love, and my life, in the name of the Father, and of the Son, and of the Holy Spirit. Amen." He placed the ring on Nessa's finger and touched it with his lips.

Nessa bowed her head as the preacher pronounced a short prayer of benediction. Then he laid a hand on each of their shoulders. "I now pronounce you man and wife. Whom God hath joined together, let no man put asunder. Amen." The preacher smiled. "Sam, you may now kiss your bride."

Nessa lifted her face and smiled at Sam as he lowered his lips to hers.

THE END

About the Author

⚘

Arlene J. Warner received the Lord Jesus into her life as a child. She has taught Sunday School, worked as an executive secretary, taught in a Christian school, and home schooled four of her children. The last several years, she has dedicated herself to writing. She is the author of several children's stories, two novels and a cookbook in the *Amanda* series, and is currently working on another historical. She is an active member of American Christian Romance Writers. In her spare time, Arlene enjoys gardening, painting, quilting, and reading. She lives in Kansas with her husband and two of her seven children.

Other books:

Amanda's New Song

Amanda and Rory, The Song Continues

Amanda and Rory's Favorite Recipes

Books available through www.iuniverse.com, www.Amazon.com, most major bookstores, and Arlene's web page: http://www.arlenejwarner.com

0-595-28708-5

CPSIA information can be obtained
at www.ICGtesting.com
Printed in the USA
FSOW01n1833240715
9213FS

9 780595 287086